The Pa

Belinda Jones's first paid j...
Pat. Since then she has writ...
newspapers including *New ...man, Empire, FHM, heat, Sunday*
and the *Daily Express*. Belinda's widely acclaimed first novel
Divas Las Vegas was voted No. 2 in the *New Woman* Bloody Good
Reads Awards in 2001 and *On the Road to Mr Right* – a non-
fiction travelogue love quest was a *Sunday Times* top ten
bestseller. *The Paradise Room* is her fourth novel.

Also by Belinda Jones

Divas Las Vegas
I Love Capri
The California Club
On the Road to Mr Right

BELINDA JONES

The Paradise Room

arrow books

Published by Arrow Books in 2005

3 5 7 9 10 8 6 4

First published in the United Kingdom in 2005 by Arrow

Arrow Books
The Random House Group Limited
20 Vauxhall Bridge Road, London, SW1V 2SA

Random House Australia (Pty) Limited
20 Alfred Street, Milsons Point, Sydney, New South Wales 2061, Australia

Random House New Zealand Limited
18 Poland Road, Glenfield
Auckland 10, New Zealand

Random House South Africa (Pty) Limited
Endulini, 5a Jubilee Road, Parktown 2193, South Africa

The Random House Group Limited Reg. No. 954009

www.randomhouse.co.uk

A CIP catalogue record for this book is avilable from the British Library

Papers used by Random House
are natural, recyclable products made from wood grown in
sustainable forests. The manufacturing processes conform to
the environmental regulations of the country of origin

ISBN 0 09 944552 2

Typeset by SX Composing DTP, Rayleigh, Essex
Printed and bound in Great Britain by
Bookmarque Ltd, Croydon, Surrey

For my beautiful muses
Tony Perry & Tezz Yancey

Acknowledgements

Firstly I have to thank Chee Mustafa – had your eyes not spied that 'boyband' blur this would have been a very different story! Thank you for taking such a fantastic voyage with me. Our time at the Big Apple Bar and those 4 a.m. Krispy Kremes have proved sublime inspiration. Couldn't have done it without you, couldn't have done it with anyone but you. (With a little bit of uh-uh!)

Tony Perry – you have touched my heart. Tezz Yancey – you make me beam inwardly and outwardly. I am so proud and in awe of your talents – thank you for motivating me to raise my game – you made me want to write a better book! Sharon Jones – you are such a devoted ally. Ta for sharing your boys! Fierce embraces to the Soul Desire band especially guitar hero Nate and Jimmy-the-Twitch plus stunning and powerful Alicia, Cheaza and Jhai.

The fabulous Vicky Legg at Orient Express Hotels – the original concept was all you, honey! Florence at the Bora Bora Lagoon Resort, merci for your help naming the villain! All at *Windstar*, and Inter-Continental Beachcomber, Sarah at Air New Zealand, Virginia and Lalla at BGB Associates and all-knowing Joel Hart at Tahiti Tourisme – ta for the introduction to Marcel Gauguin! And for knowledge of Gauguin Snr, much gratitude to Nicole Myers at Boston MFA. Also in Boston, Maya Belle – meeting you was pure synchronicity and such a blessing! I will always treasure your view from the roof terrace!

Also James Breeds for being such a charming, inquisitive, flipper-touting travel companion. Sam & Beth – for the sun and the moon! (And bad hair and mad dogs!) Petra Massey of Spymonkey – thank you for your hilarity and hospitality. And, as ever, RMB for your indispensable research skills.

This is my fifth book with Random House and I am ever-appreciative of the amazing care, support and insight from the London office! Kate Elton deserves her own private island for all the super-smart work she does! What a team – Susan, Justine, both Robs, Ron and Lizzy – big Mai Tai toast to all of you!

Also much tropical chinking to my agent Eugenie Furniss at William Morris UK and her kind and wise assistant Rowan – thanks for those pointers!

Finally to My Ty – for giving me real-love experiences to draw upon and instructing me to Be Brilliant on a daily basis! Loving your bacon, baby!

Prologue

Tahiti, how do I love thee? Let me count the waves.

My toes slip into the luminous blue of the lagoon, so warm it barely registers as water. Even as I waft my feet back and forth I am more aware of a silky sensuality than liquid. I squint open one eye to check that my legs really are immersed and discover I have been set in turquoise jelly from the knees down.

Shuffling forward on the decking, I extend my legs further, grazing my soles on the seabed, but it's only when I receive a wake-up pinch from the blanched coral that I truly recall where I am: paradise.

I know that for sure, not because of the limbo-ing palm trees, nor the musky-sweet scent of coconut oil perfuming the morning air, but because I have just been kissed in a way I have only ever dreamed about.

I close my eyes and let the sun melt across my face. And to think I had to be bullied into coming here . . .

Prologue

1

'I could be wrong, but I think you might be the only girl in the world who doesn't want to go to paradise.' Hugh rubs his bewildered brow. 'I suppose if I was proposing the North Pole you'd be jumping up and down with glee.'

I go to speak, but the prospect of a pair of swishy-furred Yeti boots and pom-pom earmuffs temporarily slackens my jaw.

'Or better yet Seattle!' he crows. 'That's got to be your dream destination, hasn't it Amber – all that miserable drizzle.'

I can't deny it, I love rain. I love how it warps wood, mists up windows, makes windscreen wipers squeak and drag, kinks fringes and besmirches the cheeks of even the most stylish women with Pierrot tears of mascara. I like rain hats that divert the occasional trickle of water down the back of your collar causing you to wince and rotate your shoulder blades so the now warm drip races down your spine. I like splashing through puddles and cowering at the heavy menace of charcoal-grey thunderclouds. I like how pavements take on a gun-metal sheen after an afternoon sluicing. I like the silent camaraderie of sheltering in a shop doorway when the wind gets so gusty you can no longer use your umbrella as a shield against the stinging tacks of rain.

And then there's all the cosy paraphernalia that partners the wet and cold: fleece-lined gloves, hats with Bassett-hound ear-flaps, scarves you can wrap around your neck three times and still have enough dangling to catch in the spokes of your bicycle. I like layering jumpers and cardis until I look like I'm wearing a comedy fat suit and can no longer rest my arms by my side. I like faux-fur hot-water-bottle covers and knitted bedsocks with individual toes.

I even like that disconcerting feeling when water seeps in through the sole of my shoe, especially if I'm wearing wool socks and there's that distinct aroma of wet sheep.

Oxford may not be the wettest city in the UK (statistically that would be Swansea, and I hope one day to retire to a sodden clod there), but it offers me sufficient licence to wear my most toggly cagoule, and that makes me happy.

'Well, I can certainly offer you a lot of moisture.' Hugh resumes his wooing. 'Eighty-four per cent humidity according to today's weather report!' He jiggles his brows temptingly at me.

'Not interested – there's never anything to do in those places except go brown.'

'You say that like it's a bad thing,' he frowns.

'It is to me,' I shrug. At age thirty-two I've basted enough chickens to question the wisdom of cooking your own skin.

'You don't have to lie out in the sun *all* day.' Hugh is sounding impatient now. 'There's snorkelling, kayaking—' He halts himself. 'Something tells me I may as well be suggesting unnecessary dental work.'

I give an affirmative nod. He's got that bit right – the only water sport that appeals to me is fishing wet leaves out of our guttering. The fact is I just don't do holidays. There's something about the pressure to be carefree and relaxed that rankles with me. Plus I'm not a big fan of having all that free time to think. In my experience thinking leads to questioning and questioning leads to . . . Well, I just don't want to go there.

'I felt sure I could get you on the art angle,' Hugh continues, harking back to his opening gambit. 'I mean, you went to Giverny to see Monet's gardens. I don't understand why you're not gagging to see Gauguin's Tahiti.'

I shake my head. 'That Monet trip was research for a specific exhibit and more importantly a mere three hours on Eurostar. You're talking about nearly twenty hours' sky-time – and you know I hate to fly.'

'You went to Boston with Abigail last year,' he grumps.

'Six and a half hours,' I contest. 'Tahiti is practically all the way to Australia!'

'I could have sworn you were really into Gauguin.' Hugh says, unable to understand why he's not gaining any ground.

'If you remember correctly, I always preferred the earlier work he did in Brittany,' I counter.

For me his Tahiti work is too lurid, too unreal. Pink sands, purple mountains, red lizards – an over-excitement of colour, and yet the poses of the natives appear languid to the point of apathy. Paul Gauguin made a pilgrimage to these remote South Pacific islands to fulfil a craving for a more primitive existence and consequently depicted his bare-breasted teenage lovers asprawl in a lush natural idyll, only occasionally showing them as they actually would have been dressed at the time: all gussied up in the starchy high-necked tent dresses foisted upon them by the missionaries. Aside from the moral issue of him abandoning his wife and children, I always felt this made him part con man – he wasn't painting things as they really were, just an escapist fantasy of how he wished things could be.

'Anyway . . .' I ruffle Hugh's shiny caramel hair, losing my train of thought as I watch the thick layers flick back into place while my fingers groove along his scalp. (This man always smells so clean, so good – my mother would have approved: £80 haircuts, hot-flannel shaves, paraffin wax manicures . . . Well, you would too if your nails were under the microscope on a daily basis.)

'Anyway what?' he asks, looking up at me.

'Anyway you'll be working most days. What would I do with myself?' I blink myself back on track. 'Learn a thousand and one ways to slice a papaya?'

'Maybe you could come with me. It's not all negotiations and money-talk. There's definitely one excursion to a pearl farm. You'd like that – getting to see how those mini-masterpieces are made.'

Hugh is a jeweller. His actual speciality is diamonds (no raggedy cuticles permitted when handling a forty-carat sparkler), and consequently his trips typically take him to South Africa and Brazil. This Tahiti gig has fallen into his lap on account of Piers the Pearl Guy breaking his ankle playing polo. (Or so he says. The rumour going round is that a Pimms-blurred game of croquet is actually to blame. One thing I know for sure is that the man is such a braying know-it-all I would have welcomed the opportunity to give him a good thwack with a mallet myself.)

Initially Hugh tried to wriggle out of the trip as pearls have never been his passion. He'll grant that in their heyday they were positively iconic – who doesn't revere Audrey Hepburn's très chic triband in *Breakfast at Tiffany's*. Jackie O's infamously baubled collar, even Madonna's flapper ropes *circa* 'Like A Virgin' – but he cannot be convinced of a viable revival. Moreover, pearls frustrate him with their wayward, determinedly individual behaviour. Diamonds you can cut and polish and define; pearls grow and form as they darn well please. They cannot be modified, even those

7

cultivated at pearl farms; whatever their flaws, you have to accept them as they are.

It's not that Hugh's a control freak, but he is a big fan of precision. And professionalism. And preparation. And two days just isn't enough time for him to become a pearl expert. Or more specifically a *black* pearl expert. Piers's specific prediction is an upsurge in demand for these lesser-known dark pearls, referencing both the latest collection from Jean-Paul Gaultier and the recent eye-catching outing by 'fashion forward' Sarah Jessica Parker at a NYC fundraiser. Hugh's having none of it, maintaining that all black pearls look like ball bearings. But the fact is Piers has already garnered substantial pre-orders from several of his regular Hey Big Spenders, including a commission for a high-profile engagement ring (ideally featuring the most expensive solo pearl that money can buy), and there is no way he can risk letting these people down. (A disappointed billionaire is not a pretty sight.)

The deal must be made by the end of the month, and it must take place in the only place in the world that black pearls call home – the French Polynesian islands of Tahiti.

I have to admit the location does seem oddly fateful considering it was a French restaurant with the fearsomely pretentious name of Quand l'Artiste Mange that brought Hugh and I together for the first time four years ago. Just thinking about it I experience an inner twang, remembering the other less palatable things that were going on in my life at the time. Thank goodness he appeared when he did, on that brittle-boned November night . . .

We actually spoke first on the phone when he called to make the reservation. I had misheard his name, writing down Garnet instead of Garner and when he subsequently arrived (with a group of five work colleagues) he laughed and pipped, 'That's funny, because I'm actually a jeweller!'

I didn't even respond, let alone laugh along with him – I had yet to master the art of meet-and-greet small talk and was sullenly preoccupied with a family matter that night so I kept strictly to business, seating his party, handing out the palette-shaped menus, draping each pinstriped lap with a paint-spattered napkin, then returning eight minutes later to take their order. Smooth sailing until he took his turn.

'So, what would you recommend?' He looked directly at me, commanding a personal response.

In the three weeks I'd been working at Quand l'Artiste Mange I'd heard a lot of jokes about '*tartes*' and endured many an extended pause between the order of '*coq*' and '*au vin*', but never once had anyone appeared to be so earnestly intent on hearing my opinion. Without thinking I found myself babbling, 'Well, the duck with plum compote is a little sticky-sickly in my opinion and I'd steer clear of the fish in general, but it's worth getting the caramelised veal sweetbreads just for the cauliflower and roasted hazelnut purée.'

Cue the sound of bemused muttering at the table. Had I gone too far?

'Gosh,' he blinked. 'I've been coming here for two years and you're the first person who hasn't said, "Everything on the menu is excellent, sir."'

'Everything on the menu is excellent, sir,' I chanted obediently.

'Oh, don't spoil the moment!' he scolded. 'I wanted an informed opinion – that's why I asked you.' Then he smiled, looking deep into me like he knew me. 'So go on, tell me, what would you choose?'

It was a policy of mine to retain a careful distance from strangers, but somehow this man had already found a way to slip under the barrier.

'Probably the corn-fed squab cooked in a salt crust,' I replied, slightly dazed, 'with a side of sugar snap peas.'

'Then that's what I'll have.' He closed the menu and returned it to my care, adding, 'Though I suspect you could cook it better yourself?' while raising an inquisitive eyebrow.

I turned away before he could see me smile. I have always loved to cook, revelling in the magical fusion of tastes and aromas and, most of all, the intricacy of recipes – I find the detail involved in food preparation so absorbing that all my other concerns just fall away. At twelve I retired my mother from all kitchen duties, though I did resent the frequency with which my teen gourmet dinners were left uneaten because my dad would come home and spontaneously decide to whisk my mum out to dinner 'somewhere fancy'. Sometimes I'd call my best friend Felicity and she'd come over and have a second dinner with me (her mum was too keen on steamed veggies slathered in margarine for her liking). She'd tell me that there was no way my parents could be eating anything as delicious as I'd cooked wherever they were, and that made me feel better. Having Hugh sense my culinary potential was like him knowing my secret password. When I returned to his table with the plates he was engaged in a debate about the computerised colour-grading of diamonds, but he still managed to give me a whimsical look that seemed to say *I'd much rather be dining with you.* I couldn't help but be flattered, yet when I arrived the next night and found he'd dropped by and left his card for me, I put it straight in the bin. It was not a good time for me. It never was.

'Are you crazy?' Maître d' Genevieve scrabbled to retrieve his platinum-embossed details before they got slurried under an avalanche of tripe. 'That man is such a catch!'

'We're not a good match,' I said simply as I secured my hair in the customary uptwist with a decorative paintbrush.

'What are you talking about – you'd be great together!' she protested, reaching out to jiggle some sense into me via my elbow. 'And what beautiful children you would have: eyes twice as hazel, hair twice as golden—' She stopped suddenly. 'Or is there someone else?' Now she looked confused. 'Would you

11

look at that – I'm the nosiest person in the whole Thames Valley and I don't know the first thing about your personal life!'

I gave a '*C'est la vie!*' shrug and headed into the dining room.

There really was no other man in my life. And Genevieve was right: Hugh was lovely – smart, clean, employed. Also handsome and possibly even rather rich. Quite the perfect man to take home to meet your parents. Any parents, that is, but mine. I hardly knew him but I'd seen enough to know I could like him. How could I knowingly lead him into the lair? Or my parents into temptation, for that matter? Let's just say his career was incompatible with theirs. It was for his own good that I had made the decision to avoid him.

But three weeks later our paths crossed again, this time at a corporate event evening at the Ashmolean Museum. I had been elected to make the presentation on the new French Impressionist exhibit and was just about to move on from Renoir to Cézanne when I noticed him. He was there with a group of male friends, one of whom had got stinking drunk on the complimentary Shiraz and, obviously having seen *Jerry Maguire* a few too many times, kept shouting 'Show me the Monet!'

It was Hugh who gracefully man-handled him out into the frosty night and barked white-breathed reprimands at him before returning, pink-nosed, to find me when the talk was over.

'I'm so sorry . . .' he began, looking fraught.

I shushed him instantly. 'It could have been worse,' I assured him. 'He could have smeared tapenade on the Degas.'

He smiled lovingly at me. Lovingly, even though we'd only spent minutes of our lives together. 'So you're a woman of many careers,' he marvelled, tapping my prompt cards. 'What is it that you actually do?'

'Well, obviously waitressing is my greatest love,' I told him, again surprisingly bold in his presence.

'Obviously,' he confirmed with a serious nod.

'But I also give talks here at the museum, basically to supplement my earnings at the restaurant.'

'Break a lot of plates, do you?' he chuckled.

I nodded. 'I'm like a one-woman Greek wedding party.'

He laughed in that 'I like you so much I'm going to burst!' way. I'd never before seen anyone look so happy while they were looking at me. It reminded me of how I look at a masterpiece when I see it for the first time – with a mixture of wonder and admiration and delight.

'Truthfully, this is my world,' I confessed, taking my eyes on a tour of the grand, high-ceilinged room with its chunky belt of ornately carved frames and all the precision dots and sweeps of paint within.

'Art?'

'Yes.'

'You paint?' he enquired, a common enough response.

13

'No.' I shook my head. 'Not really. Not professionally . . .'

'A life model?' He looked hopeful.

I smirked. Nice try. 'I'm actually a research assistant.'

He looked blank.

'Otherwise known as an art historian.'

'Wow, for a seventy-year-old crone you're looking pretty good.'

'It's a façade,' I confided. 'When I go home I take off this ridiculous blonde wig, reach for my tweed slippers and pop on a pair of pince-nez—'

'Pince-nez?' he snickered, looking incredulous.

'You know, those little glasses.' I gave a demonstrative pinch to the bridge of my nose.

'I know what they are,' he smiled, gently lowering my hand away from my face. 'It's just . . .' He shrugged, looking happily at sea. 'There are some words you don't hear too often nowadays.'

'No, I suppose you're more used to chatting about polariscopes and refractometers.'

'You speak jeweller jargon?' He reeled back, clapping his hands together as if to say *Bravo!*

I gave a nonchalant shrug, raising my eyes to the ceiling in what I hoped was an enigmatic manner. When I looked back I found he'd stepped forward; his face was closer to mine than any man's had been in a long time. I could trace the slight scent of garlic back to the crostini, and identified his aftershave as Van Cleef & Arpels Pour Homme. A classic. (I once bought

14

a bottle for my father in a bid to coax him away from the pimp-daddy scent of Fahrenheit, but he just wasn't happy unless potted plants wilted in his presence.)

'Tell me,' he whispered hypnotically.

'My parents . . .' I began, letting those two outlawed words slip out before I regained my senses and aborted the sentence.

'Your parents?' he prompted, looking expectant.

'My parents live in Florida.' I gave a curt, automaton reply, preparing to shut down and move on.

'Oh,' he said, confused by this irrelevant announcement.

'I have to go.' I pulled away from our shared space, back into my own world.

'Wait, um, can we . . .?' he called after me.

'I'm sorry.' I was already on my way, but he hurried in front of me, blocking my path.

'I know this great little arty café.' His eyes pleaded with mine.

'If you're thinking of the place where you paint your own cups—'

'And have you show me up?' he tutted. 'I don't think so.'

He got me again – got me smiling. Did I really want to walk away from this man? Something about him was suggesting an option, a different way to live. After so many years alone, was this my chance to be with somebody? I knew from his job he must be trustworthy and reliable. His clothes and grooming suggested care but not flamboyance. He was the one who had quelled the earlier scene, not created it. Was it possible, after all, that a man could make you feel safe? Still wary, I nevertheless found myself curious enough to ask, 'Where were you thinking of?'

'Do you know the Noble Savage?'

My jaw gaped. Had someone told him about my weakness for their mini croque-monsieurs? I looked around the gallery for a guilty face among my co-workers, but they were all busy flourishing at artworks and oblivious to my questioning stare.

'I do know it . . .' I faltered, deciding that if he could answer my next question I'd dare myself to go. 'That's actually the nickname of a famous painter – do you know which one?' I tried to sound more casual than quiz-show-host but failed.

He shook his head.

My heart sank. It was too much to hope for.

'But if you made me guess I'd have to say Gauguin.'

My heart sprang back to life.

'Am I right?'

I nodded vigorously.

'Huh! I always wondered why they had his portrait over the espresso machine and now I know. What an enlightening woman you are!' he teased. 'Tomorrow, then, for lunch?'

'One o'clock,' I asserted, strangely thrilled at the prospect.

'You know the address?' he checked before turning to leave.

'Yes I do,' I confirmed. 'Actually, I thought I was the only one who did. I can't believe you know that place, it's so hidden away.'

He gave me a giant smile. 'I live above it.'

And now I live here too.

Initially we were squirreled away in a snug one-bedroom, but now we've expanded across three floors – the two-storey above us was put on the market so we clubbed together and bought that and created one big unit. Hugh's idea. I wouldn't have minded if it had stayed as two separate entities – I do like my own space, somewhere to stare at the wall and not have anyone ask me 'What's wrong?' – but I didn't want to be a spoilsport, and Hugh had been advised that he could greatly increase the value of the overall property with the modernisation he was planning; and the majority of the money was his, after all.

As it happened, despite losing a few walls, we have both ended up with our own dens. Right now we're in his. Since Jasper's permitted him to work from home a couple of days a month (so the commute from Oxford to London doesn't grind him down to dust) he's transformed what was a sports shrine into a sleek office done up in cool beiges and dove-greys replete with inset ceiling lighting, scoured silver fixtures and the fastest internet connection in the land.

My den, on the other hand, is unlike any other room in the house. Should we ever sell, I know it would have to be redone before it went on the market, but I appreciate Hugh letting me deviate from his ultramodern design plan. When I first asked if I could do something a bit different, I think he was expecting me to vandalise his neutral colour palette with a psychedelic mural, but what I'd always craved was fabric wallpaper – the kind of heavily textured burgundy wall-covering you might find in a stately home. It's one of the first things that registered with me as I entered the Ashmolean Museum as a schoolgirl. Most hands wanted to reach out and touch the small bronze of Rodin's 'The Thinker'; I wanted to stroke the wallpaper!

Hugh complains that it's too fussy and dark and oppressive, but I think it's comforting, in a decadent kind of way. Mostly I sit in the dark anyway. I look all day; at night I like to listen. I'm always in there with my headphones on, playing the records my mother left me. Even when the stereo is off, I keep the headphones on. And sometimes when Hugh calls to me I pretend I haven't heard him. I don't know why I do that.

'Wooohooo!' I'm yanked back to the present moment as Hugh bounds from his leather desk-chair and begins swinging me around in a clumsy celebratory swirl. 'Gotcha!' he hoots triumphantly. 'You can't say no to Tahiti now!' He stops to clamp my face in his hands as he delivers the words, 'It's the rainy season!'

'It is?' I manage to query through my slightly squooshed mouth.

18

'Look!' He pulls me on to his lap in front of the computer. 'See – bucketing down today. Nearly six inches this month alone.' He gives the screen an emphatic rap before muttering, 'Whatever that means.'

I peer a little closer at the statistics. It does look pretty wet.

'Think of all those tropical storms,' he leers, nuzzling my neck, snail-trailing with his tongue.

'Ew, get off!' I squirm away from him, wincing like I've just bitten into a lime.

'Oh, come on, just imagine it – slate-grey skies ripped apart by phosphorescent daggers of lightning . . .' he hams it up.

I roll my eyes. 'All right, Thomas Hardy!'

He presses his mouth to my ear and rumbles, 'Thunder. Deep, booming, heart-pounding thunder,' and I feel his hand slip beneath my thermals and start drumming on my breastbone.

I can see where this is going. If I don't say yes soon, we're going to end up having sex. (Not something I feel should be sprung upon my body after such a long hiatus.)

'I don't have a swimming costume,' is my feeble last-stand protest.

'We'll get one out there,' he pants, knowing my acceptance is but one grouch away.

I prise myself away from him, walk over to the window and watch the panes of glass rattle and tremble as the wind buffets them. Outside, straggling shoppers shiver at the bus stop, desperately seeking asylum on the no. 2 to Kidlington. A passing pedestrian curses out loud at the winter weather as if it's being wilfully spiteful. This is my favourite time of year. I can't believe I'm considering abandoning all this for some postcard-perfect beach on the other side of the world.

'I'll talk to Gilly tomorrow,' I tell him, adding a rueful, 'but I don't know how she's going to react to such short notice.'

Gilly is my boss. Much as I might wish to make her out to be a tyrant, she is in fact a hippy at heart and an absolute pushover. As Hugh is well aware.

'Gilly will be fine,' he soothes, holding his voice steady as if any sudden whoops or quavers might provoke a change of heart in me. 'It's only ten days – you'll be back in plenty of time for the Turner exhibition. Why don't you have a word with her first thing tomorrow, then give me a call at the office.'

He sounds so reasonable. So why do I feel so resistant to my core? There doesn't seem to be any logical reason for it.

'Okay,' I finally acquiesce, trying to get my head around the ever-increasing possibility that, before the week is out, I could be swapping my slightly itchy polo neck for a coconut bra.

2

Anyone would think I'd just received an abduction tip-off from the Royal Society of Kidnappers & Carpetbaggers: *Amber Pepper to be snatched away at a moment's notice, never to see fair Oxford again.*

Walking to work I find myself pausing beside my most beloved sites – the Christ Church quads, the domed Radcliffe Camera, the graceful Bridge of Sighs – paying my respects and securing a visual memory to sustain me. Just in case. I still can't believe I'm seriously considering leaving. What do I want with Tahiti? All the sunshine I need is right here in these eternally golden bricks. When I was a child their gentle ridges reminded me of Farley's Rusks. Now my hand brushes the gritty, textured slabs on Turl Street with as much care as one would offer a lover's cheek. I never cease to marvel at all the honeyed hues ranging from palest Sahara sand to St-Tropez tan. No matter how muddled and moody the sky, these buildings glow.

I turn down a narrow street, surveying the courtyard ahead – the bicycles strewn like metal graffiti on black-glossed railings, the floppy-haired students chattering theorem, the moss-embedded cobbled streets all too often accessorised with cigarette butts and scrunched chewing-gum wrappers. I pick up at least three of these scrappy little offenders each day, partly to do my bit for community cleanliness and partly because when these modern-day reminders are gone and there's a lull in the human traffic, I can truly believe that I've stepped back in time. The tangible sense of history gives me tingles: I love knowing that Lewis Carroll based Alice on the dean's daughter, that J. R. R. Tolkien once worked as a lexicographer at the old Ashmolean Museum and, best of all, that Oscar Wilde used to walk his pet lobster along the same streets I take to work each morning.

Today is a library day, so I stop short at the Bodleian. The fact that I have to squeeze past surges of tourists to get to the entrance reminds me how lucky I am: people, especially Americans, pay money just to sneak a peek at where I do my fact-finding. I can't help but delight at their gasps of disbelief as they learn that this library holds a copy of every book ever published.

'*Every* book?' asks one young girl. 'Even chick lit?'

'Even chick lit,' the thick-stockinged guide confirms.

Hurrying up the stone staircase, about to enter a world of creaky, leatherbound tomes, I stop for a moment and gaze out of the leaded window. Every spire on the skyline seems to prick my eyes with tears today.

This sentimentality is absurd, I chide myself, continuing up one more flight. I'll not even be gone two weeks. Everything will be here when I get back, exactly as I left it. They'll still be selling crested mugs and navy university sweatshirts at the gabled gift shops, still sploshing out hot, strong, working-man's tea at the Covered Market, and you'd better believe the abundance of bicycle-clipped calves are here to stay.

But what about me? What if I change? Why do I get the feeling that if I go, it means goodbye? And is my anxiety, though I don't want to admit it, partly about the prospect of spending so much time with Hugh without having a private den to run to?

I forge ahead through the doors into the reading room, knowing that the sanctuary of silence will soothe me. *People go on holiday. And then they come home. Everything is going to be fine.* I take a moment to compose myself in one of the more shadowy alcoves before I meet the girls.

'Where exactly is Tahiti?' My pushover boss/top curator Gilly looks mildly concerned when I reveal my imminent holiday plans over our illicit Costa Coffee and Rice Krispie Treats.

'That's exactly what I said to Hugh!' I hiss, as if our mutual lack of geographical knowledge somehow proves a point in my favour. 'I know it's eight hours from Los Angeles because that's where we have to change planes, but mostly I'm just picturing scenes from *South Pacific*.'

'That's my favourite musical!' Gilly gasps before warbling, '"Some Enchanted Evening!"'

'"There is Nothing Like a Dame!"' I parlay back with a sailor swagger.

'"Happy Talk!"' Gilly giggles, miming chirruping mouths with her fingers.

'Are you ladies kidding me?' We turn to find Abigail, the real brainiac of the Ladies Who Crunch, looking at us like we've lost our minds.

I can't blame her, the subject matter is quite a departure from our usual gossip – pretty much whose projector jammed and which department's nouveau filing system has failed again. More *Index and the City* than *Sex and the City*.

'I have just one word for you.' Abigail leans in close, looking uncharacteristically threatening.

I roll my eyes, knowing what's coming next. 'Paradise?' I smirk.

'No! GAUGUIN!' she explodes.

'Oh, I know, I know!' I bleat, suddenly ashamed. We've all been so embroiled in the upcoming Turner exhibit I'd forgotten that she's the big G's number one fan.

'How can you be so blasé?' she wails. 'It's where he did all his most important works, and you're actually going to see it with your own eyes.'

'Yes, yes.' I reply, trying to calm her.

'You remember the show in Boston last year?'

'Of course!' I say. And not just because Hugh brought it up last night. The Boston Museum of Fine Art is a stunning building – vast and light and bright with innovative use of exhibition space and it was a credit to their prestige that they had amassed over a hundred and fifty of Gauguin's key Tahitian works for a show that was five years in the making. Abigail positively swooned at the aesthetic choices the design team had made for the display of Gauguin's largest canvas (and the one that would have been his last had he not bungled his attempt to kill himself with arsenic). *Where Do We Come From? What Are We? Where Are We Going?* was placed on a dark chocolate wall with only the softest of lighting, all the better to appreciate the subtleties of the painting's moody blue hues. Abigail was so besotted she would have rolled out a sleeping bag and slept in the gallery beside the imported Tikis if she could have.

'I can't believe you're getting to go to Tahiti!' she continues to wail. 'Are you visiting the Marquesas?'

'The what?'

'Remember, the Marquesas Islands?' she says impatiently. 'Where he set up his studio? Where he died,' she adds sombrely.

'Um, well, I know we're scheduled to visit Manihi, because there's a pearl farm there, and Bora Bora—'

'Bora Bora?' a voice snaps from behind an adjacent bookcase.

This is getting out of hand. Allegra Montefiago has

been coming to this library for five years, and this is the first time she has ever deigned to speak to me. (Until now she's maintained a strict Curator Only conversation policy.)

'That's right.' I attempt a light smile in her direction as she stalks over and takes an uninvited snag of Gilly's Rice Krispie Treat.

'You, on a research assistant's salary, are going to Bora Bora?' she scowls as she chews. '*How?*'

'Well, I'm not exactly paying – Hugh is going for work and I'm just tagging along. Why? Is it expensive there?'

Allegra attempts to give a scandalised snort but instead half-chokes on her stolen Krispie and is forced to give herself the Heimlich Manoeuvre. (Because, let's face it, no one else is going do it for her.)

'Just give me a moment,' she wheezes, holding up her hand.

I knew I wasn't going to get the sympathy I deserved over this trip, but is all this drama really necessary?

We wait patiently while Allegra attempts to regain her dignity. It's not a pretty sight watching an already horsey brunette braying and whinnying, and ultimately I crack, offering her a slurp of my chai tea.

'You were saying . . .' Abigail nudges her.

'Oh yes, my brother—' A now revived Allegra coughs out the beginning of a sentence.

'The paparazzo or the priest?' Gilly demands, seeking clarification before she continues.

26

'Paparazzo,' she replies. 'He wanted to go to Bora Bora on his honeymoon because he'd heard that all these A-list celebs sneak off there on their private jets—'

'Like who?' Abigail butts in.

Allegra heaves a testy sigh. 'Pierce Brosnan, John Travolta, Colin Farrell—'

'Colin Farrell? Colin freakin' Farrell?!'

'Abi, calm down.' I've never seen her like this over a living person before.

Allegra battles on. 'Freddie was looking into getting an over-water bungalow at the Bora Bora Lagoon Resort—'

'That's where we're staying!' My turn to interrupt. 'Sorry,' I mutter as I watch what little blood there is left in her face drain clean away. This can't be good.

Abigail looks wide-eyed at me, then at Allegra, demanding, 'How much?'

'Four hundred and fifty,' Allegra croaks. 'Per night.'

'Four hundred and fifty *pounds*?' Abigail gawps.

Allegra nods.

'Full board?' Gilly suggests.

'Not even breakfast.' Allegra swallows hard.

'And you don't want to go?' Suddenly everyone is staring at me like I'm the anti-Christ.

'Well . . .'

'Because if you're serious, I could have reconstructive facial surgery to look like you and still come out of this quids in,' Allegra snarls.

'You jammy bugger,' is Abigail's retort.

'"Bali Hai . . ."' Gilly comes over all Rogers & Hammerstein again.

I can see I'm going to have to act positive about this. 'Actually, there is one good aspect to this trip!' I volunteer.

Three sets of eyebrows arch in unison.

'Last night I discovered that Tahiti is just five hours' flight from New Zealand—'

'You mean Middle Earth,' corrects Gilly, the ultimate *Lord of the Rings* aficionado.

'And that is thrilling because . . .' Allegra drawls.

'It's thrilling to me because my best friend Felicity lives there.'

'I've never heard you mention her before,' Abigail frowns.

'That's because I haven't seen her since I was fourteen.'

Now, I'm fond of Abigail and Gilly – we keep each other ticking over socially, not that I see them much outside work – but I wouldn't lay down my life for them like I would have done for Felicity. I only knew her for two years, but her star shone brighter than any I have known . . .

We met at Headington School for Girls, a wonderful red-brick realm with a sweeping driveway, grassy quads, vast wood-trimmed playing fields and a gem of a headmistress called Miss Dunn, who was always escorted by her snuffly Norwich terrier Dougal. (Very odd sensation to be lost in logarithms and feel a wet nose on your calf.) Funnily enough, tweedy dog-trainer Barbara Woodhouse was the school's most famous ex-pupil. I remember the chaos when she came to visit – we tore out of our history lesson like Simon le Bon was in the building.

I dread to think now what my dad did to pay the fees, but at the time I was too distracted by this new world to worry. I was particularly entranced by the United Nations aspect of the classroom – a third of the school were boarders, so I studied alongside girls from Hong Kong, Switzerland, South Africa (one black, one white), France, Peru and, of course, New Zealand. Felicity and I were friends from the word go. In fact she was an instant friend with everybody – who doesn't want to be around the personification of sunny and fearless? But I remember the day she and I connected on a new level: our p.e. teacher – Miss Fit, I'll call her – was timing each of us in the 200-metre sprint. One by one we took our turn pelting down the cropped grass (pulling a thigh muscle in my case), and then came Carla Dollop, probably the least likely Olympic candidate in the class. Off she stumbled from the starting block, huffing and puffing and tummy-jiggling towards the finishing line. My heart went out to her. Especially when Miss Fit started hounding her.

'Move it!' she screeched, face instantly puce. 'You're not even trying!'

'I am!' she whimpered as she stumbled along the track.

'You could try a lot harder if you weren't so *fat*!' she spat, flaring scarlet to the roots of her limp perm.

Why was she getting so crazed over this? It was clear Carla was never going to earn a living from running so what did it matter?

'You're a disgrace,' she sneered as Carla stumbled to her knees. 'Get up.'

Carla started to cry.

'Get up!' she bayed.

I couldn't believe anyone could be so deliberately mean. What warped satisfaction did she get from bullying poor Carla in front of twenty-four impressionable girls, twenty-two of whom just seemed relieved it wasn't happening to them. I was fuming inside, but my protestations amounted to nothing more than a muttered, 'What a bitch!'

But Felicity spoke louder. 'I don't think she's running slow on purpose,' she announced dryly, causing Miss Fit to swing around, eyes flashing, ready for her second victim. But she had to bite back any further abuse because Felicity was the school's Most Valuable Player – a lithe six-footer who excelled at everything from hurdles to hockey. So instead she turned back to Carla and screeched, 'Again!' adding, 'and this time put some effort in.'

The message was clear – any more comments and it would get worse for Carla.

Goddamn p.e. teacher Nazis!

Everyone else forgot about it over lunch but Felicity and I couldn't let it lie. Something about the injustice of the situation lit a fire within us both, and we ditched the runny shepherd's pie in favour of concocting a way to make Miss Fit pay. I favoured a simple garrotting with the string of her stopwatch, but Felicity had a better idea. 'We have to take away the one thing Miss Fit prizes above all else – *winning*.'

That Saturday there was a major netball match against our arch-rivals, Cheltenham Ladies' College. The A-team list had already been posted, with me as Goal Shooter and Felicity as Goal Attack. And Captain. We just needed the other five players to back us up and we could really get our point across.

'Do you think verbal abuse of Carla Dollop is acceptable?' Felicity urged, rallying the key players on our next break.

'No,' they replied.

'Do you think that if we say nothing and do nothing Miss Fit will realise the error of her ways and apologise?'

'No,' they choroused.

'Well then, since this is a school,' Felicity concluded, 'I suggest we teach her a lesson!'

Felicity's confidence was contagious and, thinking nothing of the potential consequences, we marched en masse to the staff room to confront Miss Fit.

'You know the game on Saturday?' Felicity began.

'Yes,' she nodded eagerly, apparently anticipating a strategy debate.

'Well, I just wanted to let you know that we – the A-team – won't be playing.'

'What?' She flinched.

'We don't feel we can go out there and give one hundred per cent for a coach who has shown so little respect for one of our classmates.'

She looked confused. I don't think she had even registered the awful things she'd said two hours before.

'In short,' Felicity continued, maintaining an almost blithe tone, 'we will be on strike until you apologise to Carla.'

As realisation dawned, Miss Fit turned a sweaty rouge, sputtering, 'I'm not going to apologise to a pupil!'

'Okay,' Felicity shrugged, turning to leave. 'Good luck with the B-team.'

She'd need it, they were dire.

'If you think you can blackmail me—' she frothed, but Felicity kept walking, swiftly followed by the rest of us, eager to get the hell out of there before we got clawed back by our scalps.

Within the hour all the strikers were called before the headmistress. And all seven of us went. I realise now that in the real world it is a rarity to have such a show of solidarity – when there's a salary at stake it's hard to get people to stand up for their fellow man – but we were young and bold, with infinite faith in Felicity. Miss Dunn asked us to explain ourselves. We did. And then she asked Miss Fit to apologise. And it was a triumphant result, even though she tried to kill us with three consecutive 1500-metre runs.

'That felt so good,' Felicity confessed to me later.

'I think I need new legs.' I was still preoccupied with agonising shin-splints from the run. 'Don't you hurt?'

'It's worth it,' she shrugged. 'I'd do it again.'

I stopped my whingeing and thought, She's got a point. This feels good on the inside. And from that moment on I was looking for a chance to test myself and see if I could be equally valiant.

My defining moment came two weeks later during an afternoon English lesson. The week before we'd been given a big essay assignment, and Mrs Stafford began our lesson by handing back our graded notebooks. Instead of my usual A/B there was some scrawl telling me I'd misunderstood the brief and would therefore have to go unmarked. I was disappointed, but it was no big deal. Until it transpired that I was not the only one to have gone off at the wrong tangent; Melanie Delaney had done the same.

Now, Melanie was to writing what Carla was to sprinting, i.e. the perfect target for a mean-spirited teacher to garner a cheap laugh, and Mrs Stafford wasted no time in mockingly relating to the rest of the class how Mel had misinterpreted the question, making her sound like that era's equivalent of Jessica Simpson. Everyone tittered at her foolishness. Except me and Felicity. It just didn't seem fair; I had made exactly the same mistake. Why wasn't I also being ridiculed? The answer was simple – much like Felicity with Miss Fit, I was Mrs Stafford's prize pupil. But at what cost? I was just about to stand up and take equal brunt when Mrs Stafford went a step further, stunning everyone by ripping the offending pages from Mel's book and branding her 'Stupid girl!'

A rage swelled inside me. In front of a now uneasy class, I stood up and extended my notebook to her, albeit with a wobbly arm.

She looked confused.

'Excuse me, Mrs Stafford. I made the same mistake – are you going to tear up my notebook too?'

'Er, no,' she flustered, shuffling her papers. 'That won't be necessary.' She opened the textbook and prepared to begin the lesson.

I looked back at Felicity. She nodded at me to stand strong. It was all the encouragement I needed.

'Why not?' I persisted.

'What?'

'Why won't that be necessary? We both made the same mistake. I think we should both be treated in the same way.'

I hardly knew Mel, but it was the principle of the matter that bothered me, and I was not about to back down. I took a deep breath and added, 'And while we're on the subject, do you think I'm stupid too?'

'No, of course not,' she blustered.

'But Mel is?'

She gawped back at me.

'Isn't that what you said?'

Again she was at a loss for words, utterly snookered.

'Well, considering that two of us interpreted your brief in an identical way, I think it's fair to say that it

34

may be *you* that was at fault. Perhaps you should be more clear in your wording of questions in the future.'

At which point she burst into tears, ran out of the room and locked herself in the toilet howling noisily for the rest of the period.

I did feel a bit bad about that. It's never good to hear someone sobbing on your account, but she had been so deliberately mean, something had to be said.

From then on, if any girls had a problem, they came to us. Felicity specialised in sports and science. I did arts and the bookish stuff. We chose our battles carefully. Nothing for the sake of it; only when it really mattered. Always reasonable, always calm, never shouting. Felicity's mum was a human rights lawyer, and everyone joked that if we joined forces no one would be able to withstand the power of our righteousness! But our time together was cut short when Felicity's father announced that the family was returning to New Zealand.

You might have thought Miss Dunn would have been glad to see the back of a fire-starter like Felicity, but in fact she was devastated, and said she had hoped that Felicity might one day become head girl. She even tried to persuade her parents to let her stay on as a boarder but ultimately she understood that, for both Felicity and her family, a more relaxed and outdoorsy way of life held more lure.

She left herself the following year, replaced by one Miss Tucker and we pupils went from being known as Dunn's Nuns to Tucker's . . . well, I think you can imagine. It was quite a shift in reputation. Nothing was the same after that.

Felicity and I made a big effort to stay in touch, and though international phone calls were practically taboo back then, I got to hear her Kiwi accent getting more pronounced with every month that passed, thanks to the letter-tapes she'd send. I'd play them over and over and imagine she was chatting away in the same room as me. I missed her so much. I had other friends, but none could compare. Her spark was unique. But gradually the inevitable happened – the letters got less frequent and soon we were down to Christmas and birthday cards, albeit ones with scribbled summations of recent events. I found myself laughing less, and my once bold alter ego dwindled to meek.

Then, when I was twenty-eight, my parents died. You'd think she'd have been the first person I'd turn to – she knew them better than any of my other friends – but at the time I knew from my birthday card that she'd only recently split up with her boyfriend and I couldn't see the sense in putting her through losing them too, so I didn't tell her. I just leant a little harder on Hugh.

Now it's four years on and we've completely lost touch. I wonder what she's doing with her life today? Way back when, the plan was for me to have an exhibition at the Tate the same year she won Wimbledon, but I think it's more likely that she's become New Zealand's answer to Erin Brockovich . . .

'Just imagine how different things might have been if she'd stayed in Oxford . . .' Gilly ponders when I've finished reminiscing, voicing a thought I've had many times. 'You two might have had your own TV show by now – the Kim and Aggie of consumer rights!'

I chuckle. I did feel so invincible when we were together. The power of two! People think I'm a two with Hugh, but it's not the same. With Felicity we were in the game together, not playing opposite each other. Not that Hugh feels like opposition exactly. How can I explain it? I know he loves me but sometimes I think he's just selected a few aspects of me to love, not the whole package. It's not his fault – in the beginning I was reluctant to show him everything about me; then, when my parents died, I lost the will to flirt and we got to a stage where he didn't seem to be looking for any more from me than companionship and cooking and being polite and blonde at the occasional work do, so that was that, I was off the hook. Consequently, I sometimes feel I'm not entirely myself with him. In fact, I'm not sure I'm even myself with myself any more. I wonder if Felicity will be able to remind me who I once was? Who I am capable of being.

Oh God, I have to see her again!

There's just the small matter of finding her.

'And how are you going to do that?' Abigail wants to know as she rolls her empty latte cup into a cardboard cigar and stuffs it in her bag, ready to head back to the museum.

'Well, last night I went on Friends Reunited, and

37

I've emailed everyone and anyone from Headington School, left messages on every possible virtual noticeboard . . .'

'And you're hoping to locate her in the next two days?' Gilly looks unconvinced. 'You'll be lucky.'

'She *is* lucky,' Allegra snaps. 'She's going on an all-expenses-paid trip to paradise with the man of all our dreams. Everything else will be a breeze.'

And she's right. I get home to an email from one of our former best friends, Jackie Loh, who's kept meticulous tabs on all our old school chums from her base in Hong Kong and has furnished me with a phone number. I do a quick check on the time difference: 7.30 p.m. now means it's 7.30 a.m. in Auckland. A tad early for a blast from the past, but I can't wait a moment longer . . .

3

The phone rings twice at the other end but I cut the call before anyone picks up, suddenly nervous. What am I going to say to her after all these years? Will she even want to speak to me? What if she's changed? I tut myself – of course she's changed, it's been eighteen years since we last saw each other. But what if we don't get on any more? What if she has kids? I won't know how to relate to her if she's a mum.

Above all, I don't think I can bear to hear the disappointment in her voice when she hears about the person I've shrunk into.

I slump for a moment then, afraid of losing my impetus, I scrabble through the contents of my special secret drawer. There it is! I pull out a photograph of the two of us in blue aertex shirts on the hockey field. The sight of my fourteen-year-old self beaming like a beacon fortifies me: friends like Felicity come along once in a lifetime. If there's even a small chance that I can connect to feeling that happy and pally again, it's got to be worth a shot . . .

I pick up the phone and press redial . . .

'Hello?' The voice is female but sounds too subdued to be Felicity.

'Um, yes, I do hope I haven't woken you,' I begin in super-polite phone voice, 'but is it possible to speak to Felicity Lacey?'

There's a pause and then she says, 'This is Felicity . . .,' speaking slowly, as if her memory cogs are creaking into motion. There's another pause and then she says the first letter of my name – 'A—' – then halts herself.

'What were you going to say?' I encourage, on tenterhooks. Surely she can't be recognising my voice after all this time?

'No, it can't be . . .'

'It could be!' I beam, holding my breath.

'Amber?'

'Yes!' I squeal.

'Amber Pepper?' she shrills. 'No way! NO WAY!'

She screams. I scream. We both scream together – a banshee howl of excitement and rediscovery. At which point Hugh comes hurtling around the door looking stricken.

'What is it?' I start, jumping to my feet.

'*What do you mean, "What"*! I thought you were being attacked.' He bends over to catch his breath. 'God, Amber, you scared me! I've never heard you make a noise like that before.'

He's got a point. I'm not quite sure where the energy came from to summon such a soul-rendering clamour. It's left me feeling like I've just been mildly electrocuted.

'It's Felicity!' I hold up the phone as if he can see down the wire to New Zealand.

'Right!' he nods, looking unconvinced. 'Good. Well, carry on!' and with that he slopes back to his den, shaking his head.

'Everything all right?' Felicity checks.

'Everything's marvellous!' I grin down the phone, spinning on my desk chair. 'It's so good to hear your voice!'

'So tell me!' she commands.

'Tell you what?' I come to a halt.

'*Everything!* God! Where do we begin?'

'Well, how about I start with my most recent news?' I suggest, eager to cut to the chase and tell her about the trip that may just reunite us.

'You're pregnant!' she jumps in.

'Noooo!' I scrunch up my nose.

'Getting married?'

'Nope!'

'Getting divorced? Oh God, it's been so long it could be *anything*!'

I quickly begin telling her about Tahiti, but before we can get into the logistics I find myself gingerly enquiring, 'So are you any of the above?'

'Above what?'

I roll my eyes. 'Love life?'

'Don't taunt me!' she groans.

'That bad?'

'That nothing. But he's on his way, I can feel it. You?'

'He's already here,' I laugh. 'That was him just now.'

'Really?'

'Yup, and he's the guy responsible for getting me to within just a few hours of you.'

'Then I love him already!' she decides. 'What about your mum and dad?'

'Gone,' I say simply.

'Gone *away* or gone gone?'

'Both. In that order.'

'Oh, Amber,' her voice drops.

'It's okay.'

'No it's not,' she counters.

My heart belly-flops into my stomach. 'No, it's not,' I echo, eyes instantly welling up. Oh the relief of not having to put on a brave face! Suddenly all the feelings I've squashed and shushed over the past years start rushing up to the surface, eager for their chance to be aired and acknowledged. But now is not the time. I have to be patient just a bit longer.

'We're going to talk about *everything* when we see each other,' Felicity assures me, and in her voice I hear *I need this as much as you do!* 'We just need to work out where and how.'

I squirm a little at this point. Knowing the islands are crazy-expensive I've tracked down some £40-a-night pensions on the web, but how can I suggest she stays there when I'll be in the lap of luxury? I'm about to offer up my life savings (£857) as holiday funds when she cuts in: 'It's not a problem – my cousin Brian works aboard *Windstar*. I can stay with him!'

Windstar, she tells me, is an elegant and exclusive cruise ship – just 148 passengers per voyage and a berth with her name on it. Apparently the timing couldn't be better because the ship is enjoying her final stint in Tahiti before moving on to Costa Rica and whereas the original route took in five islands, from now until the end of the month she is mooring exclusively at Bora Bora. Brian has already offered Felicity the chance to share his cabin, but as food and beverage manager he works long shifts throughout the day and rarely has time off the boat, so, until now, she hasn't thought it worth it.

'But this is perfect!' she whoops. 'I can see him and you and Bora Bora!'

There is one potential fly in the sunscreen. 'What about getting time off work?'

'No worries,' she breezes. 'I just got fired!'

Now, some folk might find this fact inhibiting to their spending, but, having just received her final pay cheque, Felicity is feeling flush and more than happy to blow £500 on a flight. (After some lost years in telesales I thought she'd got back on track as a suburban tennis coach, but apparently the club members were just too hoity-toity to appreciate her sometimes brash demeanour and the fact that she never let the men beat her.)

'I mean, we could easily drop a few hundred on this phone call if we *really* took the time to catch up!' she reasons. 'Honestly, this is a bargain!'

Arrangements locked down, I bound into Hugh's den and tell him the good news. 'She's coming!' I cheer. 'And she's only going to be ten minutes from where we're staying so I can see her every day!' I take a breath and tentatively add, 'If that's okay with you?'

He looks up from his computer, still trying to tie up the Larrabee diamond deal before we leave, and smiles patiently. 'If this will keep you happy while I'm at work, I shall be for ever in this woman's debt.'

'Really? 'Cos she's about to book her flight and everything.'

'I would just ask one thing.'

'Yes?' I pip.

'One night, while we're away, could you possibly look as excited as you do right now at the prospect of watching the sun go down with me?'

My heart twangs. I think I need to take a class in being a good girlfriend. With Hugh working such long hours, even when he's at home, and then obsessing about cricket and rugby for the majority of his free time, I'm often off-guard and forget to soften my voice and call him darling. Not that he seems to interpret this as neglect – his parents have always led a very ships-that-pass-in-the-night existence, so our 'see you at dinner' set-up is a familiar routine for him. Actually, I'm not sure his parents even pass in the night any more, because for as long as I've known them they've had separate bedrooms. I wonder sometimes if Hugh and I will end up with a similar arrangement. I know some people would find this a rather sad reflection on the state of the relationship, but I can definitely see the upside – not every couple was made a jigsaw-perfect fit for each other. Hugh and I have long since given up trying to sleep with dead arms and tickly breath on the back of the ear during spooning. I'm lucky I got a non-needy guy. This is really the first time in a long time he's asked something of me. I think that's why I've said yes to this journey, against my better judgement.

Looking at him now, seeing the tiredness in his eyes, I feel a smudge of sympathy and lean over and kiss him on the lips. This is a big trip for him; he's going to be under a lot of pressure to prove himself. The last thing he needs is to be worrying about coming back to a grizzling girlfriend on a sun-lounger. In this moment I make a pledge to do everything I can to make the trip easier on him.

'It's going to be wonderful,' I assure him. 'You're going to get the best pearls at the best price and come back to find that Piers has got stuck down a fox-hole and you're the new head honcho.'

His arms reach up around my waist, pulling me closer. I let his head rest on my chest and hear him exhale as I stroke his forehead, massaging away the munched-up tension with my thumb.

'So, what do you want for dinner – I'll do anything.'

'Anything?' He turns his face upwards to guage my reaction.

I nod down at him.

'Twice-baked-potato-with-sour-cream-and-chives-and-bacon-bits-anything?' He looks like a little boy chancing his arm by asking for a turbo engine for his toy racing car.

I smile fondly at him. He may be the one to spoil me with expensive gifts but at least I can give back a little with my cooking. 'Be ready in an hour.' I turn to leave, but he pulls me back and sighs earnestly, 'You know, my stomach loves you very much.'

'I know,' I tell him, ready as ever with a deflective remark. 'You'd better make the most of it – we've got an awful lot of airline food coming up . . .'

As usual I begin my kitchen ritual by dimming the lights and putting on some mellow music. I carefully procure each item from the fridge and vegetable rack and then set them out like a still life on the central island before I begin to methodically prep and chop, eager to surrender to the sense of peace and focus. Yet tonight I repeatedly find myself distracted. First by packing issues: other than a stack of books and the flimsy items Abigail is insisting I borrow, I really don't know what on earth to take with me. And then there's the prospect of seeing Felicity. The yearning to be with this friend who truly gets me is so intense, I have to close my eyes to seal in my tears.

I feel like I've been meditating for the past four years or so, maintaining a numb state through repetition and familiarity, making sure that no emotions get

46

the better of me, and now the time is coming when I'll no longer be able to get away with my regular 'everything's fine' bluff. It makes me feel a little on edge, afraid of what I might unleash, but I know Felicity can handle it. She was the first person I told the truth to about my parents, and even though it was a big step, I wasn't worried because I knew she wouldn't be fazed. She listened, took everything on board and accepted it. No judgement. No googly-eyed tabloid fascination. In fact, whatever I talked to her about, I always felt better for it. I've missed that feeling. I've only just realised how much. It's going to be so great to be able to talk about Hugh without seeing the other person's eyes glaze with 'What are you complaining about? The man's a saint!' indifference.

As I set the bacon asizzling in the frying pan, I again experience the unsettling sensation that change is ahoy. Only this time some tiny forgotten part of me appears to be relishing the shake-up.

But mostly, I just feel sick.

4

Two unexpected things happen on the way to Tahiti. Firstly, the airline food is good. And not just 'not bad for micro-blasted astronaut snacks in a silt of gravy' but tasty noisettes of New Zealand lamb sautéed and served with Portobello mushroom duxelle and a sundried tomato and thyme jus, serenaded by a glass of a Pegasus Bay Pinot Noir. This could possibly have something to do with the fact that I'm travelling business class for the very first time. All that leather and legroom is wildly decadent, though I did miss peeling hot tin foil off my food. I think that's a fun tradition airlines should maintain no matter how rich you are.

Secondly, when we deplane to replane in Los Angeles, I spot a familiar face in the departure lounge.

'Hugh.' I tug at his sleeve, trying to coax his head up from his pearl research papers.

'Grade A pearls have less than ten per cent surface

flaws,' he mutters, trying to commit at least one fact to memory. (Not his forte, bless him.) 'Are we boarding?'

'Not yet.' My eyes remain trained on the far corner of the lounge. 'Hun, isn't that Sandrine Volereaux?'

'Where?' he gasps, his attention well and truly nabbed.

I point over to the winner of the Best Hair In Terminal award. 'See?'

I can almost hear my mother, ever the hairdresser, cooing, 'Look at that – not an unsubmissive follicle on her head!' Personally, if I wear a high ponytail I look like I'm preparing for an aerobics class or a facial steaming. With Sandrine the skilfully aligned up-sweep merely accentuates the elite angle of her cheekbones and the cat-like flair of her eyes. Everything about her is sleek and feline-sexy. I'm in flip-flops and the closest thing I could find to pyjama bottoms, she's in a chic, pert-bottomed trouser suit and a pair of gleaming Gina heels. As always her clothes look like they are being worn for the very first time and are thus on their very best behaviour. It makes me want to pin a badge to her silk scarf declaring, 'Don't hate me because I'm French!'

'Are you sure it's her?' Hugh says, leaning forward to try and get a clear view through the milling pre-boarders.

'Yes,' I insist. I know it's her because only Sandrine would travel in her flashiest jewels. Whereas my lobes are studded with a pair of simple cream pearls (a gift from Piers last birthday – he may be a sleaze but he loves to treat the laydeeez), Sandrine is jangling chandeliers. Every finger is loaded with gems and even from this distance I can see she's wearing the kind of necklace that comes with its own bodyguard.

'Oh my God, you're right!' Hugh reels as she finally turns in our direction. 'Piers knew they were hosting a couple of rival buyers on this trip, but he isn't going to be happy about this.'

Sandrine was the Pearl Girl prior to Piers. She broke all the company commission records then walked out the morning she got head-hunted by a Parisian jeweller and now lives in a penthouse atop the Eiffel Tower, or so we like to believe. As far as I'm aware, Hugh hasn't seen her since, so that's at least two years of catching up for them to do. (Cue much Gallic husking and overuse of the term 'cherie'.)

'Might this be a problem for you?' I ask, fretting on Hugh's behalf. 'I mean, aren't these black pearls pretty unique? What if you're both after the same one?'

'The Koh-I-Noor of the pearl world?' Hugh grimaces visibly at the prospect. 'There is supposed to be one gobstopper in existence, but even Piers doesn't know if it's just a myth. Of course she could be going to Tahiti on her honeymoon . . .' Hugh looks at me and then we both burst out laughing. The woman is untameable. A man-eater extraordinaire. Only one individual has managed to resist her highly-polished charms, and those honorary Underpants of Steel belong to Hugh.

Despite the fact that she made a blatant play for

him, I almost like her – she's so much larger than life, so shamelessly selfish, so label-addicted, and yet she never makes you feel anything less than splendid. I know she's going to claim she's in love with my flip-flops and must get a pair herself, so I'd better prepare a better response than 'I got them free with a copy of *New Woman*'. (It amazes me what magazines give away in the lead-up to the summer holidays. I can't wait for the day they try binding a ready-inflated lilo or a Mr Whippy ice-cream van to the cover.)

'Let's go and say hello,' I dare Hugh.

'*Mon dieu!*' she shrills at the sight of us. 'It can't be!'

'It is,' Hugh intones, gravely enduring a barrage of chi-chi kisses. 'You remember Amber?' he says, attemping to divert the attention to me.

'But of course!' she says, cupping my jaw in her hand. 'A woman to be faithful to, *n'est ce pas*?'

Like I said, shameless.

'Where do you two fly to?' she enquires, looking around the terminal for an appropriate destination to pair us with.

'Tahiti,' Hugh replies.

'*Tahiti*?' she exclaims, grabbing my hand, pre-sumably to check for a wedding band.

'Business,' I assure her.

She massages my bare ring finger with obvious relief. 'Oh,' she smiles, then suddenly starts, 'OH! *Not pearls*?'

Hugh nods.

'But where is Piers?' Her eyes make a swift identity parade inspection of the other passengers.

'He's back in London,' Hugh replies. 'Laid up.'

'Laid?' Sandrine looks scandalised at the prospect of Piers having sex. I pretty much feel the same way.

'Up,' I clarify. 'Laid up as in off sick.'

'Ah, *sick*, yes.' Sandrine is much happier with that explanation.

'So, did you fly in from Paris today?' I ask, deciding her first class seat must have come with its own sunbed.

'Oh no, I arrive last week to visit with my friends in Malibu. Now I am revived!'

Oh dear, that nudges it up to three factors playing to her advantage: with only a three-hour time difference to contend with from here on, her jet lag won't be as debilitating as Hugh's; pearls are of course her speciality; and French is her first language – quite a plus when you're off to French Polynesia. Unless Hugh is secretly fluent at Tahitian, the poor blighter doesn't stand a chance.

'How funny that you two will be working together again!' I pip nervously.

'Together?' Sandrine gives Hugh a wry look. 'No. Now he is the enemy!'

Hugh looks so queasy that for a moment I think we're within shot of heading straight back home, but then Sandrine pulls him into the embrace of a woman who knows how to wield a hand-weight and tinkles, 'I joke, of course! There are plenty of pearls for the both of us, *oui*?'

'I hope so.'

'And maybe, if you're really good –' she leans in close, brushing his ear with her Chanel-embossed lips – 'I share a few trade secrets with you, *non?*'

A normal girlfriend might find this peeving, but I can only laugh because in the same breath she turns to me and says, 'Cherie! *J'adore* your flip-flops – you must tell me where I can get a pair!'

Initially we take our assigned seats – Hugh and me in a pair by the window, Sandrine alone in the row in front of us – but her constant turning around and chattering to Hugh about people I've never met and designers I've never heard of takes its toll and I realise I don't stand a chance of sleeping if we stay like this, so I persuade the jewelling duo to sit together. Better that they get the big reminisce out of their system now than make me feel the odd bod out later over dinner. She is, of course, also staying at the Bora Bora Lagoon Resort and is already insisting that we join her. (In fact, by the sounds of it, that could be the beginning of many a dinner-à-trois: Sandrine's and Hugh's entire itineraries are aligned – same meetings, talks and tours – so she'll actually be spending a good deal more time with him than I will. Not sure how I feel about that.

Within minutes of swapping seats Sandrine has downed a bottle of Cristal, slipped on a satin eye-mask and entered a deep, dribble-free sleep. Hugh, mean-while, nods off two pages into his pearl homework sending a sleet of sheets into the aisle. I, frustratingly wide awake, jump up and shuffle them back together, retrieving the cover page from under the heel of our assigned flight attendant.

As the pages are not numbered I find myself reading the last and first sentences to get everything back in order. Ten minutes in I realise I am feeling calmer than I have done all day. Research. This is my game. I fan the stack of pages, assessing just how long it would take to read the whole lot. It's quite a hefty collection, with sections on history, cultivation, design, grading, certification . . . I know Hugh hasn't taken in a word so far, and he'll never have enough time to get through all this before his meeting tomorrow. Perhaps it would help him if I secured the basics, maybe even drew up a crib sheet for him? I know a little about Japanese Akoya pearls from my father's 'private collection', but until this trip I didn't even know black pearls existed. Other than in legends. I think I'd better start at the beginning.

Easier said than done. As I rifle through the file in search of the opening section, I find myself distracted by a glossy colour photograph. Well, look at that, these pearls aren't black at all. Hugh's right in that they do resemble ball bearings or metallic marbles, but the fact is that the most noirish they get is a shimmery charcoal grey. Others come in surprisingly vibrant pistachios, aubergines, blues and purple-green peacock colours. There's even a beautiful champagne-gold hue. I'm in awe: there must be something pretty magical in the

Tahitian waters to conjure up these colours. Maybe that's what happened with Gauguin: he dipped his brush in the lagoon and when it met with the canvas it turned the sand pink.

The caption tells me that the prices vary according to the rarity factor and fickle fashion. Reading Piers's margin notes, the blue is currently the most coveted, then the peacock, then the fly-wing green, with grey the most common and thus least valuable. There's also a reminder for Hugh to look out for any buddha-shaped pearls for Glenn the Spiritual Stockbroker.

'Buddha-shaped?' I mutter, thumbing onwards in the hope of finding some visual examples. Ah. I locate a sheet displaying the potential variations in form. Apparently only a tiny fraction of every harvest are spherical: in the mix you'll find gourd shapes, tadpole, button, papillon, egg, twin (which looks to me like a snowman) and the exotic-sounding 'forme fantaisiste'. There are also ones with grooves like spinning tops and misshapen curios sporting clusters of tiny wartlike pimples. As a consequence, it can take as long as ten years to match enough pearls in colour and size to make up a single necklace. Now that's patience.

I look closer at the images of the grooved ovals with their distinct middle ridges. Personally I think these 'baroque' pearls are the most beautiful. They have a unique charm and detailing to hold your interest. When I look back at the flawless spheres they seem dull in comparison.

Highly polished and perfectly formed; lustrous but ultimately dull.

By the time we arrive in Papeete – pronounced Pa-pee-ay-tay – on the main island of Tahiti, I've also discovered that the larger the pearl, the more internal layers it has, and the more layers, the more radiance. (Lustre is a highly prized quality, and you must consider both the action of the *reflected* light which bounces off the pearl and the *refracted* light which passes through. Fascinating!)

While we wait for our connecting flight to Bora Bora, I also glean that if you keep a pearl locked in a safe you need to place a glass of water beside it or else the pearl will crack. The mantle that is, not the nucleus—

'Okay, you've got to put that away now.' Hugh takes back his file, strapping it into his bag alongside his laptop. 'It's time to start admiring the view.'

'My, what a lovely runway,' I mumble as we trek tarmac to board the Air Tahiti Nui flight which will take us to Bora Bora.

Three aeroplanes in one day is three too many for me. Hugh is getting all zingy at the prospect of actually reaching our destination, but despite my pledge to be an exemplary travelling companion, I can't match his enthusiasm. Even the prospect of seeing Felicity seems more ruse than reality at this point. I rest my head on the plastic framing of the window and let it judder as we rev up for take-off. Now I'm really tired. Now I wish I'd slept and not stayed up cramming for a pearl exam that I don't even have to take.

'Here we go!' Hugh takes my hand, leaning heavily over me to look out of the window. 'Up above the clouds.'

These are not the bulky puffs I'm used to but ghostly wisps like lingering cigar smoke or breath on a frosty morning. As I make a sleepy study of them, I notice a rainbow ring surrounding the plane. Gilly would probably put it down to the collective auras of the passengers within, but I decide it's a sign from my mum and dad to let me know they've come along for the ride . . . Now they've actually got some free time, I like to think they would want to spend it with me.

'Do you know that there are a hundred and eighteen islands down there?' Hugh asks, straining to spot at least one.

'Really?' I am surprised – in my mind I'd pictured five, max.

'Yup. In fact, if you laid Tahiti over Paris, the spread of her islands would cover the whole of Europe.'

'You're kidding!' This is weird, knowing so little about where I am in the world. Also a little disconcerting that Hugh should know more than me. 'When did you pick that up?' I quiz him.

He holds up the in-flight magazine. 'Read it two seconds ago!' he chuckles, giving me a sweet kiss on the cheek.

I sigh to myself. It's not just Sandrine who would like to be in my flip-flops right now. What girl doesn't want to be spirited away by a handsome man for some long-haul loving? I pull hard on a loose strand of my hair, as if tweaking my crown will reset my brain. What's wrong with me? Why am I wishing I was at home alone in my den, listening to my mum's records in the dark? I think this country may be simply too bright and peppy for my sensibility: we've just been sent on our way not by a stern announcement to remove all sharp items from our hand luggage but by the plinkity-plink plucking of a ukulele. Even the flight attendants' uniforms are jazzily informal – cute little purple batik numbers worn with clashing flowers behind the ears. And look at that, I've just been served a glass of Day-Glo pineapple juice. What I really want is a murky cup of tea in my own mug. And a fleece instead of this all-too-sheer FLY ME TO LAGOON T-shirt Abigail designed for me. I shiver as I watch the aircon visibly dispersing like dry ice from the overhead panel.

'Cold, honey?' Hugh enquires, rubbing my goose-pimpled arms.

I want to tell him that they may as well hang us from freezer meat hooks and have done with it, but instead I murmur, 'I'm fine,' and turn back to the window.

'Oh my God!' I yelp suddenly.

'What?' His eyes are still on me.

I reach out and stub my finger on the plexiglas. The only word my slack jaw can form is 'Blue!'

58

5

They say Eskimos have thirty words to describe snow, well Tahitians need a hundred or more to define the colour of their waterworld. (Which is frankly never going to happen, seeing as they only have thirteen letters in their alphabet – something else Hugh just garnered from the in-flight mag.) The fact is, I have never seen an oceanic palette so vibrant and diverse. The main expanse of sea is a ruffled jelly of rich navy with intermittent crests of white. Then, literally out of the blue, it appears as though someone has Tippexed a freehand circle on the surface of the water and splashed a little bleach and blue curaçao within the outline. This is Bora Bora's legendary lagoon: luminous turquoises, palest mint greens and dark seepings of royal-blue ink, all keenly distinct from one another.

'It looks like abstract art,' Hugh decides.

'Abstract Aquatic I think would be the official

term,' I tell him, now concentrating on the assorted land formations within the ring, trying to make sense of the shapes. If this were an ink-blot test I would see the outer banks as the flexed arms and clenched fists of a Mr Universe muscleman protectively encircling his prize, in this case the main island of Bora Bora, each peak and valley cloaked in green fuzzy felt.

The main island is in fact just the top of the cone of an old volcano – as it sank into the sea the perimeter of the base remained raised and formed a coral reef, and a magical setting for its seven thousand residents. This information comes courtesy of the man in the seat in front as he tries to explain the topography to his young son.

'And the smaller islets within the lagoon . . .' as he points to one shaped like a lamb chop Hugh and I have to stop our eavesdropping-selves from saying, 'Yes?' . . . 'they are called motus.'

'We're staying on a motu!' Hugh gasps, pinching me excitedly. 'I wondered what that means.'

'We've got our own island?' I'm incredulous.

Hugh nods. 'There's just our hotel, a new bar and a lot of palm trees.'

'Gosh.' Suddenly I feel very Girl Friday.

'But there's a shuttle across to Vaitape every half an hour,' he reassures me.

'Okay.' I nod, then add, 'What's Vaitape?'

'The main town on Bora Bora.'

'Right.' I'm feeling out of my depth again. Can't

someone ask me something about pearls? I know about pearls.

'Look, we're almost overhead now!' Hugh redirects my attention to the window.

Now I can clearly make out the bright white of the outer crust, the adjacent ribbon of green land, the skeins of pale sand slipping into sapphire blue, the shadowy clusters of coral in the shallow areas.

I try not to look too envious as we fly over a resort made up entirely of over-water bungalows snaking out into the lagoon like the ridged tail of a reptile. That's the one thing I expressed some curiosity over, but it turned out there were only garden and beach bungalows available at the Bora Bora Lagoon Resort. Those darn honeymooners beat us to it.

'What's this narrow band of land here?' I ask Hugh. 'And why are we flying so low over it?

'That's the landing strip,' Hugh replies, crossing himself just to freak me out that little bit more.

One bump and we're down.

Only Sandrine sounds disappointed that the journey is over – apparently these inter-island flights are too short for even a woman of her sexual velocity to persuade a stranger to join her in the Mile High Club.

Clattering down the metal steps, I inadvertently cause a passenger collision by stopping in my tracks – apparently, when I can't believe my eyes, I also have trouble moving my feet. The airport is nothing more than an open-air shack! Yes, it has a gift shop and a petite café and toilets, but it has no outer walls. (I'm sure this would be lovely if there was anything resembling a breeze to whistle through it.) But what has me really stupefied is what lies beyond. From the air I thought I'd seen turquoise in its truest, cleanest form but I was mistaken. As I stumble forward, nodding respectfully as I pass the Tiki sentries, I gasp at a marina brimming with the brightest, most intense blue I have ever experienced. The only thing I've seen anywhere near that colour back in Oxford is a squirt of my Colgate gel toothpaste.

'Wow,' Hugh says, just as transfixed as I am. 'This must be one of the only places in the world where an airport could actually be the ultimate destination.'

Better yet, floating atop this mirage is a glossy white yacht, assigned exclusively to transport the three of us to our hotel. I catch sight of myself reflected in Sandrine's Dior sunglasses and want to laugh out loud, both at the newly acquired volume of my hair – darn that humidity! – and at the absurdity of seeing myself in this über-glamorous setting. However did I end up here?

'Isn't this just amazing?' I sense that Hugh is about to smother me with joyful, sun-drunk kisses, but Sandrine intervenes.

'I must have a ciggie before we board, cherie.' She taps Hugh's forearm. 'Will you get me a light?'

'I'm going to the loo!' I say, and scoot off, eager to take a moment to give my eyes a chance to adjust to the new colours and to tame my hair, just in case my mother is doing a little celestial spying from above. But when I enter the bathroom I'm so thrown by the sight of a sink counter lined with fragrant pink frangipani that for a moment I forget what I came in for. I mean, can you imagine finding the Ladies at Luton airport strewn with rose petals?

Five minutes later I'm wearing similar garlanding around my neck as the beautiful Tahitian guardian of the yacht presents each of us with heavily-scented welcome *lei*. I have a feeling Sandrine called ahead to coordinate her outfit with today's choice of flowers: she looks fashion-magazine-stunning in the cerise halter neck and white flared skirt she switched to on the last flight. I can't even be jealous. She's in a different league. I haven't learnt to be comfortable in my own skin let alone a backless top. Like right now the leaves on the *lei* are scratching at my neck as if I've left the plastic tag in the label of a new shirt, and yet Sandrine seems entirely untroubled by the decorative prickles. You know the type – can run/dance/play squash in high heels. I've yet to see her in a swimsuit, but I'm guessing she's had her legs specially elongated for the occasion.

'All aboard!' Captain Hugh salutes us as we take our places on the deck.

The heat is searing and I'm grateful for the rush of air as we gather speed, churning up the water in our wake and leaving a fishtail-shaped legacy of froth. I'm still having trouble registering that I'm here. I'm used to sludge-green rivers and trailing weeping willows, not endless lapis lazuli lagoons and towering palm trees. It really is another world.

In an attempt to feel less overwhelmed I decide to look for the similarities to my homeland, rather than the differences. See, the Tahitians live in houses too, I begin, grasping at straws as I spy the conventional single-storey homes nestling along the water's edge. No Hawaiian high-rises here. In fact they don't seem to build up at all – the mountainside is entirely green and untamed. If anything it appears to be easier to extend out into the lagoon than to create a clearing inland. And whereas Sandrine may be eagerly awaiting the completion of the Ritz-Carlton in the hope of being reunited with some marble and chandeliers, even that has a look entirely in keeping with the island style of wood and thatching. I suppose in many ways Oxford has a uniform look too – all those sand-coloured buildings with their studded timber gates and closely-cropped lawns. I can't help but wonder if we did a house swap with a Tahitian, what they'd make of Hugh's metallic minimalism, or indeed my burgundy flocked wallpaper?

'Well?' Hugh sidles up to me with wide, expectant eyes.

'It's dazzling,' I say, squinting at the sun. 'And very, very hot,' I add, disturbed by the sensation of sweat wiggling down the backs of my legs.

'I know, I can't wait to get in that water.'

'Me too,' I tell him as I eye the lifesaver ring tied to

the back of the yacht, wishing I could be dragged the rest of the way with the ring around my waist.

'Motu Toopua!' yells the yachtsman, distracting us from our temperature issues by veering away from the main island towards a bushy green islet, home to the Bora Bora Lagoon Resort. I see a main circular building clad in grey volcanic rocks, an immaculate curve of beach, a cluster of kayaks, a splash of snorkelling guests and a track of over-water bungalows that appear to be wading out to greet us.

As we slow to approach the wooden jetty, I tell myself that this is essentially the Tahitian equivalent of a bus stop, with its very own thatched shelter that just happens to shield you from the sun rather than the rain. Or maybe it serves both purposes? Hugh did promise the occasional downpour and you don't get vegetation this densely, lavishly green without a pretty effective sprinkler system.

'*Bonjour! Maeva!* Welcome!' The young French hotel manager, François greets us, directing us along the walkway towards the shade of the main building, leaving our suitcases to be off-loaded by the strapping porter.

'Oopla!'

I turn back to see that my tattered heirloom of a case has caved under the pressure of three consecutive flights and the contents are now spilling willy-nilly over the jetty. Including an overly-optimistic umbrella.

'Oh no!' I cringe, despairing that I've embarrassed Hugh so early on. He wanted to buy me one of those new Helium Lite cases from Delsey but I stubbornly refused. All I can do now is mouth 'Sorry!' at him.

'Please don't worry, madam, we will handle,' François soothes, utterly unfazed as he bids us continue.

'Really?' I falter for a second, feeling like I should reclaim my items and take the next shuttle home.

'*Oui!*' François insists. 'Please follow me.'

Once inside the lobby, Hugh's clammy hand is replaced with an iced flannel, and I quickly release my bag to accept a tumbler of chilled tropical juice accessorised with a corsage of leafy origami.

'*Asseyez-vous, s'il vous plaît . . .*' François motions for us to take our drinks into the sitting area, all wicker sofas and chairs with plump cream padding.

As Sandrine and Hugh absorb themselves with the check-in paperwork, my eyes rove beyond the robust display of spiky orange birds of paradise, and I find myself startled by a life-size carving of a Tahitian warrior with attention-seeking nether regions. Swiftly I divert my gaze to the elaborate shell chandelier overhead – string upon string of dainty brown and white sundial shells cascading down from a knotty beam, itself bound in place with attractively woven roping. I've never seen a five-star hut before. It's really quite something.

While Hugh copies the hieroglyphics from his credit card on to the registration form and Sandrine tries to shield her passport details – too late: I see that it's her fortieth birthday in a month – I wander over to study the images carved into the reception backboard. The style is symmetrical and graphic, depicting squat, bulgy-eyed, wide-mouthed creatures like a Tahitian PacMan. Already I'm intrigued by the local art. Over in the corner there's a set of three gurning masks, one giving an exaggerated gay-biker-moustache of a frown, one with snarly bared teeth and one pointing out his tongue and flicking it upwards to touch his nose. They remind me of the gargoyles back home, but instead of resenting my separation from them I suddenly realise how lucky I am to have them to go back to. Besides, I predict my time here is going to pass quicker than I imagined. It's only 6 p.m. but the day feels done now that night has pulled its dark curtains around us. I return to Hugh's side, leaning my head on his shoulder with a mixture of affection and relief.

'So, you would like a tour of our facilities?' François offers, stepping aside to allow various lamps and candles to be illuminated by his staff as he gathers up our passports.

Unless he's proposing to vault us directly into the swimming pool using the decorative bamboo rods stacked in the giant terracotta vase by the door, I just can't face the trek – the heat is still wilt-inducing even after dark. Fortunately Hugh and Sandrine now seem of the same mind.

'*Domain!*' 'Tomorrow!' they overlap, laughing as they play international snap.

'You are tired,' François nods sympathetically. 'You would like to retire to your rooms and I arrange for a light dinner to arrive there?'

'*Oui!*' Even Hugh can speak French when there's food at stake. '*Merci!*' he adds enthusiastically.

'My pleasure,' François nods. 'Anything else you need, I am here for you.' With that he hands us our room keys, each dangling the hotel's motif of a small carved wooden turtle, a symbol of fertility apparently. Hugh and I avoid making eye contact so we don't have to acknowledge the irony and swiftly exit the lobby.

'After you.' Hugh insists I lead the way. Now I'm really flagging. Maybe it's because I know a bed is just minutes away but I'm muzzy-headed, bodily disorientated, apathetic from jet lag and peeved about my suitcase. To cap it all, just when I think I'm maintaining my stance of being immune to paradise, this man o' mine has to go and ruin everything by surprising me with an over-water bungalow.

'But you said—'

'I wanted to surprise you,' he cuts in, smiling indulgently as he bids me enter.

'You have!' I sigh, though I feel a little silly now for thinking that Hugh could settle for anything less than the crème de la crème. I used to try and reason with him that the most expensive isn't always the best, that personal taste is something to be given equal value, but he always just gave me an 'Aren't you quaint!' squeeze and told me how reassuring it was to know that I wasn't with him for his money.

'Anyway, you should be flattered,' he'd tell me. 'You know I like the best things in life, and I'm going out with you!'

I never knew quite how to take this. I hardly see myself as the dream girlfriend, but I know I'm an improvement on the women his mother recommended prior to me. (And quite possibly still does.) Posh and glossy with the number of a good caterer pretty much characterised every Serena and Harriet she'd send his way.

'Don't knock superficial!' she used to tell him. 'It means she will take great care of her appearance and rarely get depressed because there's always the promise of something new and twinkly in the shops to lure her out of bed in the morning.'

'She just doesn't get me at all!' Hugh laughed as he told me various horror stories of the women he had dismissed as having Tiffany tourettes. Despite having a touch of that himself, he claimed he favoured the girl-next-door over dowried debutantes. He wanted someone real. Actually I think the word he used at the time was 'earthy'. The only way I can see myself ticking that box is when I'm cleaning the mud off my organic root vegetables. But since his mother never liked to do anything that might compromise her manicure, maybe by comparison I am.

And though Hugh may not want to be loved for his money, he does want to be loved for his generosity. That's something I've got to work on. He gets more than a little frustrated that I can see all the beauty in an Old Master and none in a New Mercedes, but right now I'm not having to fake my bliss – these shacks on stilts are every honeymooner's fantasy and I too succumb in an instant.

As Hugh buzzes around opening drawers, sliding doors and juggling the mango-scented toiletries, I stand in the middle of the floor, slowly rotating, taking it all in. Deceptively boxy from the outside, the interior is gloriously spacious with a vaulted ceiling, hardwood floors and wall-to-wall panelling in slatted teak. What with all the wood and the sound of sloshing water beneath us, I feel like I've stepped aboard a ship in one of those old movies with sea captains sporting velvet-bowed ponytails and knee-breeches. No scurvy here, though – the place is pristine; the perfect hideaway in which to recover from an excess of sea and sunburn.

There's even a day-bed-style sofa should your beloved prove too sticky to lie next to on a hot night. (Though I'm pleased to say the air-conditioning unit offers a more acceptable level of cool than our last flight.)

'Is this the fabled over-water coffee table?' I fall to my knees and inspect the glass cube in the centre of the room, instantly filled with wonder.

'It is indeed!' Hugh grins, delighted by my reaction. 'Here, let me slide the top open.' Hugh takes the basket of bread off the top and puts it to the side.

'Shouldn't there be a light?' I definitely remember this detail from the website.

'Here!' Hugh locates the switch.

It's then that we see this ingenious feature in its full glory. The idea is that, even after dark, you can lure fish beneath your bungalow by dropping a few baguette crumbs down into the water, then watch them feed from the comfort of your own living area.

'Oh my God – there's one, there's one!' I grip Hugh's arm, trying not to get too animated for fear I'll scare it off.

The moonglow-coloured fish gobbles up our sponge-like squelch of bread, then flits to the side as three of his mates gather up the spare crumbs.

For a good ten minutes we kneel in silence, tearing off snags of bread and watching the fish take their supper.

'I wonder if they only eat French bread?' Hugh ponders. 'Do you think they'd turn their noses up if we tried a slice of Mother's Pride?'

I smile and sit back on my haunches, noticing for the first time that the flowers on the bed are in fact real, not embroidered. This extravagantly beautiful detail is repeated in the bathtub – I plunge my hand into the cool water and retrieve a floating bloom. Before I can even inhale its perfume, Hugh sneaks up behind me, takes it from my hand and tucks it into my hair.

'See how pretty you look!' He stands behind me, admiring my reflection in the porthole-framed mirror.

I wince at the sight of such a bright colour beside my pallid face. It reminds me of the scarlet beret Hugh bought me the Christmas before last. It was so soft and strokable but I could never bring myself to wear anything that festive in public. I felt I would be somehow misrepresenting myself. I feel the same way now and instinctively go to remove the flower but as I see Hugh's brow crumple I manage to curb the partypooper in me, pretending I am merely securing it before decorating him with an even bigger hibiscus lolling a long, yellow, pollen-encrusted tongue.

'There – now we match!' I beam.

But do we? Ever since LA I've been thinking, Why isn't he with someone like Sandrine? Though his mother might baulk at her supreme confidence and obviously carnivorous appetite, she's a far better match. She loves to travel, loves to tan. I know everyone who passed them on the plane thought they made a striking couple, I could see it in their covetous eyes. There was no way they would have connected me with them, other than as a handmaiden.

Yes, Hugh turned Sandrine down when she made a move on him way back when, but we'd only just met; he still believed I could be everything to him. But now that he knows the truth – that I'm distant and difficult and all too often sad – I wonder if he might start seeing her with new eyes. I believe she's genuinely fond of him, and not just because he's the one who got away, though there is a chance she's exhausted every other sexual possibility by now.

There's also a chance that, as she approaches forty, she's had enough of her man *mange-ing* and is looking to settle down. If she has even the slightest desire for children Hugh offers first-rate daddy potential. He's ready. And I'm not.

I leave Hugh to finish his unpacking and wander out on to the deck, looking up at the black sky and wondering what tomorrow will bring, only to dart directly back inside when I realise Sandrine is striking an identical pose on the adjacent bungalow deck. I don't know if it's the jet lag that's making me paranoid, but I find myself speculating, What if she got word of Hugh's trip and deliberately had herself invited along, not realising I was coming too? No, that's not possible, I reason; she was already on her way before we even confirmed.

I expel a steadying breath and walk over to the bed, where Hugh is now lying fully clothed and snoring in his very own puttery-stuttery way. Not even the thought of eating can keep him awake now. As I take my place beside him I decide that whereas I can dismiss the theory that Sandrine planned for them to be together in paradise, I can't dismiss certain facts: she wears nice shoes (Hugh's one fetish). She knows jewellery (his passion). And, as of tonight, she is The Girl Next Door.

6

I awake to the invasive *drrrrinnng-ing* of a phone. As I work up the effort to wrench open my eyes, I become aware of the sound of water lapping and swishing beneath me. For a split second I think I've drifted out to sea and sit up too fast, afraid of capsizing, but then I remember I'm in a room that stands knee-deep in water.

Rrrrinng-rrrrinng . . .

Reaching over to pick up the receiver, my elbow dents a note from Hugh: *'Couldn't bear to wake you! Back by 6 p.m. Have a great day with Felicity!'*

I set the note aside and grunt a 'Hello?' into the phone.

'Aaaaggggggghhhhhhh!' A female voice makes bongos out of my eardrums. Speak of the devil.

'Aaaagggghhhhhhhh!' I yell back, charged by the sheer force of her holler.

'You up?' she pips.

'Not quite,' I confess.

'Sorry, but I couldn't wait a moment longer. I need you to get your booty over here right now!'

'Where are you?' I ask, still not with it.

'Can you see the lagoon from your room?' she queries.

'I'm *on* the lagoon,' I tell her.

Felicity gasps. 'Not one of those over-water bungalows?'

'Yup.'

'*Spoilt*!' she exclaims.

'I know!'

'Walk out on to the balcony,' she instructs.

I duly roll out of bed and stretch the phone beyond the patio doors.

'Done,' I tell her, stepping on to the warm teak boards and squinting into the sunshine.

'What can you see?'

'A blinding yellow light.'

'And as your eyes adjust . . .?' she prompts.

I see a whole new world of blue . . . Firstly there's the vibrant cobalt of the sun-lounger pads on the deck, then the expanse of azure water skimming across to the main island of Bora Bora where Mount Otemanu rises up and strikes a pagan stance . . .

'What else?'

Over at the water's edge I see a little red-turreted church and a cluster of rooftops that look like powder-green Chinaman hats. There's just the narrowest trim of houses, all keeping a respectful distance from the volcanic peak.

'In your own time . . .' I hear Felicity drumming her fingers.

I look directly below me into the clear water and see two fish with shimmery blue go-faster stripes skitting around the crunchy coral.

'Up a bit and over to your right,' Felicity guides me.

'Oh! A long white ship with four pristine white sails!' I finally deliver the magic words.

'That's me! That's me!' she cheers.

'Wow!' I coo at what must surely be the pointy-winged swallow of the cruise-ship world. 'She's beautiful.'

'I know! I'm spoilt too!' she chuckles. 'So are you coming over or what?'

I look at the stretch of water between us. 'How exactly?'

'You get the hotel shuttle to Vaitape, which will take about three minutes, and then hop aboard the *Windstar* tender – it's bright orange, you can't miss it,' she insists. 'It goes quarter to and quarter past the hour.'

'So that's just like getting two buses, right?' I check, still feeling a little out of my depth as I go back inside to search for a notepad to jot the timings on.

'Exactly. Do you reckon you can be here by noon?'

I look at my watch. 'I can do that,' I tell her.

'Great! 'Cos I'm bursting to tell you something!'

'You've got news already? You've only been here a matter of hours.'

'I'm a fast worker!' she giggles before setting down the phone.

Which reminds me – Sandrine . . . I walk back out on to the deck and stare across at her bungalow, half expecting to see Hugh's boxers strewn alongside her bikini. Silly. They're out working today. Flown back to the main island of Tahiti for a welcome presentation at the Black Pearl Museum and a cultural dinner. Poor bugger having to endure another flight. I know he would have liked nothing better than to lie out here all day with a good book, interspersing each chapter with a refreshing dip. Oh, will you look at that! For the first time I notice there are steps that take you directly from the deck down into the water. And an outside shower—

'Ouch!' I accidentally scrape my head on the jutting thatch of the roof. As I duck away from the papery prongs I realise I'm being watched by the honeymoon couple in the next bungalow along. Jeez! Could they stare any more? Anyone would think they'd never seen a pair of tartan flannel pyjamas in paradise before.

An hour later I'm on the dock, waiting my turn to step aboard the shuttle along with the other hotel guests. They all look so jaunty in their hot pants and vest tops. I don't know how they can show so much skin and not feel self-conscious. Me, I'm positively bereamed in fabric – so much so that if I let the wind inflate my skirt I could probably have an impromptu parasail on the way across to Vaitape.

The journey is brisk, the conversation around me mostly French, so I concentrate on the rumbling of the engine and the tissue paper slash as we tear through the water. This is so surreal; I still can't quite believe I've been transported to this parallel universe. I try to picture the girls in the office back at the Ashmolean, but I can't summon a clear image. It's as if my memory slides have been blanched out by the sun; a trick to keep my attention in the present, perhaps?

With a good eight minutes to spare before the *Windstar* tender leaves, I follow the flow of tourists into the covered market, where local ladies display their hand-crafted shell necklaces and silk-screened *pareu* – the Tahitian version of a sarong. There's even one recreating Gauguin's *Woman With A Flower*. I have to get it for Abigail, and fumble with the big colourful currency Hugh left for me. 40,000 French Pacific francs. That's about £20.

'*Maururu*.' The large lady with a voluminous red floral frock smiles and nods as I pay her.

'Thank you,' I say, taking the plastic bag from her.

'*Maururu*,' she repeats, laying her hand on my arm, keen for me to learn this one word.

'*Mow-roo-roo*,' I chant back.

Back in the sunshine, I scan the pier for an orange tender – there it is, just pulled up. I watch as a surprising number of people file off, every one of them looking like they can't quite believe their luck that they're here.

'This way for the island tour.' A small Frenchman sends one group on its way before turning back to do the head count for the 4×4 ride. Side-stepping him, I take a seat in the airless interior of the boat and make an inhalation of nerves and engine oil. I wonder if she will look the same? Unlikely, considering my enduring image is of her in an aertex shirt and pleated gym skirt wielding a hockey stick with orange towelling binding. As we churn into the lagoon I get a flash of her sparkling baby-blue eyes, that milky complexion smattered with freckles and those trademark springy chestnut bunches. As for me, my mother was forever braiding and French-plaiting my hair as a kind of showcase for her skills. I wonder if Felicity will be thrown by how plainly tressed I am today? Will she even recognise me?

'AMBER!' a voice calls out to me from above as the tender draws alongside the cruise ship.

I look up to see a pair of wildly waving arms.

'FLOSSIE!' I call back, her nickname bounding from my lips before I even think it.

Up the stairs I go, along the deck and BAM!, straight into her arms! Oh my God! Is there anything better than a hug when someone really means it? Immediately I sense a lump in my throat. Just seeing her makes me feel closer to my parents than I have done in years. Afraid I might crumple and embarrass myself if I stay burrowed, I pull back and take a good

79

look at my thirty-two-year-old friend. Her freckles now have a golden backdrop, her eyes and smile are as huge and dazzling as ever, but they are nothing in comparison with the enormity of her hair, which is not unlike the tresses of the native Tahitian women, lying like a big bulky buffalo rug down her back.

'Your hair!' I gasp.

'Oh don't!' she wails! 'If I'd have known it was going to get this big I would have got a number one before I came out here! Where's your mother when we need her?' she laughs, and then stammers, 'Oh, I'm sorry, I—'

'Don't be!' I shush her. 'I wish she was here too.'

Felicity hugs me again and then yanks me up the next flight of stairs to the top deck. 'Quick! You have to meet Brian before lunch gets under way.'

Cousin Brian is one of the most immaculate individuals I have ever laid eyes on. Of course it doesn't hurt any that he's in a sharp white officer's uniform, but he takes this up a notch with his precision crop, freshly-flossed teeth and the sheeniest, cleanest looking skin I have ever seen on a man (you'd almost think he'd had his jaw waxed rather than shaved for a smoother finish). His manner is an appealing combination of polished professionalism and cheeky *joie de vivre* that clearly runs in the family. I watch admiringly as he acknowledges each of the early lunchers with a personal greeting, putting a pampered smile on their faces and a spring in their step – a skill I never did quite master at Quand l'Artiste Mange.

Felicity suggests we sit inside to take advantage of the air conditioning and leads me into the greenhouse-style veranda restaurant – all white and chrome and potted plants.

'Isn't this glorious?' she raves. 'I didn't know I had such expensive taste till I got here! There's a buffet with salads and soups, a couple of hot pastas, or you can order off the menu if you prefer . . .'

I opt for the buffet, eager to get settled and get chatting. Initially our conversation is a jumble of what movies were on the plane on the way over, a reprisal of the dramatic changes in our hair courtesy of the extra moisture in the air, a verbal tour of the ship, and a detailed account of the indulgent five-course dinner Felicity forced herself to stay awake for last night.

'I had this curried parsnip soup with a garnish of crispy apple and—' she stops suddenly and bursts out laughing. 'I can't believe I'm talking about soup! Eighteen years, Amber! My God, if we'd been teen pregnancy statistics we could have adult daughters by now! You haven't got any, have you? I mean, I know I asked before if you were pregnant and you said no, but—'

'No secret offspring,' I assure her, marvelling at her energy level. 'You?'

She shakes her head. 'Not through lack of trying . . .'

My face falls. 'You mean you can't—'

'Find a man to impregnate me?' she laughs. 'That's

81

my problem!' She takes a sip of iced water, then scoots forward, looking extra bright-eyed and wilful. 'Actually, I think my luck may have just changed.'

'What do you mean?'

'This is what I wanted to tell you: last night, when I got off the plane, I *fell in love*!' she pipes, looking exceedingly pleased with herself.

'With who?'

'I don't know!' she squeaks, throwing her hands in the air.

'Oh,' I frown, confused. This sounds a bit of a non-starter to me. Since when did Felicity get so dizzy?

'I mean, I've seen him – I know what he looks like,' Felicity clarifies. 'I just don't know his name. Yet.'

'Go on . . .' I need convincing further.

'Well, I'm not sure whether he was on my Air New Zealand flight or if he'd just come in from another island, but I was with this big *Windstar* group looking out for Brian, and our eyes met and it was like someone had just given one of those CPR jolts to my chest and I got this overwhelming urge to throw myself at him.'

'But you didn't?'

'As I matter of fact I did.'

'*What?*'

'Not on purpose! There was this sudden surge behind me and I toppled right on to him, but instead of shrugging me off or trying to dodge me, his arms went right around me and he held on tight until the crowd settled.' Felicity's eyes glaze in remembrance. 'Oh, Amber, it was just the best feeling. I felt as if I could have fallen asleep in his arms right there in the midst of all that chaos.'

'And then?'

'I opened my eyes and saw Brian, let go so I could wave at him, and when I turned back he was gone.'

I feel a little pang of loss on her behalf. 'Is there a chance that he's also a guest on the ship?' I try to establish the facts.

'Brian reckons that's the most likely scenario. He says that if I stay by the food all day I'll soon find out if he's on board.'

'And if he's not?'

'Well, Bora Bora is a small island. No more than thirty hotels here. I can find him.'

Not easily daunted, is our Felicity. I follow her gaze as she assesses the latest newcomers to lunch.

'Nope, old folks. Nope, Italians . . .' She crosses them off her list.

'Was he really good-looking?' I'm still trying to get a fix on her OTT attraction.

'No Pretty Boy Pitt, he's just My Guy,' she answers in a sing-song manner.

'I suppose he could be taking room service?' I think back to the plans Hugh and I made last night.

'Even if he is now, he won't be every day. Besides, Brian reckons you really only do that on a ship if you're ill or on honeymoon, and he certainly didn't look in love.'

'What do you mean? How can you tell?' I want to know.

'Oh, just the way they were together.'

'*They*?' My eyebrows shoot up with concern.

'Well, he was with a woman but I really don't think they were an item.'

'Oh, Felicity!' I can't help but slump.

I've been through this before with Abigail. 'But I can tell there's no real connection between them!' she'd insist as she fell for yet another already-attached commodity. I don't want Felicity going down that thankless path.

'Honestly!' she protests. 'I was watching them for a while – he didn't look her in the eye once.'

'Well, there's a lot to see when you first get off the plane. Not every airport opens on to a lagoon that looks like a swimming pool filled with luminous mouthwash,' I reason.

'Trust me, they weren't in love,' Felicity is adamant. 'If you were in love and you arrived in paradise, you'd be pawing each other saying, "Look at this! Look at that! Oh, honey, this is so amazing!"'

I think of how Hugh and I were when we arrived. He definitely used the 'amazing' word, and I know he took my hand. But what was I doing?

'If you could have seen the way he looked at me,' she says, staring out beyond the salad dressings.

'Describe it,' I urge.

Felicity opens her mouth, but no words come out. 'I can't explain,' she sighs finally. 'But it was like he *knew* me.'

'Maybe he thought he did?'

'How many six-foot freckle-faced goddesses with Diana Ross hair do you know?'

I smile. 'Only one.'

'Anyway, I just know,' she says matter-of-factly. 'Just like you did with Hugh.'

I halt my forkful of artichoke. 'What did I know?' I question out loud.

Felicity looks temporarily thrown, then huffs, 'You tell me – you're the one who's practically married!'

Ignoring her snip, I stop and think for a minute. What did I know for sure? 'I knew he wouldn't hurt me. I knew he was a safe place to go. I knew he was kind.'

'Well, what more do you want?' she challenges me.

I look at my friend. She's the first person to ask me that question. *What more do you want?* Everyone who has met Hugh presumes I have it all.

'I don't know,' I sigh in reply. 'I didn't even know I wanted more until you asked.'

'Then you probably don't,' she clips. 'You're probably just overempathising with my wantings. Don't fret it.'

For a second, things feel a little awkward between us. I wonder if we're both a little irritable from jet lag, and then I realise that when we were fourteen our relationship talk hadn't really gone beyond crushes on the boys at New College. This is new territory for us. I set down my knife and fork. Felicity takes another sip of her drink and looks out of the window. I wonder if I should go and get dessert and come back with a new topic of conversation?

'Look, I'm sorry if I'm being touchy about this.' Felicity is first to speak, her face taking on a pink hue as she admits, 'Lately I'm just so *jealous* of anyone who's found a partner.'

I go to respond but she cuts me off.

'And please don't tell me it's not all it's cracked up to be. That's like rich people telling you money doesn't matter.'

I contemplate her for a while. Uncharacteristically jittery and prickly, avoiding eye contact . . . This isn't right.

'Tell me,' I gently prompt.

She looks up at me. 'What?'

I simply hold her gaze, trying to convey the same comfort and understanding she always offered me.

Her eyes turn down again. 'You mean tell you how I got so bitter?'

My heart sinks. Then it's true. I didn't think it was possible for someone like Felicity to get beaten by life. How did it happen?

'In a nutshell, sparing you twenty case studies, it's just a build-up of disappointment,' she explains, going for bravado but instead looking ever more vulnerable. 'When the rejections hit the double digits it takes its toll. Everyone says be yourself, but when people – *men*

86

– don't like that, what exactly are you supposed to do?'

'What are you talking about? Everybody likes you. What's *not* to like?'

'I wish I knew.' She shakes her head. 'They seem so super-keen initially. "I can't believe a gorgeous girl like you hasn't got a boyfriend!" they say, acting all incredulous and paying me all these compliments, but then they don't call. I get one date and we talk and laugh and find all these things in common, and even when I can actually feel something in their kiss, there's never any follow-up and I'm always left wondering why? At what point did they decide that I am not an experience that they want to repeat?' she sighs, adding, 'It wears you down. Every time it happens you feel a little less attractive. A little less sure. Gradually you lose your ability to trust and you get nervy and needy . . . And who wants that?'

This breaks my heart – that men can taint women like this. Good women, women who deserve better. Surely there must be a way they could behave that would do a little less damage?

'Mostly I wish they would stop telling girls what they think they want to hear and just have the courage to be honest. Honesty I can take. It's the other stuff – the not knowing . . .' She looks wretched. 'There are only so many times you can bounce back. I'm so sick of that sinking feeling – getting my hopes up and then realising that I'm back to square one. I sit at home thinking, "Okay, I'm going to be positive, I'm going to have a plan!" But the thought of going out to bars on a Friday night with an agenda is so depressing. It's like you're having to lower yourself somehow, admit you are desperate, and that makes you feel even more crappy about yourself. So maybe you decide instead to get on with your life, as everybody suggests you do, and then a year passes and nothing has changed. All that bollocks about he'll come along when you're not looking is such a con. Usually told to you by women in relationships who don't want single girls out tempting their fellas, I think you'll find!'

Listening to her pain, I again feel obligated to feel grateful for Hugh. Hugh who spares me all these miseries. If only I could agree with Felicity when she says, 'Sometimes safe can be the sexiest thing in the world.'

'Your hot beverage, madam!' Brian sets a pot of peppermint tea between us, giving his cousin an affectionate shoulder-squeeze. 'You okay?' he checks, dipping to her eye level.

She lays her hand on his and assures him she's fine. 'I was just having a poor-me moment, which is nuts considering where I am and who I'm with!'

He nods understanding then pings upright, exclaiming, 'My two favourite Canadians!' as a young couple he introduces as honeymooners Liz and Steve enter the dining room. 'How was the aquascope?' he asks as he guides them to a table.

Felicity watches for a moment and then says, 'Now they *are* in love. Proper grown-up, friends-first, grow-old-together love. That's what I want.'

I sigh. If I could package up what I have with Hugh and make it a gift for Felicity I would. I've got a horrible feeling it's wasted on me.

'You know, when we were at school I never felt like I had to apologise for any part of me,' she sighs, misty with nostalgia. 'In those days I thought all that really mattered was the size of your heart!'

'That's still all that matters,' I insist, desperate for her not to let go of the wonderful principled person she once was.

'No it's not, Amber. There's something else going on now, something I don't understand. Whatever men want, I don't have it.'

'But what about Airport Guy?' Hark at me – now I'm rooting for him!

A flicker of optimism plays on her face. 'He seemed different somehow,' she dares to believe. 'Do you know what it was?' She sets down her cup. 'When he looked at me it's like he saw the real me – good heart, bad hair, the works – and he liked me anyway!'

Suddenly I believe her. That Felicity is a woman of high ideals is entirely apparent in her face. Maybe these other guys knew they weren't good enough and that's why they bailed out so early – to avoid failing in her eyes. It's possible that Airport Guy was different, that he saw someone he could reach his personal best with. Maybe he's actually someone who deserves a woman of her grade A quality.

'You know what? We're going to find him,' I assert, suddenly fired up. 'Whatever it takes. Whoever he is.

We'll do it together!' I leap to my feet, keen to get started, even if it means knocking on every cabin door.

'Let's do it!' Felicity cheers, also raising to her full height. 'But first I think we should jump ship.'

7

'I don't think I can do this.' I waver on the edge of the platform.

'Don't be such a wuss, *jump*!'

'I'm not jumping. I'm barely considering lowering myself in one rung at a time.'

Felicity rolls her eyes and pulls herself out of the water for the third time. Her mane is now dragged into a silken cloak and she looks just as capable of doing twelve laps of butterfly as she did at school.

'It's all right for you, Esther Williams!' I complain as she does yet another form-perfect dive into aquamarine.

'Is it the water or the swimsuit?' Felicity demands when she comes up for air.

'Both,' I confess, feeling even more uncomfortable in Felicity's racing-backed Speedo as a team of divers arrive and begin to prep their dinghy.

We're down in the bowels of the ship, behind a

heavy iron door. I couldn't quite believe it when Felicity heaved it open and stepped into a world of scuba and snorkelling gear, vast coils of rope and a gaping mouth leading us directly into the lagoon.

I wish I had Felicity's abandon – she looks so happy swirling in the water, floating on her back, face tilted in rapture at the sun. No man worries at this moment. Me? I just can't bring myself to take the plunge, and choose instead to bury myself in the ship brochure.

'Do you know they offer nuptials at sea? Gives new meaning to tying the knot, eh?'

'I don't get it,' Felicity frowns, swilling around at my feet.

'Nautical knots, you know—'

'Not that,' she groans. 'Your body hang-up. I mean, fair enough at school – we all felt fat compared to those anorexic Swiss girls – but look at you now.'

'Don't!' I complain, trying to cover myself with the booklet.

'Body of Heidi Klum and you're still hiding. It makes no sense.'

As Felicity disappears beneath the water's surface yet again, I find myself taking a surreptitious peak at my curves. Hugh thinks I cover up because I don't want the attention wearing something figure-hugging would bring. But it's more than that – I've always felt so unconnected to my own body. It's like someone upgraded my video system to Tivo and everyone tells me how lucky I am to have it, but I don't have the manual to get the darn thing to work. Besides, I'm scared of open water, the way it goes on for ever, not knowing what lies beneath . . .

'I think we should get on with checking the ship for Airport Guy,' I suggest, trying to lure Felicity back on board. 'I know we've just had lunch, but they're serving tea on the sun deck now and we can inspect the library and the lounge en route . . .'

'All right, but I reckon most people have gone ashore for the day.' She deliberately shakes water over me as she emerges. 'I think we'll stand a better chance tonight.'

'But tonight you're coming to dinner with me and Hugh, remember?'

'Oh yes, that's just what I need – a chance to play gooseberry under the stars.'

'It won't be like that,' I contend. 'Sandrine will be there too, I'm sure.'

We debate this arrangement on the way back upstairs, and ultimately Felicity concedes that it will be a good chance to give the guests at the Bora Bora Lagoon Resort the once-over, not to mention Sandrine.

'Don't worry, I'll tell you if anything is going on with those two,' she assures me. 'I've got an eye for that stuff.'

We do a quick circuit of the deck before settling on a pair of padded sun-loungers adjacent to the jacuzzi.

'Do you know what I could do with now?' Felicity sighs as she reclines herself further. 'Hokey-pokey.'

I quickly look around to see if anyone heard. 'Is that Kiwi slang for—'

'No!' She stops me before I blunder further. 'It's ice cream – vanilla with honeycomb bits. Delicious!'

'Shall I grab us a few bits from the tea buffet?'

'Oh, go on then!'

As I put together a plate of cake and cookies, I once again sweep the deck for possible Airport Guy contenders. I don't want to say anything to Felicity, but it does seem horribly likely that the man she saw is in a relationship with the woman he was travelling with: other than one petite blonde Lolita torturing the Filipino waiters, it does seem to be all married couples on board.

I return to our spot, and we start reminiscing about schooldays and catching up on what we know of our old classmates. Then, as I reach for a bite of cookie, I see Blondie stretching in an absurdly provocative, arched-back, teen-stripper way and before I can stop myself I blurt, 'I haven't had sex in eight months!'

'What?' Felicity splutters, expelling a confetti of lemon sponge crumbs. '*Really?*'

I nod, looking fretful.

'I thought you said Hugh was attractive?'

'He is, he's lovely. I just . . . .' I slump back into my seat. 'Lately I don't seem very motivated *that way*.'

'What about him?'

'He doesn't seem to mind. He was never that

demanding, it's just every now and again . . . Usually when it's sunny.'

'Well you're in trouble now.'

'Yeah, I know,' I grimace.

Felicity looks concerned. 'I was joking. Is it really that awful?'

'Not awful.' I pause as a waiter clears the table of empty cake plates beside us. 'I can't believe we're talking about my sex life over afternoon tea!' I hiss as he goes on his way.

'I know, isn't it great?' she enthuses. 'Well, not great that you're not having sex, just great that we can spill our guts.' She twists her body round to face me more squarely, clearly fascinated by my puritan life. 'So what exactly is the problem?'

Part of me wishes I'd never opened my mouth, but equally I feel this may be my only chance to discuss such matters. I could never have this conversation with Gilly or Abigail or, God forbid, Hugh. We've never spoken candidly about sex. I'm too embarrassed to, and I get the impression that he's too wary of offending me to speak his mind. We both seem to be of the opinion that it'll sort itself out eventually, as if it's a third party that just needs a little time.

I lean forward so I can whisper to Felicity in confidence. 'It just always feels so samey, like I'm only going through the motions. I want to feel more, but I don't know how.'

'Has he *ever* rocked your world, like back at the beginning?'

I take a moment to consider this. I was definitely nervous at first, but ultimately it was the comfort of having someone there once my parents had gone that seemed to override any passion.

'I was crying a lot at the time, so it was mostly hugging, caring stuff at that point,' I explain.

'And later?'

'I don't know,' I squirm. 'It seems he can get pretty far with just looking.'

'I'll bet.'

'So what do you think?' I demand. 'I know it's going to be more of an issue this week, but I really couldn't feel any less inclined. Am I a lost cause?'

'*Au contraire*! I really think Tahiti could be just the place to get your juices flowing – a few cocktails, a walk on the beach . . . And if that fails,' she puts on a mischievous look, 'it just so happens that I have a little something that could help you on your way.'

'I am not taking Viagra!' I gasp.

'Viagra-smiagra!' She bats away my protestation. 'This is an all-natural Kiwi remedy. The last guy I was with gave it to me, but we never got around to using it.'

She leans over and rummages in her bag, pulls out a mini-bottle of headache pills, pops the top and shakes the contents into her hand. Amid the five red capsules lies a lurid purple one. 'What have you got to lose except your inhibitions?'

I look at the pill, convinced it just winked at me, then shrink back, shaking my head. 'No, I couldn't!'

'Not right now, but tonight. You could surprise Hugh.'

'I don't think so.' Poor guy would have a heart attack if he found me swinging naked from the rafters.

'Well in that case, the least you can do is get drunk.'

I give Felicity a despairing look then slot my sunglasses back in place muttering, 'Who says romance is dead?'

Two hours later we're back at the bungalow, aiding and abetting the process of getting ready with a pitcher of Mai Tai.

'What exactly is in this?' I demand as I slosh out a second glass.

'Rum, orange juice, pineapple juice, grenadine . . . *Put that back*,' she barks suddenly.

'What?' I jump.

'Jeez, Amber, nuns have sexier outfits than you! What were you thinking when you bought this?' Felicity snatches away the dress I was planning to wear tonight.

'I like the colours,' I mumble. 'Rust and cranberry and—'

'It's just a mess of pattern!' Felicity tuts. 'If you bent over someone might pull up a chair and set their drink down on your back.'

'But—'

'Do you want to look like something out of an olde worlde tea shoppe?' she demands as she throws the dress back in the wardrobe.

I wish I had natural style like Felicity. She's in cropped black trousers and a silver boob tube with a crescent of metal at her neck, looking effortlessly chic now that her hair is knotted tight off her face.

'This is more promising . . .' she holds up Abigail's *pareu*.

'That's a present for a girl at work.'

'I'm sure she won't mind.'

'No.' I stand firm, shoving it in a drawer.

'Oh, suit yourself.' She flumps on the daybed, averting her eyes as I slip on something less busy but equally voluminous. 'Where is this man of yours anyway, I'm starving!'

I look at my watch. 8 p.m.

'Come on, let's go through and check with reception, see if he's left any messages.'

'Mademoiselle Pepper!' I am summoned the second we step through the door. '*Excusez moi*, a Monsieur Garner has just telephoned for you.'

'Yes?'

'He's very sorry but he won't be making it back in time for dinner, or indeed at all this evening. The meeting has run on and there are no more flights from Tahiti until tomorrow morning.'

'Oh. Okay.' I toy with the idea of getting paranoid about the possibility of him sharing a hotel room with Sandrine, but then the receptionist distracts me by adding, 'He says you should put dinner on the room and invite Felicity to keep you company overnight.'

'Hey, that's a good idea.' I turn and grab her hand. 'It'll save you getting the boat back and faffing around with tenders.'

'But you've only got one bed,' she frets.

'You saw how big it was,' I shrug.

'Not big enough,' she smirks as she manoeuvres me through to the bar.

'What do you mean?'

'I mean I'm not sharing a bed with you after what I just put in your drink!'

I blanche. 'You didn't?'

She nods impishly as she hauls herself up on to a bar stool.

'You didn't!' I repeat, now fully scandalised. 'Oh, Felicity! How could you?' I clutch my throat and then my stomach, wondering what stage the purple pill has reached and whether I could try retrieving it with a good old-fashioned porcelain kiss.

'Too late for that,' she reads my mind. 'It went in your first drink.'

My eyes widen in mortification. 'Well when is it going to start taking effect?' I assess myself for any alien sensations within. Is that gurgling normal? Now I come to think of it I do feel oddly floaty and loose. And very, very warm, but then it is at least eighty degrees. It's been so long since I was last tipsy I'm not even sure how to differentiate between the wooziness of the booze and any potential compromising of my decency.

'You probably won't feel it for at least an hour,' Felicity says, offering her lay-person's diagnosis.

'Are you sure about that?'

'No,' she admits, rather too casually for my liking. 'It's different for every person.'

I roll my eyes in despair, then find my gaze lured through to the dining room where a petal-like cluster of plates is on walkabout. I'm starving too, but I'm wary of committing to a table. What if the dessert is really, really good? 'I'm not going to start doing a Meg Ryan over dinner, am I?'

'Don't be silly!' Felicity is dismissive as she lops one of the complimentary canapés into her mouth.

'But you can't be sure?' I take a sterner approach.

She looks sheepish as she licks her fingers. 'No.'

'That's it!' I wail. 'I'm having a quick rummage in the bread basket and then we're leaving.'

I'm at the maître d's podium, halfway through announcing my reservation details, when I realise that Felicity is still at the bar, incapable of walking anywhere due to a sudden and disabling fit of laughter. I stomp back and hoik her into an upright position. 'Stop that!' I shake her.

'I'm sorry,' she whimpers, trying to conceal her mirth. 'I just wanted to get you in the honeymoon mood.'

'I've told you, it's not like that with me and Hugh,' I scold, surprised at how sensitive I am on the subject. 'Next time keep your drugs to yourself.'

'It's not a drug, it's all-natural,' she slurs lightly, gripping my shoulder for support.

'Rather in the way that magic mushrooms are all

100

natural?' I gripe as we approach our assigned waiter.

She thinks for a moment. 'I suppose so, yes.'

'Not helping.' I keep my eyes firmly on the waiter's heels just in case there happens to be a particularly handsome newlywed at a neighbouring table – I don't want to blink and then find myself smeared in coconut ice cream and offering him a spoon.

'This is perfect for you?' Our waiter shows us a table a mere candlewick's distance from the beach, thus offering a convenient alternative exit, I'm pleased to note. 'We have the view of Otemanu –' He directs our gaze across the bay to the now black and menacing volcano – 'and the full moon.'

I stare up in wonder at the glowing orb of pearlescence until an image of me howling naked from the rooftop comes to mind. As Felicity takes her seat, I surreptitiously run my fingers over my forearm to check that I'm not sprouting bristles. No, all is well. In fact my skin feels unusually silken – really amazingly soft. And look at that: the usual dusty crepe on the backs of my hands has been replaced by a youthful sheen. *No*! I freeze mid-caress. It's begun! I quickly grab the napkin – the crisp white fold of fabric – and lay it in my lap, trying to hold it together. I should probably down a few gallons of water to try and flush the purple wickedness out of my system.

'And to drink?' the waiter enquires.

'Two more Mai Tais and a bottle of Sancerre,' Felicity chimes.

'And water!' I croak before he turns away.

'Sparkling or still, madam?'

'Both. Please. And big bottles.'

'Certainly, madam.'

'You're going to be fine,' Felicity assures me.

I pick up the menu so I don't have to look my poisoner in the eye. 'If I wake up tomorrow the star of some low-budget Tahitian porn movie, you'll be sorry.'

'What, like *Really Blue Lagoon*?' Felicity titters. 'Or *Nudity on the Bounty*?'

'It's not funny.'

'It is for me,' she grins, shamelessly.

'And I wonder why we lost touch.' I arch a brow as I peruse the starters – lobster tail with mango vinaigrette, spicy mahi mahi ceviche with steamed sweet potato.

'Oh, come on,' Felicity nudges me. 'Have another drink, and then even if you do do something embarrassing you won't remember.'

'What are you having as your main?' I ask, deciding that the best policy is to change the subject.

'Mmmm, I think either the seafood cassolette or the fillet of thazard with poe chutney.'

'Thazard? Poe?' I stare bewildered at the menu.

'I've no idea what they are either, but I'm feeling rather daring tonight. What about you?'

'Either the brick papillotte snapper—'

'And you know what that is?' Felicity challenges.

'Papillotte is fish cooked in a little parchment pouch. I presume the brick is referring to the oven . . .'

'Oh. Or?'

'Or the ravioli with Bora Bora shrimp,' I tell her, somewhat intrigued by its accessories – sautéed fennel with pastis I can get my head around, but who ever came up with the concept of a crustacean-cappuccino sauce?

'May I take your order?' The waiter rejoins us.

Felicity nods eagerly. 'Is the thazard good?'

'Excellent.'

'Okay, that's me.' She hands over her menu, no further information required.

My turn. Deciding I should probably skip the caffeine in my current condition, I boldly announce, 'I'll have the prick—' then freeze, shocked by my own Freudian slip. As Felicity bites down on her hunk of bread, handily also mopping up the snot that has spurted from her nose, I try again. 'The brick papillote snapper,' I say, unable to look either the waiter or the convulsed and frothing Felicity in the eye. As soon as he's out of earshot I collapse in a blubber of embarrassment. 'I can't believe I said that – it's all your fault!' I swat at her.

'Oh, don't worry, it's slang, I don't think he twigged,' she mollifies me between hyena cackles. 'Though wouldn't it be great if there really was a restaurant where you could just order a man right off the menu – I'll have the Tall Dark Handsome with a side of humour and a billion-buck bank balance, please.'

We chink glasses as Felicity adds, 'Here's to you getting your mojo working again.'

I take a larger than average slurp of drink. She said 'again'. What I didn't get into earlier on the sun deck is the fact that my mojo, as she puts it, never really worked in the first place.

And that's okay – I've long since accepted that I'm not a sexually-motivated person. I mean, when I was a teenager I definitely had the regulation crushes – boys made me swoon and flutter, but I didn't ever want to tear off anyone's clothes and ravage them. If kissing were as far as things went that suited me fine. Anything beyond that seemed to be asking for trouble – look at my mum and dad. They couldn't keep their hands off each other. I'm convinced that all that heavy breathing caused the short-circuit in their brains that made them act in such irrational ways. Having said that, as Felicity and I fill in the missing years some more, I'm reminded that maybe I did feel a spark with one or two guys along the way, but I was smart enough to avoid them as a result. I'm no fool. That accidental alchemy that can happen between two strangers is a dangerous business, I'm telling you.

'You know where we should go after this?' Felicity asks, as she now dips into her dessert of baked meringue papaya and lime sorbet.

'Well, I don't know about you –' I let my green grapefruit ice parfait melt on my tongue as I speak – 'but I'm going to turn the aircon on to frostbite and have you tie me to the bed.'

Felicity looks alarmed.

'To restrain me, fool!'

'Oh!' She expels a relieved breath. 'Actually, I have a better idea.' She shuffles her chair closer to mine. 'Apparently there's this new bar about ten minutes' walk from here. It's got quite a buzz going, there's a live act—'

'What kind of live act?'

'A band. They're meant to be great. They have a Tahitian themed night on Sunday, but they mostly do R&B grooves – it should be fun. And *he* might be there . . .' She gives me a persuasive look.

'I don't know. What if I start coming over all letchy and unnecessary . . .'

'Look, men go round feeling horny all the time. Doesn't mean they shag everything in their path, does it?'

'Actually, I think that's exactly what they do, given half a chance.' My face falls further. 'And tonight I'd be the one *giving* them half a chance.'

'Okay, bad example,' Felicity clips. 'So this is what we'll do: we'll stroll by, check it out, maybe stay for one drink, but I promise I won't let you get intimate with anyone.'

'What if you can't stop me?'

'It's a little purple pill, Amber. You're not going to turn into the Incredible Hulk – *You wouldn't like me when I'm aroused*!' she giggles as she sploshes more wine into both our glasses. 'It'll be fine, trust me.'

'Are you crazy?' I scoff. 'I'm never going to be able to trust you again.'

'Oh, don't say that,' she pleads, setting the wine

bottle down with an overzealous plonk. 'I just want us to have some fun before we die.'

I narrow my eyes at her. Everyone seems intent on getting me to do things I don't want to do lately. Well, if I resisted the lagoon swim and the *pareu* outfit, I can resist this.

'So, are you in?' she asks the second the bill is signed.

'I'm in,' I sigh.

Well, the sooner we find her fella, the sooner I'll get some peace.

8

'The Paradise Room!' Felicity reads the carved inscription above the doorway while I peer inside, narrowly avoiding singeing myself on a ceremonial tiki torch. For some reason I was expecting a casually assembled shack with a stage made from stacking pallets and drinks served from a blue plastic cooler. This ambient haven is the absolute antithesis – there's a seductive glow coming from the infinite number of caramel-glazed candles and the scent of warm rum mingling with fresh vanilla as I cross the threshold.

The room itself is a large oval set with booths of hot peach suede and an assortment of bamboo screens creating nooks for those in search of a more secluded rendezvous. There's a cluster of petite cocktail tables on the main floor, each barely bigger than a coaster and draped in either white or coral linen. I can almost picture Rock and Doris making a martini toast, and suddenly I wish I was wearing a low-backed beaded dress and matching clip-on earrings.

'Where's the bar?' Felicity's eyes rove the room.

'Surely not?' I point to a shell-inspired spiral staircase that is in fact a free-standing booze emporium.

Perched three steps up is a rather extraordinary looking creation in a gold minidress.

'That's a *rae-rae*!' Felicity squeaks, as if she's spotted some kind of endangered species.

'*Rae-rae*?' I repeat, struggling with the pronunciation.

'You say it like rerrr-rerrr – you have to roll your r's.'

'I've had four Mai Tais and half a bottle of Sancerre; everything I say sounds like rerrr-rerrr!' I complain.

Felicity steps closer, pulling me along with her. 'They're like the Tahitian equivalent of Bangkok ladyboys,' she explains, unable to take her eyes off Exhibit X as he flicks his long black hair with a double-jointed wrist then surveys the room with the most petulant of pouts. Felicity chuckles. 'Isn't it funny how camp traits are universal?'

'Do you think he's the entertainment tonight?' I ponder. 'I bet he could do a great Cher.'

'I think it's polite to refer to them as "she",' Felicity corrects me. 'Oh, look – those people are leaving the table up the front!' She goes to lurch forward but I yank her back, still a little unsure.

'You do promise we'll leave straight away if I start getting—' I lean in and lower my voice – '*frisky*?'

'Absolutely,' she confirms. 'If there's even *talk* of a naked duet with the *rae-rae*—'

'Felicity!' I gasp, mortified.

'Honestly, stop worrying! I'm beginning to think you may be immune to the pill anyway – you're still not feeling anything, are you?'

I shake my head, ever so slightly disappointed. 'A little bit maybe. But mostly just catch-myself-on-the-corner-of-every-table-I-pass drunk.'

'Yes, I noticed,' Felicity grimaces. 'Well, just try not to break anything and we'll go from there.'

Felicity takes my hand and we weave our way to the front, me taking extra care not to ensnare any of the clientele in the drapes of my pashmina. (I'm mindful of this hazard ever since Hugh accidentally caught a small Chinaman in the open flair of his trenchcoat while striding down Orchard Road in Hong Kong.)

As we settle at our table and order an entirely superfluous beverage, I am aware of a swish of activity on the stage, but it's not until I look up and focus that it hits me. Apparently the pill was just waiting for a trigger. And tonight that comes in the form of two bare-torsoed men in voodoo-meets-Vegas plumage, eyes shining like darkest ebony behind matt velvet eye-masks.

'Woah!' I grip the edge of the table as the pill releases its potency along with a surge of adrenalin. There was I thinking that welly boots and a Peter Storm waterproof were the ultimate aphrodisiac when in fact it turns out I'm all about shiny black feathers and the way this duo's trousers are stretching taut across their thighs as they make predatory strides across the stage. I watch with slack-jawed awe as they fold their arms in an Indian-chief-meets-genie stance then give a double pump-grunt. It's as though they've locked into a secret fantasy of mine that I never knew I had. As they husk the chorus to 'Freak Like Me' I find myself undeniably and supernaturally *aroused*.

'It's begun!' I rasp, reaching out to alert Felicity.

'Tell me about it,' she gawps, looking equally enraptured.

'I mean it,' I insist. 'I'm feeling all sorts of crazy stuff.'

I actually want to growl. I want to reach up and pull one – or both – guys down on to me hard and heavy and feel their hands manipulating my spine as I arch into them. This is all new to me. I don't quite know what to do with myself.

'I'm going to have to squeeze your knee,' I warn Felicity as I discreetly lower my hand beneath the table.

'Ow!' she yelps, wincing at my clamp-like grip. 'Steady!'

'Sorry!' I gulp, trying to reshape her joint to its original form.

'So which one do you want?' Felicity gurgles, shamelessly reneging on her former promises to 'lead me not into temptation'.

Not that I mind. I couldn't be persuaded to leave now even if you had the aid of two burly henchmen and a handkerchief doused with chloroform.

'Well?' She jiggles me, impatient for an answer.

I take a closer look, feeling like I'm being pressured to choose between a Monet and a Manet. The guy on the right has skin as brown and smooth as Nutella with a tattoo of a wild cat prowling down his bodacious bicep and ab-bumps so nuggety-rugged they look like six rough-hewn rocks. On the left is six foot of slinky-hipped, sheeny butterscotch, his artfully plumped pectorals making a tantalising showcase for a glinting silver nipple ring. So far so sexy, but 'I need to see their faces,' I announce.

'Picky!' Felicity tuts as the guys groove off stage, allowing a pair of female foxes to strut forward and strump out 'Crazy In Love'. The heart-slamming beat does nothing to ease my ardour, and the lyrics rile me further. I'm looking around to get the waitress's attention – water! – when the band segue into the easy sway of the Isley Brothers' 'For The Love Of You' and the guys return, now in fresh white linen shirts, faces fully revealed. Oh no. *No!* Now I'm in real trouble.

'They're beautiful,' I breathe, startled by their facial graces.

'Stunning,' Felicity confirms as they take their position at the front of the stage, harmonising both vocally and visually.

Both have closely-shaven heads and finely-etched goatees, but their features suggest two very different characters: the darker one (he of the cat-tatt and the ab-nuggets) has an almost regal dignity, like a prince from a mythical land. In my altered state he puts me in mind of a brooding yet genteel Yul Brynner from *The King and I*. The other has more of the open, ebullient style of Will Smith with a squooshy marshmallow-soft mouth and a well-earned beauty spot below his left eye. I get misty as I behold them. Now these guys' parents were *true* artists.

I'm just adjusting to the feeling of being lulled and transfixed when, without warning, they break into a power-surged version of the Jacksons' 'Shake Your Body Down', hustling through precision-synchronised moves at breakneck speed. I blink and shake my head – surely that last kung-fu side-kick/see-saw/up-down/pelvic-swivel/grapevine-sprint sequence wasn't humanly possible? Even my eyeballs are having trouble keeping up; how can their feet be moving faster than I can see? Oh God, this can't be right. I think I may be having a funny turn . . .

'Fliss!' I croak, grabbing her arm. 'Did someone press fast-forward?'

'Huh?' is the best she can offer.

'Felicity?' I implore, concern growing as my heart starts yammering erratically. 'Does this pill speed things up?' The guys are now nothing more than a juddering flicker-book blur. I'm starting to feel dizzy and overwhelmed.

'So, did you choose yet?' Felicity queries, oblivious to my predicament.

'What?' I pant, trying to get a grip.

'Which one do you want?'

I swallow hard, then dare to look back at them. Why aren't they sweating? How can they move that fast and still sing? 'I don't know!' I flounder, fearing I might faint. 'Can I have both?'

'I hear that!' comes a voice from behind us. We turn around to see the *rae-rae* offering complimentary wafts of frangipani perfume in our direction. 'But don't you get any ideas, they both belong to me!'

'Oh really?' Felicity titters, tickled by the scarlet threat of his/her pout. 'And who might you be?'

'I'm Fantasia, hostess-slash-goddess at The Paradise Room!' She strikes a full-on diva pose before continuing, 'And I see you ladies aren't wearing the regulation tiare flower.' She rotates her wrist and opens her palm to reveal two milky-white gardenia buds.

Oh, look at the pretty flowers! Pale and calm and still. I feel better already.

'Wear one behind your left ear and it means your heart is taken,' she advises. 'Right ear tells any visiting sailors that you are available!'

Felicity swiftly secures her bloom behind her right, but Fantasia seems to read my predicament. 'Maybe you need an extra one,' she winks, tucking a bud first behind my left ear, then my right. 'Your heart is officially taken but you are still available!'

I gasp – is it that obvious?

'I saw some guy wearing it backwards at the airport, what does that mean?' Felicity queries.

'Follow me and you'll find out how available I am!'

'Fabulous!' Felicity is jubilant. 'I might bring this custom back home with me – it would make things a lot easier!'

'Have them strewn throughout your hair and that means you are desperate! Better hurry up!'

'I don't think there are enough flowers for how desperate I am,' Felicity sighs, sneaking a glance back at the stage. 'What's their flower situation?'

'I already told you – they are *taken*,' Fantasia snarls. 'By me.'

'Can you at least share their names?' Felicity is not easily deterred.

Fantasia hesitates, then leans forward and whispers. 'See the sexy espresso . . .' She points to the dark prince currently mellowing out to Marvin Gaye's 'Let's Get It On'. 'That's my Tony. And the pretty latte . . .' she switches our attention to the Beaming Machine – 'that's my Tezz. And this,' she reaches behind her to grab a drink off a passing tray, 'is Mai Tai!'

'*Manuia!*' We raise our glasses and chink heartily at her toast.

'Hmmm, Tony and Tezz,' Felicity sighs, deliberately rotating her flower as she sips her drink.

'Tezz and Tony,' I add, garnering pleasure simply from saying their names.

Fantasia looks crossly from one of us to the other and snaps: 'Repeat after me . . . MINE!'

'Mine!' we chorus dumbly.

'*No!*' she screeches, swatting at us with a cocktail napkin.

114

'Sorry, YOURS!' Felicity corrects our blunder.

I intend to do the same, but then Tezz catches my eye and croons 'Baby Stay With Me Tonight' like it's a personal invitation, and I once again breathe 'Mine'.

In the background I hear Fantasia telling Felicity that the guys are collectively known as Soul Desire, that they're both East Coast boys who met nine years ago on the Las Vegas production of *Starlight Express*. At which point Felicity catches my eye and mouths the word 'gay' with a hapless shrug.

'Ya think?' I mime back, waiting for the swirly yearnings to drain from my body. But they don't. Apparently the purple pill cares not what sexual persuasion these fellas favour; all it knows is that they're *hot*! And lordy can they move! During their grinding, groin-popping moments they may as well be entwined with my very own hips: I'm feeling every flex.

Just as I'm wondering how much longer I can conceal my flagrant lustings from Fantasia, she's summoned to find seats for a newly-arrived posse muddling around at the back of the bar.

'You ladies behave, now – I'm watching you!' is her parting threat.

I wait until she's safely out of earshot then quiz Felicity. 'Do you really think they're gay?'

'Musical theatre? It doesn't bode well,' she grimaces, leaning back on her chair so she can get a good squint at the new arrivals.

Me, I'm not convinced. Tony is just so powerfully masculine, and the way Tezz looked at me before . . .

and again right now! My toes scrunch in delight as he warms me with his smile.

'Oh my God – is that him?' Felicity twists further round in her seat.

'Him who?' I frown. Surely there are only two men in this room, and they are both standing before us on stage.

'The Him from the airport! I'm sure—' and with that she's gone.

'Don't leave me!' I yelp after her, to no avail.

Suddenly I feel worryingly exposed. I look at the couples on the tables either side of me – one petite and Japanese, the other bearing the kind of horrific sunburn splotches that can only belong to a Brit abroad. I'm not sure either would know what to do if I started getting out of hand. Only Felicity knows what comes next in Purple Pill World, and she's vamoosed. Bad girl.

I try to compose myself as best I can. At least all that frantic fast-forward stuff has subsided. Now the guys are simply gliding in slow motion to Craig David's 'Flava'. And when I say gliding, it's really as though their feet have turned to liquid and they are melting across the floor . . . Oh my God! I start upright – I must be hallucinating! How terrifying! I blink hard but they're still at it, now rotating in circles. Well, I guess it could be worse – they still only have one head apiece. Then I notice Tezz's champagne satin shirt has unbuttoned itself to the navel. I take a quavery breath as I imagine tracing my fingertips down the central canyon of his highly-defined chest . . . *Wa-hayyy* – there's that full-body rush again! Probably best I don't look at him for a while. I fumble for my drink, only to tip it up, splurging instant-stain orange all down my dress. Next thing I know I'm being handed a leaning tower of napkins by an efficient waitress, while up on stage the guys have become stretched to twice the height of their female dancers, dancing in three-storey-high top hats and twirling canes you could propel a gondola with. Everything's gone Willy Wonka weird. I squeeze my eyes closed – make it go away!

As it happens, blocking out the visuals only enhances their audio appeal. Tony is now crooning Al Green's 'Let's Stay Together' and the place is a-hush as his voice climbs and caresses each note. My breathing evens out. I feel transported to a state of fabulous serenity. And then the voice changes, and Tezz begins Prince's love serenade 'Adore'. I go all limp and willing. So very willing. It's as though all my senses are awakening, just for him. His is the voice I've been waiting to hear my whole life. Suddenly, instead of dreading what this pill might do to me, I'm dreading it leaving my body and taking all these amazing new sensations with it. I want to feel like this for ever.

And then the beat changes and I hear him sing the words,

> Girl in the front row
> I think I wanna know
> You

My eyes spring open and again I find him looking directly at me.

> I see you're feeling me
> Wanna see what we can be
> And do

I flush, squirming at the intimacy of the moment. Am I imagining this? I rub my fingers over my ears, expecting the song to revert to Prince, but it doesn't.

> There's no need to be shy
> Just believe this guy
> Is true

Oh, if only I could believe. If only this was real. I feel my eyes well up – despite these strange warped delusions, this all seems more real than anything I've ever known. I feel like Sleeping Beauty stirred not by a chaste peck but by the most exhilarating of kisses.

'You should see the look on your face!' Felicity teases as she slots back into her seat. 'Poor Hugh doesn't know what he's missing.'

'What?' I stumble. 'Oh, you mean the girls?' (The two foxes are now giving their own saucy version of Kelis' 'Milkshake' in microscopic hot pants.)

'No, *you*, dummy! He's missing out on you – li'l ol' sexed-up you!'

I press pause and try to imagine being with Hugh as I'm feeling right now. Would I want him to dance at the end of my bed then crawl up to me on all fours? I don't think so. I suppose it's all about context. Maybe if I'd taken this pill and then gone straight back to the room with him we'd have had a life-changing night.

'Come on, we should go.' Felicity gets to her feet.

'Hold on – what happened with Him?' I ask, remembering why Felicity abandoned me twenty minutes earlier.

'False alarm.' She goes to walk on.

'Wait – false alarm he wasn't all you thought he was, or false alarm it wasn't the same guy?' I slur.

'Not the same guy.' She shrugs.

'Oh.'

'So . . .' She tips her head in the direction of the exit.

'I can't leave,' I blurt, anchoring my feet to the ground, a picture of defiance.

'What's the matter?' Felicity looks concerned.

'I have to stay until the last song.'

'That was the last song.'

'What?' I look up, just in time to see the final ankle withdraw behind the curtain. 'How did that happen?'

'I think you're entering the blackout phase.'

'The blackout phase?' I yelp.

'It's not that you pass out exactly,' Felicity explains, heaving me to my feet and hoisting one of my arms around her neck so she can be assured of keeping me upright. 'You just start to lose track of time and your memory of what has gone before starts getting patchy.'

No! I don't want to forget. Even if I never experience these feelings again I at least want to remember what it felt like to be so elated, so *alive*!

'Do we have to go?' I whimper.

'We're the last ones here. Even Fantasia has gone.'

I look around. Where did everyone disappear to so suddenly? The place was packed, yet now there's not even the muffled sound of revellers blending into the night.

'Little bit to your left . . .'

As Felicity steers me out I look down at the tables – definite signs of drinking: half-drained glasses, half-melted ice cubes. I didn't imagine it. I reach out and pick up a cocktail stirrer and jab it into my palm.

'What the hell are you doing?' Felicity snatches it away from me before any damage is done.

'I want to stay awake! I don't want to forget!'

'Oh God, what have I done?' She rolls her eyes.

'You've given me the best night of my life!' I proclaim, legs now not remotely interested in engaging in anything so pedestrian as putting one foot in front of the other.

'Hang in there, not far now.' Felicity decides she'll fare better by marching me from behind like a life-size rag doll.

'I mean it, Flossie. You're the best!' I try to reach round so I can see her. 'And you were right there with me so you know it's not a dream.'

'Yes, yes.' She struggles to keep me moving forward.

'I mean, yes they did grow to be ten foot tall and

120

perhaps they don't have real feet but some kind of gliding mechanism . . . but it was all real, wasn't it?'

'Bedibyes. That's it. Lie down.' Somehow she's got me into the bungalow and on to the bed. 'No more talking now. Close your eyes.'

I do as she says, but the guys are still dancing in my head – snapping, swinging, sliding, bumping, bouncing, dipping, pumping . . . And then there's Tezz's ever-animated face – one minute flirty and dirty, the next joyful and fun-seeking, interspersed with exquisite moments of higher-plane purity.

'It's like he was singing just to me . . .' I murmur.

'I know,' Felicity soothes.

'Really, the words—' I go to sit upright, but she eases me back down flat.

'It's going to be okay.'

'No, it's not,' I blub, suddenly experiencing a whoosh of loss and confusion. What am I doing back here? I need to be back at the bar. I start flailing around in a panic.

'Calm down, sweetie,' Felicity soothes, restraining me. 'Everything will be back to normal by morning.'

'Don't say that!' I flump into the pillow, filling the foam with tears. 'I don't want to go back to normal. Don't make me!'

'Okay, whatever you say. If you want to dream of the guys—'

'Tezz?' I jump in, eager for her specific permission.

'Sure, if that's what you want!'

I sigh, once again filling with bliss. As Felicity

smoothes my brow like a mother would a sick child, I imagine Tezz's hand gently moving into my hair, lacing his fingers with my tresses and easing away my angst with an almost reverent sensuality. Knowing that he now awaits me in my dreams, I finally let go and surrender to sleep.

9

'Felicity!' I reach over and pummel my snuffling bedfellow.

'Wha?' she responds, part gagged by the pillow.

'There're no men in the room are there?' I'm afraid to look, consumed with the feeling that I've done something I shouldn't have.

She pushes herself upright and squints one-eyed around the bungalow, then mumbles a groggy 'No.'

'Have there been? I mean, at any point during the night, were there men in here, *doing things*?'

She gives me a withering look. 'Trust me. It was just you and me, all night. *Snoring.*'

'Thank God!' I expel a breath. 'I had some pretty freaky dreams. Pretty realistic ones too.' Even now the guys are still spinning in my head like little love genies.

'I'll bet you did,' she swallows, mouth clicking through lack of lubrication. 'Those dancing boys give a girl plenty of fodder. Where's the water?'

'I've got it!' I coax the bottle towards me and prepare to lever her out a glass. But then I flashback to my 'woman possessed' behaviour on the way home and a deep shame infuses me. 'What exactly was in that pill anyway?' I look up at Felicity as I pour, only to glug water all over the sheets. 'Agggh – sorry!'

'Woman!' Felicity scrambles out of bed, swiping the rivulets from her legs.

'Sorry!' I repeat. 'I didn't mean—'

'I'm having a fag!' she booms, grabbing a pack of cigarettes out of her handbag and lurching out on to the deck.

'I didn't know you smoked?'

'Only when I've got a hangover,' she calls back.

Meanwhile I try to prop myself into a sitting position, feeling ever more queasy and uneasy. I know it was all just amorous imaginings, nothing physical but I feel as if I'm being punished all the same – my fluctuating nausea is getting menacing, there's some kind of plug jamming up my throat, my eyelids are fat and heavy and my skin has puckered like a pooped soufflé. And when I think of Hugh I feel ten times worse. I try to stand upright, but a frying pan wops me in the head and I crumple back to bed.

'Urghh,' I grunt, trying to get Felicity's attention. 'Where are those Aspirin of yours?' I call out to her.

'In my bag.' She motions to me from the balcony to help myself.

Easier said than done. Hangovers make me so apathetic, I can't even save myself.

'Got them?' Felicity checks on me as she concludes the brief fumigation of her lungs and steps back inside.

You'd think I had Giant Haystacks pinning me down for all the effort it takes me to drag her leather pouch over to the bed. I lie in the recovery position for a few moments before locating the little white plastic bottle and rattling the contents out on to the dry patch of sheet beside me.

'How many do you think I can take before they actually start making me feel worse than I—' I freeze.

'What?' Felicity clocks my reaction.

'There's another of the buggers!' I look up at her. 'Another purple pill.'

'There can't be.'

I hold the offending item out to her between pincer fingers. 'See?'

She takes it from me, looking bewildered. 'But I only ever had one,' she frowns, trying to figure out what has transpired, finally concluding, 'I must have given you Aspirin last night.'

'Don't be ridiculous!' I spit. 'You saw the state I was in!'

'I took it out of the bottle, dissolved it in your drink . . .' Her brow furrows as she tries to replay the memory before plinking one of the headache pills into my glass of water. It fizzes, froths, then settles. 'Just like that,' she notes.

'What are you saying?' I scramble on to my haunches, disturbed by the insinuation that the whole thing was a fabrication on my behalf.

'I didn't mean to mess with you, sweetie, but honestly, you weren't on anything. Having said that, those Mai Tais were mighty strong . . .'

'No!' I bury a fist into the mattress. 'What I felt . . . I mean, those guys—' I fall back, stunned. What is she telling me? No, no, no. I can't accept it. Obviously there must have been a mix-up – she had two pills, that's all there is to it. I simply don't have feelings like that – my whole body charged with desire!

'Well, they were super-hot, even if they are gay,' Felicity reasons.

'But how do you explain the fact that they grew to ten feet tall?' I challenge her.

'What?'

'I told you! I saw all this weird stuff – giants, melted feet . . .'

Felicity gives me a sympathetic look. Aaaghh! I feel like one of those vexed souls in movies where no one believes their story.

'Maybe you had delayed sunstroke?' she shrugs impatiently. 'Look, if you like, you can take this pill right now and tell me if you get the same symptoms, but I promise you, this was the only one.'

I lie back on the bed, exasperated. Why won't she believe me? What I felt last night wasn't normal, not for me. As I struggle to make sense of this I feel panic mixing with irritation – I can't believe what she's put me through. Was it all a mind game?

'Of course the best way to solve this mystery is to go back to The Paradise Room and see them again – see if you have the same reaction.'

'I'm not going back!' I snort.

'How can you *not* go back?' Felicity looks confused. 'If those guys made you feel that excited for real . . .'

'All the more reason not to return. I've got a boyfriend, remember,' I say, doing an excellent job of depressing myself further.

'Oh yeah. I keep forgetting. That guy you don't fancy.'

I go to protest, to tell her how attractive he is – *and he is*. I just don't want to do with him the things I was imagining doing with Tezz. Instead I grumble, 'I was perfectly happy before I got here.'

'Were you?'

'I was happy enough,' I snap.

'Oh yeah, that's what we always dreamed of, being happy enough.' She shakes her head, adding, 'Not discernibly *unhappy*.'

'Listen,' I say, steeling myself so I can get through the next sentence. 'After your parents die, you don't particularly expect to be happy. *Ever again*. It's actually a huge achievement just to get through the day – to wake up and not have the grief bring you to your knees. Just to be able to breathe,' my voice trembles.

Instinctively Felicity reaches for me, and before I know it I've collapsed into her arms, blubbering, every breath catching in the back of my throat. I can't do this, I tell myself. I can't give in to these emotions. I can't fall apart all over again. Yet the sobs come harder and harder, racking my whole body and Felicity just hugs me tighter, like a parent trying to contain a wailing child. With her physically holding me together, I dare to let go for a second, and as I do my entire body floods with tears.

My God, I marvel at the never-ending flow. How long have I been storing this up?

'It's okay to cry, let it out,' she soothes, brushing back my hair.

'It's all too much!' I sniff as soon as I'm able to speak. 'The sun is too hot. The sea is too blue.' I start hyperventilating, something I haven't done since my parents died.

'Take a breath,' Felicity guides me. 'And another. That's right.'

Slowly I regain my composure, even though the air is still coming in snatched gasps. 'I'm okay now,' I tell her, a little prematurely.

Felicity smiles, takes both my hands and looks into my eyes. 'Amber. It's a beautiful day. And two friends who haven't seen each other in nearly twenty years are going to order themselves a $60 room-service breakfast and feed the fish croissants as a special treat.' She tilts her head kindly. 'How does that sound?'

'Good,' I nod, squeezing her fingers tight.

Just think of the fish – *and only the fish* – and everything will be fine.

Deciding that it is easier to wash away my tears than attempt to mop them up, Felicity suggests I take first turn in the shower. Now, as I stand here on the terracotta tiles lathering up mango-scented shampoo and feeling the warm water cascade around the contours of my face, part of me feels that a kind of catharsis may have taken place. The scary part is that I know this is just the beginning. I certainly don't know what's coming next. I don't even really know what happened last night. Felicity could be right – those Mai Tais were mighty strong, and who's to say one of the myriad ingredients didn't cause some kind of allergic reaction in me that made my world a little crazy. Like I say, it's been a long time since I was that drunk. Have I simply forgotten what it feels like?

I sigh. Whatever happened, I feel changed from the experience. I might wish I could go back to being comfortably numb, but the reality is my insides have been shaken up and it's going to take a while for them to settle again, if they ever do.

Hold on, is that the phone? I tilt my head away from the shower-head. I can hear Felicity's voice. I wait for a second to see if she's going to call me, but instead I hear her laugh and carry on nattering. Must be Cousin Brian.

As I resume rinsing my hair, my thoughts turn to Tezz. I think of all my wild imaginings – both in person as I watched him perform, and then overnight in my dreams – and I can't help but feel foolish. Of course he wasn't singing to me. He's just a pro, making every girl in the place feel special. That's what performers do, isn't it? Make the audience fall in love with them. But just for one night. I have something more enduring with Hugh. We have a life together. We share cutlery.

'Amber!' Felicity rattles on the door. 'Hugh's on the phone.'

Why didn't she say so sooner? How come they were chatting like old pals? I shake myself down and reach for one of the larger towels. 'Coming!' I call ahead, eager to get to him and make everything right.

'Hugh!' I drip into the receiver.

'Darling! I'm so sorry about last night, but it sounds like Felicity managed to keep you out of mischief!'

I dart her a nervous look – what exactly has she been saying to him?

'Mmmm,' I mumble and quickly change the subject: 'Where are you now?'

'I've just got into Bora Bora airport. The yacht's right here so I should be back with you in twenty minutes.'

Twenty minutes! Not nearly enough time to revert to the old Amber. He'll know something is wrong as soon as he sets eyes on me.

'I thought maybe this afternoon we could do a helmet dive. I know it might sound alarming, but they say it's for everyone from seven to seventy and you get to walk along the bottom of the ocean. How does that sound to you?'

'Wonderful!' I surprise him with my reply.

'Really?'

'Sounds great!' I overenthuse, keen to compensate for last night's wantonness.

'Okay, I'll call ahead and set that up. See you shortly. I love you.'

'See you!' I put down the receiver, and for a second a fond smile plays on my lips. That's my Hugh – sweet, kind, safe Hugh. You can weight me down and tie me to the seabed and I know I'll live to tell the tale if he's by my side.

Suddenly I feel guilty, not for anything I wished for last night but for not loving him enough. *Must try harder*. I'm just being silly and ungrateful. Everyone says he's perfect, and they're right. I never have to question his devotion. I'd be a fool to mess up what we have. Look how miserable Felicity is alone. Today I'm going to show him just how lovely a girlfriend I can be. I'm going to be enthusiastic and affectionate and . . . Mid-resolution I notice Felicity busily gathering up her things.

'You're not leaving?'

'I don't want your man's first impression of me to be as a hung-over old soak!'

'But how long do you think you can hide the truth?' I deadpan.

'Funny!' she grimaces.

'Really, won't you at least say hello?'

'Well, if I wait to see him, then it's another half an hour before the next shuttle to Vaitape and I'll miss getting back to the boat for lunch . . .'

Lunch? I look at my watch. So much for breakfast, it's already 1 p.m.

'What about tonight? Can you join us then?'

Felicity shakes her head. 'It sounds like he's got something special planned for just the two of you.'

My stomach squirms queasily in response. Can't we ever have a day without extravagant gestures? He knows I can't compete. 'Like what?' I ask her.

'Don't worry,' she says, dismissing my concerns. 'I'm sure it's no big deal.'

I continue to look fretful.

'Look,' she sighs. 'The poor guy is in paradise with his lady-love, and he's yet to have a proper night out with her. I don't want to intrude.'

'What about tomorrow? I'm not sure if Hugh's free, but we could try for lunch?'

'Lovely,' Felicity chirrups a little too cheerily. 'How about I meet you at your dock at noon?'

'Then afterwards we can scour the island looking for Airport Guy!' I suggest.

'Which reminds me – I got you this.' She pulls a CD from her bag. 'Last night at the bar when I was on that wild goose chase for him, I found this nook at the back where they were selling Soul Desire CDs.'

My heart does a little jump. 'Oh, thank you,' I gush, reaching for it.

'Unless you'd rather not have it . . .' she taunts, holding it out of my reach. 'I would completely understand.'

'No, it's fine, it's just a memento.' Apparently a few traces of crush remain, even after the purging shower.

Once in my grasp, I flip the plastic casing to locate the cover, eyes shining as the guys' laughing faces greet me. Even in 2-D, their smiles are contagious.

'Look, it's called *Beautiful Day*! Just like you said just now – "*Amber, it's a beautiful day . . .*"'

'I wonder where they took that shot.' Felicity leans over my shoulder to inspect the image of a lemon sherbet-painted house with a powder-blue convertible parked outside. 'Could be Key West.'

'Thank you, honey. It's the perfect memory of a very special night.'

'Just not one to be repeated any time soon.' Felicity looks apologetic.

'It wasn't so bad.' I no longer feel the need to guilt-trip her. 'I mean, we did have fun.'

'We always do,' she chimes as she gives me one last squeeze.

I watch her tackle the walkway like she's a drunk-driver doing the walk-in-a-straight-line test (and failing), then look down at the CD like it's contraband. I definitely have mixed feelings about playing it. It goes somewhat against my mission to show sole devotion to Hugh. And what if it acts as some kind of audio hypnosis and I fall under their spell again? Besides, I've only got ten minutes or so before Hugh gets back . . . I should at least dress and tidy up before I decide whether to chance one song. As I pull on my white linen trousers and the blue boat-neck T-shirt Abigail insisted on lending me (gratefully received now I'm here and all my other clothes make me perspire just looking at them), I scan the track listings. Then, as I straighten the bed and clear away the debris of last night's outfit dilemma, I mull over the titles in my head. In spite of my inner turmoil, the song that seems to be calling my name is 'Lucky One'.

I lie flat-out on the daybed, telling myself I could just as easily be listening to Lemar, then adjust the headphones and press play.

It begins with a strummy acoustic guitar and dreamy 'do-dup-do-do, do-dos'. I feel my shoulders relax and my heart levitate. Then he sings.

> They say you're lucky if you let true love find you
> Once in a lifetime maybe twice
> Well I have to be the luckiest man alive
>
> It feels like you came right out of nowhere
> Just when it seemed all hope was gone-

I press pause – woah! I don't know if I can do this. Just the sound of his voice – so gentle, so sweet – is having an effect. I take a breath and centre myself, unable to resist another bar or three.

> Life was just existence until you came into my world
> Was it my resistance that kept you away so long?
> But now I'm the lucky one

That's beautiful, I swoon, as I listen to the chorus. To treasure someone's love like that, to feel that appreciation in the very core of you.

Never will I take your love for granted, no,
no
Cos you make me feel so alive, yeah
And for that I'm yours, I'm the lucky one

I picture Tezz – those dark eyes, that beauty spot –
looking at me as he sings the words 'I'm yours', and my
heart swells with the promise of a new kind of
pleasure. It's almost like I can feel his touch. I breathe
in. Is that Van Cleef & Arpels?

My eyes flicker open and I find Hugh gently
stroking my arm. Instead of starting and jumping
back, I contemplate him for a moment, as if he too is a
phantom.

'Wow, now that's a look I haven't seen in a while!' he
smiles, looking deep into my eyes.

Oh God. Poor Hugh. It wasn't him I was thinking
of.

He leans in and gives me a soft, you-know-what-
comes-next kiss . . . I try hard not to freeze, not to
noticeably pull away. I've missed you, his lips say. I
need to touch you, I need you to *want me* to touch you.
I need you to love me back. I feel a tug at my heart and
my eyes well up as I press a kiss hard into his cheek so
that it registers with him that I am responding, but
then, right on cue, my stomach lets out a yowl of
neglect.

'Oop!' Hugh laughs, looking down at my belly. 'I
take it you haven't had lunch yet.'

'I haven't even had breakfast,' I tell him truthfully.

135

'I'm sorry, hun, but do you mind if we grab something to eat, I'm feeling a bit faint.'

'Of course,' he says, seemingly unfazed. 'I bet the poolside café could rustle up something nice and quick.'

'Perfect!' I smile, cupping his face in my palm. This man really takes care of me. Could I really want for more?

'Up you get!' He hauls me to my feet. 'You want a piggy-back?'

'No, I'm fine,' I laugh.

'Come on, saddle up!' He reaches round and slaps his lower back. 'Remember how we used to do the Oxford Triathlon with Jacqui and Richard?'

I do remember. It wasn't a real triathlon, we made it up. There was a piggy-back race, followed by a punting challenge, then a frisbee contest. And which-ever couple lost had to buy the drinks.

'Come on, Amber, your steed awaits!' He stands with his back to me, looking like a cowboy about to reach for his guns.

I sigh to myself. Having just got out of having sex, I suppose the least I can do is jump on his back.

No sooner have I locked my thighs around his waist than he charges out on to the walkway, giving a full Ascot opening race commentary as we bound towards the main building. Such is the way he won my heart way back when. I knew that come the end of our days out with Jacqui and Richard he'd lend me his big sweater to walk home in, and that one chapter into

136

whatever book I'd taken to bed, there'd be a delivery of a steamy Horlicks. I appreciated every caring gesture he made. I knew I was lucky. So why now, as he propels me over an imaginary water jump, does it feel so awkward and inappropriate? And why am I hoping that Tezz won't see us?

I knew it was a bad idea to come here. As I suspected, paradise brings out the worst in me.

10

I've never begun my day with deep-fried calamari before, but I wouldn't hesitate to do it again. I may even consider permanently switching my chai tea to a grande gazpacho. Those tangy green peppers really get you going.

Initially I felt a little conspicuous being the only fully-clothed individual as far as the eye could see, but gradually I accepted that the flesh-to-fabric ratio in a poolside café is rather different from the drafty dining establishments I frequent back home. Hugh informed me that in less classy joints you'd just get plastic chairs so your wet swimmers can drip through the slats, whereas here at the Bora Bora Lagoon Resort the chairs are super-comfortable padded affairs constructed from some kind of miracle gauze that absorbs the wet yet leaves you dry. Interesting concept.

While enjoying a puffy calzone and telling me how

great Sandrine has been translating everything from French to English for him, Hugh made a heroic effort not to look at the pair of candy-thonged bottoms to our right, and I tried not to eavesdrop on their owners' conversation. However, when Hugh went to the loo I couldn't help but catch wind of the heated analysis of their respective tans.

'But your feet are so much browner than mine!' wails Bubblegum Pink Thong.

'Yes, but look at my shins, they're all speckledy.' Opal Fruit Orange hoiks her leg up on to the table for closer inspection. 'They've been going like that for the past three years. It's probably cancer.'

'At least your face is really, really dark,' consoles Bubblegum.

'What about your stomach!'

'I know but I'm hardly going to be able to show that off in Chicago.'

'Oh, I do hope the weather is good when we get back so we can wear something skimpy – everyone will be sooo jealous!' toots Opal Fruit as if her greatest mission in life is tormenting pale people.

I wonder if they even know where they are. Why didn't they just check into the local tanning salon for a week?

'I really want to get a bit of colour while I'm here,' Hugh announces as he settles back into his nappy-tastic seat. 'Make the guys at work jealous!'

I look at him, then back at the girls, and wonder, Am I missing out on one of life's great pleasures?

'Suncream?' he offers. 'Better butter-up before we head off. Can you do my back?'

I do so, effusing as much love from my fingertips as I can, only to discover that we'll be wearing wetsuits for the dive. Besides which, even Paris Hilton would be hard-pushed to catch a ray twenty-thousand leagues under the sea. Actually it's more like ten metres down. Even so, I'm happy to watch three other pairs of holidaymakers get fitted with a giant leaded helmet and make the dive ahead of us. Hugh takes my hand, sensing my nerves as I watch them easing themselves down the ladder and disappearing under the water. If someone offered to take me back to shore now I'd leap at the chance. I don't want to do this. Even though face after face emerges looking delirious with glee, spouting, 'That was the most incredible thing I've ever done!'

All the while, Hugh chats easily with the tour guides and the other punters. It's rather handy that he's such a chatterbox in public, I just have to tag along and smile dutifully, which leaves me plenty of time for my own thoughts. Like how come, when the dive instructor tells us to adjust the pressure in our heads by popping our ears when we're about halfway down the ladder, the water isn't going to rush up into our helmets along with the hand that is reaching in to squeeze our nose. Apparently it just doesn't.

'So thumbs up for okay,' he tells us when our turn comes.

'What about not okay?' I gulp.

'Trust me, I know every symbol for not okay.'

Gotcha. I take one last breath of natural air and then stumble a little from the sheer weight of the helmet and its heavy yoke. I check again that there's actually a tube connecting me to the tank of air and start my descent. The diver sinks into the lagoon alongside me. Five rungs down he motions for me to pop my ears. I reach my hand up into my helmet and water does indeed seep in, but only halfway up my neck, so that's something. Suddenly there are no more rungs and I bob down on to the sandy bottom of the ocean. Seconds later Hugh is by my side reminding me of my attached pouch containing a French stick. No sooner do we tear off a sodden snag than we're bombarded with a zillion convict fish – appropriately named for their bands of black and white – nipping the bread from our fingers. There are so many of them Hugh is entirely obscured from view, in fact in my line of vision there seem to be more of these finned humbugs than water. Occasionally I feel a slither of their gel-smooth scales, reminding me that this is not some fancy visual effect – I really am hanging out with fish in their natural habitat. Finally they disperse and I get my bearings, heart pumping with the privilege of being able to dip down into their living quarters and meet their neighbours – the yellow-ended saddle butterfly and the glimmering green parrot fish – while admiring their fancy coral carpets. Then I see Hugh moving towards me with all the lumbering grace of a man walking on the moon,

141

miming the taking of a photograph and pointing to another couple with an underwater camera. I instinctively reach up to check my hair, clunking my hand on the helmet before I realise that that's not a real concern at this time. As we pose side by side, I'm glad that we'll have a record of this unique moment. Hugh looks so happy it was well worth the risk of drowning. I feel like I've finally done something right. And then I go and spoil it all by realising that a teeny part of me is impatient for this miraculous experience to be over so I can get back to the room and carry on listening to the CD.

I thought I might have time before dinner, but after we emerge from the water, it turns out Hugh has booked us on a sunset cruise on a catamaran. Or a cat-meringue as he likes to call it. Apparently it's a swanky champagne affair so he insists we dress to impress, then quickly discovers that no man, however well brought up, can withstand a blazer and tie in this heat.

'Do you think it's okay if I wear my khakis and a nice shirt?' he checks with me.

'You know you're asking the wrong person, but yes, of course. The main thing is to be comfortable.'

I then use that disclaimer as an excuse to don my beaded flip-flops and what he calls my Chelsea hippy skirt (salmon silk tie-dye with ruffles and a sequin trim) which promptly billows up like a crinoline the second we step outside, making me feel I should be squatting decoratively over a toilet roll.

'You look lovely,' he tells me all the same.

I smile back at him, link my arm in his and nuzzle into him as we walk, determined that we should look every inch the perfect couple.

The boat is sleek and white and flat – more hydro-planing sci-fi raft than yacht – and as we step aboard I wonder exactly where we're supposed to sit; it seems to me to be all surface and no seats.

'Right here,' says Hugh, motioning to the raised central ridge.

'Won't we skid off when the boat gets going?' The narrow chrome bar trimming the deck perimeter is not nearly enough to rein me in.

'I'll keep a hold of you, don't worry,' Hugh assures me as he nestles me close to his side.

Tilting my head back on to his chest, I look up at the mast above us, wondering if a sudden change in wind direction might cause it to swing round and take me out.

'Relax!' Hugh rubs my arm, sensing my concern.

'Also is possible to sit here.' The skipper points to two trampoline triangles on the ledge jutting out at the front of the vessel.

'You're kidding?' I gasp.

'No really, is safe, see?' As he steps on to the taut fabric, the interlaced ropes creak in a disgruntled fashion.

'I'm fine here, thank you!' I bleat. 'Hold on, are we moving?' I look back at the rocking jetty. 'What about the other guests?'

'It's just you and me.' Hugh pulls me closer still. 'Sailing into the sunset together.'

'Oh!' This must be the treat Felicity hinted at. 'How nice.'

Hugh starts humming Duran Duran's 'Rio' as we glaze forth, and I have to admit this is pretty darn glamorous – a whole catamaran to the two of us, and nothing but an eternity of sea and sky ahead. We're so far removed from any humdrum concerns and yet I can't escape the uneasy feeling that he's gone too far again. Sometimes I feel that my only role in these situations is to be grateful, like it would be almost rude to talk about other subjects; that I constantly have to say, 'You spoil me! I'm so lucky! This is such a treat!'

I think of the conversations I've had with Felicity since we were reunited and how there's interaction back and forth and real emotion. With Hugh the gist of our exchanges seem to be, 'See what I do for you?' and 'Yes, darling – you're a wonderful boyfriend.'

'Warm enough?' Hugh checks, as the most welcome of breezes ruffles our clothes.

'Perfect,' I sigh. And really everything is. I'm with a man who goes to great lengths to make me happy. It's obviously my problem that I have a problem with that. So for now I'm going to set aside any navel-gazing and give my full attention to the lagoon waters as they respond to every subtle change in the light. What was once a turquoise glow is now a muddle of blues and greys like a painter's water jar, with a slash of emerald freshly seeped from the brush. Then, as the sun sinks

144

lower, the water darkens to dense pewter with gold accents on the ripples. All the while the catamaran is moving with such grace I find myself imbued with an unusual sense of dignity and peace.

Following the curve of the motu, we're presented with a startling new scene: a row of over-water bungalows and a solitary palm tree set like black paper cut-outs against a hallelujah sky of shimmering pearl and moody charcoal. It puts me in mind of a magnificent etching on polished brass. So bright in parts, I'm forced to squint at the gleam.

'It's like that *Ray of Light* picture of Madonna!' Hugh observes.

I laugh. He's right! 'This is incredible,' I sigh. 'I've never seen anything like this before.' The way the sun is now touching the horizon, creating a golden path for us to follow, takes my breath away. If Gilly were here she'd say this was a sign to stay on course with Hugh. But I'm now barely aware of his presence, so lost in wonder am I as dune-like drifts of apricot and violet suffuse the sky.

I hear Hugh talking, but not the words, and then just when I think the sky is about to succumb to night, new colours flare up – dazzling blasts of orange and pirouettes of pink.

Behold: sky art!

Every effect is so tantalisingly fleeting! An infinite, never-to-be-repeated slide-show of masterpieces. I find it almost frustrating to think that we can't capture this beauty and share it with other people. Though

Hugh is doing his darndest with a mini-movie on his digital camera, there will be no Bora Bora Sunset Exhibit coming to a gallery near you. Every second seems all the more precious for knowing that.

'Champagne?' The skipper offers us two slender flutes with which to toast each other.

'Thank you!' I smile, happily preparing to chink and sip when I see Hugh's face contort with horror.

'Don't move!' he blurts. 'There's something on your shoulder!'

'What?' I panic, swatting blindly, sending my champagne slopping on to the deck. '*Get it off! Get it off!*' I feel my knuckle knock against a hard corner of leather, sense something flying past my eyes and then there's a splash.

Hugh stumbles back, looking aghast.

'What was it?' I shudder, slightly confused. It didn't feel like a bug.

Hugh blinks twice then swallows hard. 'That, my dear, was a somewhat exquisite £30,000 Asscher-cut diamond engagement ring.'

'What?' I choke, hurtling to the edge of the catamaran in time to see the brown cube disappearing from view. 'Hasn't he got a net or a scooper or something?' I turn and wave madly at the skipper.

'It's okay.' Hugh lays his hand on my champagne-slopped forearm.

'No it's not!' I panic. 'People are supposed to go in search of sunken treasure, not sink it themselves.'

Hugh sets my miraculously unbroken glass down

on a safe part of the deck, then takes my hands and turns me to face him. 'I was just kidding. The box was empty. Thank God.'

'What do you mean?' I frown, still in shock.

He releases my left hand, reaches into his pocket and pulls out a sparkling band of square gems – £30,000-worth of Asscher-cut diamonds, if I'm not very much mistaken. It's only at this point that it dawns on me that he is in fact proposing. At least, I presume he's just suggested something along those lines – I haven't actually heard a single word he's said since the ring came into view.

'C-could you repeat that last bit?' I blunder, wondering how a man I thought I knew inside out could catch me out like this.

'You're still a bit flustered, aren't you?' he sympathises. 'It was a stupid joke, I shouldn't have scared you like that. I'm just nervous. I was trying to break the ice.' He gives me a 'Geddit?' look. 'Ice,' he repeats, tapping the diamond. 'See, now I'm just going for really bad puns.'

I manage a weak smile, then lurch despite the steady passage of the catamaran. 'I have to sit down.'

'Yes, yes. Let's just take a moment.' Hugh helps settle me.

The relief that I haven't just sent the family fortune to a watery grave is now overwhelmed by the 'Will You Marry Me?' newsflash. Did anyone else see this coming? Why now? Other than the fact that we're in the most romantic setting in the entire world. I suppose that's it. I look up at the sky, now a shimmering pageant of gold and rose. There couldn't be a more romantic backdrop in all creation. I feel inspired and utterly enraptured when I look at it, yet this sensation dwindles when I look at Hugh. I don't understand. I've seen proposed-to faces on TV – there's the initial shock/surprise (that bit I seem to have mastered), but where's my teary-eyed joy and surrender? Where's the instant unstoppable cry of 'Yes, of course I'll marry you!' as if I've been poised for this moment, on tenterhooks since the first 'I love you' was uttered. Suddenly I feel both sad and inadequate. What's wrong with me? Why can't I rise to this occasion? Everything is in place – the setting, the man, the woman, the ring. So what's the deal with my temperamental heart? Have I trained it so keenly to avoid pain that I've also limited its capacity for pleasure? Oh God, why wasn't it me that went overboard? I shake my head in regret.

'Amber?'

I turn to the man who could have been my fiancé by now.

'You're shaking your head,' his voice trembles. 'That's not a no, is it?'

I study his hazel eyes, so earnest, so fearful. This is all wrong! I want to make it right, to tell him what he wants to hear, to make this good man happy, but how can I get engaged when my heart is not engaging? My brow crumples in despair – there's no denying it: I just don't feel buoyed with love. And if not now, when?

'Are you all right?' Hugh asks, looking under-standably disconcerted by my inability to speak.

'I'm sorry.' I force out an apology, desperate to make light of the situation. 'You know me – I'm a rainy days and Sundays kinda gal. All this sunshine and colour . . .' I look down. 'I think I'm a bit over-whelmed.'

Hugh nods, obviously hungry to gobble up any explanation of my distracted behaviour. 'You're probably still a bit jet-lagged.'

'And hung-over,' I mutter.

'Oh, really?'

'Just a bit,' I lie.

'*Excusez-moi.*' The skipper bids us move aside as he adjusts the sail. Despite all his manly wrenching, it sounds to me like he's running something up on a sewing machine.

'So?' As Hugh takes my hand and presses it to his chest I can feel his heart rattling nineteen to the dozen.

What to say to him? It's not fair to either of us if I say yes without truly meaning it, but how can I possibly say no? I can't hurt him after all he's done for me. But just the fact that he would propose to me now and me not see it coming shows me that we must be in two very different places. Besides which, I can't take any more gifts, let alone one worth £30,000. I think I must have receive-fatigue.

Whatever it is, he needs an answer.

'Um. Gosh. You've really caught me out with this!' I try a little forced laughter.

'I've been thinking about how I was going to do it ever since I was offered the trip,' he confides. 'I wanted it to be really special . . .'

'Oh, it is, it's incredible,' I assure him. 'It's just—'

'Tell you what,' Hugh jumps in, apparently sensing the bad news and eager to shoo it away. 'Why don't we pretend that this didn't happen?'

'What? No!" I go to protest. Poor man. When he's gone to all the trouble of creating this magic moment, the least he deserves is some kind of coherent response.

'Really,' he insists, squeezing my hand tight. 'I'll try again later. Maybe on dry land next time?' He gives a hopeful raise of the eyebrows.

I don't know what to say, so I kiss him. Not an 'I'll marry you!' kiss but a 'God bless you for being so patient' kiss. I trust he knows the difference.

'Here, come back to my arms,' he says, pulling me to him. 'Everything's going to be fine.'

'I'm sorry I spoilt—' I wriggle round to speak to him.

'Hush!' He puts his fingers on my lips. 'I love you, Amber. I'll wait.'

As we both turn to face the view, my heart slumps. I know it's not a question of waiting. I always hoped it was, but for four years now I've been waiting to feel as much for Hugh as he seems to feel for me, and it hasn't happened. Now this proposal, and, worse still, the promise of more to come. I honestly can't think of anything worse than waking up every morning wondering if this is going to be the next P-day. Besides, can I really let him go through all that again when I suspect my reaction will be just the same?

I wonder if my uncertainty about all this has anything to do with my experience at The Paradise Room last night? I didn't know I had it in me to feel that attracted to a man without feeling threatened by it until I laid eyes on Tezz. I wish I could rechannel those souped-up sensations towards Hugh, but I can't. I don't know what this all means, but I feel it's something we should talk about, not brush aside.

It's then that I realise that every time I've ever wanted to talk about our relationship in any depth (and I'm only talking about a couple of millimetres deep, because I don't believe in stirring the pot unnecessarily), Hugh has made some excuse. 'Do you mind if we talk about this tomorrow?' he says, giving the excuse that he still has work to do. And then the next night he comes home with a present. And I feel that my concern is trivial because look how much he loves me. And I cut him some slack by keeping schtum and cooking a nice dinner. But now he's talking marriage, and the mere thought of it is making me feel trapped and anxious.

I really feel I should say something now, but as I turn to him I see a new animation on his face and he beats me to the punch by babbling, 'Hey, check this out – the sun and the moon in the same setting!'

'What, honey?'

Scrambling for his digital camera, he points ahead

to the bright white disc now peeking out from behind Otemanu, then back behind us to where the last trace of yellow is seeping into the liquid horizon. 'That's because we're practically on the Equator here,' he explains, sounding exceedingly chuffed.

My eyes flick between the two.

Well, will you look at that – this man gives me the sun and the moon, and it's still not enough.

11

I can't sleep. My mind keeps going over and over the proposal farrago. Repeatedly I attempt to play the scene with a different ending, but I can never muster a convincing, 'Yes, Hugh, I'll marry you!', despite the fact that I've had four years to prepare myself for this moment. Four years. I must love him or I wouldn't have stayed so long, surely? I think back to when we first met – there was definitely a mutual attraction, certainly a curiosity on my part. I just can't help wondering how far that interest would have carried me had my parents not died just three weeks into the relationship.

But then look at the character he showed at that time of crisis. When I felt like I was drowning in grief and confusion, he was the one who kept my head above water. He opened his arms and let me cling on to him for dear life, seamlessly taking control of everything, from the funeral arrangements to making sure my bills were paid when I was too lost and despondent to care. Even today the only thing I really have to worry about is what to create for dinner. Not that I'm with him for an easy life. I've never had extravagant tastes so I wasn't struggling before I met him, even on my meagre salary, and it's not like I've ever partied too hard to get around to the hoovering.

He told me he wanted to be with me on a daily basis and it seemed like a reasonable proposition – none of that obsessive you-and-me-against-the-world behaviour that ultimately led to my parents demise. We're together, but not in each other's faces. We never argue. Occasionally I'll see frustration in his eyes but he'll never voice it. At least not directly at me. He'll grumble about black pearls being ugly, along with my taste in wallpaper, and ask when am I going to donate my Puffa jacket to charity and start wearing the cashmere coat he bought for me . . . I sigh. Maybe we could get Felicity to counsel us while we're here? She's so excellent at getting to the nub of a problem and sorting it out. She's never even heard of biting your tongue.

Feeling like I might go crazy from trying to figure out a way to coax my emotions into submission, I try to focus solely on the way the water beneath the coffee table is projecting white-blue pulses across the ceiling. It's really quite absorbing tracking these reflected sprites, and I'm feeling something approaching contentment when Hugh turns in his sleep, strapping an arm across my waist. Instantly I feel claustrophobic and my feet begin twisting and scrunching. I can't lie here wearing a human seat belt! I have to escape!

Gingerly I lever Hugh's arm upwards like a drawbridge while simultaneously finding the floor with my right foot. As I lower first my bottom and then the rest of my body on to the bedside matting, I set his arm to rest on the mattress. For a full ten seconds I lie flat out on the floor, waiting for the searchlights to make their sweep. No sirens. No unleashing of rabid Alsatians. All is well.

I begin rising in slow motion as if I'm portraying 'awakening' in a modern dance production, then tiptoe across to the daybed where I resume staring at the square of pale water framed in 3-D by the coffee table. If this really were a prison cell and all the doors and windows were sealed, I might try using the sliding table top as an escape hatch . . .

Having said that, I did get off pretty lightly following the aborted proposal. A pleasant dinner across the water at the Bamboo House (all the other couples there ate in companionable silence, so we actually looked quite the chatty young things), then we both agreed on an early night. Hugh was out for the count before I'd even finished flossing, but I knew I wouldn't be able to settle.

Perhaps I'll have better luck over here. I pull a cushion beneath my head and extend my legs, already feeling more at ease, but also aware that I mustn't get too settled and actually fall asleep – if Hugh woke and saw me here it would seem too much of a statement.

He'd imagine the worst, and I'm not ready to rock the boat that much.

Turning to face the wall, I reach up and tilt the slats of the shutters open just enough to see out. My fingers graze the mesh of the mosquito netting as I lean closer and consider the subdued elegance of the night waters advancing upon the shore. Maybe I just need some fresh air. That definitely sounds appealing right now. I feel around in the darkness to find my shoes, whisk my hair up in a clip and grab the room key. I'm nearly out the door when I inadvertently send the hotel umbrella slamming into the floor with a crack.

'Mmm . . . Amber!?' Hugh muffles into his pillow.

'I'm right here!' I soothe. But a minute later it's a lie – I'm already out the door, heading for the beach.

As I feel my way along by the ropes of the walkway, I realise my feet are responding to some piped music and I get an image of Jennifer Grey surreptitiously practising her steps in *Dirty Dancing*. I quickly look around before throwing my head back in homage to her, when suddenly my stomach spasms and I jolt forward – that sounds like Tezz singing! I look around for him before I realise that his voice is being wafted from afar. Or The Paradise Room, to be precise. And there's that feeling again! I know it's merely a flash-back to last night but it feels so intense. I take a moment to take control of myself and curb the desire to run in the direction of his voice, but then decide that maybe I'm feeling compelled to return to the bar for a reason: maybe I need to confirm for myself that it was simply booze and an overactive imagination that lit that fire within me?

Perhaps if I can face that disappointment head-on, then I can let go of whatever it is that's holding me back from Hugh? It could work. It is possible that I've always secretly wondered if my parents were on to something with that passion lark. I don't want to spend the rest of my life wondering if I'm missing out. This is good! I'm going to face this right now. Yes!

I turn to face the path. Then halt again, gripped by nerves. 'Come on!' I urge. 'This is the right thing to do – it's going to get everything back in perspective and give me the peace of mind to look Hugh in the eye and say—'

And say—

Again the words stick in my throat. But before I become further paralysed with indecision, my feet set themselves in motion.

From faded walkway to flagstone path, through the tiled reception past the pool, over the lily pond, beyond the tennis courts, gathering speed and momentum as I go. I feel more optimistic with each scurried step – this is going to clarify things for me. I'll see that Tony and Tezz are just normal guys earning a buck shaking their thang and then I'll be able to move on or let go or do whatever needs to be done to free myself from my aggravating inner jumblings.

I want to squeal under my breath as I ruffle the foliage en route. I can't quite believe I'm doing this. I can't believe I'm drawn like this . . . As I slow down to approach the bar entrance my stomach loops with nervous excitement, but this time I don't hesitate . . . I have to find out if lightning can strike twice.

Merging with the shadows at the back of the room, I cautiously raise my gaze towards the stage. Instantly I feel like a surfer who just caught a wave – my face lights up and I find myself awash with elation, too happy to register the implication of my reaction. *Just look at them go!*

I thought the pill was fast-forwarding them, but they really do dance that fast – kicks and squats and side-shuffles all impeccably executed at 90 m.p.h. I stare agog as each of my hallucinations is proved to be based in reality: the melted feet effect? Rollerblades. (Of course! Now I remember Fantasia saying they met in the cast of *Starlight Express*.) My insistence that they stretched to ten feet tall? Stilts worn beneath extra-long black satin trousers! And the way they had me combusting with lust? Nothing more than good old-fashioned sex appeal!

And it just keeps on coming. Last night there was all too much to take in, but now I see that Tony not only has nuggety abs but also a divine Action Man ridge running from his hips down to his groin as if he has been slotted together from an easy-assemble Perfect Body Kit.

As for Tezz . . . I take a moment to re-admire the smooth elliptical definition to his upper arms, then notice his exquisitely elegant hands for the first time, and take specific note of the bands of silver encircling both his thumb and ring finger. I don't know why I find that so potently alluring but I do. As he raises his right hand for a finger-click and then returns it to rest on his thigh, I can't help but emit a giddy whimper. If he made the slightest beckoning motion I know I would find myself stumbling forward towards him. Instead, as they announce a short break, I choose to divert to the spiral bar and order a Mai Tai, albeit a virgin one tonight.

And to think I used to tut at my schoolfriends and their pop-star crushes. I remember Becci Gwyther being so utterly nose-pressed-against-the-TV obsessed with George Michael that I thought she had become psychologically unhinged and suggested she see a doctor. Now, age thirty-two, I finally get it! I wonder if part of the appeal is the fact that certain songs in the Soul Desire repertoire remind me of my mother – Stevie Wonder, Aretha Franklin, Al Green. I smile to myself, remembering her face as she sang along with the Reverend, earrings glinting and rocking inde-pendently, eyes closed, the palms of her hands shaping and smoothing the air around her as if blending her own breath with the breeze. I find myself looking around at the women in the audience, half hoping I might find her sat amongst them, perhaps on a little night excursion from heaven. My dad would be by her side, of course, spivvy in a suit even in this humidity, holding her hand.

'Can I get you another?' The waiter offers me a second drink and I accept, this time with booze'n'all.

Everything about being here just feels so good. I never thought this after-dark world would hold any appeal for me; I don't suppose I've even seen 2 a.m. more than a few times in my life. Getting up at six always seemed such a great head-start on the day. Though if you asked me precisely what I've achieved with all my sprightly early mornings other than a feeling of virtue, I really couldn't tell you. All I know is that right now I am feeling so very relaxed and exactly where I need to be.

But then I remember the one mystery from last night that remains unresolved – didn't I think Tezz had sung directly to me? I was actually convinced he'd invented a new set of lyrics just to get a secret message across. If everything else I saw was real, could that be too? Could it be that he really had noticed me?

Suddenly I flush with embarrassment. Of course not! Who do I think I am? Look at me sat here on a chi-chi bar stool thinking I'm Natalie Wood. I feel so foolish when I look down at my shapeless shroud of a sundress that I'm tempted to leave, but then the lights dim and both the guys and the girls steal on to the stage in Philip Marlowe detective raincoats with upturned collars, shiny black Ray-Bans and tilted trilbies. My self-consciousness is forgotten as I watch them prowl around singing in low, understated voices. Gradually it dawns on me – and the rest of the audience – that they are about to blast into Tina Turner's 'Proud Mary'. Conversations are halted and drinks set down in anticipation. Still moving with tantalising stealth, first the shades come off, then the hats, then flasher-mac-style the raincoats are flung wide and we're assaulted with a frenzy of fringe-swishing as the fab four shimmy and shake like their life depended on it. The appreciative whooping gathers momentum as they hot-step it around the stage, the girls revealing white-fringed minidresses and red patent leather boots, the guys in mesh tops and black-fringed trousers.

'Rolling!' I find myself chanting while inadvertently hunching then throwing back my shoulders in time to the music. The atmosphere is electric. By the time they're done, I'm actually panting. I look around for someone to squeak at, definitely feeling the absence of Felicity's knee to squeeze, and see that every face in the room is equally ecstatic.

'You guys are great!' calls out the kind of man you'd expect would only cheer at his favourite sports team on TV.

'Woo-hoooo!' yodels every woman in the room.

I laugh, giddy with elation, wondering how any of us are supposed to go back to normal life after this.

'Back for more?'

I turn to find *rae-rae* Fantasia voguing in pink satin.

'Hiiiii!' I beam, delighted to see a familiar face, especially one elbow-deep in iridescent make-up. 'You look gorgeous!'

'Now that's what I'm talking about – a little attention on *me*!' she struts, slumping her sequinned purse down on the bar next to me.

'Everything all right?' I ask, a tad concerned.

'Well, all anyone ever wants to talk about is my boys,' she pouts, making a dismissive swipe in the direction of the stage.

'Mmm,' I muffle, biting back the million-and-one questions about to spill from my lips.

'I mean it comes to something when a cross-dresser doesn't even prompt a second glance.'

'I see your point,' I sympathise.

'Besides,' she huffs, eyeing me up and down, 'you're in my bad books.'

'I am?' I blink.

She taps the side of her head. 'What did I tell you about the flower behind the ear.'

'Oh yes, I know, I'm just not really in the flower market right now,' I frown, confused by my own phrasing.

'So where's your friend?' Fantasia queries as she signals to the bartender to get her a glass of water.

'She's back on *Windstar* tonight with her cousin,' I explain. 'I couldn't sleep, so I thought I'd pop along for a drink.' I raise my glass in cheers.

'You'd better watch yourself – they're addictive.'

'Oh no, I'm just having one tonight—'

'Not the booze,' she cuts in, giving me a penetrating look. 'The boys.'

'Well, I suppose that's the idea,' I shrug, averting my eyes and trying to sound blasé. 'If you're a performer, you want people to keep coming back for more.'

162

Fantasia studies me further, then cautions, 'This isn't real life, you know.'

'No, I know. It's far too good for that.' I meant that as a jokey aside, but as soon as the words fall from my mouth I feel as though I've been slapped. Is that what I really think? Is Felicity right? Have I got so used to my mediocre existence that I can't even imagine the possibility of feeling this good on a regular basis? Suddenly I decide I'd best get out while I'm still on a high.

'Well, nice to see you. I should be getting back,' I say, standing up, ready to descend the spiral staircase.

'You can't leave now.' She bars my path. 'They've got a new number in the next set.'

What is her game? One minute she seems to be warning me off, the next she's insisting I stay and get further addicted.

'It's Tezz tap-dancing,' she entices, talons cuffing my wrists. 'Another ten minutes – what can it hurt?'

I chew my lip. The question is not so much what, as who. Or should I say Hugh? Not that I'm doing any-thing wrong – technically I just couldn't sleep so I went for a walk and had a quick drink in a bar. He doesn't know all the other stuff that's been going on in my head. But does that make it all right? It doesn't feel like it.

'Here they come!' Fantasia senses movement in the wings.

Well I suppose it would be rude to exit mid-performance, I reason to myself, and sit back down. I only wish Felicity was here with me – we actually took after-school tap lessons one year. It would have been a hoot to see if we recognised any of Tezz's steps.

I take another slurp of my drink and twist my body towards the stage. Oh my God! He's staring right at me! His face illuminates with a smile as our eyes connect. I quickly check behind me in case he's actually directing his beauteous full-beam at someone more deserving, like Halle Berry – but no, it's really me. I look back to find him laughing and mouthing, 'Whassup?' at me. It's more than I can handle – my heart pogos so high it hits my throat, and the contents of my head begin to spin and flurry like a whirlpool.

I want to cry out, 'Don't do this to me unless you really mean it! Don't let me be one of a thousand fans screaming and squished at the front of the stage. Don't let me be the one who faints and has to be carried off by Red Cross stretchers!'

Actually, I remember Becci saying she almost envied those girls because it somehow made them special. She also suspected it was just a ploy to get backstage and that, once they'd recovered, they'd sneak off and find their way to the band's dressing rooms. Once she even said she wished she had a terminal disease, because pop stars were always shown visiting hospital wards of children with leukaemia. She felt it was so unfair – why them and not her? That's when I told her she needed help.

My gaze returns to Tezz. I watch him slam-dunk a

few fancy moves then BAM!, his eyes are upon me again, and with a playful grin he pulls his shirt to one side giving me a flash of his nipple ring. Or am I just projecting my own desires? I feel like I can't differentiate between fantasy and reality with this man. Every time I look at him my mind teases me with erotic images and sensations. I turn away, focusing on the chill of my drink, trying to clear my head, but then I hear him breathe these words:

> I like it when you're in the room
> It gives me a sexy vibe
> Imagine if I was your groom
> And you were my bride tonight

My eyes flick to Fantasia. Judging by the scowl contorting her face, she heard it too. Wow! I want to laugh out loud – this has got to be the best chat-up technique ever. The extra allure a person exudes when raised just a few feet above the populace is astounding. As he raps the chorus, my heart rate reaches a dangerous excess.

> Welcome to my honeymoon hotel
> Honey you know I'll treat you well
> Welcome to my honeymoon suite
> Gonna kiss you from your veil to your feet

I feel weak with submission as my eyes trail his hand manoeuvring deftly down his torso, over his stomach, down . . . *oop*! The seduction is swiftly aborted as Tony strides up and gives Tezz a 'quit your flirting' swat.

Resplendent in a long, strokable, leopard-print coat, he cues the band to strike up 'Stray Cat Strut' then effects the most amazing balletic slow-mo barrel-jump, pausing in mid-air like some *Matrix* special effect. Where are the hidden harnesses and spring-boards that make these moves possible? I'm just wondering how these guys have dodged becoming international phenomena when Fantasia gives me a 'Here we go!' nudge.

Straining forward for a better view, I see Tony bid the band slow to a low-level underscore before turning his attention to Tezz. He points to his feet, now atop a mock doorstep, then challenges him to reinterpret the 'Be-dee-dup, be-dubba-da-dup, be-dee-da!' scat-sounds he's making as tap steps. Tezz takes the challenge, echoing 'Be-dee-dup, be-dubba-da-dup, be-dee-da!' using only scrapes and slaps of his metal-soled shoes. Not bad, Tony seems to be saying. Now let's see you do this! And so he taunts and tests him, making his scats increasingly long and more complex. If Tezz misses so much as a 'da', Tony shakes his head and has him do it again. The audience is rapt as their to-ing and fro-ing escalates into a rat-a-tat-tatting blur. Just as Tezz seems invincible, Tony puts on a mis-chievous look and requests Tezz to tap down the steps, double-time-step across the stage and then propel himself on to the bar-top below.

'Are you crazy?' Tezz reels, checking out the chasm that lies between stage and bar.

Tony gives a blasé shrug and calmly repeats his request: 'Doop-doop-doop-doop-CRASH!'

'A brother could break his leg doing that!' Tezz protests.

'There's ice down there,' Tony parlays. 'Just pack some on when you're done.'

'Are you trying to kill me?' Tezz wants to know.

'Well, I got some friends coming in tomorrow night and I told them I was a solo act, so . . .' Tony looks sheepish.

'Well, you're right there,' Tezz sasses back. 'You sing *so low* no one can hear you!'

The audience chuckles at their banter.

'Come on – y'all want to see him do this, right?' Tony calls out, turning to enlist their support.

The audience is bewildered, half egging on Tezz, half concerned that shins will indeed be splintered.

'Okay, okay, I'll do it!' Tezz holds up his hands.

'You're going to "Doop-doop-doop-doop-CRASH?"' Tony confirms.

Tezz nods an affirmative.

'Okay, let's see it!'

I lean further forward, not wanting to miss a trick.

Tezz begins with the standard tap, but instead of moving forward, darts into the wings, continuing to make appropriate sound effects into his microphone as he dashes around and enters the bar via the lounge area. In one swift move he's up on the bar-top making the casements of cherries and olives quake with his riffle-and-spank combinations. First the drummer, then the bassist assist him in building to an almighty crescendo, at which point even Tony concedes he's well and truly foiled. Tezz throws his arms up in triumph! Everyone cheers. Then, as he jumps down, he casts a barely discernible 'You like that?' wink in my direction. I cannot believe my luck! I almost feel guilty getting so much attention, especially when Fantasia huffs to her feet and tells me she's going back to work.

'Well, it was nice to see you again!' I smile, trying not to flaunt my glee.

'I'm sure you'll be back,' she notes dryly. 'Just make sure you make the right choice.'

My lips part, ready to demand clarification, but she's gone before any words are formed.

The right choice? She doesn't know about the proposal, so she can't be referring to that. Then again, I suppose I did infer a certain ambivalence in my relationship status last night. What else could she mean? Certainly not a choice between Tezz and Tony. The more mysterious half of the partnership hasn't even looked in my direction, other than to raise an eyebrow at Felicity and my pitiful 'seat dancing' last night.

I'm confused. I feel like I've experienced more emotions in the last three days than I have in the past three years. If not longer. It's probably best that I step back and take a breather at this point. There are only so many nerve-tingling thrills a novice like me can take. I slide from my seat and slip out through the exit without once looking back at Tezz.

Half an hour later I find myself sat with my feet in the hotel pool, fascinated by the ghostly glow my shins take on when submerged. The boys' music serenades me still, sent to me now upon a jasmine breeze. I lean back on my hands and take in everything around me – the eerily deserted pool café, the sleeping sun-loungers, the dainty spotlights accenting every frill and frond in the undergrowth. There's such a different atmosphere here at night. By day it's all about Day-Glo *pareu* and tanning scandals. Under the reign of the moon, all hues are subdued and secrets come out to play.

I smile to myself. Sitting here alone, I no longer feel like the outsider. This world belongs to me. Even when the music ceases and I am released from its spell, I stay where I am, wondering how 160 guests and an equal number of staff can be so still, even in sleep. I have never known such tranquillity. Outwardly at least. Inwardly those troublesome qualms are starting to undulate again. I try to ignore them and stay tuned into the Zen calm, but it's too late – questions need to be answered . . .

How is it that a stranger on stage can feel more relevant to my heart than my long-term partner? Is this just a premature bout of wedding-day nerves? Does Tezz seem so very appealing because I have yet to learn his flaws? This really does seem to be my belated version of a teen crush – you pick someone with abundant and obvious talent and then dream up the rest to suit your heart's needs, isn't that the idea? Given the chance, I'm sure he'd be just as disappointing as every other mortal. Not that Hugh has disappointed me, probably because I went into our relationship with zero expectations. I wasn't looking for *anyone*, let alone The One. But now he's brought it to the point of marriage and love-for-all-eternity, and as I take a closer look at the concept of 'us', I find myself questioning him. Or rather 'us'. Exactly how are we doing as a couple?

All this ruminating nudges awake a long-forgotten voice in my heart. 'Look, I was fine dozing until now,' it seems to say. 'You didn't need me, you asked nothing of me, so I've had a lovely long kip, but if you're going to start seriously talking marriage then I'm afraid I have to be involved. It's my thing and I won't be ignored. In fact, I guarantee you one helluva hullabaloo for the rest of your life if you persist without me. Or maybe I'll just niggle at you, that might be worse – constant questioning: *Is he really the man for me? Have I done the right thing?* One way or another I'm going to get you!'

Wow. I guess my heart means business. In response my head demands: 'What do you want then? Tell me!'

And all my heart says is: 'Tezz.'

'He's just appealing because he's new – unexplored territory!' my head battles. 'Yes, he seems to have an

170

irresistible sense of humour and a sexiness that could invoke a climax at twenty paces—'

'Hey!' I cry, 'I thought you were supposed to be opposing him?'

'Oh yes! The thing is, these assumptions about his character are not based in real experience; you've never even spoken to him.'

I can't dispute that. But then my two feuding internal voices surprise me by agreeing on one thing. *There's only one way to find out . . .*

'Hold on!' I exclaim. 'Are you giving me permission to pursue Tezz even though I'm here with Hugh?'

The voice in Hugh's corner heaves a testy sigh. 'Well, I can see you won't be truly satisfied until you know for sure that he's not some being sent to earth for your exclusive pleasure, so I suggest you get a move on, get him out of your system and get back in time to make a real commitment to the man who truly loves you.'

Am I really giving myself permission to consider Tezz as an option? Aside from the infidelity issue, that would require considerable daring on my part and suddenly I'm not sure I've got what it takes. Maybe this is what being star-struck feels like – he actually seems on a higher plane than me. I mean really, how could I possibly get it on with someone so vibrant and honed? I have to face facts – men like that are designed as a dream. Good double-bluff on behalf of my anti-heart, I'd say.

I get to my feet, leaving a trail of dark, wet

footprints on the blonde paving as I head back to the bungalow. Only this time I decide to take the beach route, and soon my soles are coated in the minuscule fragments of shell that pass for sand here. I wiggle my toes, enjoying the gentle abrasion. Back in Oxford the only recollection my feet have of summer is leather sandals and the occasional tickling of grass as I kicked off my shoes under the big oak tree in the park. It felt good when the grass was long and soft and green, but by the end of the season it would be stubby and yellowing and itchy to the touch. That's when I would long for the rain again.

Suddenly I feel disorientated. Where am I?

I look up to see the bungalow walkway just a few feet ahead and realise my steps have become smaller and slower. I thought I was ready to go back but apparently I'm not ready to be cooped up just yet. I look at my watch – 3 a.m. Only three hours till sunrise. Maybe I'll stay up and watch the new day emerge. The sunset was so magnificent I'm sure it'll be worth a few yawns along the way. I turn back and scan the beach for one of the nearly horizontal palm trees to straddle, just in case the sand is alive with late-night revellers of the creepie-crawlie variety. I see one up ahead and stride forth, so focused on my target that I nearly miss the gift of a forgotten beach towel scrolled up beside it.

'Perfect!' I shake it out, patting it back into place in the sheltered nook beneath the stooping palm.

Maybe I'll just close my eyes for five minutes. Even if I do conk out, the sun will wake me up. I settle on to my back, loving the feeling of the warm air enfolding my body. So I've had a bit of a crazy day; it's okay now. I just feel drowsy. Nothing is a big drama any more. What will be, will be.

I breathe in, then slowly exhale. In and out, following the pull and splay of the water. I'm sensing myself dipping into unconsciousness when three droplets splash on to my skin – one on my cheek, one on my shoulder and one on my forearm. Is that rain?

As I reach to wipe my face I open my eyes, and there, looming over me, is the dark, tapered silhouette of a man.

12

'Tezz!' I scramble upright with shock, giving myself an almighty thwack on the head with the low-slung tree trunk as I do so. 'Yow!' I howl, slumping back on to the towel in a skew of limbs.

'*Damn!*' His face winces in empathy as he reaches to steady me. 'I didn't mean to scare you. I wasn't sure if you were asleep.'

'Wha—?' I feel dizzy. What just happened? Did he just hit me?

'Are you okay?'

I look up at him and think: *I may never know*. First it was imaginary drugs and hard liquor, then possible hangover delusions, now concussion! All I can do is stare back and hold on to the throbbing in my head.

'I just needed my towel,' he continues. 'I didn't mean to—'

It's only then that I twig: his beautiful body is

glistening not with infinite teardrop diamonds, just water. He's been swimming and he needs to dry off.

'Oh God, sorry!' I attempt to lurch upright and WOP! Same head, same tree, double the pain.

'Woah!' he says, swiftly guiding me out into the open, shielding me from a possible third collision with a protective arm. 'I think that's enough head-banging for one night.'

I don't know what the hell is going on – the sand is spinning around me like I'm hanging off a round-about. I reach out for something – anything! – to keep me upright, then gradually, through the woozy nausea and the smarting and the stinging, I become aware that my hand is gripped on to his upper arm. And his bicep is unexpectedly large. And sleek and taut and damp.

'Can you hold on for just a second?' he asks.

I nod. I can hold on for ever.

He reaches back, retrieves the towel from under the tree and lays it out in front of me.

'There,' he says with a flourish reminiscent of Sir Walter Raleigh.

'But don't you need to dry yourself?' I waver.

'It's not like I'm going to catch cold,' he shrugs.

I smile but still hesitate.

Again he flourishes: 'My lady?'

My lady? I couldn't stand any longer if I wanted to. I crumple on to the towel in a stupor. It's probably a good thing I'm so spaced out. If I was *compos mentis* I'd be babbling with hysteria from being this close to a man I was deliberating about pursuing moments earlier, not to mention the fact that his sheeny six-foot frame is clad only in a pair of shorts. As it is, I'm too distracted by my innumerable inner voices to speak. The majority are going 'OWW!', but the one that claims to have slept through my relationship with Hugh is jumping up and down clamouring, 'My turn! My turn!'

Tezz kneels beside me, gently smoothing his palm over my skull. 'I think we're looking at a golf ball,' he grimaces, giving his opinion of the dimensions of my impending bump.

To think that only this morning I was imagining his hands in my hair. Just not quite like this. 'Could be worse, right?' he continues. 'Could be a cricket ball – you're from jolly old England, aren't you?'

'Yup,' I nod, still discombobulated, which could explain why I then say, 'You know, I got hit on the nose by a cricket ball when I was six. Do you see how it's wonky on the bridge?'

I offer myself for inspection and he duly runs his finger along the detour the bone took as a result. 'Ah yes, just a tad off.'

'What about you?' I query.

'It's just like this naturally,' he replies, pulling his soft nose to a point.

'No,' I laugh. 'I mean where are you from?'

'Oh right!' He throws his head back in a big Pezz-head laugh before answering, 'Boston.'

'Ah!' I say, as if I've spent many an afternoon at tea

176

parties there, as opposed to two days shuffling around the Museum of Fine Art. 'That's practically English, isn't it?'

'Not South End, where I'm from,' he clarifies with a rueful headshake. 'There have been a lot of renovations recently, but back in the day it was rather more *ghetto*,' he says, pronouncing the word like he's Prince Charles while running his hands over his own scalp, 'You know, maybe I need a few knocks to get my skull up to size. I'm such a Peanut Head.'

'What are you talking about?' I hoot. 'You're perfect!'

'No, really,' he insists. 'Whenever I get my picture taken with someone, I'm like this tiny shrunken head next to their big baseball bonce.'

'Well you should just stand more in the foreground then!' I roll my eyes. 'The other thing –' I point back to the tree – 'wouldn't work. You'd just have all these bulbous swellings and no hair to hide them with. You'd look like an alien.'

'Thanks very much.'

'You know what I mean!' I'm laughing now. Even though it hurts me to do so. He's warmer and more playful than I expected. The seductor who delivered the loin-tingling rap about the Honeymoon Hotel is allowing the goofball from the tap sequence to take centre-stage.

'Anyway, you don't look a Peanut Head in the feather headdress . . .' I say quietly, submitting a compliment.

'Yeah, that gives me about an extra foot in every direction!' he acknowledges.

'It's amazing,' I sigh, experiencing an instantaneous stab of lust as I recall the virile pump'n'grunt combo that goes with that particular costume.

'An heirloom from our Vegas period!' Tezz confides.

'You guys performed in Vegas?' I sit upright too quickly and again he reaches out to make sure I don't keel over. I love the feeling of his hand on me. It makes me feel like the Chosen One.

'Yup – four hours a night, six nights a week for ten years,' he confirms.

'Gosh, that's a lot of show time,' I marvel. 'Which casino did you perform at?'

'The New York, New York.'

'And now you're on Bora Bora!' I chuckle, then lower my voice. 'Do you have a secret stutter?'

'Like K-K-K-Ken?' he enquires.

I blink in disbelief. I'd swear this beautiful man just channelled poodle-permed Michael Palin from *A Fish Called Wanda*.

'The Ca— The Ca—' he strains, re-enacting the agonising scene where lawyer Archie Leach is trying to elicit the name of a hotel, the Cathcart Towers, from poor speech-impeded Ken.

'Slowly, very slowly . . . No hurry!' he does an impeccable frazzled-but-courteous John Cleese. 'Plenty of time!' and I fall about laughing.

The man is a hilarious mimic and finishes me off

with a contemptuous Kevin Kline spitting, 'You English think you're sooooo superior!'

'Ohhh I love that movie,' I sigh, wiping a mirth-induced tear from my eye before lowering myself into a more relaxed reclining position.

'Me too,' he says, mirroring my pose. 'But I think you probably guessed that already.'

Now we're lying facing each other, just a few inches apart, knees touching, both acting like we haven't noticed.

'So what brought you here to B-B-Bora B-B-Bora?' I tease, loving the easy intimacy between us.

'Well, my partner Tony – you know, from the show?'

As I nod a yes, my insides desiccate – he said *partner*. So they *are* a couple. How nice for them both. No wonder they're so synchronised.

'He always wanted to have his own place. And when this venue presented itself—'

I can't help but snuffle incredulity. 'You make it sound like it came knocking on your door with a cane and a calling card!'

'Actually it was a little bit more complicated than that,' he admits.

'I'll bet it was. But I like that you're so nonchalant about it.'

'Well,' he shrugs, 'I live to be nonchalant.'

'Oh me too,' I agree, not really knowing what I'm saying.

For a second we just grin at each other. Maybe it's a

good thing he's both gay and taken. A girl could get a lot of crazy ideas about a man like this.

'How long have you been dancing?' I ask, trying to get back on track, delighted that I'm getting to watch his exquisite mouth move in response to my questions, beguiled by the soft husk in his voice.

'I was born dancing!' he laughs. 'As a kid me and my sister were always making up routines. Then I had my first tap class—'

'Oh my God, you are *so* amazing at that!' I can't help but interrupt.

'The funny thing is, I never knew it was in me until I had that lesson. Then it became the *only* thing for me,' he confides. 'Where I grew up, we lived about ten minutes' walk from the Prudential Centre and they had a café on the ground floor with a wooden patio area. I would sneak in there at night and tap. That became my getaway – tapping and dreaming. That's when I felt most free.'

Our worlds are so different, yet there's something in what he says that finds an echo in me. Add to that the image of his little feet going tickety-tickety-tickety solo in the moonlight and I'm hooked.

'So your parents weren't in showbiz?' I ask, eager to discover more.

'Well, my dad can certainly sing – he has a beautiful voice – and he was in groups, but he didn't earn a living from it.'

'What was his profession?' I get nosy without meaning to.

'Um . . .' Tezz falters, looking a little thrown.

I recognise that look. At least I've felt that look. Before he can speak again, I take a chance.

'Was it illegal?'

'What makes you ask that?' He's taken aback by my directness.

'Personal experience,' I state, still dangling out on a limb.

'Really?' he tilts his head at me.

I'm about to backtrack madly when he announces, 'As a matter of fact my dad spent most of my childhood in prison.'

'Oh mine too!' It's my hand reaching for him now. 'My mum even did a two-year stretch!' I beam.

'I've never seen anyone so happy to have jailbird parents!' he chuckles in disbelief.

'I'm not happy, exactly – I just . . . I never get to tell anyone!' I peep, all excited. And then I feel sad as I hear myself say, 'I rarely get to talk about them at all.' It's my mum I miss the most, but the last thing I want is to sound like I feel sorry for myself so I quickly pull myself together and start a new sentence. 'It just . . .' But I can't find the words.

'It just feels good to be open?' he suggests.

'Yes, it does,' I nod, feeling properly understood.

'So what were yours in for?' he asks, cocking his head. 'If you don't mind me asking.'

'Jewellery theft. Which if you knew—' I cut myself off. I was going to tell him about Hugh's job, but that would mean telling him about Hugh, and the denial part of me still wants to believe that he's not really gay, so instead I bounce the question back to him. 'What about yours?'

'Petty crimes, burglary,' he shrugs. 'He would always say, "*It's not stealing because . . .*" and come out with some involved excuse to justify it, but after a while that's all I heard. "*It's not stealing because . . .*"'

I nod, totally getting it. I don't think my dad ever felt he was actually in the wrong, because everything he did, he did for my mother, to make her happy, to make her glitter. It was her trying to return the favour and acquire a much-coveted gift for his sixty-fifth birthday that led to her incarceration and, shortly afterwards, their fatal demise.

'Repeat offender?' I continue, quizzing Tezz.

'Yup. You know, seven months here, three years there . . .'

'Mine too.'

We look at each other with shiny eyes, like we've just discovered that we both bought *Thriller* as our first album.

'Makes you kind of jumpy to hear the doorbell ring, doesn't it?'

'You're not kidding,' Tezz concurs. 'For a while it seemed like every weekend we'd have cops on the doorstep and I'd be like, "Just one weekend, can we do something different, please?!"'

'It was that regular?' I wince, feeling like I got off lightly.

'It certainly seemed that way.'

'Tell me,' I encourage, lapping up this new-found bonding experience.

As he readjusts his position to get into story-teller mode our knees lose contact, but as he settles again he's right back there where he belongs.

'Well, everything revolved around this four-storey brownstone building that's been in our family for generations,' he begins. 'When things didn't work out at home or my dad got into *things*, my mum always knew there was room there for her and her kids. My room was at the top at the back,' he adds, giving me an image of a little prince tucked away in a turret. 'Anyway, the family would work hard all week then come to party at the weekends. My grandmother had the record player in the bedroom for some reason, and all the adults would bring in their chairs and be jamming and drinking beer and smoking and laughing and playing cards. Meanwhile us kids used to play this game called Don't Touch The Floor – starting at the top of the house, we had to find a way to get to the bottom without—'

'Touching the floor?' I jump in.

'You got it! We'd climb down the banisters, throw down a coat as a stepping stone to get to the next level – whatever it took.'

'For the record, and I don't mean to interrupt again, but if you have a sleeping bag and put the shiny side down, you can go down whole flights of stairs in seconds, like you're tobogganing.'

'Good to know!' he twinkles.

'Carry on.'

'Well, they'd always be yelling at us to stop jumping around, but we were having fun dodging this constant influx of people – Aunt Rochelle and Uncle Jay and all these relatives . . .'

I can't help but smile at the image of the ever-burgeoning household.

'The atmosphere always started out festive and great, everyone partying, alcohol being consumed, alcohol being consumed . . . . Suddenly it's 2 a.m. and out of nowhere it goes from "You're my baby!" to "Ya need to get your shit together!" then "Don't tell me what I need" – and next thing you know there's arguing and commotion and fisticuffs.'

'And the police?'

He nods. 'It felt like every single weekend. Always fighting. Always drama. Now, I know my family is dysfunctional, but there's a lot of love there. But back then, I used to pray over and over, "Get me away from here!"'

'And look at how far you've come,' I say, brimming with admiration for the kid who tap-danced his way to paradise.

'You too,' he holds my gaze.

I go to insist that he's come much further when he hushes me with the words, 'We're in the same place.'

I blink back at him. I've heard about having an instant connection with someone, but I always thought I was too shut off to have it happen to me. Besides, didn't you have to be American? I guess it's sufficient that one of us is. Now I'm experiencing this for the first time, I'm finding that the best part is not feeling alone any more. It's like I was brought up by lions, and now finally get to be with my own kind.

We talk about prison visits and the impact of the 'absent father' and the lack of information you're given as a child. And then I surprise myself by confessing that, as much as I disapproved of what he did, I secretly wished my father would steal something for me – it seemed to be his way of proving his love. But he never did. He only had eyes (and thieving hands) for my mother.

'Sometimes I felt like she had to hide her love for me from him,' I say, realising that I've never actually said this out loud before. 'When he was in the room he needed every iota of her attention.'

'I bet that was lonely sometimes,' Tezz suggests.

'It was,' I say simply. 'When he went away . . . I used to feel so guilty because I knew she missed him so much but I liked it better. There was no competition and she would spend all her free time with me.'

'And now?'

'Now they're up there,' I point heavenward. 'He went first, and without him she had nothing to live for.'

Tezz looks horrified. 'She had you.'

I don't know how to reply without triggering a torrent of emotion, so I say nothing, hoping that we can somehow resume our lighter banter.

'I'm sorry.' Tezz caresses me with a compassionate gaze, then narrows his eyes as if it's just dawning on him that we got into all this on account of him finding me kipping under a tree. 'You know, you're out awfully late for Bora Bora,' he notes. 'Do you have a hall pass?'

'I've got it here somewhere, sir!' I say, pretending to search my pockets before explaining, 'I'm actually staying in one of the bungalows . . .' I point over yonder, but before he can ask me who I'm sharing with I ask, 'What about you – is this how you wind down after a show?' I motion to the ocean.

He nods, eyes lingering on the glimmering waters. 'Every night. It's even more magical when no one else is around, don't you think?'

'Absolutely,' I confirm, feeling for the first time the full woo-potential of the setting.

'So I take it you're not on your honeymoon?' He turns back to me.

'Nooo,' I laugh nervously, my heart pounding that he's even asking a romance-related question. 'I think this would be a terrible place for a honeymoon – it's far too hot to have sex.'

'You think?'

The sultry look on his face gets me all flustered. I feel like such a frump and a wimp as I blabber: 'Well, I just can't imagine having the energy—'

'You know, Gauguin was dying from syphilis the whole time he lived here and he still managed it!'

'You know Gauguin?'

'Well, not personally. But I know his grandson,' he shrugs.

'You know Gauguin's grandson?'

'Marcel.'

'Marcel?'

'I'm beginning to think this bump might be taking its toll – you're repeating everything I say.'

'Sorry,' I laugh. 'It's just . . . My friend Abigail would freak. You actually *know* Gauguin's grandson?'

'Well, he's really more Tony's friend. I just smile at him.'

'You just smile at him?' I raise a quizzical brow.

'I don't speak French,' he explains. 'Do you?'

'No.' I wonder if Sandrine could get me fluent in a day.

'We're seeing him tomorrow, as a matter of fact. You can come with us if you like – he's got an art project he's looking to promote. The more visitors the merrier.'

This is too freaky. 'You know that's what I do?'

'How do you mean?' Tezz frowns.

'I'm an art historian.'

'Well then, I think that makes it compulsory,' he grins.

'You'd actually take me to meet Gauguin's grandson?' I remain incredulous.

'As long as you promise not to steal anything.'

I hoot with mirth, then counter, 'Well, if I did I'd know just who to get to act as the fence!'

'Oh, that's so wrong!'

'No, *that's* wrong,' I say, pointing at a member of the resort housekeeping staff tramping by with a rattling bucket of cleaning products.

'People going to work and we haven't even gone to bed yet!'

I look up at the sky, now a soft blue streaked with peach. The sun has risen and I didn't even notice.

Tezz gets to his feet, then reaches back to pull me up. My hands remain clasped in his while he informs me of the arrangements for tomorrow, or should that be later today? I try not to be distracted by the fact that I'm level with his nipple ring as I repeat back, 'Noon at the dock. I'll be there.'

'Okay,' he confirms.

Then we hesitate. Neither of us seems to want to read our next cue card – the one saying, 'Goodnight.'

'Well, you take care of that cricket ball,' he says finally, giving my bump the lightest touch.

'You take care of your Peanut Head,' I smile, giving his Fuzzy-Felt scalp an affectionate rub.

'I don't know why I told you that,' he mutters as he turns and strides on his way.

I stand on the sand, grinning my head off for a good thirty seconds before I prance back to the bungalow, strangely alert despite my lack of sleep.

'Told you! Told you!' yippees my heart, getting in a swift gloat before I put the key in the door. 'Are you loving him or what?'

Before I can form a reply the handle gives way and I get a cold jolt realising just how many notches I need to take my happiness down so as not to arouse suspicion in Hugh. He probably wouldn't even recognise me in this uncharacteristically radiant state.

Oh God, this is all wrong, I fret, hand still gripping the door handle. I go back to The Paradise Room to confirm that my fixation with Tezz is entirely fanciful and I end up finding him twice as attractive second time around and then proceed to have *the* most intimate and entertaining conversation I've had in ages. Darnit! Seconds ago I was feeling so joyful, but already my mood is tainted with confusion and guilt.

What does this all mean? Is it acceptable to be planning outings with one man, even though he may be gay, when I'm sharing a bed with another? Am I playing with fire? Or worse still, live human hearts?

'Enough with the drama!' I scold myself as I step into the bungalow. 'You haven't done anything wrong.'

As the door closes behind me, I swear I hear the latch click the word *'Yet'*.

13

'So off I go for a hard day's work at the Black Pearl Gem Company,' Hugh informs me as I putter around the room rounding up our empty water bottles in a bid to look busy and normal. 'It's such a palaver having to scrutinise every single pearl when you're dealing with these kinds of numbers,' he sighs as he slots his eyeglass in his briefcase. 'Piers wants at least three hundred beauties.'

'Is Sandrine being any help?'

'Actually she's being great – she dismisses whole cases at a time and just steers me towards the grade As.'

'Well, that's something.'

'Yes, it is,' he says, trying to look on the bright side. 'So what are your plans for today?'

'Oh, you know: a little swim, a little coconut juice, a little rendezvous with Gauguin's grandson!' I want to answer. Instead I say, 'Meeting up with Felicity.'

190

It's simpler. Then I realise I really do have plans with her.

'I am, I'm meeting with Felicity!' I blurt, spinning round to face him.

'I didn't say you weren't,' Hugh frowns.

'At noon!' I baulk at the double-booking.

'Is that a problem?' Hugh looks concerned.

'No, no.' I shake my head. Yes, yes! I want to howl. I try to think how I can keep my date with her *and* Tezz then remember Tezz saying Marcel's art project was a more-the-merrier event and decide she'll just have to come too. Not that anything shy of Da Vinci's David could hold Felicity's attention for more than two seconds. And even then she'd want to know why the model didn't use a fluffer. At least Tony will be there to keep her occupied. Oh God, how did my life get this complicated? And to think I scoffed at those bronzing babes by the pool! Oh for the simple pleasure of doing long division with your SPF numbers.

Hugh sighs heavily as he steps towards me. 'I hate that I have to keep abandoning you like this—' he begins.

'It's fine,' I cut in. 'You're working. I understand.' I quickly pull him into a hug so that I can bury my shifty face in his shoulder. In all our years together I've never had to hide anything from him beyond the odd bar of cooking chocolate. Not that I've exactly been an open book. I've had plenty of feelings (and tears) he's not been privy to, just no secret assignations with sexy men with shaved heads and thumb rings. Although I feel sick at myself for deceiving Hugh, I also feel strangely protective about this potential new friendship with Tezz. I might not be able to put a label on exactly what's going on between us but I'm fairly certain that when something feels this special, it's not supposed to be cut short. Besides, seeing as he's gay, there's no harm in it, is there?

'I thought tonight we could go to dinner at Bloody Mary's,' Hugh tells the top of my head. 'It's where all the celebs go – Cameron Diaz, Keanu Reeves, Steve Martin . . .'

'Great!' I muffle, picturing the Hollywood A-listers seated on a raised platform looking down on the regular punters, rather like the top table at a wedding. Oh no! I tense up. I hope he's not planning another proposal. Without the element of surprise he stands even less chance of me accepting, and I don't think I could handle letting him down again.

'Felicity can come too, if you like.'

'Lovely!' I sigh with relief, cheek to his collarbone. 'I'll invite her when I see her. At noon.'

'Okay. Well, better be off!' he chirrups before haplessly peppering the top of my head with kisses.

'Youch!' I scream, leaping from his arms.

'Look, if you don't want me to kiss you—' He gets immediately defensive.

'No, no, I forgot to tell you – I've bumped my head. Feel this . . .' I reach for his hand then guide his limp fingertips over my cricket ball. Every time I accidentally knocked it in the night (or rather, during the brief

192

period when I lay down upon my return), the pain would actually make me smile because it made me think of Tezz. But not this time. Hugh did a real Woody Woodpecker number on me.

'God, it's grotesque!' he gasps, reeling back as if it's some ugly growth.

'I know,' I say a little proudly.

'Are you okay? How did it happen?'

'I bumped it on the jutting-out bit by the steps,' I lie, pointing out to the balcony.

'When?'

'Last night. I couldn't sleep. I stepped out for some air, thought I'd have a little paddle and THWACK!'

'Easily done,' he cringes. 'I've got a little scratch off that myself.'

He does indeed have a tiny graze on his temple. Who'd have thought Hugh would be the one to authenticate my story?

'But that –' He touches my bump again just to freshen up his revulsion. 'Amber, that's gross.'

'I'm only going to worry if it sprouts a mouth and starts talking back to me!' I tease. Heaven knows I've got enough lively debate going on in my brain as it is. Unsurprisingly, the loudest voice belongs to my mouthy heart. For the past few minutes all I've heard is its repetitive clamour of 'Is it noon yet? Is it noon yet?'

'You should go,' I say, planting a reassuring kiss directly on his lips.

He gives me a sympathetic smile and tells me he'll

be back by 6 p.m. 'Oh, and try to have fun today!' he adds.

'Okay, will do. See you then,' I wave him off, feeling like every housewife who's about to have an affair with the milkman.

11.50 a.m.: I'm on the jetty and wouldn't you know it? Tony is the first to arrive.

He looks cool in every sense of the word in a short-sleeved white cotton shirt, long khaki shorts and black flip-flops. I look down at my tie-dye sundress and fussily laced espadrilles wishing, not for the first time, that I was a boy. Or at least a girl with better dress sense.

'Hi,' I smile, feeling a little awkward.

'Hi.' He takes a seat a polite distance from me.

I wait to see if he's going to speak. *Tum-te-tum* . . . Apparently not. Uh-oh, here comes the babble: 'Um, I don't know if Tezz told you, and he probably hasn't had a chance yet, but he said it would be all right if I came with you to meet Marcel?'

'Yeah, he told me.' Tony remains impassive.

'Is that okay?' I ask, the definition of tentative.

'Sure. Why not?'

I let his words sit for a second before broaching the next hurdle. 'The thing is, well, I'd forgotten that I was also meeting my friend Felicity, so I was wondering . . .'

'If she could come too?' He puts me out of my misery. At least I think he does.

'Is that okay?' I ask again, wanting to be sure.

'Of course. As long as she doesn't mind swimming alongside the boat.'

'Oh! If there's not enough room—' I stumble, flushed with embarrassment.

'There's enough room,' he smirks, reminding me of the mischievous element of his stage persona.

'So you were joking?' I confirm, still unsure of where I stand.

'Yes. Hilarious, aren't I?'

This man makes me nervous! It's probably best I stop talking. Probably best, but *so* not going to happen.

'Tezz says that you speak French,' I offer.

'Well then, it must be true.'

'Tell me, just how many consecutive mornings have you got out of bed on the wrong side?' I want to ask, wondering what he's so miffed about. Or maybe this is his natural state. I think back to what I've seen of the guys interacting with the audience during the breaks – Tezz all effusive and animated, delighted by the attention, Tony moving among the tables in slow-motion, always maintaining a regal distance. People touch Tezz and he touches them back. But not Tony. It's as though he's shielded by an invisible force field. I'm guessing this a man who doesn't like people in his face or in his business. I hope he doesn't think I'm trying to cross the line here. Oh God, please let Felicity be on this approaching boat or I have a feeling I'm going to make things much, much worse.

Mercifully she is. Now it's her turn to get on his nerves.

'Oh wow – it's you!' She points at Tony as if he's a landmark. 'Amber, look!' she says, as if I might have missed Tony despite the fact that he's sitting just a few feet away from me on an otherwise empty jetty. 'You guys are so phenomenally sexy!' She scurries up to him and extends a hand. 'I'm Felicity!'

He responds with a minimal 'Tony'. The man who put the curt in courteous.

'I can't believe we've got you here all to ourselves!' she beams, squeezing on to the bench beside him. 'How about you give us a private serenade!'

Oh no. I close my eyes in full cringe mode.

'Go on,' she implores, unfazed by his self-contained man-in-a-glass-box demeanour. 'Give us a tune!'

'Felicity!' I hiss, mortified.

'What?' she asks, wide-eyed.

'Um, I just wanted to let you know that Tony here has kindly agreed to take us along to meet Gauguin's grandson. He's working on this new art project . . .'

Her face reads, 'And this would be interesting to me because . . . ?', but she says, 'Great!' Then adds, 'Do you mean now?'

'Yes.'

'Oh,' her face falls. 'So we're not . . .' she jiggles her eyebrows meaningfully (this being her subtle way of referring to our Airport Guy mission, I presume).

'Oh no. We'll be doing that too. Just later.' I look

apologetically at Tony. 'We've lost a friend and we need to find him.'

'Are you sure he wants to be found?' he asks.

Woah – barbed!

'Of course!' Felicity chimes, adding 'He just doesn't know it yet' under her breath.

I for one am saying nothing more until Tezz gets here. A person could get hurt around here.

'So about that song!' Felicity turns to face Tony.

My head falls into my hands. Never was there a woman more in need of a skin peel.

'Did you have a particular favourite from the show?' he asks, obviously fairly confident that she won't remember a note.

'What about one of your own compositions?' she betters him. 'One from your CD!'

He gives her a wry once-over, then says, 'Well, there is one track that springs to mind – "She's Banging".'

'Banging?' Felicity laughs. 'How romantic!'

'It's about the prostitutes that frequented the bars we used to work at in Vegas.'

Was that another dig at us? It certainly feels that way to me.

'Oh God, I love prostitutes!' Felicity raves, oblivious. 'And Vegas prostitutes are practically legendary! What calibre are we talking here?'

Tony shrugs. 'Your basic big shoes, little handbags, cellphones at the ready, sitting alone, drinking Hypnotic.'

'Hypnotic?'

'It's this fluorescent blue liqueur. Practically the colour of the water here,' he says, nodding beyond the decking. 'Gets a girl noticed.'

'Good tip!' Felicity chuckles. 'And did these girls ever proposition you?'

'As a matter of fact they did,' he reveals, lowering his voice. 'And they offered very generous terms.'

'Freebies?' Felicity gasps delighted.

He nods. 'But that's not my style.'

'No.' Felicity nods, giving him a knowing look. 'But it must have been fun to talk to them. Were they beautiful?'

'Stunning, some of them.'

'Makes you wonder why they do it, doesn't it?'

He pauses for a minute, probably wondering how he got himself into this conversation, then confides, 'As a matter of fact, I wondered so much I once wrote a paper on Sex Addiction.'

'You didn't!' Felicity gawps.

'I did.'

'No way! Me too!' she reels.

It really is bizarre what people find to have in common these days. I'd actually forgotten that Felicity had had a brief spell as a psychology major.

'I used to go trawling K Road in Auckland looking for case studies,' she remembers. 'It wasn't pretty – my girls were pretty low-rent, barely getting by.'

'Mine were mostly high-end. Gucci handbags, designer clothing.'

I can't believe this – they sound like a couple of

pimps comparing staff! Suddenly I feel like I've led a very sheltered life. Which is bizarre, considering the jailbird parents conversation I was having with Tezz last night.

I tune back into the conversation, somewhat startled to hear Felicity tell of a girl with peg-like nipples who was hired on a weekly basis as a centrepiece for a guy's poker night.

'So there she is, lying flat out on the table, naked body heaped with all manner of snacks and dips, some idiot playing hoopla with the onion rings—'

'Damn, I always miss the good stuff!' exclaims a familiar voice.

I turn around and see Tezz approaching, looking lithe and breezy in crumpled linen trousers and a sheer tan shirt.

'Hey!' he grins as our eyes meet.

'Hi!' I squeak, feeling my face light up as if my skull was encasing a giant 100-watt light bulb.

'How's the bump?' He touches a safe spot above my ear.

'Bigger and better than ever!' I boast.

'Bump?' Felicity frowns, no doubt wondering how we got on head-touching terms.

'Oh, this is my friend Felicity.' I turn to introduce her. 'She's coming too, if that's okay?'

Before he can reply, a voice calls out in French and we turn and see a small canopied boat approaching, captained by a stocky, nut-brown man with a wavy raven bob. Though his colouring is native Tahitian, the hook of his nose gives him away. I get chills on behalf of Abigail. I suspect I'm about to set sail with some very illustrious French genes . . .

14

'Marcel!' Tony greets Gauguin's grandson with surprising gusto and they begin chatting eagerly in French, laughing and manfully slapping each other as they go. Apparently Mr Fly-under-the-radar is quite a different person around people he actually likes. Maybe it's just women he prefers to hold at a safe distance.

'Tu te rappelles Tezz?' Tony makes a gracious sweep in the direction of his partner.

'Oui, oui, comment vas-tu, mon ami?'

'Bien, merci!' Tezz responds, nodding respectfully. *'Très bien!'*

'I thought you couldn't speak French,' I hiss at him.

'That's as good as it gets,' he says in a confidential whisper.

'Et les deux filles – Amber et Felicity,' explains Tony.

'Enchanté!' Marcel dips his head then beckons us on board, *'S'il vous plaît . . .'*

Marcel and Tony huddle around the helm continuing to chat earnestly, while the non-French-speaking among us take a seat on the fibreglass seat moulding at the back. As Tezz and Felicity get acquainted, I find myself studying Marcel. I was expecting him to be surly and eccentrically attired, but his smile is warm and his stout frame tucked into a simple white T-shirt and brown-belted jeans. Jeans! I feel like a bemused time traveller – I can't quite believe I'm looking at the real live offspring of one of the Great Masters.

'So that's quite some accent you've got going on,' I hear Tezz comment on Felicity's vocal cocktail.

'Oh, I know, it's a mess!' she grimaces. 'Bit Brit, bit Kiwi and as of last night a bit Japanese.'

'What?' I laugh out loud.

'Spent the night talking to this lovely couple from Tokyo,' she explains. 'I've always wanted to go there . . .'

'But you're originally from the UK?' Tezz checks.

'Oxford,' she nods. 'That's where Amber and I went to school, a long, long time ago . . . In fact, this is the first time we've hooked up in eighteen years.'

'Wow! That's so cool,' he grins, casting a fond glance at me. 'So what prompted the reunion?'

Well, that wipes the reciprocal smile off my face. Felicity and I dart an unsettled look at each other.

'Well . . .' I begin, deciding I should be the one to lie about Hugh.

'We heard there was this really hot band playing at

202

The Paradise Room!' she jumps in. 'Turns out the rumours were true!'

Good save! And just to make sure Tezz is sufficiently diverted, Felicity keeps it coming.

'You know, we were so impressed with your moves,' she raves, sliding a little closer. 'Is it true you guys met in *Starlight Express*?'

'That's right,' he confirms. 'Tony was actually already in Vegas working on a big production show at the Stardust, but that was my first major gig.'

'How exciting!' she coos.

'Actually, I was terrified,' he confesses as we continue to bump along the waterway. 'We had this hard-core instructor with a big cane and he'd be yelling, "Skate, skate, left, right!" and banging on the ground with this stick—'

'Sounds like *Fame*!' Felicity interrupts.

'It was more like being in the damn army!' Tezz laughs. 'Except the sergeant had this really nasal voice . . .' He does a squeaky-camp impression that sets us giggling, then continues, 'Dude would have us skating in circles, and if someone fell we just had to jump over them and keep going and he'd be yelling "*Get up!*" at them, banging his stick by their side. I mean, I get it now – during the live show someone would inevitably fall and you'd have to keep going, so there was a method to it, but my God it was intimidating. I went through many phases where I questioned whether it was ever going to click with me, whether I could cut it . . .'

I shake my head, having trouble imagining Tezz being less than effortlessly adept at anything he turned his toes to while at the same time finding his frankness profoundly endearing. Why does it feel so good to hear that someone else finds life tricky at times too? I've missed being around that. Hugh comes from a long line of men who'd rather die than cop to a weakness.

'All that pressure and I was only chorus,' Tezz continues. 'Tony was one of the leads – you know, Electra, the AC-DC train?'

'AC-DC . . .' Felicity repeats, shooting me a 'Say no more' look.

She's really convinced they're gay. Suddenly I'm not so sure. I feel so different around them compared with the gay guys I've worked with in the past. But then again, I didn't fancy them in the same way. Could it be that what I'm longing to interpret as a mutual attraction is merely my own pheromones bouncing back at me? Well, I'm guessing I'll have an answer shortly – Felicity seems intent on amassing potentially incriminating information.

'You've got a lovely straight back, Tezz,' she simpers. 'Did you ever study ballet?'

'Briefly, when I was at dance college, but as a kid it was mostly jazz and Afro-Cuban. That guy was the real child prodigy, though.' He nods towards Tony.

'Little Billy Elliot?' Felicity ponders out loud. 'Well, that explains the poise.'

Tezz honks a laugh. 'If only you knew . . .'

'What?' Felicity blinks back at him. 'You guys are a vision of precision – you hit every mark—'

'*On* stage,' he agrees. 'Tony's unchoreographed moves are a little less, shall we say, exact!'

'Really?' Neither Felicity nor I can believe it.

'I'm telling you – we've lost count of how many times Nureyev there has put his size nines through the changing screen or tripped on one of the props.'

'So the girls in your show—'

'Malia and Lexi,' he chips in.

'They're not actually there to give you guys a breather, just a chance to administer First Aid?' I hear Felicity query.

'You got it!' Tezz laughs.

This is fascinating to me. I remember the first time I looked at a Modigliani painting and thought that the painter must have such a serene disposition to paint those elegant almond eyes and elongated necks, only to discover that he had a nickname that translates to mean 'accursed', once threw his girlfriend out of a window and died of drink and drug excess at thirty-five. What goes on behind the scenes, eh? Not that a little clumsiness is on a par with that, but I wonder if Tony has any dark secrets? I mean, you certainly don't look at Tezz and presume he's the offspring of a burglar, and yet . . .

'Is the scar on your knee the result of a backstage incident?' I ask, rejoining the conversation.

I see Felicity thinking, 'What scar? What knee? We've never seen his knee.'

'Oh, you noticed that?' he gives me an intimate look.

I nod back.

I sense Felicity's eyes darting between us, aflame with curiosity.

'I wish I had some great story about how that happened – how we worked some disco knife-throwing routine into the show – but in fact I was taking out the trash aged nine and there was broken glass in the bag and as I—'

'Enough!' Felicity yells, holding up a squeamish hand.

'Let's just say I had to have six stitches,' he concludes neatly.

'You know you're ruining all my illusions!' Felicity flinches. 'I thought you guys were flawless.'

'Just keeping it real,' Tezz winks.

Real? I look up in delight. That word again. I smile to myself – Fantasia was wrong! She made me think that my new-found exhilaration couldn't exist outside of The Paradise Room, that I was deluding myself with a dimly-lit dream, but here I am in broad daylight and I feel just as high. Suddenly it occurs to me that I've been living the wrong way round. Everything about my life with Hugh appears to be a magazine-spread ideal (with the possible exception that the stylist forgot to dress me), but *this* is real life – no covering up the mistakes and the fears and smiling prettily for the camera; instead embracing your flaws and smiling on the inside. Now *I* feel like dancing! And I might just get the chance – Marcel has slowed the engine and is heading for land.

'*Alors! C'est Matira Beach!*' Marcel gestures to the sandy shore, taking us as close to the narrow strip of ivory as he dares.

'Are we going to need machetes to get to the exhibit?' Felicity enquires, contemplating the network of choking foliage that lies ahead before swinging her legs over the edge of the boat and sploshing down into the shallow waters.

'Mind your head,' Tezz warns as I prepare to follow her.

I was so busy gathering up my yards of skirt that I'd forgotten about the metal-framed canopy above me. 'Thank you!' I give him a sincere look as he helps me go overboard, murmuring 'Peanut!' as I pass him.

He goes to give me a playful wallop but I slosh out of his reach into the arms of an indignant Felicity.

'I'm beginning to feel like I've missed a vital episode of *Amber in Tahiti*,' she complains, eyes narrowed at me. 'What's going on with you two?'

'What do you mean?' I blink wide-eyed at her, yet am unable to curb my grin.

'Hmmm,' she growls, studying my face for clues, only releasing me so she can retrieve her sunglasses from the waistband of her cut-off shorts. 'You're up to something . . .' she mutters, casting a glance back at the boys busily securing the boat. 'Don't tell me you've shagged—'

'Don't be silly,' I shush her, steering her towards the shade. 'I mean, I may have lain beside his half-naked form in the starlight, but—'

'What?' she squawks, jumping round to face me. *'What?'*

'Later!' I hiss, postponing our gossiping as the menfolk approach.

'Now, this is just a temporary setting for the exhibit,' Tony explains, bidding us follow him through the raggedy trees to a small clearing where he pauses outside a basic single-storey building. (Apparently one man's garage is another man's art gallery.) 'Marcel is touring the paintings around to show local hoteliers and concierges, but the permanent site will be near his home in Fa'aa.'

'Far-ah-ah?' I repeat, attemping the word. That rings a bell.

'It's the name of the international airport in Tahiti,' Tezz explains, reading my mind. 'Hopefully he'll get a lot of the thru traffic that way.'

'Good plan,' I acknowledge.

'Vous êtes pret?' Marcel unlocks the door and steps back to allow us to file in. For some reason I'm first in line.

Once inside, I'm instantly dizzy: the four walls are crammed floor-to-ceiling with a hundred or more of Gauguin's most vibrant and celebrated Tahitian works. Everywhere I look I'm greeted with naked cinnamon skin, waist-length, raven-black hair and Crazy Color

208

versions of a now familiar landscape – all virtually overlapping each other, making me feel as if I've stumbled
into the warehouse of some kleptomaniac art thief.

It takes me a second to realise that the majority of
the paintings are a little off, a strip of scenery or the
occasional elbow or foot clipped, a familiar face slightly
distorted.

'Copies,' I murmur. 'Did you—?' I turn back to
consult Marcel.

'Paint them? No. He commissioned a local artist.'
Tony anticipates my question.

'Are they—'

'For sale? No, purely for exhibition. What do you
think?' He stares pointedly at me.

'I think they're amazing!' I answer truthfully. 'I've
seen several of the originals in Boston – *Hail Mary*, *Are
You Jealous?*, *Where Do We Come From?*' I point to each
corresponding copy. 'The Museum of Fine Arts had
this incredible exhibit last spring but they were
conventionally spaced along the wall, as they have to
be to allow crowds to flow, but this hotchpotch, this
patchwork of canvases . . .' I turn around trying to take
it all in. 'I don't know if it's the ultimate plan to hang
them this closely aligned, or if it's simply the space
constraint, but I love it!' I grin. 'Seeing the whole
collection almost within one frame, I feel like I'm
getting Gauguin's full vision of Tahiti, instead of just
four-foot-by-five-foot snapshots.'

'So you really are an art historian?' Tony looks
genuinely surprised.

'Tell me, is that something people would actually lie about?' Felicity interjects, looking confused.

Ignoring her, Tony concentrates on translating my words to Marcel. I ask how the project came about. He explains how an Austrian curator was visiting the islands and invited Marcel to be guest of honour at a Gauguin exhibit in his homeland and how he accepted – it was his first opportunity to see one of his grandfather's paintings 'in the flesh'.

'There are none in the family?'

Tony shakes his head. 'I know there is a Chinese guy in Tahiti who owns one, and a Pissaro and a Van Gogh for that matter, but it's his private collection.'

'So what happened in Austria?'

Marcel talks at length, leaving Tony to distil the information.

'Well, obviously when he first saw the exhibition he had a sense of pride that this was his grandfather's work, but little more than that – he had always been more passionate about plants than paintings. But then, on the third day, one of the lesser-known self-portraits captured his attention . . .' Tony directs me to a moody image of Gauguin sporting what looks like a Dennis the Menace jumper, jaw clasped in contemplation, staring out from heavy-hooded lids. 'No matter where Marcel went in the room, he felt his grandfather's eyes locked on to him. It was then that he knew he was meant to find a way to continue this legacy. Since then each of the paintings has come alive to him, and he now considers them to be company!'

'Gosh.'

'He's a spiritual guy,' Tony confides. 'Everything to do with this project is done with great humility and respect.'

'How ironic that he should have to go all the way to Austria, of all places, to get a real sense of his heritage,' I muse.

'Sometimes you can feel things more acutely when you are displaced,' Tony translates, passing on Marcel's wisdom.

For a moment Marcel and I hold eye contact. I feel as if he can sense that I, too, am experiencing some kind of awakening, so far from home.

Despite the fact that every conceivable colour is charging my peripheral vision, all I want to do is gaze upon Tezz. This is something of a turnaround for me. Hugh always used to moan that he became invisible when I was in the presence of great art, but Tezz indisputably has the edge in this room. Though whether copies count as great art is debatable.

'Don't you think it's a bit of a con?' Felicity whispers, taking me to one side as we wander unescorted for a moment. 'I mean, he's basically just bought a load of wonky forgeries!'

'Actually, I think it's a great idea,' I confess. 'Abigail tells me that the most common frustration for people going to Tahiti's Gauguin Museum is that the only original pieces on display are etchings and woodcuts – and the big disappointment is that those works are monochrome, whereas for most people Gauguin is all about his intuitive use of colour. This is what people want to see. They'd never get the funding or the resources to do this for real, so I reckon it's a pretty good second-best.'

'Okay, I'm bored now,' Felicity clips. 'Can we go?'

I'm about to rebuke her with a 'You heathen!' pinch when Marcel nestles between us.

'You see we have no signatures?' He's pointing ahead as Tony again speaks for him. 'We cannot put Gauguin, nor do we want to use the name of the artist, so we have decided that we will use the Marquesan name for Gauguin – Koke!'

'That's cool!' I acknowledge. 'So if someone sees "Koke" on a painting, they'll know it's a copy from *your* collection – kind of like a brand?'

'Exactly,' Tony confirms as Marcel nods back at me.

'I'm going to wait outside,' Felicity announces, darting off, unable to take any more. She's always been more of a 'doing' person than a 'looking' person.

'Do you have a favourite painting, Marcel?' I turn to face him, eager to prove that he has my attention, at least.

Tony goes to translate my words, but Marcel halts him, understanding me and leading me to the opposing wall.

'*Te Tamari No Atua*,' he reads.

'The Birth of Christ,' Tony translates, following behind.

The scene has a nativity feel – there are cattle lowing in the farm-building background, but the foreground offers a carved wooden bed with a Tahitian woman, half draped in an indigo *pareu*, lying exhausted upon a pale lemon bedspread. Another figure sits beside her, tending to a newborn baby.

'The woman on the bed is my grandmother Pahura,' Marcel informs me via Tony. 'She gave birth to my father Emile.'

My eyes widen and then well up. 'That's amazing,' I breathe, taking a moment to enjoy the tangible sense of history in the air.

Suddenly I want to apologise out loud to Gauguin Senior for being so dismissive of his Tahitian works in the past. Now I've had the chance to really put them in context, I can see how incredibly powerful they are.

Feeling Tony's eyes upon me, I turn to find his expression has softened. Apparently his hooker concerns have been put to rest. He certainly seems fully relaxed as he goes on to explain how Marcel custom-makes each picture frame, but now it is I who am tense. I know that we're close to wrapping up, and that as soon as we're done here Felicity's going to want to shoot off, but I'm not ready to leave – I have a craving for some time alone with Tezz. I want to recreate the cosy confidentiality of last night and find a way to lock down this new optimism for life so that it becomes a part of me.

Excusing myself for a second, I stick my head outside the door to check on Felicity. She seems fine, happily chatting to another girl on the beach, so I return inside and take the opportunity to approach Tezz.

'Tell me about this painting,' he requests, head tilted in curiosity.

'As if it were the original?' I smile, preparing to indulge him.

He nods, eager to play student-teacher.

'Okay, then!' I clear my throat, dust off a little in-house lingo and begin. 'Well, this is one of many of Gauguin's works which takes a traditional religious image and gives it a Tahitian spin. In this case we're looking at Eve's temptation in the Garden of Eden.' As I say the words I find myself blushing slightly, as if the painting is mirroring my own flirtation with sin.

'Go on,' Tezz encourages, looking at me in a not entirely dissimilar way to how I look at him when he's on stage.

'Um . . .' I try desperately to concentrate. 'As apple trees are not native to Tahiti, he has her picking a feather-like flower, and instead of a serpent whispering temptations, there is a winged red lizard hovering by her ear.'

'And the girl?'

'That's Tehamana – his fourteen-year-old mistress-slash-muse.'

'Fourteen?' he gasps. 'And he was what?'

'In his fifties. I'm not condoning the relationship, but it's worth knowing that fourteen was the marrying age for women in Tahiti at the time, and it was actually her mother who introduced the two of them – she met Gauguin, presumed that because he was European he must be wealthy, and said, "Come meet my daughter!"'

'Gosh!'

'I know, it seems scandalous now. Actually, it did then to his contemporaries back in Paris, but according to my colleague Abigail, he really did love her – he found her so beautiful and mysterious, and in many ways she was his initiator into the culture and the language. He said every day was an adventure with her.' I step closer to inspect the detailing in her face. 'She is beautiful, isn't she?'

'Yes, she is,' Tezz concurs in a whisper.

'Gauguin adored her golden skin tones. He used to speak with such poetry of "the sun rising in her skin", and though he painted on rough burlap, her face was layered with so much detail that if you reached out and touched it, you would find it had a smooth, almost luminous quality.'

Suddenly I become aware that I am the only voice in the room. I turn to find Tony and Marcel staring patiently from beside the door. Time to go.

'Well, Marcel, I'm so honoured to have seen this collection,' I say, adopting my most ambassadorial tone. 'I'm looking forward to spreading the word back

215

in England. I have one friend in particular who I know will be on the next plane out to visit you! I wish you every success.'

I practically go to give a little Germanic click of my heels, but settle instead for a handshake and the acceptance of a sweet kiss on the cheek.

'Are you done?' Felicity looks strangely excited as I emerge.

'What is it?'

'I think I'm getting warmer!' she grins.

'I couldn't be any hotter if I tried,' I complain. 'I've literally got rivers of sweat teaming—'

'No, I've got a lead!' She grabs my arm.

'A lead?' I frown back at her. It's too hot for ambiguity.

'Just down the beach there's this jet ski camp – this girl was moaning 'cos her husband's disappeared off to it every afternoon. Apparently it's Testosterone Central there, so if Airport Guy's not on today's ride, chances are he was there yesterday or the day before . . .'

'So you want to go along and ask a few questions.'

'Questions are for Miss Marple,' she snorts. 'We're about to circumnavigate the island!'

'On a jet ski?' I verify, more than a little daunted.

She nods joyously.

'Ow-ow-OWWW!' Out of nowhere a skinny tattooed scamp with straggly long black hair starts beating his chest and howling wildly.

'That's Coco. He's our guide.'

Okay, now I'm scared. Coco doesn't look like the type who'll be tootling along at 5 m.p.h. to accommodate the beginners of the group. I look back at Tezz, now deep in conversation with Tony. How can I leave him? But equally how can I stay? Felicity's already halfway down the beach trying to keep up with Coco's accelerated gait. I feel torn. Maybe if I linger at this neutral mid-point the decision will be made for me? Suddenly Felicity turns back, gesturing for me to follow; but I can't move. Indignant, she stomps two paces back towards me, slams her hands on her hips and hollers like a fishwife: '*Amber, are you coming or what?*'

15

Much as I would have loved to take the 'or what' option and stayed with Tezz, I couldn't *not* follow Felicity. I made her a promise that we'd spend the day looking for Airport Guy and she's already given up precious man-hunting time to indulge my fancies, so now it's time to return the favour. Even if I am, as ever, entirely inappropriately attired.

'Just hitch up your skirt a bit and twist it into a knot at the side,' Felicity advises as she gets kitted out in her lifejacket and told to put her mini-rucksack in the jet-ski equivalent of the glove compartment.

'Stay at least ten metres apart from each other – these machines have no brakes,' Coco instructs as he wades over to me, fully aware that his other charges are getting restless at the last-minute hold-up. 'If I put my arm up straight, that means follow me. Out to the side like this, slow down. Arms crossed, cut the engine.' He continues his briefing while placing what looks like a red telephone-cord coil around my wrist. He tells me it's connected to the ignition key – should I get catapulted into the sea, the engine will stall and I won't get abandoned like a jockey dumped by a horse intent on finishing the race regardless.

'Okay, let's go!' Coco whoops, hurdling the shallow water, pouncing on his jet ski and yanking it round into the leader position.

'That's it?' I gasp. 'That's the extent of the instruction?'

One by one the other jet skis take off after him. All at about 150 m.p.h. Well, officially it's closer to 60 m.p.h., but every single one of them is going full-tilt. Felicity squeals and charges forward – she hasn't had the chance to properly check out the group yet, and she has no intention of letting them out of her sight. (He could be one of them!) I start slowly, but my fear of getting left behind is far greater than my fear of doing some kind of Evel Knievel wave-wheelie, so I too wrench the handlebars round and find myself skimming the surface of the water at an alarming rate. As I power straight ahead into the blue, I feel a sudden surge of elation. Aside from the pressure to keep up, this is fab!

In the distance I see the group weaving to the left and follow suit, only to get wopped, jolted and jarred by the now oncoming waves. That'll teach me to get so cocky! My bottom actually leaves the seat three bumps in succession, leaving me feeling like some wisp of a thing that needs to be weighted down to stay on board.

I desperately want to stop and catch my breath, but everyone else is blasting ever onward, so I grip tighter and scream to release the tension as I continue getting splattered and battered by the choppy water. And then a funny thing happens. My screaming turns into singing, and I realise that every song I belt out has the word 'free' in the title.

I'm just doing George Michael's 'Freedom' in Becci's honour when I see Coco's arm waving to the side. We're in the middle of the sea, but he wants us to slow to a stop. We draw up into a wobbly cluster, and I can see now that we're about fifty-fifty men and women. I'm watching Felicity's face for a reaction as she studies the men around her, but it's Coco who makes her eyes start from her head – he's just stepped off his jet ski and is standing thigh-deep in water. How is this possible? I could have sworn we were miles out to sea! He bids us join him, grinning 'Sand bank!' as he begins handing out sections of outsize grapefruit as a half-time refresher.

'Let me help you,' Felicity offers, using the prop as an excuse to approach the rest of the group – six Americans, all in couples, and a group of eight party people from Brazil. No Brits. No Airport Guy.

'I thought there were more of us . . .' Felicity sighs.

'Two groups,' Coco explains. 'We pass the others in five minutes. You married?' he says, sucking mischievously on his grapefruit pith.

She looks at him. He's such a scamp, clearly the type to try it on with any single women he encounters, but his shiny-shiny eyes are so beguiling it doesn't matter. She shoots me an 'always good to have a back-up' glance, then leans towards him and husks, 'If I had a flower, I'd be wearing it behind my right ear.'

You'd think Tahiti had just won the World Cup from his response.

'Let's go! Let's go!' he chants, as if to say, 'The sooner we get this over, the sooner the real ride can begin!'

Now confident enough to let my mind wander as I slice through the surf, I allow myself to think about Tezz and imagine frolicking with him in the water, gently splashing each other and then submerging and entwining for the best kind of wet kiss. And then I feel a bucket-of-iced-water shock of guilt. I can't believe I'm even thinking such things! Whatever realisations I may have come to about how I want to live my life, I can't dismiss one significant fact: that I am already living with Hugh. He's the reason I came here in the first place. Not to mention the fact that he has only just laid his heart on the line with a proposal. I could never dishonour him, no matter how desperate I am to start living out loud.

In a bid to outrun my inner conflict I dare to accelerate further, actually starting to enjoy the sensation of my face being pummelled by the breeze. Perhaps it'll beat some sense into me.

I'm just marvelling at the flashing sprinkles of water dancing and spinning before me when Felicity turns and shouts something to me, gesticulating over to her left. But the wind captures her words, tossing them in the air and casting only a few nonsensical syllables in my direction.

'What?' I yell back to her, increasing my speed to get closer, only to have the spray splat back at me. 'Pah!' I spit, shaking my head, and attempting to blink the ocean from my lashes, inadvertently giving my eyes a salty glaze. Now half blind, I'm forced to cut the engine, afraid that the seamlessly clear lagoon will suddenly become awash with honeymooners bobbing on lilos and sharks holding up *Caution:* SQUID CROSSING signs. I reach for a dry layer of skirt, pressing the material into my face, squinting and squeezing until my vision is restored, then I look ahead. Uh-oh. The group is disappearing fast, following the curve of the island around to the right. I can just make out the last jet ski and there's a couple on board. No Felicity. I can only presume she followed her pointing hand to the left, having caught a glimpse of Him, though how she saw anything is a mystery to me – the sunlight is so dazzling I can't even make out the horizon. Oh well, in for a penny, in for a French Pacific franc. I settle back into position and go to rev up the engine, but it gives me no response. Oh no. Increasing my grip on the handles, I twist firmly and repeatedly. Nothing.

'Wait for me!' I call out, though I know nothing but a passing parrot fish could possibly hear my request.

Okay. Calm. Rational. Maybe it's like my old Mini – somewhat temperamental. You have to talk nicely to it, coax it and try not to flood the engine. Flood the engine indeed, I tut, acknowledging that I'm sat in a giant pool of water. I try again. Nothing. Wait, pretend I'm not freaking out and then give it another go. Not even a bubble or a whirr. I reach my hands up to peel the tickling tendrils of hair from my face and resecure my ponytail, only then realising that I must have tugged the key out of the ignition while drying my eyes – it's dangling from the coil around my wrist. Hoorah! I slot it back in, turn it on . . . yes! There's a grinding burr and we're off. Not having a single clue where I'm headed, I bear determinedly into the sun-spangled water, pounding and thumping the waves, yelling '*Felicity!*' at the top of my lungs. I feel like I'm doing the aquatic version of the charge of the light brigade when suddenly I see a jet ski coming straight for me. Instead of my life flashing before my eyes, I conjure up the scene in *Mission Impossible* where Tom Cruise and his nemesis hurtle towards each other on motorbikes, only to leap off and launch into combat in mid-air as their bikes crash beneath them. Not keen on that outcome, I swerve, he swerves and the next thing I know is that I'm drenched and disorientated and no longer in an upright position. I cling for dear life to what feels like the seat of the jet ski, convinced that if I so much as readjust a finger, my excess of dress fabric will drag me down to Davey Jones's locker.

When the anarchic rocking subsides and I dare to open my eyes again, I expect to find Felicity trawling Airport Guy behind her in a fishing net. But instead I see Tezz. His already sheer shirt has gone translucent and is suckering to his skin, highlighting the designer curves of his body. I can't help but stare – it's as if his muscles have been vacuum-packed for extra definition.

'Damn, that was close,' he understates, pulling up alongside me. 'You okay?'

I nod a breathless yes.

'Need some help getting back on?' he offers, reaching over to hold the jet ski steady.

I shake my head and summon every bit of my strength to haul myself and my sloppy, water-weighted skirts back into position. When I've caught my breath and wrung out my dress, I get up the nerve to look back at him, finally twigging that it's an unlikely coincidence bumping into him like this. Of all the lagoons in all of the world . . . 'How come—' I begin.

'Tony wanted to talk business with Marcel, so I thought I'd catch up with you,' he shrugs happily. 'I found Coco easy enough, but then he told me you girls had gone AWOL . . .'

'So you're the search party?' I suggest.

'Yes ma'am,' he confirms, giving me a military salute.

I grin back at him. 'Well, one down, one to go.'

'Oh, I already got Felicity.'

'You did?'

'It wasn't easy – she was hell-bent on jet-jacking some poor guy from the other group!'

'Did she catch him?' I gasp.

'Yes she did.'

'*And?*'

He shakes his head. 'She threw him back.'

'Why?' I bleat, defeated on her behalf.

'I don't think he was quite what she was hoping for,' he muses.

Oh, poor Felicity.

'Big thrill for the kid, though. Fourteen-year-old from the Mid-West on holiday with his parents. He couldn't believe his luck!'

Then it wasn't Airport Guy. There's still hope!

'So, you ready to go on?' He nods his head to the right.

'Do you know where to find them?'

'Sure. I said we'd catch up with them at the Coconut Show.'

'The Coconut Show?' I raise my eyebrows quizzically. Other than a lot of horsey clip-clopping noises, I really can't see it.

'Just you wait!' he teases, leading the way, constantly checking that I'm keeping up and treating me to innumerable big grins. I know I shouldn't be thinking such things, but it occurs to me that to the untrained eye we must look like a couple, out on the tropical version of a Sunday afternoon bike ride.

'You want to see monkey?' Coco quizzes the assembled masses as we jostle for shade in a small clearing beside the shore. 'Yes? Yes?'

'Yes! Yes!' we cry catching his caffeine-buzz enthusiasm.

'Come out! Come out!' he calls up the nearest palm tree. 'You see?' he turns back to us, pointing skyward.

While we're craning our necks, Coco launches himself at the trunk and starts skimming upwards, feet pressed inwards, knees akimbo, hands slapping the trunk one after the other with rhythmic confidence. He's the monkey! Or at the very least, Mowgli. He halts halfway to give us a 'Ta-daaa!' flourish. It's good enough for us – this tree has to be ten storeys high – and we praise him with our cheers. But it's not over yet.

'Have to get a coconut!' he explains as he demonstrates his excellent head for heights, continuing upwards until his hair tangles with the upper fronds. 'Yow-ow-owww!' he howls as he starts pelting the jungle floor with coconuts.

I dodge out of the way, having had enough concussion to last the trip, but Felicity stands agog. Whereas watching Tezz and Tony perform an exquisitely synchronised routine (bare-chested) proved to be the ultimate aphrodisiac for me, Felicity appears to be responding to the Spiderman/Tarzan motif.

'Just look at him!' she gawps as he scuffs back down at breakneck speed, then manoeuvres his pickings over to our feet with Pele-like precision.

Having only ever seen the brown bristly supermarket variety of coconut, I'm surprised to see a number with smooth green casings. These are the young coconuts, spilling forth a clear liquid Coco has us convinced will get us tipsy, yet it's the juice from the mature coconut that has the more distilled, alcoholic taste and, as Coco delights in telling us, is effective at loosening the bowels!

Having wooed everyone with drink samples, Coco picks up a new nut and tears at the outer fibres with his teeth, throwing what looks like husks of orang-utan fur on the smouldering fire Tezz has prepared for him.

'Keeps away the mosquitoes,' he explains as he invites the most macho-looking dude in the group to copy his act.

The guy grabs a coconut, locks his teeth on to a corner and pulls. After several attempts the best he comes away with is a web of whiskers he'd have a job flossing with.

'Now that shit is tough,' the guy concedes, shaking his head and patting Coco on the back in acknowledgement of his superhuman skills. 'Your teeth must be made of flint, dude!'

Once Coco has gnawed through to the familiar brown shell, he cracks it neatly in two and places the two halves over his nipples. 'For the titties!' he giggles, adding, 'For ladies only. Unless you man playing football!' he jests, cupping his groin. 'Also for utensils and ornaments . . .'

I feel ashamed of our wasteful Western culture as I listen to Coco reveal ever more resourceful uses for every aspect of this remarkable plant.

'The trunk is timber for construction and for carvings, the roots we toast and grind for coffee substitute and extract for medicine, from the coir fibre we make ropes and matting, the blade of leaf we thatch and weave and make bundles for torches . . .' he rattles on as he straddles a wooden bench with a metal spoke on the end and starts scraping out the white flesh from the inside of the shell, heaping his quarry on a tray. He works diligently through a heap of coconuts and then nods to Tezz to remove a sheath of leaves camouflaging a table of pre-prepared bananas – petite two-inchers, sliced lengthways and arranged in a decorative fan.

'Here, here!' He beckons us over, instructing us each to pick up one half banana, sprinkle liberally with shredded coconut, then place the other half banana on top.

'Like a sandwich,' one lady observes.

'No, no,' Coco corrects her, looking grave. 'Tahitian hot dog!'

Ha!

'Taste it!' Tezz encourages me.

'Oh, wow!' The banana is sweet and smooth, with none of the starchy bulk of its larger siblings. And the coconut? So fresh and moist – delicious!

'You like?' Coco enquires, reaching past me to take a plump handful of pulp. 'See what else we use this for?' He puts his hand beneath his chin, tilts his head back and squeezes. The effect is like a sponge emitting a milky wash over the gleaming mahogany of his chest. 'Cream for my body!' he announces, inviting Felicity to rub it in for him. She doesn't need asking twice.

'Here – you try on Tezz!' Coco reaches over and stuffs a wodge of coconut into my hand.

'Oh no!' I squeak, trying to dodge out of the way.

'Yes, yes – is good!' He rounds me up, clamping my hand in a vice and guiding it over to Tezz's torso.

I can feel myself turning a raging pink and look despairingly at Tezz.

'It's okay,' he soothes.

But is it? Would Hugh think this was acceptable behaviour? I doubt it.

'Squeeze! Squeeze!' Coco urges.

'Go on!' Felicity hisses.

I can't believe I'm going to do this in front of a group of tourists. I feel like a Thai sex show. I take a last look at the group in their logo T-shirts and jelly shoes, still shovelling down native hot dogs, and then shut them out.

Now it's just me and Tezz. I take a breath, lift my hand and squeeze hard. As the white liquid races over his honey-brown skin, a gasp of lust escapes my lips and my eyes dart every which way trying to follow the streaky patterns sprinting around his chest like an abstract painting in the making. The way the rivulets remain raised and shiny rather than being absorbed fascinates me. It's almost as if his sheer skin has been polished with wax.

Instinctively I reach out and gently slide the liquid down his side, causing him to shiver. Afraid I'm being too provocative, I quickly move my hand to his arm and try to ignore the enticing gullies streaming into his

229

waistband. His chest is heaving hard and I long to reach up and press my lips into the dip beside his collarbone, to taste the sweet coconut milk on his sea-kissed skin, but the voices of the group distract me. Are they talking about us? I venture a peak up at Tezz, and he looks right into me, taking my breath away as I become aware of his body calling to my own.

'Okay, okay!' Coco claps. 'Now we ride home!'

The best I can do is stumble two steps back. Meanwhile Coco engages Tezz, marching him over to the shoreline, but I'm in too much of a daze to follow. Only Felicity's words register: 'I don't think he's gay any more.'

I emit a low whistle and croak, 'Me neither.' I can still feel the sensation of his skin on my fingertips, the presentiment of how our bodies would be together. If I had my way, I'd stay put and lean against a palm tree and revel in the moment for the next hour at least. I don't want to get back on the jet ski because I know the wind will blast the delicate nuances away. I want to sustain this feeling for as long as possible, because I have never before experienced such a heady mix of sexual and sensual.

'I know how you feel,' Felicity coos. 'I think I'm going to do it with Coco!'

'*What?*' I snort, jolted out of my reverie. 'When exactly?'

'Tonight – he's asked me over to his house!'

'And you're going to go?' I gasp.

She gives a naughty nod.

I open my mouth to complain that she's supposed to be coming out with me and Hugh, but realise that that prospect was really only ever going to be fun for me. Besides, sex never sounded so good.

'So is that Airport Guy out of the picture now?' I ask as we slosh over to our respective jet skis, preparing for the last stint.

She stops suddenly, looking insulted, as if I'm accusing her of being unfaithful to her phantom fella.

'I just meant—'

'What?' She pouts. 'Don't you think you can be attracted to two people at once?' Her words are pointed.

'I just wondered if the chase was back on for tomorrow, that's all.' I try to make things better, with little success. 'I wasn't making any judgements.'

She doesn't look convinced. 'I know you think I'm being ridiculous, but I know Airport Guy is The One.'

I can't stop my eyes straying to Coco.

'Coco is just someone for me to practise on,' she blurts defensively.

'I see.'

'No you don't. How would you know how I feel?' she snaps. 'You haven't been single for the past four years.'

There it is, the oh-so-familiar 'it's all right for you' sting.

'Just because I've been in a relationship doesn't mean I haven't been lonely,' I begin.

'What do you want – sympathy?' she scoffs, sud-

231

denly consumed by her bitter alter ego. 'You've already got one person who loves you madly and now Tezz is falling for you, I can see it!' she cries, thrashing at the water, apparently in lieu of throwing a vase against the wall.

'Felicity.' I say her name but don't know what to follow it with.

'Do you know what I really want?' She turns to face me. 'I want what you have with Hugh. Only with more sex,' she adds sheepishly.

I can't help but smile. I've heard it all before, usually from people who've actually met Hugh. Despite our problems, apparently I still sell him as Mr Perfect. Is it worth me trying to explain, *really explain*, what it's like for me? That I'm beginning to see now that we've never really communicated. That from the word go he took the role of protector and pamperer, and got so filled up with that he didn't notice that my needs had changed. And I didn't know how to tell him.

'No! Don't say anything!' She holds up her hands, apparently predicting what is coming next. 'I'm being horrible, I'm sorry. God! I keep flaring up like that girl in *The Exorcist*. I don't know what's wrong with me.' She looks down at the water. 'I don't want to be this person! The Unhappy Happy Girl.'

Now I'm concerned. Felicity was always proud of who she was and looking forward to who she was going to become. I feel we need a hard-core heart-to-heart, but in the meantime I try a little light guidance.

'Maybe Coco isn't such a great idea,' I venture. 'You might end up feeling worse.'

'What's the alternative, Amber?' she flares up again, all too easily. 'Keep holding out for this mythical man of honour that I so desperately want to believe is still out there, waiting for me to come into his life?' She hangs her head. 'I need to feel someone wanting me. I wish it was Him, but it's not. There's a good chance it never will be.'

'Don't say that—' I step towards her.

'I hate to tell you but I think you got the one good guy,' she smarts.

'Oh, come on,' I try a little false cheer. 'There's got to be at least two out there – one for each of us!'

'Cute notion,' she shrugs, clambering on to her jet ski. 'But for now I'm going to go for flesh and blood.'

A rev of the engine and she's away, practising turns and spins while the rest of the group get themselves in line.

I'm too depressed to move. I don't want her to give up on Airport Guy and settle for Coco. And part of my reasoning, I have to admit, is selfish: for a while there it was as if we were both reaching for the moon together: her for Airport Guy, me for Tezz. Is that dream really over so soon? I look over at my moon-boy, still chatting to Coco, and wonder what on earth I'm doing. For all I know they could be comparing their imminent conquests.

But then Tezz looks in my direction, and even at twenty feet the warmth of his eyes slays me. I can't help but smile back. Without breaking eye contact he wades up to me and takes my hands, interlocking his long brown fingers between mine, filling me with a lovely sense of unity.

'See you tonight at the show?' he enquires.

I open my mouth to say 'Of course', but then remember I'm spending the evening with Hugh. You know, my boyfriend. 'Um . . .' is all I can manage.

His eyes shade with disappointment. 'Otherwise engaged?'

'I'm not engaged!' I blurt, knee-jerk reaction.

He gives me a quizzical look. 'I meant busy – you know, forging your own Gauguin, that kind of thing.'

'Actually I promised I'd help dye the lagoon turquoise tonight,' I joke, giving a faux grimace and praying facetiousness will get me off the hook.

'Right, right. Can you believe some people actually think it's that vivid blue naturally?'

'I know!' I laugh delightedly. 'Suckers!'

Oh, I'm just so content around this man. Even talking nonsense seems strangely satisfying. Everyone's always telling me what a witty guy Hugh is but his posh-boy joshing just doesn't tickle me the same way. I'd happily stand here, knee-deep in lagoon, chitchatting with Tezz till my toes shrivel to raisins, but Coco has just issued the final 'Ow-ow-OWWWW!' departure howl. It's time to flare our engines and vamoose.

'Come tonight,' Tezz urges, issuing a final invitation. 'I want to sing to you some more.'

My heart pirouettes with pleasure. I thought my father had the monopoly on romantic gestures, but I never once heard him *serenade* my mother. This is all for me! As I board the jet ski and surge forward amid a frothy frill, I'm forced to admit that, though technically I'm not 'allowed' to want more from Tezz, I do. At the very least the chance to be alone with him one more time. But what if I get my wish? Say we do reunite under the stars and he takes my hands and draws me close . . . To kiss or not to kiss, that is the question.

Or is it?

I'm no longer sure I have a choice in the matter. For the first time in my life, I feel like my heart is running the show.

16

Three hours later I'm stood betwixt Hugh and Sandrine, contemplating the set of wooden panels acting as a guest book for Bloody Mary's, and my thoughts rebound to Felicity. If she were here she'd be freaking out that Patrick Swayze once dined within these very bamboo-poled walls. Johnny Castle was her soulmate – the guy who would both protect and stand up for his fellow man, no matter the personal cost. It would do her good to be reminded of the values she used to hold so dear. If only she was here with me now, stepping into the sandy-floored restaurant, picking out her cut of fish and matching marinade instead of doing whatever she's doing with Coco. Unless she's having fun. She could be having fun. He's a fun guy. Maybe the sexual attention will do her good. Better yet, maybe she bumped into Airport Guy on the way back to *Windstar* and her happy ending is already underway.

I sigh heavily. Is that really too much to hope for? I fear that it is. The Happy Ending myth seems to be the emotional equivalent of the American Dream: every citizen is eligible for a shot at it, regardless of background, education or finances, yet only a small percentage will achieve star-spangled success. The good news is that your looks and the size of your bottom really don't matter a jot; when it comes to love, cupid is as undiscriminating and random as the lottery. And just as with the lottery, the grand prize won't always go to the most deserving recipient. After all, no one is more deserving than Felicity. So why is she alone? And why is Hugh squandering his good love on me? I feel a strange, testy negativity seeping into me as I knock back another Kir royale ananas (champagne and pineapple liqueur) and decide that – mmm, tasty – this is in fact the new love of my life. Because Tezz . . . well, chances are he's nothing more than a disappointment waiting to happen. I mean, realistically, who am I to him? The Brit holiday-maker he met on the beach? The woman who took liberties with his towel? Some chick to flirt with for a few days? How can I really be thinking it's any more than that?

'Amber? Is everything all right?'

I look up and find Hugh looking concerned. Slowly he reaches over and removes the knife from my stabbing hand. 'The food won't be much longer, I'm sure. Have some of my salad to keep you going . . .'

I have never known my emotions to be so all over

the place. It's a good thing that Sandrine has joined us or poor Hugh would probably have found himself arguing with me for the first time, over nothing.

'What do you think of these seats?' Hugh asks me.

I haven't even registered them. I shift position so I can inspect what's propping me up.

'Chunks of palm tree trunk!' Hugh announces. 'Planed and varnished!'

'Very cool,' I acknowledge.

'You have to see the bathroom,' Sandrine insists, laying a bejewelled hand on mine. 'You wash your hands in a waterfall!'

'Lovely!' I chime, wishing they'd go back to talking business so I can zone out again.

Instead they begin reciting the names of all the celebrities that could well have ordered wahoo fish in a teriyaki sauce, just like they have.

'Pierce Brosnan, Harrison Ford . . .' Hugh lists a pair of personal heroes.

'Goldie Hawn, Racquel Welch, Dorothy Lamour . . .' Sandrine counters with a trio of impossibly glamorous women.

'Jack Daniels, Bombay Sapphire!' I announce, making it clear where my interest lies tonight. 'Hey, wouldn't Bombay Sapphire be a wonderful name for a Bollywood star?' I slur to no one in particular. Then I catch Hugh looking at me. 'What are you doing?' he seems to be saying. Not in an accusatory or disapproving way, just concerned. Like he always is. That's probably one of the reasons it felt so refreshing with Tezz – there was no pity in his eyes when he looked at me.

'So, Sandrine,' I say, taking a deep breath as I try to muster some pep, 'does it look like there are enough grade-A blues to meet both your needs?'

Her eyes start from her head, but before she can speak, Hugh corrects me. 'It's the peacocks that are the most desirable, sweetie. That's what we're after.'

'But I thought Piers—'

'Oh, cherie, look at your shoes!' Sandrine exclaims suddenly.

For once she has good reason to fawn: a pair of strappy metallic Jimmy Choos, would you believe – a present from Hugh back when *Sex and The City* was all the rage and Hugh still believed that Charlotte and I had something in common because she also worked in an art gallery.

'Hugh chose them,' I tell her.

'You have such good taste,' she coos at him. 'They look like something I would wear!'

She's right. I did wonder what on earth Hugh was thinking at the time; they are so not me. Now I come to think of it, the gift came around the time Sandrine made a play for Hugh . . .

'Hoorah, the food!' he cheers as the waiter arrives bearing fragrant gifts.

'Wahoo?'

'That's me and Hugh!' Sandrine pats their respective place settings.

'Your mahi mahi will be out in just a few minutes,'

239

the waiter says, updating me on my odd-one-out platter.

'Okay, thank you,' I nod to him, trying not to look forlorn. 'Don't wait for me,' I urge the others. 'You two get stuck in.'

I seem to have lost my appetite anyway.

When we get back to the hotel, Hugh suggests a nightcap at the bar but Sandrine feigns an elaborate yawn and excuses herself. I'd love to know what's going on in her head right now. How is it affecting her, spending so much time with a man she once desired? After all, if desire is not sated, does it ever really go away? Does she find it galling to be around us as a couple? Not that I'm giving a particularly convincing portrayal of the doting girlfriend. Whenever Sandrine is around, I find myself deferring to her and behaving like they are the primary partnership. As if she has more right to him than me.

It's such a confusing game, this decision about whom we choose to spend our lives with. It rarely seems as simple as 'Who do you want to be with the most?' or 'Who makes you happiest?' Maybe that person is already taken, maybe they don't feel the same way, maybe they don't even exist.

But Tezz is real, I remind myself. And now that we're back on our motu and The Paradise Room is once again within reach, I feel an unignorable pull to be with him. All the girlie neuroses that were plaguing me at Bloody Mary's fade away as I have a moment of clarity: Tezz has come into my life and awoken my heart, and when I close my ears to all the negative jabbering, my gut instincts say I've touched some part of him too.

I sigh to myself. If only I had one of those rotten, lying, cheating boyfriends then people would cheer me on as I reached out for something more positive. As it is, Hugh's behaviour is so impeccable I could wait a year and he wouldn't give me the slightest justification for doing him wrong.

'Coffee or brandy, darling?'

'Baileys, please,' I request, taking a squooshy seat by the window as he orders our drinks at the bar. The barman says he'll bring our beverages to us but Hugh continues to stand there, seemingly adjusting himself via a hand in his pocket. He too must be tiddly from the cocktails; he's rarely so indiscreet. I wonder, could this possibly be the beginning of his decline into an abusive philistine?

Any false hopes are dismissed as he walks towards me and I notice some distinctly angular ridges at groin level – it's with a chill that I realise there's an all-too-familiar cube in his pocket. Oh no, surely not? I'm just about to excuse myself to the Ladies, never to return, when he takes my hand, places the box in my palm and closes my fingers securely around it.

'Hugh—' I begin, unable to hide my discomfort.

'It's just a little gift.'

'Oh?' A flicker of hope. Please let the box contain the world's smallest coconut.

241

'I noticed you're still wearing your white pearl earrings, and frankly that seems sacrilegious in Tahiti!' he winks.

I open the box and discover a pair of shimmering peacock studs.

'I know you prefer the ones with the pimples and the grooves, but I wanted you to have the best.'

I look at the earrings, then I look at him. On the one hand I'm relieved – at least it's not an engagement ring! On the other hand, I feel utterly disheartened. His choice is so telling: despite his certain knowledge that I am drawn to the flaws and quirkier characteristics, he is only capable of giving me grade A quality.

'That's so sweet of you, thank you!' I say, dutifully putting them on and dropping my white pearls into my purse.

As he sits down, my eyes suddenly open up. I was looking for some kind of sign or 'permission' and he just gave it to me – gift-wrapped no less!

Hugh may be wonderful and generous and kind, but he's not giving me what I want.

Now I'm convinced of what I must do. For one night I'm going to quash my feelings of loyalty and obligation to him and I'm going to try something new: I'm going to go to Tezz, and whatever I feel when I see him, I'm going to act on it.

But first I need Hugh to fall asleep.

'Ready to call it a night?' I take my last sip of Baileys as he drains his coffee cup.

'I'm really not tired yet, are you?'

I give a non-committal shrug. 'Maybe we could get a video from reception?' I suggest, knowing there's a far better chance of him zonking out if I can get him horizontal.

'I don't know . . .' He chews his lip, looking around him. 'All this and we sit in and watch TV.'

'We could see if they've got anything actually set in Tahiti. That way it would enhance our experience of "all this"!' I look imploringly at Hugh, surprised by my conniving alter ego. 'What do you say?'

He caves in with one caveat: 'Okay, but not *South Pacific*.'

'Deal,' I confirm, feeling like he's succumbed to step one of my evil plan.

We end up with two videos – *Love Affair*, the remake of witty, weepy *An Affair to Remember* starring Cary Grant and Deborah Kerr, this time with Warren Beatty and Annette Bening in the lead roles, and the classic Marlon Brando version of *Mutiny on the Bounty*.

'Aren't you going to get into your PJs?' Hugh asks when I lie down beside him, still in my beaded evening dress, another of Abigail's loans.

'I'm too sleepy to get undressed,' I sigh, nuzzling deep into the pillow, pretending that the detailing isn't digging in, much as I deserve its needling.

'Do you want me to help you out of it?' As Hugh reaches for me his knee presses down on the remote and we're bombarded by a French-speaking news debate.

'I'll get it!' I jump up and silence the TV, resetting the video while I'm at it. 'There!' I clamber back into position. 'Oh look, Portsmouth!' I'm surprised to see the Old Country in the opening scene.

'Jeez, what's Brando wearing – he looks more like Prince Charming than a naval officer!' Hugh is soon equally distracted.

By the time the *Bounty* anchors in Tahiti (with a warning from Captain Bligh that the natives have 'no ordinary concept of morality'), I realise I have my eyes as much on Hugh as the screen. It's a risky business, because every time he catches me looking, he kisses me and snuggles me closer. This is the closest I've felt to an out-of-body experience – my shell is encased in his arms, but my spirit is already at the door. At one point I'm resting on his chest, convinced his breathing has become sufficiently slow and relaxed, and raise a hand and flicker my fingers in front of his eyes.

'What are you doing?' he laughs, grabbing them.

Oh no. Still awake.

'Just stretching,' I tell him. 'Got pins and needles in my hand.'

'Poor baby,' he says, adjusting position so I can free up my blood-flow.

As we watch the relationship between Fletcher Christian and Captain Bligh grow ever more fractious, my eyes flick to the clock. I'm seriously running out of time here. Half of me is feeling sick with impending deceit, and half of me is consumed with impatience. This is beyond boy/girl stuff. I feel like I'm at a crossroads and I need to decide how I want to live the rest of my life. There's so much at stake here. I don't want to make a decision based on lust or holiday hedonism, but I feel compelled to find out more about Tezz and what is going on between us. And there's only one way to do that.

'Shall I nip to the bar and get us a couple of hot chocolates, just to be extra cosy?' I suggest, ready to swing my legs out of bed. 'You can keep watching, just tell me what I've missed.'

'Don't be silly, honey,' he pulls me back. 'We can order room service.'

'Well, if you're sure . . .' I muffle into his pyjama top.

I want to scream in frustration. I've never done anything bad to him before, never given him a moment's cause to feel jealous or insecure in four years. But I need this one thing. Just to know . . .

'Mind if I turn off this light?' I enquire as an abundance of Tahitian babes once again crowds the screen. 'Hugh?' I'm just about to nudge him to get a response when I see a small bubble appear at the corner of his mouth. Can it be? Tentatively I lean forward so I can see his eyes. Closed. I reach for the remote and click off the movie – can't risk any mutinous caterwauling waking him. I hold my breath as I watch his chest heave. Dare I do this?

'I'm sorry,' I whisper as I tip-toe away from him.

*

Once on the path I quickly pick up speed, and a renewed sense of hope and excitement infuses me. A flashback to the coconut milk flowing down his chest just makes me run faster.

There he is! Moving around the stage, part-man, part-panther. I want to watch him for a while before he sees me, so I hang back in the shadows as he announces the last song of the night and proceeds to buckle my knees with a tantalisingly rumbly version of Tony Toni Tone's 'Let's Get Down'.

Five minutes later he's switched his stage clothes for a smooth chocolate-brown shirt, tan strides, tinted shades and a hip-hop cool hat. The man has style! I watch him moving among the audience, warmly acknowledging the return customers, posing for pictures with excited admirers, illuminating every face he encounters with his joyful banter and attentive demeanour. I smile to myself – he's just as entrancing to watch off-stage as he is on.

'Excuse me!'

'Sorry!' I apologise to the waitress whose path I'm blocking, and then gag in panic as my eyes lock on to a distinctively blinged brunette to my left – *Sandrine!* What the hell is she doing here?

Frantically trying to dodge her line of vision, I propel myself into the Ladies. Oh my God! I can't risk her reporting this back to Hugh, even if it means sacrificing my audience with Tezz. I have to get out of here!

I go to recce an escape route, but then hear voices

approaching and quickly retreat into the nearest cubicle. Convinced I'll be thrown out if I'm discovered using the facilities merely as a hideout, I give the toilet paper a vigorous yank, instantly creating an Andrex puppy effect on the fast-spinning toilet roll.

'Apparently he was engaged just over a year ago,' the first, somewhat familiar voice begins.

'What?' the other gasps as I attempt to halt the fast-growing tissue streamer I've created.

'Yup. Body and soul in love with this girl. When she broke it off he was devastated. Emotionally he's shut down, says he couldn't conceive of even *wanting* to feel so much for someone again.'

'But he looks so happy on stage!' the other voice protests.

I snap upright. Are they talking about Tezz?

'Well, he's a pro – he's been singing and dancing since he was a little kid,' First Voice explains.

It is! It's him! I gasp to myself, quickly shaping the paper into a cushion-size bundle stuffing it into my bag rather than clog the toilet, not wanting to miss a word.

'It's amazing, what you said before about his dad and everything . . .'

'I know. What doesn't kill us makes us stronger, right?'

I continue to listen, but they've changed subject now so I take the opportunity to flush and emerge from the cubicle. The girls look up and smile. I recognise one as the sassy backing singer Malia as I

247

squeeze past her to wash my hands. I want to compliment her on the show, in particular her rabble-rousing rendition of Melissa Etheridge's 'Only One', but then the door opens and I spot both the back of Sandrine's head and a clear run at the exit and find myself bolting while I have the chance.

A couple of paces down the path I'm regretting the unnecessary aggravation I've brought upon myself tonight – all for nothing! I can't help but wonder if Sandrine was sent as a kind of caution to me, to make me slow down and really take stock before I go too far. I'm about to start questioning everything, including my entitlement to be truly happy, when my fortune changes: there, just a short distance ahead of me, is Tezz.

We're still too close to The Paradise Room for me to call his name out loud, so I concentrate on trying to keep up with his extended strides until I deem it safe to speak.

'Hey, mister!' I attempt a playful tone as we turn a corner.

No response.

Obviously not loud enough, but I don't want to risk bellowing yet, so I lope onwards, expecting him to veer towards the beach but instead he heads directly into the dense jungle, advancing purposefully through its dark tangles.

'Tezz?' I call his name, projecting the best I can, but still to no avail. I'm wondering whether for some

248

reason he's deliberately blanking me when I see moonlight glint off the silver domes covering his ears – he's lost in music. I'm going to have to draw level with him if I want to get his attention. But I'm not as sure-footed as he is – he's moving fast, and already the light of The Paradise Room is dwindling and ducking behind the foliage. I stall for a second. This could be dicey – I daren't lose sight of the club. There must be something I could throw at him to cause him to turn round? Reaching into my bag, hoping to find a pen or even the turtle room-key, my hand is instantly bound by the reams of toilet paper. I'm cursing the added bulk to rummage through when it dawns on me that I can use the paper!

I quickly find an end and loop it around the waist of the nearest palm, tying a loose knot, and then, breath quavering, I scramble onward, leaving a long white ribbon in my wake.

17

Scratched, yanked and stumbling, I repeatedly wince at the prospect of being thwacked in the face with a pinged-back tree branch or catching my foot on a humpback root, yet continue regardless, a woman on a mission.

There's just one small snag – I'm running low on paper. I push my hand into my bag to assess how many more metres I can safely travel, and when I look up, Tezz is gone.

What? I spin around.

He was right there in front of me, but now nothing. Suddenly I'm fully freaked. The leaves seem to be creeping and twitching about me, my breathing is patchy and there's a creaking sound I can't quite place.

'T-Tezz?' I call tentatively into the night. My heart appears to be thumping louder with every beat.

As I scour the foliage, there seems to be a cloaked figure and glinting eye lurking behind every tree and

I'm sure I can hear the snuffly whine of a beastie. Oh God! I must be crazy! What have I done? If I get eaten by wild boar it'll be no more than I deserve. In exasperation I cry out loud: 'I must be mad!'

'Amber?'

It's him!

'Tezz?' I call back.

'What are you doing here?'

I turn 360 degrees, but still can't see him. 'I just wanted to say hi . . .' I squeak, feeling like I've arrived at a woodland confessional – a place you can come to whisper your desires to the night.

'I didn't mean to follow you,' I continue. 'It's just you couldn't hear me calling, so I kept going.'

There's a pause, and then his disembodied voice enquires, 'Do you want to come up?'

'Up?' I frown.

'Up here . . .'

I hear a rustling from above, tilt my head back and raise my eyes, finally locating him on a ledge between two knotty Banyan trees.

'How—?' Before I can complete my question, a rope ladder unravels clunkily down the spine of the nearest trunk.

Wow. I step back, daunted. He may as well be asking me to make my own way up to heaven. The last time I attempted anything like this was in P.E., and Felicity was always on hand to give me a boost. Nevertheless I reach for the ladder and, in the most ungainly manner, set an unstable foot on the bottom rung. As I pull myself upward I feel the rope getting taut and squeaking as it bears my weight and swings off to the left. I try another step but feel decidedly wobbly. How am I ever going to make it up to the penthouse?

'You might find it easier to climb sideways,' he suggests. 'Hold the ladder at right angles to your body, that's right, move your left leg around to the other side – CAREFUL!'

I wobble precariously, clinging on for dear life as I wait for the ladder to settle again.

'Hand over hand . . .' Tezz coaches as I get closer. 'Amber, are you trying to do this in heels?'

I look down at my feet. Ah. The Jimmy Choos.

I give him a sheepish look. He shakes his head. I shrug them off, watching them clip the trunk as they fall into the undergrowth.

'That's better,' we both agree as I master the last few rungs.

'Here.' He holds out a hand and heaves me on to the wooden platform.

I step forward and enter a charming Polynesian-style tree house. The teak flooring is softened with raffia matting and heaps of red and turquoise cushions bearing the traditional hibiscus print. There's a wooden bowl of ripe papayas, a jar of honey beside a hot-drink flask and clusters of tiny tea lights illuminating the free-form pillars of books and CDs. The look couldn't be more different from the Victoriana of my den back home in Oxford, but the feel is the same – this, it would seem, is Tezz's personal hideaway.

'I hope I'm not intruding,' I fret, suddenly self-conscious. 'You know, infiltrating your secret retreat . . .'

'Semi-secret,' he hushes me. 'There are at least two other people in the know. Well, three now including you.'

I make a speedy assumption: no doubt Tony is one, and I'm guessing the other would be his ex.

'Get comfy,' he says, motioning to the cushions.

I lower myself into the nest, not quite sure what pose to adopt. I feel prissy if I sit upright and too presumptuous if I splay out in recline so I settle for an awkward tilt.

Well, I did it. I followed him. I climbed. Now what? He seems to be waiting to take his cue from me.

I could opt for a casual conversational gambit like, 'You know how your heart got completely mangled when your girlfriend broke off your engagement? Well, I want to do exactly the same to my boyfriend so I can run off with you!'

Perhaps not. I almost wish I hadn't inadvertently gleaned that private bit of information about him: it's making me overly tentative in his presence, wary of doing anything that might scare him away. Yet I have so little time to find out whether or not the rapturous feeling he conjures up in me flows two ways. Before I can get further embedded in my quandary, I'm distracted by a picture postcard resting atop the nearest stack of books and hear myself blurting, 'Is that allowed?'

'How do you mean?' He raises an eyebrow.

'Well, that's a Rubens painting,' I begin. I recognise it as *The Toilet of Venus* from an exhibit we hosted two years ago – a nearly naked woman tending to her image in the mirror. 'I thought Tahiti was All Gauguin, All The Time,' I tease.

Tezz grins as he lolls beside me. 'I just liked the idea that this woman had one black pearl earring and one white.' He offers it to me for closer inspection. 'They say the white symbolises purity and the black represents the pleasures of the flesh.'

I feel a wobble of lust as his words tempt my ears.

'That's right,' I gulp, trying to recall the phrasing of the placard we placed beside the picture at the Ashmolean. Ah yes: 'This portrait symbolises the reconciliation of both "comforting mother" and "dangerous seductress" in one woman, an idea sublimely desirable to Rubens,' I quote.

'Well, he was on to something – it's all about balance, baby!' Tezz notes.

As his words register, I feel yet another inner shift: with Hugh I suppressed any passionate impulses because I was terrified they would lead me to the fever-state of my parents' relationship. Ever since I was a child, passion in relationships has equalled danger. But now I see things really aren't so black and white. With Tezz the heat is undeniable, but I don't find it worrisome, perhaps because there's no sense of him trying to own me or control me. Hugh always wants to make things right and make them better and as a result, though he means well, I just end up feeling wrong. But when I'm with Tezz, I'm not afraid of him seeing my flaws. Ever since our conversation on the beach I've felt a liberating sense of acceptance and understanding. So why am I suddenly charged with an electrifying surge of nerves? Is it because he's close enough now to kiss? I said before that I would act on whatever feelings I have in his presence, but really, do I dare?

'So what about you, Amber?' he says in a low voice, tantalising me by leaning closer still. 'Are you the "comforting mother" or "dangerous seductress"?'

I search for an answer but then get a better idea and turn my back on him so I can forage in my purse without him seeing what I'm up to.

'What are you doing?' he asks, craning his neck in bewilderment.

'Patience!' I order, twisting away from him as I locate one of my discarded white pearl earrings and swiftly switch it with one of my new black ones (I try not to think of what Hugh might say if he knew I was using his latest gift for such an effect).

'Ta-daaa!' I trill, turning back to him. 'See – I too have one of each. I think that makes me the perfect woman!'

He laughs delightedly as I showcase my lobes.

'A yin and yang Venus,' he sighs, raising his hands to gently run a finger over the two contrasting globes, replacing my peppy smile with a swoop of yearning. As the warmth from his hands transfuses my face, my lips part and my eyes flicker closed in surrender.

'Amber . . .' He breathes my name and then I feel his lips melt on to mine, so soft yet so charged with emotion, every nuance taking me closer to the point where I'd swear we're actually levitating.

As the kisses deepen and intensify I start to feel dizzy. I'm not used to this spiralling desire. And then it hits me: it's broken – the trust I had with Hugh. Suddenly I can't stop a barrage of images of him showing me consistent kindness and care and, sick with guilt, I pull back. I am not free to do this. Hugh saved me when I was in despair, this is not the way to repay him.

'I – I can't!' I stammer, turning to run away, remembering only just in the nick of time that there's a fifty-foot drop at the door. 'Oh God!' I gasp, lurching to grab back at the bamboo post, trying to shake off the image of the earth charging towards me. Talk about making a dramatic exit – I could easily have smashed every bone in my body! Was this my final warning: Passion Kills!

'Are you okay?' Tezz gasps, securing his arms around me. 'I won't kiss you again, I promise – just don't jump!' he urges.

As he clasps me closer, I try to seal a resistant layer over my heart, but before I know it I'm squeezing him back, wanting him closer to me than anyone I've ever met. This is all too hard. I know what I want, but I'm going about it in the wrong way. I'm in danger of corrupting everything with my deceit: Hugh doesn't know where I am and Tezz doesn't know about Hugh. I have to make my peace with my guardian angel before I can even contemplate going any further with Tezz. I don't want to lie any more. I want my life to have passion *and* purity.

Finally regaining my composure, I croak, 'I really have to go.'

'Can you tell me what's wrong?' he enquires softly.

I look back at him, appreciating the lack of pressure he's putting on me, seeing the child who learned when not to ask too many questions.

'There's just something I need to do,' I tell him.

'Okay,' he nods respectfully. 'Give me a minute and I'll walk you back.'

'No need!' I chip too quickly.

'It's no trouble, I'm going to the beach anyway . . .'

'Your nightly swim?' I smile fondly, softening again.

He nods, and without thinking I find myself reaching to place a single kiss on his cheek. 'I'll be fine,' I insist, preparing to make my descent. 'I left a trail.'

'Very festive,' he notes, taking in the garlanded branches below as I systematically retreat down the ladder towards where my shoes lie twinkling like treasure in a magpie's nest.

A couple of rungs early I let go of the ladder, land with a thud, give a quick goodbye salute and forge ahead, hastily retrieving the paper trail, caring nothing for the slicing fronds and whipping vines keen to ensnare me. I'm nearly back at civilisation, eager to get back to the bungalow so I can process everything that has just happened and work out the best way to explain to Hugh what— I stop suddenly.

'What's this?' I question, distracted by a slackening in the paper.

I pull it taut and it pulls back. There's something on the other end. Not something, *someone*. A woman.

When my eyes first adjust to her silhouette, I think she's one of the backing singers – her physique is similarly Amazonian, her hair equally afrotastic – but then she steps from the shadows and her face is new to me: a high-cheekboned high priestess.

'Oh, thank you!' I giggle nervously as I relieve her of the final ream of paper. 'I don't want you to think I was littering. I just didn't want to get lost – it's a jungle out there!' I quip.

She looks at me, then looks beyond me, then looks pissed off.

'Were you with Tezz?' Her eyes narrow to two poison darts.

There's something so proprietorial in her voice I stop myself from answering a truthful 'Yes' and instead bluff a 'Huh?', swiftly embellished with 'I've been playing late-night paperchase with my friend. There she is now!' I point over her shoulder at nothing and call, 'Felicity!', then hurtle ahead, heart pounding as I escape a potential lynching.

What the hell was that? Now my head is reeling. I

thought Tezz was supposed to be emotionally shut down, but he didn't seem to have any problem kissing me, and now there's another chick on the way! Could it be his ex, realising she can't live without him and returning to reclaim him? I buckle at the prospect. No. It can't be. He certainly wasn't expecting her or he wouldn't have said he'd leave with me. Nor would he have wanted to have been caught doing what we could well have been doing by now. I experience a jab of nausea. Oh, thank God we didn't! Thank God I left when I did! Or maybe I left too soon! Maybe now he'll think I don't want him and in his rejected, vulnerable state he'll fall prey to her!

This is all way too much for my brain and heart to cope with alone. First thing tomorrow I'm calling Felicity to see if she can help me make sense of this madness.

That's if she's even talking to me . . .

18

'I'm not talking to you,' Felicity pouts down the phone to me.

'Oh,' I say, deflated, ready to resign myself to a day of muddle-headed misery.

'Ask me why,' she challenges.

'Why?'

'Because you were right,' she sighs.

'About what?'

'About Coco.'

'Oh no!' I gasp. 'Was it awful?'

'It would have been if I'd stayed. The minute he kissed me I just panicked and ran.'

'Funny you should say that . . .' I mumble, quickly bringing her up to speed on my night.

'Okay, stop right there!' She halts me before I even get to the mystery woman at the end of my streamer of toilet paper. 'This is clearly a conversation we need to have in person. Is Hugh working today?'

'Yes.'

'How soon can you get here?'

'Half an hour?'

'Make it twenty minutes and you can come on the Circle Island Tour with me.'

'What exactly does that involve?' I ask, fearing a power trek in ninety-degree heat.

'Sitting on an air-conditioned bus pretending to look at the sights but actually seeing if we can catch a glimpse of Airport Guy.'

'He's back in favour?' I perk up.

'Yes ma'am. I'm not giving up on him yet. Yesterday I may have been a bitter old hag. Today I'm going for relentless optimism!'

I laugh and cheer 'I'll be there!', grabbing my bag before I've even set down the phone.

For some reason I'd got it in my head that we'd be touring the island on a National Express coach, but in fact we're travelling aboard an old wooden-sided 'le truck' with air conditioning in the form of open windows. Fortunately we're rattling along at quite a pace, and the resulting breeze is bliss. The only snag is that there's too much to take in and not enough time to gossip – we learn that what look like elongated mailboxes at the end of every driveway are actually designed to accommodate the twice-daily delivery of French sticks from the bakery; that stray dogs abound and one hapless mutt can trigger a canine chorus enduring for several miles;

and that local Tahitians bury their dead in their back yard.

Felicity makes a mental note never to purchase property here. 'Other people's gerbils in cigar boxes I could live with, but knowing someone else's granny and granddad are in a coffin under the lawn?' She shudders. 'Or do you think they dig them up when they move?'

We finally get to gabble nineteen-to-the-dozen when we stop for a *pareu*-painting demonstration and are allotted ten minutes to rifle through the gauzy rainbow of cloths stencilled with fish and shell motifs.

'So firstly, Coco.' I kick off the questioning as we duck behind a densely pegged clothesline for a bit of privacy. 'What exactly was the deal there?'

'There's nothing to say. It just felt wrong,' Felicity winces. 'I thought it might get me back in the game, but I can't seem to bring myself to do it now unless there are some genuine future prospects on offer.' She absent-mindedly smoothes a mottled mauve *pareu*. 'I'm not saying I'm going to wait until I'm married to have my next sex, but I at least want to know there's going to be a chance of a second date!'

'Gotcha,' I nod.

'So what was the problem with Tezz?' she asks, turning to me. 'Did kissing him make you realise how much you really love Hugh?'

'Not exactly,' I cringe.

'The opposite?' She looks fearful.

'It's complicated,' I sigh. 'At the time it felt so right

262

– absolutely the best feeling ever – but then there was the guilt and, on the way back, there was this girl . . .'

Felicity listens agog as I describe my brief but disturbing encounter with the high priestess.

'Well, she's definitely after him even if he's not reciprocating,' she concludes as we file back on to the truck.

'So you think it might just be her chasing him?' I follow her to the rear bench where we can talk without disturbing the rest of the posse.

'Could be.' She thinks for a moment. 'But you say only three people know of his tree house?'

'That's what he said.'

'So there is a chance he did once have something going with her. But maybe not lately. He's supposed to be all broken-hearted and steering clear of the ladies, isn't that what you heard?'

I try to recall Malia's exact wording. 'Well, it definitely didn't sound like he was ready for a relationship. I don't know about shenanigans.'

'Hmmm,' she muses as we continue on past an abandoned construction site for a hotel that ran out of funding, then stall for the guide to run a quick errand at a friend's house. 'And this girl, you say she was striking, with big hair?'

'Braided at the front, fluffed out at the back.'

'With a silver ankh at her neck?'

'Yes, how did you know?' I'm only just remembering that detail now.

Felicity taps the window and I immediately drop to

the floor. The high priestess is stood right there in the garden across the street.

'Oh no!' Felicity gasps.

'What?' I hiss from seat level. 'Tell me she's not getting on the bus!'

Felicity quickly shakes her head. 'Tezz is with her.'

'What?' I go to bounce upward but instead Felicity lands on top of me, equally keen to hide herself.

'What are you doing?' I squeak, crushed. 'I need you to tell me what's going on between them!'

'I know!' she growls. 'But I don't want him to see me or he won't act natural.'

The bus lurches forward, guide presumably back on board.

'Quick! Look back!' I beg her.

She peeks up, but her face falls as she does so. This is so not good.

'Were they kissing?' I scramble back on to the seat the second we round the corner.

'No.'

'But it looked like they were about to?' I carry on earnestly.

She looks uneasy, then concedes a yes. 'But not for sure. They might just have been tickling each other or something.'

I'm devastated. How could this happen? How could he be so intimate with me one minute and then frolicking with her the next? My stomach contorts into a pretzel of envy at the mere thought of him touching someone else.

264

'Oh Amber, it could be perfectly innocent,' Felicity rallies as we drive past a pharmacy and a basketball court. 'Long-lost friend, sister, cousin, anything . . .'

The bus stops again.

'This is where the land crabs live,' announces the guide, directing our attention to the dirty, shady sandbank to our left.

'I can't see them,' I complain sullenly.

'Watch to see what happens to this flower . . .' The guide takes one of the bright red hibiscuses decorating the window of the bus and casts it on to the earth. Instantly two giant clipping, snapping crabs scuttle up to it and latch on to a petal each, vying for the bloom like two housewives fighting over a scarf in the Harrods sale. Suddenly it seems to me that the crab with the more exotic markings represents the high priestess and the one with the bleached-out shell is me – pale and not-so-interesting Amber – with Tezz, of course, the vibrant prize. As the tussle continues I'm on tenterhooks to see who will win. Dust flies, claws are brandished, but neither crab is willing to back down. Finally, wretchedly, the high priestess triumphs, instantly dragging her prize down her hole, leaving the other crab dazed and alone. I slump back in my seat, defeated.

'Maybe it's a good thing you saw them, Amber,' Felicity begins. 'Just imagine if you'd thrown away all you have with Hugh on a holiday romance with the local Casanova.'

'He's not—' I go to protest and then sigh, 'I can't believe he's like that.'

'How can you be sure?' she probes.

'Because I'm never sure of anything, but I was sure of him.'

'And how do you feel now?'

'Part of me still believes, but that girl . . .'

'Look, you know, I think you should stick with what you've got with Hugh. You don't know how lucky you are to have a man like him, *really*. But,' she sighs, trying to muster some empathy, 'if Tezz has really rocked your world as you say and you want to give it your best shot, then you're going to have to be direct and ask him about her.'

'Really?' Right now I can't think of anything worse.

'Mind you, if he's a cad and a player, he's not going to tell you the truth. He'll just say you've got it all wrong, that they're just friends and she tripped on something and fell into his arms. Hmmm. There must be some way you can find out for sure.'

'If I had enough Mai Tais I'd ask *her*, but she could have her own agenda.'

'Indeed,' Felicity agrees.

'Anyway, I don't even know how I'd get to see him again. I can't go back to The Paradise Room and risk Sandrine being there.'

'Do you think you could find the tree house by yourself?'

'Not a chance.'

'That's a shame. That would have probably provided the quickest answers to all your questions.'

'You mean if I'd gone and spied on them?' I scoff. 'To get a good look I'd need Coco's tree-shinning skills, which I definitely don't possess.'

'I could probably get up there.'

'Honestly, there's no way I'd find it again. It was deep in the jungle. Deep.'

We both fall silent. Until something occurs to me.

'He does go the beach every night after the show.'

Felicity looks up at me.

'Never misses a night. That's how I first got to chat with him.'

'Well, that's perfect! It's not even far from your bungalow, so you won't look like you've gone out of your way to see him!'

'I think he might be a bit suspicious that I'm out strolling at 2 a.m. . . .'

'Not if he doesn't see you!' Felicity glints.

'Are we back to the spying idea?' I sigh.

'Is this important to you?'

I don't answer.

''Cos I could have sworn we were talking about your future life happiness here.'

'We are.'

'So then you want to know the truth?' Felicity reasons.

'Yes.'

'Well, as of right now I don't really see an alternative,' she humphs. 'If you're going to make a

267

decision this serious, you need to have as much information as possible.'

I give her suggestion some thought as we trundle the final stretch of the island, back to the jetty. She could be right. I really want to know what's going on, and I don't know how else to find out.

'You don't think it's morally wrong?' I ask, trying to assuage my concerns as we alight from the bus and amble over to the nearest cold-drink vendor.

'Compared with blindly cheating on your would-be fiancé, I don't think it's too bad.'

'Felicity!' I gasp.

'I'm just telling it like it is.'

'I don't want to do this to Hugh,' I complain.

'But you *do* want to kiss Tezz again?'

'In an ideal world . . .'

'Yes or no?'

'Provided I'm the only one he's kissing, *yes*,' I sigh.

'Interesting dilemma.' Felicity strums her fingers on her chin. 'In a way, this is a bit like seeing a beautiful designer dress in a shop window – you fall instantly in love with it, but you tell yourself you can't possibly afford it so there's no point in even trying it on. But then you can't stop thinking about it. You become obsessed by it. And in actual fact, if you had tried it you would have realised it made your stomach look paunchy or the colour made you look jaundiced, and then you would have let it go. But only if you'd tried it on.' She looks confused by her own analogy. 'Which doesn't mean I'm condoning or even encouraging you to get it on with Tezz, but I do think the smart thing to do is to see if it's even available.'

'So, really, I'm not so much trying him on as checking the price.'

'Exactly!'

'Well, when you put it like that . . .' I smile at her then link my arm in hers. 'I'm sorry we didn't have much luck today as far as Airport Guy goes . . .'

'No worries,' she chirrups, giving me a friendly nudge. 'I've got a back-up plan.'

'Oh?'

'Tonight Cousin Brian's going to introduce me to this local know-everyone, know-it-all guy. He reckons if Airport Guy has ever been to the islands before, he'll know him. And if he hasn't, he'll know a way for me to find him.'

'Sounds promising,' I tell her, hoping against hope that he'll come up trumps.

'Well, good luck with tonight's mission,' she says, giving me a hearty hug as our respective water shuttles arrive. 'Call me first thing and let me know how it goes.'

'Okay.'

'You are going to do it, aren't you?' she checks, turning back to me.

I fake a big, confident smile in her direction but murmur a rather more weedy 'We'll see' under my breath.

Come the evening, I'm even less convinced of the wisdom of Felicity's plan, but sneaking out has become the norm for me. It shocks me to admit that not once since I've been here have I lain next to Hugh the entire night. I look down at his sleeping head beside me, justifying my departure as a quest for truth, then place a traitor's kiss on his brow, hardly recognising this duplicitous person I have become.

Once outside I assess the beach, searching for a suitably sheltered vantage point. For a second I consider adopting one of the upturned canoes as a kind of shell, but fear the pair of them might come sit on me to watch the stars. Unbearable!

What, then? I rotate on my heels. Ha! The towel hut! Perfect! It's like a bamboo Wendy house with a front flap that opens up fully during business hours and just enough now to let me in. Even if I do have to go in head first. For a second I fear that I'm going to get trapped with my legs sticking out, but I manage to claw myself along the floor, dislodging only a hundred or so snorkelling masks in the process.

'Okay.' I calm myself, settling into a position that allows me a clear view of the stretch of beach where Tezz takes his swim. 'I can do this,' I reassure myself. And so I wait. And wait. I look at my watch. An hour has passed already.

When a further thirty minutes creep by I'm beginning to think he won't show. Of course, just because he's not here doesn't mean he's definitely with her. Maybe he didn't feel like swimming tonight. Maybe he had to learn a new routine or use the hotel computer to send an email to his mum in Boston. I'll wait just a little longer. I lean my heavy head against the bamboo. So very tired. If I shut my eyes then maybe my hearing will be enhanced? Ah yes, there are the waves, slipping back and forth on the shore. Back and forth, back and forth . . .

'Ms Pepper?'

Huh?

'Ms Pepper!'

Is someone saying my name? I open my eyes, blinking up at a blinding light, just able to make out François the hotel manager and Hiro the Towel Guy looking down at me in confusion.

'Is everything okay?' François enquires.

It takes me several seconds to register the shift in time and recognise that the blinding light is in fact the sun.

'Oh, morning! *Morning!*' Yup, it's definitely morning. Would it kill them to have the occasional cloud here? My retinas are scorched!

'You know, you can always bring one of the towels from your room if you fancy an early swim.'

Processing their words in the nick of time, I bluster, 'Ah, yes, hadn't thought of that. Good advice. That's what I'll do next time.'

As I clamber out of the booth, I feel like I'm emerging from a birthday cake at the wrong party.

'And we have a lovely range of swimwear in our boutique . . .' he trails off, taking in my outfit – patently evening attire.

271

'Super. I look forward to having a look.' I straighten my dress, preparing to march off at high speed. I can't believe I fell asleep – I'm still none the wiser about Tezz!

'Ms Pepper?' This time the voice belongs to Hiro.

I turn back. 'Yes?'

'Your towel.'

'Right! Lovely, thanks.' Again I go to leave.

'And one for the lounger?'

'Yes. Thank you.' Will the humiliation never end?

I know they're watching me walk in the opposite direction to the pool, but I can't fake it any more – my nude knicker and bra set simply won't pass as a bikini and I can't go shopping for swimwear at 7 a.m. wearing a black evening dress.

Miraculously I don't see any other guests on the way back to the bungalow but I do see Hugh up bright and early, out on the deck. Uh-oh. Now what? How can I possibly show up in last night's outfit and not arouse suspicion?

There's nothing else for it. I divert from the walkway back on to the beach, quickly strip down to my inappropriate undies and wade into the water until I'm deep enough to lean back and dunk my hair. Then I scurry out again, praying no one is watching, wrap the first towel around my body, roll my dress in the second and hurry along to our bungalow.

'Hugh!' I give a jaunty rap. Please say he's only just woken up!

As the lock turns I feel totally shifty and on edge. I

try to tell myself that my only crime is that I slept in a towel stand, but it just doesn't wash.

'Thank God you're all right!' His first words are of relief, but as I go to step inside, he blocks my path, his face darkens and, in a voice I barely recognise, he glowers, 'Where the hell have you been?'

19

For a second I can't even speak. I feel like I've just been slapped. I've never seen Hugh's face contorted with anger and suspicion before – it's the worst kind of wake-up call.

'I thought I'd go for a swim while the pool was nice and quiet,' I bluster. 'I actually got there before the towel guy, would you believe – that's even better than beating the Germans, isn't it?'

Oh, please let me be able to carry this off. I have to do whatever it takes to stop him looking at me this way.

'What time did you leave?' he asks, voice stone cold.

'Gosh, I really don't remember. I don't think I even looked at the clock . . .'

'I woke up at 3 a.m. and you were gone. I've been awake ever since.'

I gulp to myself. How the hell can I explain away the time?

'And since when did you swim without your

274

costume?' he continues, holding up my one and only one-piece.

Quick Amber, *think*!

'Well, when I first went out it was just for a walk, and then I lay down to look up at the stars and I think I must have dozed off, and when the sun came up it was so lovely I went in the water in my undies . . .' I prise open my towel to give him a flash. 'See?'

'Who were you with?'

'What? No one!' For once I can tell the truth. 'It was just me, the whole time.'

'And you didn't go any further than the beach?'

'No, why do you ask that?' I'm starting to get defensive now.

'Yesterday Sandrine said she thought she saw you at a local bar.'

My stomach wrenches guiltily. I'm so screwed. 'What bar?' I bleat, frowning confusion.

'She didn't say. Apparently it was just a fleeting glimpse, but she said she could have sworn—'

'No, of course not!' I snort, vigorously shaking my head. 'She must have had a Mai Tai too many.'

'That's what I thought. Until now . . .'

He maintains an interrogatory stance. I don't know what to say. It chills me to think that the night before last I was ready to break it off with him. Had I not encountered the high priestess on my way back from the tree house, I would have definitely gone through with it. But now everything feels messy and nasty and all I want to do is smooth things over and go back to

275

how it was before. I should have listened to Felicity when she told me how lucky I am to have Hugh. She knows how hard it is to be alone. She can see my ungrateful behaviour for what it is. Suddenly I feel ashamed, as though everything with Tezz has been the whim of a spoilt child. Felicity only wants the best for me. If I can't trust my own judgement at this time, I have to trust hers.

'Come here!' I step forward and open my arms out to envelop Hugh. At first he is stiff and resistant, but gradually he begins to yield. 'I'm sorry you were so worried,' I tell him. 'But it's okay now. I'm back.'

He grips tightly to me. 'You've been behaving so out of character lately, I thought—'

'Shhhhhh,' I hush him, not wanting to hear any close-to-the-bone accusations. 'I know I've been distant and weird, but it's over. Everything is going to go back to normal. What do you say – shall we go to Manihi and have a fresh start?'

'You still want to go?' He sounds almost surprised.

'Of course.'

He looks plaintively at me. 'I love you so much, Amber. I don't know what I'd do without you.'

I feel a stabbing pang of guilt. How did I ever think I could hurt this man? Thank God I've been given a second chance to make things right.

'You know we've only got an hour before we leave?'

I didn't. I'd lost all track of time along with my rationale. 'Well then, I'd better get in the shower!' I pip.

'I'll order breakfast,' he brightens. 'What juice do you want – orange or grapefruit?'

'Pineapple.'

'Tea or coffee?'

'Hot chocolate.'

'Danish or brioche?'

I pause with my hand on the bathroom door. 'Croissants.'

'I love you!' he cheers, as though our standard breakfast banter has restored his faith in the relationship.

'I love you too!' There, I said it. It can be done.

Fortunately I'm in the bathroom with the door closed before he sees the expression on my face. But I see it reflected back at me in the mirror. I'm actually cringing.

How did this happen? I frown to myself. I do love this man, I'm sure I do. Maybe I haven't exactly been head over heels lately, but I certainly wasn't this confused back in Oxford.

There's a tap on the door. 'Darling?'

'Yes!' I still haven't made any progress towards the shower.

'Papaya or kiwi?'

'Watermelon if they've got it.'

'Okay!'

He sounds so upbeat, so ready to believe that everything will be all right. If I can just match his enthusiasm . . . First things first, though. I have to let go of Tezz. Instantly I feel a painful wrench deep within. But my mind is made up: I'm gonna wash that man right outta my hair.

I take hold of the shampoo and study the small print: 'effectively removes all daily grime, styling products and fixations with beautiful phantoms'. There, that should do it.

20

Though I appear to have sufficiently appeased Hugh, I feel more than a little self-conscious around Sandrine during the flight. She did see me at The Paradise Room. She knows it, I know it. Now I get the sense she's waiting for me to put my next foot wrong. Well, if I do I'm going to do it in style – she's insisted I trade my *New Woman* flip-flops for her pair of Gucci slingbacks . . .

I've just decided that Abigail will be the next beneficiary of these high-class hand-me-downs when we bump into land and Sandrine exclaims '*Mon dieu!*', raising her Dior shades to make sure she's not seeing things.

'What is it?' I lean across Hugh to the window and find myself equally stunned. '*That's it?*'

Manihi's airport makes Bora Bora's open-air emporium look like Terminal 3 at Heathrow. I say 'airport', but there is literally nothing more than a raffia shelter propped over a couple of benches. No check-in desk, no security, no conveyor belt, no luggage carousel, definitely no duty-free. Not even any staff, save the guy with the earmuffs who waves the plane on to land and then buggers off the second the job is done. Nevertheless, we are still greeted with lavishly ornate *lei* as the representative from the Manihi Pearl Beach Resort guides us over to the golf cart that serves as the shuttle service.

Remembering how my first *lei* prickled my neck, I decide to rest this one on my knee, only to watch it bound overboard as we bump over the first of many potholes. Manihi has a very different look from Bora Bora. The land seems pale and parched with barer, spikier branches and the route to the hotel is nothing more than a dirt track. Despite the lack of initial gloss, we've once again managed to score ourselves a pair of deluxe over-water bungalows. I'm not sure I'm ever going to be able to go back to having mere earthen foundations beneath me. There's just one catch – there is no air conditioning, not in the rooms or the bar or the restaurant or reception. The only relief to be had is to wade out into the surrounding water or stand neck-deep in the elegant sprawl of hotel pool.

Alternatively you can do as I do and lie very still on the top cover of the bed while your boyfriend unpacks and shouts descriptions from around the room.

'Hey, they've got a glass panel by the sink here so you can watch the fish while you're cleaning your teeth!' Hugh calls from the bathroom. 'Did you know this was the first hotel to have the over-water coffee tables?' He pokes his head around the screen door.

I turn my eyes but not my head in his direction. 'Really?'

'Nice little writing desk over here. Great uninterrupted view. So how do you like the blonde wood vibe compared with the dark teak of the Lagoon Resort? Quite a different feel, isn't it?'

He's right – even the exterior here with its golden bamboo batons is in stark contrast to the heavy panelled wood we left in Bora Bora. Captain versus Castaway, I label the contrasting styles, and then fall silent, channelling every ounce of concentration into convincing myself that I'm lying in a chest of ice. My body just wasn't designed to simmer at these temperatures. I was thinking of opting out of the visit to the Pearl Farm, but now I can't wait to get on the boat for the hour-long ride because at least I know that means sixty minutes' breeze.

En route I'm sufficiently cooled to risk a bit of Hugh's body heat, closing my eyes and leaning my head on his back as the wind binds my hair across my face like cotton on a bobbin. Tonight could be a good night to experiment with a little romance – new island, new resolve. My minor aberration with Tezz is in the past – nothing more than a seven-year-itch come three years early. I run my hand over his shoulders, kneading at some residual tension and telling myself this could be just the kick-start our relationship needs. If I can just stay awake long enough . . .

'We're here!' Hugh rouses me from my semi-slumber as we pull alongside a wooden platform where three women in matching hibiscus-print dresses greet us as if we're their favourite relatives. The pearl-buyer consultant explains to Hugh and Sandrine that we'll be sitting in on a talk along with a small group of cruise ship tourists, and then she will take them through to a private room to make their selections.

'Sounds great,' Hugh enthuses as we seat ourselves on the long wooden benches in the classroom-style hut on the water's edge.

The 'teacher' is a savvy Tahitian woman who finally illuminates me on why Tahitian pearls are uniquely black – it's all down to the colouring of a certain type of Polynesian oyster called the *Pinctada margaritifera* . . . But first we get a little history. In ancient times the oyster shells were carved and polished up and used to make fish hooks, lures and ceremonial jewellery. Later they proceeded to do a roaring trade in the button business, up until the sixties when mother-of-pearl was replaced with the more versatile plastic. It was then Polynesians turned to culturing oysters for pearl production.

Going back to basics, she then explains how pearls are created when a grain of sand or some kind of foreign body sneaks into the shell and, in a bid to isolate this, the oyster coats this nucleus in nacre (mother-of-pearl). The pearl farmer basically reproduces this process in a semi-controlled environment, beginning by attaching young 'seed' oysters to underwater rearing lines. He will then choose one healthy 'donor' oyster, remove a fragment of its mantle and divide this into fifty teeny-weeny particles to be reinserted one a piece into his collection of seed oysters.

'Everyone understanding so far?' Teacher asks.

'Yes!' we chorus.

'Next stage is grafting,' she continues. 'This is like going to the dentist for the oyster!' She shows us the contraption that holds the oyster shell in place and the forceps used to prise it open, and then passes around a sample with jaws ajar, exposing its gloopy-sinewy interior.

'See inside?' she asks me.

I nod, slightly repulsed now she's compared it to a throat.

'With a scalpel we make an incision into the gonad and insert this bead.' She holds up the piece of mantle, now honed to a perfect sphere. 'Then we return the oysters to the lagoon.'

'How long before the nucleus becomes a pearl?' a man with a New York drawl enquires.

'It takes about a year to grow a one millimetre-thick layer around it. The more layers the better. Big pearls, many many years. All the time we check on them and clean them . . .'

'Why do you check on them?' One thirtysomething Brit gets nosy. 'What are you looking for?'

'Well, this process is like surgery – not everyone survives,' she replies gravely.

'Oh?' We all lean in, gagging to hear the grizzly statistics.

'Thirty per cent will not survive the shock of the operation.'

'You mean they die?'

'They die,' she confirms. 'Another thirty per cent will reject the inserted nucleus. And of the forty per cent success stories, only around three per cent will produce perfect pearls.'

'Only three per cent?' The audience are aghast.

'So of the fifty pieces you insert,' the Brit does a quick bit of maths, 'you're lucky if you get one or two of the valuable round pearls from the harvest?'

'Yes,' she says, seemingly wondering how she ever wound up in this disappointment-riddled business.

I remember reading these statistics in Hugh's notes on the plane, but hearing them announced in this context, from the mouth of a woman whose livelihood depends on freak perfection, really brings home to me what a gamble this industry is.

As she hands round a series of polished shells, I study their ridges of oil-slick shimmer and I can see where the distinct hues originate. 'And you have no control over what the final colour will be?' I find myself asking as my thumb smooths the glossy finish.

'None,' she confirms. 'Every one is a surprise.'

I love that nature insists on having the final say. On the boat ride over I was afraid I'd drop off during the talk, but frankly I'm finding the whole thing fascinating. I just wish Sandrine would stop wittering on at Hugh during all the vital bits of information, I know she's trying to be helpful and talk it back to him in jewellery-buying terms, but couldn't she save it until after the woman is done?

'And so now I would like to invite you to enjoy our shop.' Teacher concludes her talk by directing us to a surprisingly chic boutique, one that wouldn't look out of place in Bond Street, were it not for the sand on the floor. Meanwhile Hugh and Sandrine get their cue to step behind the scenes.

'We shouldn't be more than half an hour,' Hugh whispers to me as he disappears into a room set up with high-tech viewing and drilling equipment.

'Okay,' I tell him, feeling my dad's eyes straining to see where the safe is located. 'No rush.'

I mooch around the shop, taking in all the wares, amazed by the range of designs on offer, many of which are supplemented by other gems. (Shame there are no black diamonds to really complement these pearls.) Some are gaudy, doing little more than justifying their price tag, others are starkly hip, set on geometric curves of silver. My favourite are the baroques strung on lengths of fraying silk. There are even some masculine offerings – simple cufflinks and pearls bound with leather thongs for the surfer dude in your life. But the pièce de résistance seems to be a necklace comprising thirty perfect-match pewter pearls, each the size of a Malteser. Judging by the dimensions and the obvious quality, I feel I may be looking at the Tahitian equivalent of the crown jewels.

'We call it Wilma,' the sales lady reveals as she joins me beside the display case. 'Like the Flintstones!'

I chuckle back at her. 'Is it actually for sale?'

She nods. 'It's one of the most expensive pieces in the islands.'

Oh Lord, don't tell Hugh or he'll feel compelled to own it.

'But with pearls, it is not always about the price.'

'How do you mean?' I ask, my interest secured.

'I always tell the women who ask my advice, don't ask which is the most precious, which is the best buy, tell me which one you love!'

I smile back at her, understanding fully.

'Of course there are factors to consider – perhaps which colour will best complement your wardrobe and your skin tone . . .' She studies me for a moment. 'With this green-brown in your eyes and the blonde of your hair, I would say pistachio for you,' she decides, holding out a sample of a gleaming creamy-green.

I take it in my hand and then study her in return. Black hair, dark navy eyes with a necklace of charcoal baubles. 'I would probably have put you with the blue,' I venture.

'Ah, yes,' she nods. 'I have a beautiful blue necklace at home, but I cannot wear it here.'

'Why not?' I'm curious.

'Customers see it and then they want one the same and we just can't get it for them.'

'Because . . .?'

'Blue are the most rare and the most expensive.'

'Not peacock?'

'Peacock are very popular, especially with the Japanese, but they are not the most exclusive.'

That's weird. Sandrine is still emphatic that the peacocks are premium. Maybe there's a difference in status or demand in France. I make a mental note to check that Hugh is aware of this possible discrepancy just as soon as Sandrine is out of earshot.

'One more question . . .' I turn to ask the sales lady whether it is true that there is one extra special giant pearl in existence, but she's moved on to a customer who actually intends to make a purchase.

We get back to the hotel in time to watch the sunset and the nightly parade of the fumigation tractor pumping out mosquito spray as it putters along the beach. Then we get a little spritzed ourselves on the restaurant terrace, this time courtesy of a dainty rain shower. Though we have to wipe a few specks of rain from our menu, no one makes a move to go inside – it's so warm and muggy, the light misting is most welcome. The only real problem is that I'm exhausted. Apparently a few hours' kip in a towel stand just doesn't cut it.

I order the prawn bisque, followed by the steamed swordfish with egg-plant millefeuille and citrus butter, and have my eye on the aniseed crème brûlée for dessert, but I couldn't tell you whether any of it lived up to its delicious promise because the wine I drank before I was served went straight to my head, and frankly I don't recall anything much between leaving the restaurant and waking up the next morning.

When I do stir, however, I notice something distinctly different about my person. There's a big peacock pearl ring on my wedding finger.

21

I reach out and jab the purple-green globe just to make sure I'm not hallucinating. It's real all right, shiny and smooth and lustrous. I rotate the band on my finger like a psychic hoping for some clue. I have absolutely no recollection of how it got here.

'Do you like it?' Hugh slides to my side and rests his chin on my shoulder.

My heart patters nervously. 'It's beautiful,' I murmur, wondering if I dare admit that I don't remember the presentation and thus risk hurting his feelings. Again.

'I put it on while you were asleep,' he tells me. 'I didn't want to mess up this time.'

I feel a pang of sympathy. Though I feel somewhat shanghaied, I know that after yesterday's wobble he's in search of some surety that I'm not going to slip away. I turn and cup his face and say my standard 'It's lovely, thank you'.

'I don't consider this a real engagement ring, obviously, but I thought it could act as a kind of Tahitian test run, see how it sits with you,' he explains, stroking my hair into the pillow. 'In fact, I was wondering . . . They do these ceremonies here. They're not legally binding or anything – you have to be resident for a month to have it count – but it sounds great . . . there's singing and flowers and canoes—'

'You mean a *wedding* ceremony?' My throat tightens.

'Well, I was thinking of it more as a fun romantic thing to do, you know . . . when are we going to get a chance to go native like this again?'

I open my mouth to speak.

'Unless you think it's cheesy?'

'No,' I find myself saying. 'Of course not, it sounds charming.'

Anyone would think he'd just presented me with a lace parasol and an invitation to take an afternoon stroll in a rose garden. Did I just agree to a mock wedding ceremony? He made it sound so casual, as if it was a toss-up between that and a snorkelling excursion.

And maybe it is no biggie. After all there are no documents, no relatives, no witnesses.

'Can it be just you and me?' I check. 'No Sandrine?'

'Of course.' He snuggles closer.

Well, if no one sees, then what harm can it do? Besides, this is a good deal for me – he's offering me the chance to play commitment without consequences. I should be counting my lucky stars.

'And if you feel comfortable with this, then when we get home . . .'

I feel a muffle of claustrophobia as he makes reference to our real life back in Oxford. For a second my mind flashes to Tezz and I am consumed with unfulfilled longing – for all the good it does me. He's not the one proposing, after all.

'So what do you say?'

It's very clear to me that if I say no, our relationship may never recover. He needs me to make this leap.

I take a deep breath and smile. 'Let's do it!'

'Fantastic!' he whoops. 'I'm going to pop off and make the arrangements.' He swings his legs out of bed, then leans back to kiss me, but suddenly jerks away as if the close proximity to my lips has alerted him to some innate resistance.

'What?' I gulp, guiltily.

'I guess I shouldn't really be looking at you before the ceremony!' he teases, stumbling towards the bathroom with his hand over his eyes.

I chuckle along, but already I'm wondering how I'm going to get through the eye-to-eye contact *during* the ceremony. Would it be acceptable to keep my sunglasses on during the vows? I mean, it is awfully bright out there . . .

'You want me to bring you breakfast, honey?' Hugh calls back to me before he exits.

'A chocolate croissant would be divine,' I tell him.

'You're divine!' he sings before closing the door.

Well, at least one of us is feeling good about this.

Jeez! *I have got to perk up!* This is the first of what sounds like a whole string of wedding days! I need to work on my attitude.

Shuffling up into a sitting position, I gaze out beyond the deck. In Bora Bora we overlooked majestic Mount Otemanu and the ragged greenery of the main island. Here there are just acres of glassy lagoon and seamless sky.

I feel as though I'm trying to look into my future, but I can't see what lies ahead.

There must be some clue out there . . . I get up and shunt the glass doors aside. It's hotter yet out here, but I'm thankful for the occasional breath of air as I lean over the knotty pine balustrade to study the fish. Maybe they want some breakfast too? I crumble a few pieces of baguette into the water, quickly finding myself absorbed in a new game – pick a favourite fish and try to target him. I opt for the one stray clown fish amid the indistinct masses of grey mullet, but apparently this little Nemo is blind, stupid or has an eating disorder because he actually seems to be avoiding the bread – while all the others dart straight for each morsel, he gets confused and shoots off in the other direction. Maybe he's not hungry. Maybe he just came to party. Maybe he's like me and doesn't want what everyone else thinks he should want?

I decide to try an alternative strategy – scattering a big handful over yonder where the marauding masses scrap and bustle and head-butt, I lop a separate piece directly before his mouth. But before he can open and inhale, a maverick high-speed fly-by snaps up the bread for himself. There's only one thing for it. I'm going to have to get in amongst them.

I slip on my jelly shoes and wade in, intending to cast the crumbs right at their expectant mouths. Woah! I didn't think they'd get so close to me! These chaps are infinitely more tame – and abundant – than their relatives on Bora Bora. Within seconds I have a hundred or so foot-long fish swarming around me. I blink in astonishment as they fall into formation, swimming in a rapid anticlockwise circle just a few inches from my waist. Half freaked out, half enchanted, I laugh out loud – I feel like I'm rotating a giant mullet hula hoop! Preparing to shred the bread I hold my hands up in the air, but this only seems to draw them in closer – they are now swimming in a four-deep band around my midriff.

I look up to see if anyone else can see this bizarre phenomenon taking place and spy Sandrine out on her deck, breakfasting with a dark-haired man. Blimey! She didn't waste any time! Even on a remote island she can find a stranger to seduce. I'm surprised she's wearing her glasses, though. They definitely age her, and I thought she only sported them for work. But then I see her hold something up to the light and carefully study it. Is this a business meeting? I jump suddenly as I feel the slimy sensation of a fish against my hand. While I was distracted, my right arm had lowered into the water and now all the fish are ram-raiding the baguette, clambering over each other and rising out of the water in a bid to get a bite. For a moment I dare myself to hold my hand steady to see if a fish will suck the ring from my finger and give me a sign that I need to cancel this wedding *now*, but then I see a big ugly brown and white speckled fella coming right for me with a menacingly gaping gob, and I can't help but squeal and slosh back to the steps and up on to the deck.

When I look up again Sandrine and her guest are gone. Weird.

As for the ring on my finger . . . still very much there. It's ironic: my parents went to such lengths to acquire jewellery, and I seem so keen on repelling it.

'Groom service!' Hugh calls ahead of entering the room, chortling at his own joke as he sets down the croissant on the side, all the while dutifully averting his eyes. 'They can do the ceremony in an hour,' he tells the floorboards, 'if that's enough time for you to get ready?'

Ready? I hadn't really thought this through. Exactly what vision am I supposed to be conjuring up?

'One of the staff ladies is going to help you dress.' Hugh is one step ahead of me. 'If you shower and do your make-up as you wish, she'll do the rest.'

'The rest?'

'You'll see.'

'W-what about you?' I falter.

'I'll get cleaned up and changed over at the main building. Add a little suspense to proceedings!'

Like I need any more tension.

'Okay,' I squeak.

He's gone before I can (a) quiz him over Sandrine's visitor and (b) request the Tahitian translation for 'I do'. Or rather, in my case, 'Do I?'

For a moment I stand still, bewildered. Most girls have a year or so to build up to their wedding day; I've been allotted an hour. I feel like I haven't done even basic homework on this. Don't most girls picture themselves in fantasy wedding dresses from the age of ten? For me there was only ever one woman and one dress – my mother in form-fitting lace. Pictures of her and my father outside a little church in Thame took pride of place in every room of the house. She said she'd never felt more beautiful than she did that day, gleaming with freshly pilfered pearls. She really suited the authentic Sixties styling – even her veil looked like it had been back-combed. I wonder what she'd say if she could see me now? Most likely, 'A sheet? You're getting married in a *sheet?*'

It's actually a *pareu*, mother. I raise my eyes heavenward, smoothing the length of coconut-white cotton patterned with vanilla-cream hibiscus flowers. Well, I guess every island visitor succumbs sooner or later. Vaihere allows me to retain my bra while she carefully folds and drapes the fabric, creating a cowl neck-effect top with a knee-length skirt.

'Now . . .' She makes a magician's flourish.

I take it she means me to remove my upper

undergarment. I do so cautiously, concerned that with one false move the whole thing, which to me feels like little more than an outsize napkin, could end up heaped over my bare feet.

'Pretty!' Vaihere encourages as she sets a three-tiered crown of greeny-ivory tiare flowers on my head.

Beneath it, my hair is barely dry from the shower and sitting in natural waves. Again, definitely not what my mother had in mind. I'd lost count of the number of times she would come home from work and say, 'Now this is how I'm going to do your hair on your wedding day.' And dinner would get sidelined as I sat there, rumbly-tummed, letting her pin and primp and coil some fancy new experiment until I made the women on *Come Dancing* look like they favoured the natural look.

But I did enjoy the spin around the floor once she was done.

Once again my mind strays to Tezz. I wonder if I'll ever find out what his intentions were? Even though I know I'm doing the right thing by Hugh, I'm finding it so hard to consider Tezz 'past' when he's still so very present in my heart.

'Don't look so sad!' Vaihere places a hand on my arm. 'This is happy day!'

My eyes well up.

'Happy! Happy!' she sings.

'Happy! Happy!' I quaver, trying to convince myself.

Vaihere looks concerned. 'He is good man, your husband?'

I wish she'd stop calling him that. 'The best,' I assure her.

'Okay, then we go . . .' she slowly leads me to the door.

I give a final glance back at the lagoon. If it looked like there was anything out there to swim to I'd probably go, but as it is, it's just a big blank. The only thing I can do right now is cling to the shoreline. And my sure thing – Hugh.

I follow Vaihere to a private curve of beach where a trio of musicians squat in the sand – two strumming ukuleles, the other striking a chunk of hollowed-out tree trunk with a stick. Quite a contrast to the traditional wedding band back home. Not sure I'd like to see most of those pasty individuals get their man-boobs out during the ceremony, but these guys look and sound great.

'Little bit nervous?' Vaihere continues to check on me.

'Little bit,' I confess, sneaking a glance at the Tahitian priest standing solemnly by.

I look down at my feet and then around at the pillar-like palm trees. I guess in this culture it's the bride who waits at the altar for the groom. I don't mind; it gives me time to come up with one positive aspect to this ceremony – that there's no expectation to have parents present. Not that I wouldn't give my right arm to have my mum and dad here on earth for one more day, but I can certainly live without Hugh's. His mother in particular wouldn't stand for this ceremony. It's like she can see what no one else can see – that I'm not right for her son. Hugh says he doesn't care what she thinks, but perhaps he should. I suspect she knows a thing or two about loveless marriages.

'Here he comes!' Vaihere points out across the lagoon to a white-painted outrigger canoe, its distinctive balancing bar bound with spiky palm fronds and floral adornments and Hugh sat on board wearing a crown of tiare flowers. He whistles and waves as he strides ashore with what looks like a bathroom towel tied around his waist.

As he gets closer I see he's actually sporting matching fabric to my dress. Again, not something you'd find back home – few grooms can carry off a tuxedo made of ivory organza.

Do it for him! I force myself to smile, numbing all opposing emotions as he takes his position opposite me. For four years he's given me a soft place to fall. Never once so much as left a stray hair in the soap.

He smiles back at me, but for the first time I can see something other than love in his eyes. I could be imagining it, but to me he looks anxious, like he needs to nail this procedure so he doesn't have to worry about me leaving him any more.

Things get positively trippy as the priest begins intoning ancient sacred rights with strange savage-sounding incantations. I pray that we're not angering

298

any Tiki gods by going through with this for all the wrong reasons and hold my breath until the blessing is complete and the priest motions for us to exchange the pair of extra-long tiare *leis* Vaihere is holding out to us. I go first, garlanding Hugh and setting the flowers neatly to rest on his shoulders. He then raises the loop above my head, but as he lowers it past my ears he seems to be distracted by my eyes and as he lets go the loop falls straight over my shoulders, brushes past my hips and crumples on to the sand by my feet. I step back to try and retrieve it, inadvertently crushing a section of the dainty blooms.

'Oh no!'

'Here, let me help!' Hugh tries to pick it up at the same time as me and the whole thing comes apart in our hands.

I see Vaihere exchanging a concerned look with the priest, but he glosses over the fiasco by baptising us with Tahitian names and then wrapping us up in a *tifaifai*, a handmade wedding quilt – a lovely symbolic touch were it not for the 100-degree heat.

'Sorry about the *lei*,' I muffle into his neck.

'Don't worry, you can share mine,' he says, binding me closer still as he hooks it over my head.

There is no avoiding it any longer: we kiss . . .

But instead of releasing reciprocal joy, I am keenly aware that I am still holding back. For whatever reason, some vital part of me will not submit to this union.

'Shame we've got a flight to catch,' Hugh sighs,

pulling my hips into his groin. 'I'd like nothing better than to go back to the room and have a conjugal visit.'

My heart sinks like a stone. It's not a great realisation to come to on your wedding day, but I have to be honest with myself: I'm not in love with this man and I never want to have sex with him again.

22

We arrive back at the Bora Bora Lagoon Resort in time for dinner.

'Are you sure you don't mind Sandrine joining us?' Hugh asks again. 'I mean, this is our wedding day . . .'

'No, no, of course not,' I assure him as we await her pleasure in the hotel bar. I had originally instigated the invitation thinking Felicity would be joining us (I'm still keen to get her take on the French fox), but instead Flossie elected to stay aboard *Windstar* for their deck Bar B-Q, as for once Cousin Brian will be free to mingle rather than standing behind a podium match-making diners with tables.

'It's the only night I get to sit down and eat with him. Do you mind?'

'No, no,' I assured her, feigning a carefree attitude when we spoke on the phone.

'We can have a proper catch-up tomorrow,' she told me. 'I'm hoping to have some news first thing. That know-it-all chap thinks he's got a lead on Airport Guy!'

'Oh wow! That's so exciting!'

'I know, can't wait!' Then her voice lowered conspiratorially, 'Dare I ask about Tezz and Operation Beach Bunker?'

'You may, but I have nothing to report – I fell asleep in the towel stand and I'm none the wiser.'

'Oh, Amber!'

'Not to worry,' I chirrup falsely. 'You have a good night and I'll see you tomorrow.' No point in burdening her with the whole Hugh/wedding saga now – she deserves a night off from my emotional dramas. Besides, I think I'm going to have to start tuning into my own feelings instead of relying on her guidance if I'm going to find a way through this. After all, I took her premier advice and 'chose' Hugh, but regrettably that's just not working for me.

I look at him sipping his pre-dinner cocktail, oblivious to all my inner angst. There was a time when he was my world, but I no longer feel connected to that life. It seems strange to me that he can still consider me so right for him when 'we' feels so wrong to me. Our nuptials have really rammed home that I am not a fully functioning member of this relationship, but I don't quite know what to do with the information. I know now that I don't want the separate bedroom love-style his parents have, but it seems that if I stay with him that's where we're headed. But what's the alternative? More than a fear of being alone, it seems that I simply don't know how *not* to be with Hugh.

Aside from all the practicalities of the house and our entwined lives, it's just so sad. I want so much for him to be happy. If only a painless transition could be made. Part of me wishes another woman would walk up and offer to love him right so I could release him into her care.

'Ah, here she is now.' Hugh turns to greet Sandrine.

How he is able to stop his jaw dropping is a miracle to me. Ms Volereux is barely wearing a black drape of fabric, the kind of design that demands much contemplation on how it is staying put, and exactly what might be revealed should the wearer either lean forwards or turn sideways-on.

'*Bonsoir*!' She air-kisses us both.

I place my hands behind my back as I lean towards her for fear of hooking a fold of fabric and unveiling her. Not that she'd probably mind. She's so confident, she'd go to dinner wearing nothing but a strategically-placed string of black pearls.

'Where are you going, sweetie?' Hugh calls me back as I turn to lead the way to the restaurant, making a mental note to steer clear of the brick papillote fish this time.

'The dining room's this way.' I point down the steps to my left.

'Oh, we're not eating here,' he breezes. 'Hiro insisted we try this new place – apparently the desserts are out of this world.'

Sandrine glances at her watch. 'I'm afraid we've just missed the shuttle to the mainland, *cherie*.'

303

'I can't wait another hour to eat,' I confess, giving Hugh an apologetic look.

'No need,' Hugh chirrups. 'This place is walking distance.'

Sandrine and I freeze. This can only mean one thing.

'Follow me to The Paradise Room,' Hugh flourishes, oblivious.

'They do food there?' Sandrine and I query in unison.

'You've heard of it?' He looks back at us, intrigued.

Sandrine gives a nonchalant 'of course – I've heard of everything!' shrug, while I find myself saying, 'I thought it was just a bar.'

I'm waiting for Hugh to make the connection – that The Paradise Room is where Sandrine saw me on late-night walkabout – but instead he rattles on, 'Restaurant until 10 p.m. then a bar till 2 a.m. They've even got a live act there – Desirable something. They're meant to be great!'

Nothing from Sandrine. Nothing from me. What does her silence mean? Could she too have something to hide? If she does, she's not nearly as accountable as me. Oh God, this is a disaster! Why wasn't I more honest with Hugh while I still had Felicity as an alibi?

As we proceed along the path that I have previously staggered, skipped and sprinted along, all the feelings I've been trying to repress get stirred up again. I can't even imagine what effect it's going to have on me to see

Tezz again, especially with my current company. If only Hugh and Sandrine were the couple and I was free to find out if our connection was real. Somehow I've convinced myself that the high priestess isn't really a factor any more yet, as we pass the Tiki torches and enter the papaya-glow of the room, she is the first person that I see.

Positioned on a prime table adjacent to the front of the stage she looks like the cat that got the cream. I like to think she won't recognise me – it was dark, and she only saw me fleetingly. But then I realise she's not the only femme fatale I have to worry about. What if Fantasia bounds over and lets slip that I've been here multiple times? How on earth would I explain that to Hugh?

And while we're at it, what exactly will I say if either Tony or Tezz acknowledge that we've met before?

'Oh yeah, this is some guy I once doused in coconut milk and his hooker-obsessed best friend.'

All of a sudden I find myself wishing I'd stayed in the room and dined on leftover French bread. I'm sure the fish could have done without for one night . . .

'Hey, this place looks cool!' Hugh enthuses as we're led through to a corner table.

I consider 'oo-ing' and 'aahh-ing' over the spiral bar and all the intricate shell-detailing but feel it's only a matter of time before I'm exposed as a regular, so decide to keep my mouth shut. No sign of Fantasia – but then she probably just hosts the nightclub portion of the evening – and no Tony or Tezz. Thank God. Probably limbering up backstage. I smile as I picture Tony tripping over every available prop while Tezz busily polishes his tap shoes. In my mind I see him stepping out on stage and his face lighting up as he spies me in the audience. I hear the music swell and then crumple and cringe at my foolish fantasy: much as I might wish it, I have to accept the fact that Tezz is not going to stride up to me and growl, 'No one puts Amber in the corner.'

'After you.' Hugh steps back to allow Sandrine to slide in first, then bids me do the same.

'No, you go – girl-boy-girl!' I insist.

'Well, aren't I going to be the most envied man in the room,' he grins, puffing up as he takes his position between us.

'You men and your threesome fantasies,' Sandrine tweaks his cheek between her long copper nails.

There's still hope – *they* could be the couple, I could be the gooseberry! It's too hot for hand-holding anyway, so if I just adjust my body language so that all my pointy bits are facing in the opposite direction to Hugh . . . I extend my legs away from the table, practically tripping up the waitress in the process.

'Oh, sorry!' I scrabble back to the confines of the table feeling like I just got a little smack for my underhand behaviour.

'So what do you fancy, darling?' Hugh peers over at my menu.

'Um, I'm really not that hungry,' I mumble, grip-

306

ping my sickened tum. I really am starting to feel extremely anxious.

'What?' he hoots. 'Two minutes ago you were demanding instant and immediate sustenance! What about the coconut-crusted sea bass with wasabi and sour cream mashed potatoes and spicy asparagus. Doesn't that sound good?'

'Yes, it does.' I go for the easy option and take his suggestion.

'Or the New Zealand lamb chops,' he salivates. 'We may never have the chance to get them this fresh again!'

'Good idea.'

'You don't have a preference?' Now he looks concerned. 'You know I rely on you for guidance in these matters.'

'Why don't we get one of each and share,' I suggest, forcing a smile and adding, 'You order for me.' Already I've forgotten what the proposed choices were.

'Are you not feeling well?' Hugh frowns, getting ever more cloying. 'Can I get you some iced Perrier, or maybe blow on your neck?'

'I am a bit hot!' I jump to my feet. 'I think I'll go and splash my face with water.'

'Are you taking the menu with you?' Hugh laughs, reaching to retrieve it from my hands.

'I think I'll keep it as a fan,' I explain, giving a demonstrative waft. It'll also make an excellent facial shield should I encounter any high priestesses en route.

Back in my familiar cubicle, I pull at the toilet roll, wrap my hand in paper and recall my journey to the tree house and the beautiful kiss I found there. Whatever Tezz's situation, I felt what I felt – an amazing sense of dreaming and waking in the same moment – and I can't unfeel that. Now that I know I have the potential to feel that way, I don't think I can settle for anything less. I just hope I don't have to wait another thirty-two years until I feel it again.

I must have been lost in thought longer than I realise, because when I return to the table our food is being set in place.

The meal is extraordinary – utterly melt-in-your-mouth fish with an inventive array of accompanying textures and tangs, keeping our taste buds on their toes at every bite. Hugh is in raptures; so much so that he asks the waiter if we might compliment the chef in person?

The waiter looks confused until Sandrine translates into French. He has us wait a moment and then guides Hugh and me through to the kitchen.

'Monsieur Perry?' The waiter coughs discreetly.

'*Oui?*' The chef turns to face us, wielding a butcher's cleaver.

'Tony!' I gasp, shocked into incriminating myself by the size of his knife.

His face, as ever, is unreadable, but Hugh's eyes are busily ping-ponging between us. 'Do you two—?'

'Know each other? No, no!' I gabble. 'I just . . . um,

on the menu it said Chef Tony Perry. And here he is –
Tony!'

Is that a flicker of I-know-your-game I see in Tony's
eyes? He's got to be wondering why on earth I'm
pretending we've never met before.

'The puréed potatoes were so creamy and
delicious!' I blather, trying to move the conversation
on. 'How do you get them so smooth?'

'Crank them through a food mill then apply the
immersion blender,' he says quietly.

'Really? Really.' I nod overly vigorously. 'So, how
long have you been chefing for?' I rattle on.

'Well, obviously it's not my first career—'

'Obviously,' I nod.

'Obviously?' Hugh is confused.

'I'm a performer,' he explains to Hugh. 'Singer,
dancer—'

'So you're part of the act here too?'

'Me and my partner Tezz . . .'

'Doesn't happen to be your sous-chef, does he?'
Hugh joshes.

'No, no. Tezz's idea of fine cuisine is Papa John's
pizza.' He rolls his eyes.

Hugh laughs along, then says, 'Well, I really have to
congratulate you on the food tonight, Tony. It's been
the perfect meal to complement a very special day.' He
looks dreamily at me.

'Every day is special in Bora Bora!' I shrill,
desperate to move on. 'We really should let you get
back to work,' I note as an assistant appears and alerts

309

Tony to the fact that the dessert orders are starting to come through.

'Thank you for your kind words.' Tony dips his head as we turn to leave.

'And you for your discretion,' I want to respond.

'Well, that's impressive,' Hugh coos as we step back into the main restaurant. 'You don't get too many dancing chefs, do you? Bet he does a great Mashed Potato. *Get it?*'

As we turn towards our table I spot Fantasia leaning over talking to Sandrine and nearly turn round and slam back into the flapping kitchen doors.

'Um! Shall we get a quick breath of fresh air before dessert?' I say quickly, manhandling Hugh out on to the terrace.

'I think you'll find it's the same air inside and out,' Hugh observes. 'Not overly keen on windows here, are they?'

'No,' I say, profoundly on edge. Could this day get any more stressful?

Away from the hustle of the restaurant the night seems all too quiet – the kind of quiet that makes people say what's on their mind.

'So. Amber. How's married life treating you?' Hugh tries to play off the question as a joke, but I know he's desperate to hear whether I'm ready to say, 'I do' for real.

Is this the time for me to speak the truth? To tell him how I'm really feeling? I know there's never a good time for these things, but this is the happiest I've seen him all trip, albeit a little flushed and tipsy. Can I really bring myself to spoil his night? Surely it can wait until tomorrow?

He lifts my chin, giving me a sympathetic look I don't deserve. 'It was a mistake bringing you here, wasn't it?'

I open my mouth to protest, but he has more to say.

'If I'd just popped the question when you were pottering around the kitchen one evening you probably would have said yes, no worries.'

He's right. I probably wouldn't have given it any thought. The offer would have been 'More of the same but legal, darling?' and not knowing much else, I would most likely have said, 'Lovely, book the church and I'll be there. And by the way, could you take the melon out of the fridge, it should be sufficiently chilled by now.'

'You know, if you're tired we could go back to the room?' Hugh slips a comforting arm around my waist.

There it is – the get-out clause. No need to put myself in a situation where both he and Tezz are in the same room. But then I glance back through the window and catch a glimpse of Tezz making his way to the stage, and even though I know I'm making it worse for myself, I can't bring myself to leave without seeing him one more time.

'And miss trying the infamous dessert – are you kidding?'

'Adda girl!' Hugh cheers, clearly happy to stay. 'And

we should really see this fellow Tony jump out of the frying pan and on to the dance floor!'

I do my best to chuckle along with him as we return to our table.

The room is now dark with a single spotlight trained on the stage.

My heart begins to tremor as the musicians take their position. I close my eyes and sink deep into the booth.

Let the show begin . . .

23

Eyes still closed, I prepare my face to react as if I'm seeing the show for the first time. If they stomp in on stilts I'm going to reel back and gasp, 'No way!' If they rollerblade into position I'm going to take a few seconds to twig the source of their fluid movement and then clap along with Hugh as they spin on the spot. However, if they make a pelvic advance in the 'Freak Like Me' feathers and leather, I cannot be held responsible for my actions.

Suddenly the drums begin to pound and my eyes flash open. It's an unfamiliar beat – a frenzied staccato that gets progressively more rhythmic as one by one four men charge the stage: Tony, then Tezz, then two native Tahitians. Each wears a band of shiny green leaves roped above both biceps and below each knee and a patterned loincloth with a traditional design that puts me in mind of a brown and white 1970s kitchen tile.

Tezz and his Tahitian counterpart take a wooden stick to a carved trunk and reinforce the beat as Tony and the other fella rattle their knees together and expel primitive howls. Even with my eyes trained on Tezz I can't help but notice the naked, perfectly-rounded buttocks of the Tahitian men, particularly the one inked with a spherical pattern that could double as an astrological chart.

Then, just when I think I might be palpitated into a trance, the drumming stops as abruptly as it started and a new more seductive rhythm begins, followed by a distinctive rustling which is gradually amplified as Malia, Lexi and two beautiful dashboard hulas swish on in ankle-length red grass skirts with coconut bras and flower garlands in their hair. Visions, all four of them. Slowly hips rock right to left, right to left, reminding me of the motion of the mezzaluna I use for chopping herbs. Each switch begins with a graceful swoop and concludes with a precision snap. As the music gathers pace they go double-time then triple-time until perspiration glistens on their backs. There can't be a man in the audience who's not wishing his wife could do the same.

'You like these moves?' Tezz takes centre-stage to address the audience.

'Yeah!' everyone hollers back with wild abandon.

'You wanna try them?'

The audience is suddenly self-conscious, barely emitting a whimper, with the exception of three guys and two gals who've charged the stage and are already shaking everything they've got.

'Come on, we need two more ladies and one more man,' Tezz cajoles.

Cue much deliberate avoidance of eye contact, especially from our table, which fits the bill exactly. Having said that, I think Hugh could be persuaded, if his work Christmas parties are anything to go by. As for Sandrine, if she did get up there in her drapey dress they'd have to slap a couple of coconuts on her just to keep the show from going X-rated with her first shimmy.

'Don't make us come and get you!' Tezz threatens in vain. Still no volunteers. 'Okay – press gang!' He jumps off the stage, enlisting Malia and Lexi on his recruitment drive while Tony tries to control the over-zealous new additions to his dance troupe.

'He's coming right for us!' Hugh gasps, half excited.

Oh God! Where's that darn menu when you need it? I try to pull my hair over my face like Cousin It but it's too late – I've been spotted.

'My lady?' Tezz says the magic words as he extends his hand.

Once again I'm powerless to resist. My fingers interlock with his like a perfect-fit puzzle and he smiles right into my soul as he raises me to his level. It's only when I'm halfway to the stage that I turn back to direct a sheepish look at Hugh. But he's not there. That'll be because Malia has nabbed him and he's currently on the other side of the stage having grass bands attached to his knees.

'*Lei*?' Tezz places the second garland of the day over my head, standing unnecessarily close as he adjusts the flowers around the back of my neck and then carefully settles the blooms over my chest. Good grief, if my hips could shimmy at the speed of my heart I'd probably acquire Tahitian citizenship on the spot.

My eyes furtively flit to where the high priestess was sat but I find her chair empty, giving me the freedom I need to savour this moment. Even though I try to dismiss him as a player, Tezz's presence thrills me still.

'No movement in the upper body,' he instructs by placing his hands firmly on my hip bones, 'just your hips. Take little steps on the spot – right, left, right, left, less of a march – raise up on your toes, that's right,' he encourages. 'Feel the rock?'

I most certainly do.

Tezz nods to the musicians to take it up a notch. We all do our best to keep up – me and the other three girls doing our straight-backed hippy-hippy-shake while the boys hunch over and get all knock-kneed, Hugh in particular looking like he could do with a flat cap and couple of spoons to play on his thigh. Then, just when I think I might be in danger of dislocating my hips and watching them dance off into the night, Tezz raises his hand and the music stops.

It's over.

'Woohooo!' The audience raves at the visual fiasco, whistling and cheering as we are led to the side of the stage.

I'm just thinking that it was actually worth the

humiliation to have Tezz's hand on the small of my back as he guides me to the steps when my feet get snatched from under me and I find myself hoiked up into Hugh's arms.

'Darling, you were great!' he gushes, smearing my face with a sweaty kiss and inadvertently pinching the skin under my knee as he clutches me tight to him.

I try to get back to my feet but his grip is ferocious. 'Pardon me, newly-weds coming through!' he hollers, clearly buzzed from being on stage and seemingly hell-bent on making as much of an exhibition of us as possible as he parades the length of the room.

By the time we get back to our seat I'm in the foetal position, pretty much wishing I'd never been born.

'What a fun night! Let's have another drink!' He gesticulates at the waitress as he sets me down.

I can't bear to look up and yet I want to know if this has provoked any kind of reaction in Tezz. From what I can tell in my munched-up, mortified state, he's too busy singing to be displaying any kind of reaction. I listen for a moment. If I'm not mistaken they're doing a hip-hop version of 'There's Nothing Like A Dame!' (What would Gilly make of that!)

Warily I raise my gaze. The guys are in full boister-ous serenade, in raptures over the girls' womanly charms. Either he doesn't care about what he just saw or he's a lifetime subscriber to The Show Must Go On. I just can't tell which.

I'm expecting the girls to twitter back some feminine-flirty ditty, but instead they start belting out

317

Anastacia's 'Not That Kind of Girl', and the boys slink to the back of the stage, advances thwarted. I know Tezz has the acting gene, but isn't he looking a little too sad? All the playful theatrics seem to be gone from his face. I look over at Tony to see if he's going for the same expression. Nope, just a neutral mask. And then I catch the two of them exchanging a look. If I was to guess the message, it's 'I told you' from Tony. Could I be reading too much into this? But then Tezz turns his troubled eyes to me and I feel my face burn with shame.

'Be Careful With My Heart . . .' The boys step forward to open the next song, sidling up behind the girls.

'Who sang this again?' Hugh asks, swaying from side to side as their voices parlay back and forth, bugging me with every bump into my shoulder.

'Madonna and Ricky Martin,' I reply without looking at him.

I feel heavy with remorse. Even if Tezz was available to me I've well and truly blown it now. I try to think how I could have played things differently, but realise the situation was hopeless from the beginning. How were we ever going to get the chance to get close? I came here with another man.

And then Tezz begins to sing a new song:

> I'm seeing things I can't believe
> I look at you and I can't breathe
> I wanna know what lies beneath
> Tell me the truth before you leave

318

I blink at him, startled, again feeling like he's communicating directly with me.

'What's this?' Hugh frowns, frustrated that he can't tap along.

'I don't know.' I swallow hard.

'Maybe we'll recognise the chorus . . .' Hugh listens closer.

'Was it all in my mind?' Tezz sings.

'Wishing,' the girls husk.

'Was it all in my head?'

'Hoping,' they coo.

'Am I really so blind?'

'Denying,' they breathe.

'I guess I misread.'

I slump into my seat, feeling awful. I've played with two men's affections and I'm hurting both of them.

Tezz lulls himself into a state of acceptance, soothed by the piano solo, and then finally concludes:

> If this is all it's meant to be
> Me looking at you, you looking at me
> Then that's okay, I'll treasure each glance
> But in my heart we'll dance and dance

I nearly pass out with the bittersweet agony of it all. When he lays his palm on his chest and closes his eyes, I feel like I know where he's gone because he's taken me with him – back to that first private encounter on the beach.

Or is my mind playing tricks? I give my drink an

accusatory stare. Is this your doing, making me think he's creating lyrics just to speak to me? The ice cubes jiggle indignantly. *You're the one doing the drinking!*, they seem to say. Maybe I should stop. It's making me want Tezz more, making me want to risk everything to be with him again.

'The chef guy, what was his name again?'

'Tony,' both Sandrine and I chorus.

'Remarkable!' He shakes his head in awe.

'What about the girls – they're really good aren't they?' I try and divert him before he starts critiquing Tezz. I don't want those two worlds colliding.

'They're fantastic, but not as pretty as you!' He lops a sloppy arm around me, feeling so clumsy and burdensome after Tezz's deft touch. 'Hey, there's Tony! I'm going to tell him what a great show he put on! I love this place!'

I watch as he lunges over in Tony's direction, now on a break, leaving Tezz solo on stage.

But not for long . . .

'We have a special guest here tonight,' Tezz announces, looking adoringly down at the high priestess. 'Joining me on stage now is Tiara.' He reaches out a hand to her and draws her to his side.

'Tiara? As in the diamanté headband?' Sandrine frowns.

'That's what it sounded like,' I shrug, miserable as they start moving to Janet Jackson's obscenely sexy 'All Nite (Don't Stop)'. Her voice, so husky I want to nick-name her the hoarse-whisperer, taunts me with words like 'X-rated' and 'stimulated' as their hips move in explicit synchronicity.

'She's hot!' Sandrine coos.

How did I ever think I could compare to that? My body simply doesn't slink and pop that way. With burgeoning nausea I watch the pair of them work the song to a breathless climax. And then their heads rock together and they consume each other in a hungry embrace.

I must have drunk too much because I only just make it to the bathroom in time before I throw up. For a good five minutes I slump beside the toilet, spitting out the poison and letting hot tears stream down my face. I feel like he did that just to spite me – *so you think you can wreck me by producing a husband? Well, check this out!* Okay, so I get it – Tezz is categorically with Tiara. There's nothing between us; all hope is vanquished.

When I emerge, still visibly shaken and dishevelled, Hugh is, of course, first to my side, still with Tony in tow. 'Sandrine said you didn't look well.' He smooths my hair back from my face, forgetting that I've still got a sore bump and generally making me feel worse. 'I think we'd better get you home.'

This time I'm more than ready to leave. I turn to bid Tony a feeble goodnight, but his eyes are averted, closely watching Tezz and Tiara.

'Sandrine! Over here!' Hugh is momentarily distracted as he waves over to our abandoned dinner companion, thus giving Tony the chance to whisper something to me.

'Don't hurt him any more than you already have,' he says simply.

'Him who?' I ask, my mouth working faster than my brain.

'Well, I guess that's up to you now,' he shrugs, before disappearing into the night.

24

'Sweetie. *Sweetie?*'

'Huh?'

I'm aware that Hugh is trying to communicate something to me. I just can't figure out what.

'Amber?' he persists, lightly jostling my shoulder.

'What is it?' I ask, surprised at how gravelly my voice is. And how raw and ragged my heart feels.

'I just wanted to make sure you're okay before I leave.'

'Where you going?' I'm still disorientated.

'To work,' he smiles. 'Another day, another motu. They're actually putting on a fashion show for us today, showing off some of the new designs . . .'

'Mmm,' is the best response I can muster.

'Well, I'd better get going. As long as you're feeling all right?'

'Yup!' Why is he fussing like this?

'Not feeling sick any more?'

Sick? For a moment I don't know what he's talking about, but then my memory returns to me, along with a pervasive sense of sadness. 'I'm fine,' I lie, wanting him to leave so I can fully submerge myself in misery.

'Good, glad you're feeling better. So don't forget you're due at the kitchen at 11 a.m.'

I want to say 'Yup!' again and get the conversation over with, but I have no idea what kitchen he's talking about.

'The cooking class?' he prompts. 'With Tony?'

'Tony?' I startle myself upright.

'The chef from last night,' Hugh tuts as if my problem is purely memory-related. 'See how you feel, but it's all arranged, he's expecting you. Said he'd teach you how to make the coconut-crusted sea bass so you can do it for me back home.'

Now I do feel queasy. Those two obviously had quite a chat last night, and you can bet they discussed more than my culinary skills. I think back to Tony's 'Don't hurt him any more than you already have!' warning and then picture the wide range of kitchen utensils that could double as implements of torture – the cheese grater, the meat mallet, the flame-thrower that burns the sugar on a crème brûlée, but none so terrifying as a disapproving glare from the master-chef himself. Why on earth would I want to put myself through that?

I close my eyes and shrink into the pillow.

'That's right, you just go back to sleep for an hour.'

324

Hugh smooches my brow with a tad too much saliva. 'I'll see you later. Might even have a little treat for you . . .'

Oh no. No more treats. *Please!*

Once Hugh is gone, I drag myself and the telephone out on to the balcony and flump on to the sun-lounger. As I dial Felicity, I realise there is no *Windstar* on the horizon today. I peer around the lagoon as I wait to connect, curious as to where they may have relocated to, and then walk the phone back inside so I can answer the knock at the door. It's a message from Felicity.

Tried calling but you're engaged.

I look at the phone, roll my eyes and set the receiver down.

Sailed last night for Huahine. Will be back by 6 p.m. Join us on board for dinner tonight. Hugh and Sandrine welcome. Love you!

I sit down on the corner of the bed feeling thoroughly bereft. So today it's just me, alone with my thoughts. I can't think of anything more depressing.

I'm tempted to pull the covers back over my head and try to sleep the anguish away, but having done such a thorough job emptying my stomach last night, I decide I need a little breakfast first.

'Orange juice, caffé latte, croissant and fruit plate.' Room Service repeats my order back at me.

'Actually, maybe not the orange juice.' I change my

mind, deciding it might be a little too acidic. 'How about mango?'

'You want the special?'

I don't know how special a mango can be, but I decide to give it a go.

'Serving just one person?'

'Just one,' I confirm.

Is this what my life is going to be like if I do succeed in prising myself away from Hugh? Eating alone, sleeping alone. I smooth the sheet where Hugh so recently lay and once again feel hideously conflicted about where to go from here. It seems like a no-win situation to me: if I leave him I know I'll miss him horribly – just the everydayness of our lives, always having him there at the end of the phone, someone to cook for at night. Not to mention the guilt I'd feel over hurting him. But how can I stay if it means carrying this uneasiness within me, knowing that I will never feel truly fulfilled while I'm with him?

I don't even know what to hope for from here on. Even if Hugh and Sandrine miraculously got together and relieved me of my girlfriend duties, what would I want for myself? I can't help but feel this whole episode with Tezz has been some kind of cautionary tale – letting passion into my life even for a few days has acted as a wrecking ball, just as I always feared it would. Just like it did for my mum and dad. Mind you, they got away with it for a good many years, unfazed even by my dad's intermittent spells in jail. It was only when my mum was sent down that things really fell apart.

I have to say I saw the whole thing coming. I remember the night she told us that she feared Lord Rathbone, her one titled client, was losing it. She'd gone to his house to give him his usual monthly trim and noticed he'd taken to poking the fire not with the provided tong but with his ridiculously foppish jewelled walking cane. We were eating dinner at the time, artichoke pesto pasta I recall, and my father set down his fork to tell my mum about how he'd always dreamed of owning a cane like that. How, when he was a little boy, he thought that would be the ultimate sign that he had become a gentleman. I saw in her eyes right there that she meant to get it for him.

As far as I'm aware it was the very first time she ever stole anything, but this was for Dad's sixty-fifth birthday – a special occasion – and after all those years of having gifts heaped at her feet it was the least she could do. And all too easy – there she was in his house, there he was old and doddery, probably wouldn't even miss it. He was on the verge of incinerating it as it was.

I think it was actually a relative who alerted the police, obviously having an eye to acquiring the piece for themselves one day. My dad never should have stepped out with it so boldly, but he was just so excited he wanted to take it to the dinner-theatre show they'd booked for the following weekend. He even dug up a black cape from somewhere, never looked more dapper. My mum wore a floor-length African violet dress and her most sparkly necklace. I've still got the picture they took just before leaving the house, ready to step out in style. Just their luck that they were seated at a table with a local copper and his wife. He made a call in the interval and they were picked up after the show. Of course my dad insisted my mum had nothing to do with it, but she didn't want him going inside again at his age. Long story short, they both got sentenced.

That all happened just before I met Hugh. I'd actually been to visit both of them the day we bumped into each other at the Ashmolean exhibit. I remember feeling particularly low that evening. It seemed all they wanted to hear about was each other – is he taking his medicine? How did she look? – never about what was happening with me. I never felt I was as precious to my parents as they were to each other. My name says it all. Not Ruby, or even a semi-precious stone like Jade, but Amber, fossilised tree resin. Appropriate to me, perhaps, but not of any great value to them. No wonder I fell into Hugh's arms when he treated me like gold.

I avoided telling Hugh that my parents were in prison until, after just a few weeks inside, my dad died of pneumonia. That was a big enough strain to put on a new relationship, but then, within the week, I received my last phone call from my mother.

'Is it all right if I leave you now, darling?' she asked me, sounding oh-so-calm. 'I really need to be with your father.'

'Mum!' I wailed, sick with panic as her words hit home.

'Hugh will take care of you,' was the last thing she said before the line clicked dead.

Since then I've felt like something she bequeathed to Hugh in her will.

I take a breath and step on to the balcony, ready to address the heavens.

'Mum, I have to ask you something.' I blink upwards. 'Is it okay if I leave him now? He's done a wonderful job of taking care of me, but I think it's time for me to go it alone.'

In response I hear the distant sound of a woman singing. I try to make out the melody – is it one of her old favourites? Is that Dusty? As I listen closer, the voice gets louder and distinctively more Tahitian. It appears to be coming from across the water. I turn full circle and then, from behind one of the other bungalows, I see a native woman and man gliding towards me in a canoe. She is singing and smiling at me and bearing my breakfast on a tray on her shoulder.

'The special,' I breathe to myself as she disembarks and steps up on to the balcony, lovingly transferring my order on to the table and bordering it with an abundance of flowers. I've never seen a more colourful presentation – pink petals, yellow fabric, orange and red fruit, bright blue lagoon – I feel like I've stepped into a Gauguin painting.

As I take my seat, my heart wells up with optimism: not a bad introduction to solo dining!

I wave off the canoe and then lift my glass to the sky and toast her. 'Thanks, Mum!'

25

Considering I expected to be languishing in my pyjamas all day, I'm not doing badly. It's 10.45 a.m., I'm up and dressed and my eyes haven't leaked in at least ten minutes. I'm about to write some postcards to the girls at work when there's another knock at the door. This time it's the maid wanting to know when she might clean the room.

'Ummm . . .' I pause to consider my plans for the day, then remember I don't have any. Except . . . I look at my watch again. I could still make the cooking class. I can be assured there will be no *9½ Weeks* shenanigans in front of a blue neon fridge, but other than that, how bad can it be? Suddenly I'm not so fearful of facing Tony.

'Now is perfect. I'm just leaving,' I tell the maid, grabbing my bag and a hairband and heading off down that oh-so-familiar path.

*

As I approach the main entrance to The Paradise Room, I pray Tezz won't be around rehearsing a new routine or sneaking snacks from the kitchen. Everything has gone so very pear-shaped between us and I just want to leave it in the past now.

As it happens, he is nowhere to be seen, but Tony, of course, is prompt.

'I hope it wasn't my food that made you sick last night?' He gives me a challenging look as he unlocks the door and bids me enter.

'No, no, it was delicious. I'm afraid I mixed my drinks.' I avert my eyes as I step inside.

'That's a dangerous thing to do,' he warns, ladling on the foreboding as he leads the way to the kitchen.

'I know,' I stumble after him. 'I'll be more careful next time.'

'So there is going to be a next time?' He stops to give me a loaded stare.

My heart patters nervously. 'Well, you know, you always say, "I'm never going to drink again!" And then, before you know it . . .' I trail off. 'I've got a very resilient liver,' I tell him.

He studies me for a second longer, then says, 'Hugh was really worried.'

What, are these two new best friends?

'Yes, well, I didn't mean for that to happen.' God, why can't we be making a Tahitian hot dog? The whole thing would be over by now.

As he flicks on the overhead fan, he can't resist one more gibe. 'I always think people should take a little

331

more care when in custody of another's heart,' he preaches.

I go to shout 'enough!', but something about the resonance in his voice prompts me to blurt: 'It was you, wasn't it?'

'What do you mean?' he frowns as he ties on his apron.

'All this time I thought it was Tezz, but now . . .' The penny has just dropped. 'It was you who was engaged.'

'Who told you that?' He looks up, suddenly exposed.

'No one. I overheard—'

Seeing the pain in his face makes my heart go out to him. He was madly in love and she left him. No wonder he has such empathy for Hugh.

'Do you want to talk about it?' I make a gentle offer.

'To you?' He sounds incredulous.

'Well, I don't think the chopping board is a great listener.'

He shakes his head. 'I'm not really one for spilling my guts.'

'Why not?' I question him, having no fear of falling from grace, seeing as I'm already damned in his eyes.

'It's not in my nature,' he says, still clearly off-balance. 'Trust doesn't come easy to me.'

'Why not?' I demand again. Something about this man makes me want to challenge him. To reach inside him and pull his heart up for air, get it breathing and pumping again like mine so recently started to do.

'What do you mean, "Why not"?' he blinks back at me.

'Well, that "don't trust" attitude has got to have started somewhere.'

He looks for a moment like he's not to be drawn, but then he says, 'In this business, it's not always easy to judge people's intentions.'

'You think people have bad intentions towards you?'

'Sometimes.'

'Well, how bad can they be?' I don't get it.

He sighs heavily. 'Well, for example, women will come up and tell Tezz and me how much they love the show and what talented performers we are, and the next thing I know they're emailing us nude pictures.'

'So?' I laugh.

'So they were only paying us compliments to try and get us into bed.'

'You don't know that.'

'Yes I do.'

'No you don't. Isn't it possible that they think the show is phenomenal, and that maybe it's because of your talent that they want to shag you?' I propose. 'Besides, you can't do the moves you do and not expect to be viewed as a sexual object. I mean, it's a very sexy show.'

Did I just say sexual and sexy in the same breath? This is so unlike me.

'All I know is that I'm more comfortable behind the scenes, choreographing and—'

'Cooking?'

'Exactly.'

'Well, that's your choice, but you can't fight the fact that you are born to perform. Oops, sorry. You don't want to hear any compliments, do you?' I find myself getting all sassy. 'You'll only think I want to sleep with you.'

'I think you've got your hands full at the moment,' he says dryly.

I go to dispute his accusation, but instead quietly concede, 'Maybe I have.'

It would seem he's aware that something went on with me and Tezz, probably assumes it was more than a kiss, but then I suppose the details are irrelevant – it's the intention that counts. No doubt he's less-than-impressed that I didn't mention Hugh prior to his appearance last night. I layer on a little more shame along with the white chef jacket he hands me, noticing that, as with last night, he's favouring royal blue cloth.

'Any significance in the colour?' I ask him, keen to change the subject.

'White is traditional. I don't want my food to be traditional,' he says matter-of-factly.

I look down at my jacket, suddenly feeling rather insipid.

'I want my staff in white so I can be assured of their cleanliness,' he explains. 'I'm fanatical about hygiene, so I don't have that concern.'

'What are the plastic forks for?' I point to the shiny white prongs sticking out of his top pocket.

'I use these if I want to taste the food. No double-dipping – one mouthful then discard.'

Wow. This is a whole different league of cooking etiquette.

'Humans are the most dangerous presence in the kitchen,' he adds as he swiftly sanitises the surfaces. 'Unconsciously rubbing your eyes or your nose, itching your scalp . . .'

I shrivel up my face, imagining all the nasties. 'Where I used to waitress, the chefs sneezed into their own jackets,' I say.

'Crook of the sleeve.' He demonstrates, burying his face into his bent arm. 'It's the best way to stop the germs spreading.'

'I think I'd better wash my hands!' I volunteer.

'Twenty seconds with hot water will kill the surface micro-organisms.'

'Right!' I salute him with the soap, feeling like I'm preparing for surgery.

For the next half an hour we concentrate exclusively on the food preparation. While the sea bass fillet is marinating in a mixture of coconut milk, lime, honey, garlic, salt and pepper, we toast the coconut flakes on an oven sheet until they are light brown, then, working side by side, we trim and strip the asparagus, peel and dice the russet potatoes, seed and julienne the jalapeño peppers and render the maple bacon. The way he handles the ingredients, the precision of his instruction and the absolute passion he has for the process is so beguiling. He may not be my number one fan, but I have nothing but respect for this man.

'Okay, now the asparagus is perfectly al dente we're going to shock it with an ice bath.'

I watch him douse the slim green stalks, mesmerised.

'And then we're going to cut them into one-inch pieces and set them aside. Do you know how to clarify butter?'

I nod. 'Do you want me to use a spoon or pour it through cheesecloth?'

'Cheesecloth.' He nods at the appropriate drawer.

This teamwork is fun.

We continue ticking off tasks until the time comes to learn the secret of his exquisitely succulent fish. 'We're going to sear both sides of the fillets and then bake them in the oven for between twenty and thirty minutes, depending on the thickness of the fillet.'

I stand in studious silence as he sets the fish asizzling, and then, once they are both evenly browned and in the oven, my mind starts to wander. Not having itched my ear, set anything on fire or peeved the maestro since we started cooking, I feel sufficiently emboldened to broach a non-food-related topic. I know relationships are off the menu, but there's one thing I remember Tezz mentioning while we were aboard Marcel's boat that I've been dying to ask about.

'What about ballet?' I tiptoe towards the subject.

'What about it?' Tony counters, eyes never leaving the fillets.

'Can we talk about that?'

'Sure,' he shrugs. 'Seen any good Carlos Acosta productions lately?'

'Actually, I meant you.' I narrow my eyes at him. 'Tezz said you were quite the prodigy.'

Eyes still averted, he murmurs, 'What do you want to know?'

'I want to know everything,' I chance, encouraged by his near compliancy.

'Everything?' he scoffs.

'We've still got at least nineteen minutes before the fish is done,' I shrug. 'Why don't you start at the beginning?'

At first his tone is dismissive and he's sparing with the details, but as nostalgia claims him, his story gets more personal, and I start to feel less like the enemy and more like a confidante.

'It was actually singing that led me to dancing,' he recalls. 'When I was seven years old I joined the cherub choir, and the director went to my mother and told her that he wanted to give me a solo – an old spiritual song called "You Can't Beat God's Given" – and I remember my voice seemed high and squeaky, but the congregation was clapping and encouraging me and I liked the way it felt. Not the applause, but the music.'

'Can your parents sing?' I quickly interject, wanting to get the full picture.

'My mother sang in church every week, but my father would only sing when he was home. I used to sit and lean against the bathroom door listening to him sing Nat King Cole when he was in the shower – a voice like melted chocolate it was so smooth! – but ask him to do it in front of people? Oh, he would freeze up!'

'But not you?'

He smiles. 'I would sing all the time – I knew every song on the radio from Cat Stevens to Donna Summer! I would even sing without realising it. One time in class I started singing, "Cat's in a cradle and the silver spoon, little boy blue and the man in the moon". Do you know that song?'

I shake my head, amazed at how gentle and melodic a grown man's voice can be.

'I remembered it from when I was little, and my teacher said, "You like to sing, huh?" And then he said "You *should* sing!" He probably didn't even mean it, but his words stayed with me and I started going to the young adult choir at church and won a place with the Killian Singers at school. Then, when I was in tenth grade – that's when you're fifteen – we began adding choreography to the singing numbers, and the dance teacher who came in to coordinate this noticed Mr Over-Achiever/Mr Needing-To-Shine really going to town on it. She pulled me to one side and asked if I'd ever taken dance lessons, and I snapped, "No, and I'm not going to, so don't even go there. *Not ever!*"'

I chuckle at his petulance.

'It's not that I didn't want to,' he confides. 'Inside I

338

really did, but it was the stigma of that in High School. "Oh, you're a dancer? Mmm-hmm . . ." And then you were beaten up every day. But she stayed after me for weeks:

"'You're such a natural!"

"'Leave me alone – I don't want to!"

"'Just come to one dance class . . ."

'So eventually, out of curiosity, I stopped by. I watched the class and I was just dying inside, thinking, *I want to do that*! But there was only one guy, and he was *extremely* effeminate – feathers were flying everywhere! – and I knew I didn't want to look like that. "I'm no sissy! I'm not doing it!" I told the teacher, but she said, "Don't think the way other people do. Think for yourself – do you want to dance?" And I told her that, as long as she didn't tell anybody else, yes, I did.'

I smile, feeling the triumph the teacher must have felt persuading this little Leroy, with all the associated attitude, to give it a try.

'She set me up with a ballet instructor who taught a Russian-based style where men danced like men, none of that hands flipping and flopping around!' He laughs, leaning back on the counter, eyes filling with wonder as he recalls his first class. 'It was in this big warehouse studio with a live piano and all these beautiful high-school girls in pink. I was surrounded by all this grace and beauty and I felt so awkward, but I kept going back, and gradually it started to attach itself to me. Football and academic studies fell by the wayside, and I went from taking two classes a week to one every day then three classes a day! My muscle groups moved and everything got ballet-dancer shaped.' He pauses to peek through the glass on the oven door to check on the fish, then continues. 'Next thing I know I'm at home doing bar in my room, and I progress out into the hallway between the living room and the family room and I'm practising my pirouettes and then there's my dad.' He pulls a face.

'Uh-oh!'

'He was very passionate about sports, as am I, so this wasn't exactly what he was hoping for from me.' His face clouds over. 'He got into so many fights in the neighbourhood with people calling his son a little faggot, even lost friendships over it.'

'Really?'

'He was a very angry person,' Tony observes, wincing as he recalls the rages he endured as a child. 'Never really got to spread his own wings . . .'

My heart goes out to him realising how hard it must have been for Tony to pursue his dancing while living under the same roof. And how brave he was to move to New York at seventeen because everyone said that was where he had to go to make a career for himself.

'So I rented a room in a dicey neighbourhood in Harlem and put myself out there, but I was too wet behind the ears, no street savvy, and some unfortunate things happened . . . people tried to take advan-

340

tage . . .' He looks uncomfortable. 'I got freaked out, so I came home and got a job in a bank with the same company that my dad worked for, different branch though. My dad had an accounting degree and I was going to follow in his footsteps and study business because I thought the dance industry was nothing but bad.'

'No!' I cry. Even though I know that this phase didn't last, I'm nevertheless appalled at the thought of him cooped up in an office like a caged animal.

'It's okay!' he laughs. 'I was still dancing on the side, I never lost a beat.'

I heave a sigh of relief. 'So what got you back out there?'

'A Pepsi commercial with Gloria Estefan. My agent projected I could make $75,000 from it, so I quit my job at the bank, but in the end I got cut from the final edit and made just $5,000!'

'But kept dancing?'

He nods. 'I was lucky, I always got work.'

'So what's your relationship like with your dad now?'

'We don't speak. I've actually changed my surname to my mother's maiden name.'

'Gosh,' I gasp. 'That's pretty severe.

'No animosity, it just seemed the natural thing to do. We never identified with each other. I'd say we're pretty much done.'

The finality in his voice is absolute.

I feel sorry for the father who's missing out on

knowing such a remarkable son. Perhaps with a little extra poignancy since my own father never really knew me. From lack of interest, really, rather than disapproval of my career choice. It incenses me to think how damning parents can be of a child's dreams. Look at how dedicated and diligent Tony proved himself to be in discovering his true self. Surely all that hard work is something to be lauded?

Then I remember that first night on the beach, with Tezz telling me how disappointed his dad was that his son was such a goody-two-shoes – he wanted him out playing rough and tumble and being Jack-the-lad, and clearly this hurt him. Like every child the whole world over, he wanted to be loved and accepted for who he was, not forced to fit someone else's ideal.

No wonder these guys formed such a bond! They both followed their heart and escaped from a stifling home situation. Something I am, in a way, attempting to do a little later in life.

'So you understand, then, the importance of following your heart,' I venture, somewhat tentatively. 'Even if it sometimes hurts other people?'

Two can play at the poignancy game.

He looks up at me, knowing exactly what I'm getting at, and yet I feel compelled to get more specific, even if I am risking riling him.

'You didn't deliberately set out to hurt your father but you had to follow your own path. I would never intentionally hurt Hugh – he's been nothing but wonderful to me,' I insist. 'But I feel like I'm hanging on to him for the wrong reasons. Even if this whole trip and everything I've felt here proves to be a fantasy, he is no longer my reality.'

Tony looks sad. There's a leaden pause before he concedes, 'If you honestly feel that—'

'I do,' I tell him, ever more certain of what I have to do – *and soon*.

I know that if I leave breaking up with Hugh until we're back in Oxford, then I'll never do it. I'll step through the door on Willow Terrace and it'll be like I've never been away. I'll look around at all I would have to give up and imagine the hassle and heartache of putting the house on the market, packing my things, finding somewhere new to live, removal men, solicitors fees, cooking for one, and it'll seem like too many miseries and obstacles and I'll start telling myself I don't have it so bad. I have to ensure that doesn't happen.

'I don't want my heart to have a desk job,' I tell Tony. 'I'm going to tell Hugh today.'

Tony looks ever more wretched. 'Just what the world needs – another broken heart.'

'You could look at it as one more heart set free to find its true destiny,' I propose.

'I'm sure that's exactly how Hugh will see it,' he sniffs.

'Well, not immediately,' I concede.

'Not any time soon, I assure you.'

I flash with indignation. This is no flip decision on my part. I don't know why it's so important to me for

343

him to understand that, but it is. 'Would it be better if it was my heart that got broken?' I query.

'What do you mean?' Tony looks defensive.

'I mean that you think I'm the bad guy because I'm breaking up with Hugh, but if I stay I will continue to feel lonely and unfulfilled and ultimately my heart will be just as broken as his because I stifled it.' I swallow hard. 'Would that be better?'

Tony blinks at me, clearly a little thrown by my argument.

'Look, I'm really sorry that your girlfriend hurt you,' I continue. '*Really*. But the fact is, she probably didn't feel she had a choice. Nobody likes to be the cause of another person's pain. But her first responsibility had to be to her own heart.'

I pause, deciding I may as well go the whole hog now that I've well and truly rattled his cage.

'And while we're on the subject, you could do with taking a bit more care of your own.'

'More care of *my* heart?' he scoffs. 'I couldn't be any more careful,' he insists.

I shake my head, knowing his pain all too well. 'Taking care and being careful aren't the same thing. I get that you're not ready to put yourself out there yet, but don't tell your heart that it's never going to love again,' I implore him. 'You want it to rest and heal, not give up altogether.'

I look around for a raw onion to start chopping as an excuse for my shiny eyes, but there's none to be had.

Tony emits a long breath. 'I don't know why I keep letting you in my kitchen.'

I chuckle and relax my shoulders, equally keen to let the subject drop now. 'Nobody clarifies butter like I do.'

'And nobody tells it straight like you do.' He gives me a sincere look and then sighs. 'It's been a while since anyone called me on this stuff.'

'It's my new hobby,' I shrug. 'Telling the truth.'

He opens his mouth to speak, but the oven alarm pings, disturbing his train of thought.

'Come on,' he chivvies, returning to the matter of the food and in particular its presentation. 'Let's see how you are at piping potato!'

I end up staying way into the afternoon helping Tony prep for the evening ahead, losing all track of time until Hugh turns up, wondering where I've got to.

'Hope she hasn't been too much trouble!' he teases, patting me on the bottom.

'Actually she's been a great help,' Tony admits, nudging my heart with his sincerity.

'So, tell me what you've learnt today!'

Though Hugh is clearly in a chatty mood, Tony is patently uncomfortable knowing what lies ahead for him and quickly excuses himself.

'Busy man!' Hugh looks a little disappointed. 'Well!' He turns to me, clapping his hands together. 'We've still got a couple of hours before dinner with the masses. What do you want to do?'

I take a deep breath. The time has come – now or never. 'Shall we take a walk along the beach?'

His face lights up. 'You don't know how long I've waited for you to say those words.'

I cringe inwardly. This isn't going to be easy . . .

26

It's a scene you've seen a hundred times in holiday brochures and commercials for couples' resorts – a man and a woman strolling hand in hand along a deserted strip of beach, her in a wispy sarong, him in an unbuttoned shirt. Their love is as golden as their surroundings, and their only concern is where their next cocktail is coming from.

Not once have I looked at those pictures and suspected that the girl is about to break up with the guy.

My mood fluctuates with every barefoot step, switching between clear determination to respect my true feelings and waves of sympathy for this dear man who has done no wrong.

Back home I swore to myself that I would do everything in my power to make this trip easy on Hugh, and here I am with my finger on the button marked DEVASTATE. It's strange to be teetering on the brink like this, still having a choice, almost in awe of how much damage just a few words can do.

Right now the question seems to be, what am I more afraid of losing? The stability and security I have with Hugh, or the thrill of discovering the real Amber Pepper, so ignored and subdued over the past few years.

As we walk, I wonder, can I live with myself if I strive to be the person I really feel is me, only to find that the experience falls short of my expectations and leaves me all alone? Equally, can I live with myself if I don't give myself this chance to find out just how happy I could be?

Or would the greatest long-term satisfaction come from Doing the Right Thing? I stumble as my inner devil's advocate hollers, *The right thing for who?* Certainly to stay with Hugh would be the more socially acceptable thing, but what am I supposed to tell my heart? *I'm sorry, you made a good argument but overall we have decided that there will be less hurt and drama all round if we just carry on as we are.* I can almost hear its plaintive response: *Please, I beg of you – one chance to fly!*

It's these words that resonate to my core, so I take a deep breath and begin.

'Hugh, about the wedding—'

'It's a no, isn't it?' he cuts in, sounding so casual, so accepting, I'm thrown. All I can manage in return is a dumb nod.

'Okay. No biggie.'

What? I can't quite believe his ears. Has he too

undergone some life-changing revelation? I wait for him to continue.

'I know you've never been in any hurry to ram-raid the altar,' he says kindly, putting his arm around my shoulder and giving me a chummy squeeze. 'And I get that with your parents being gone, the Big Day might seem like a bittersweet proposition, but if you ever change your mind, you just have to say the word and I'll be there – in top hat and tails. Or a parka and a big woolly scarf if you prefer!'

Oh dear. I thought that was a bit too easy.

I dig my heels into the sand and turn to face him. 'It's more than the wedding,' I tell him in a quiet voice.

'What do you mean?' He looks confused.

I open my mouth, but it's a good few seconds before I get up the nerve to say: 'I think what I'd like more than anything is for us to be friends.'

Suddenly he turns to ice. 'I thought we were friends.'

'Of course we are.' I blink at him, needing him to understand me. 'And I'm hoping that we always will be.'

My words hang in the air as his face drains of colour. 'What exactly are you saying, Amber?' he quavers.

Again I take a breath and force a smile. 'I realise this may seem a strange time to . . .' My eyes rove around the shells trimming my toes as I struggle to find an appropriate term.

'Dump me?' he suggests. 'Oh my God – are you breaking up with me in Bora Bora?' He half laughs.

'Um . . .' I falter, still teetering on the fence.

He looks around him, incredulous. 'Why now? What's going on?'

'I don't know how to explain,' I stammer, searching for the least hurtful rationalisation. 'Something about being here, or away from home, or . . .' I heave a sigh and speak as gently as I can. 'Whatever it is, it's made me realise that we're not right for each other.'

'You mean I'm not right for you,' he corrects, testily.

'No . . .' I flounder.

'I can't believe this!' He shakes his head, ignoring my worthless protestation. 'I thought we'd got past this culture shock or sunstroke or whatever it is that's been making you act so strange.' He gnaws on a knuckle, getting increasingly peeved as he paces the sand. 'How come you couldn't wait until we got home to discuss this? I mean, what's the big rush? You have to get away from me right now, this very second, is that it?' he snarls, smarting with hurt.

Before I can answer he gives me a self-righteous glare and grizzles, 'It's really pretty disrespectful. You know I'm out here to work, and now—' His voice catches in his throat.

Oh God, this is horrible. I feel so selfish. How can I explain that I have to do this now because I can't trust myself to leave him if I wait until we get home? I try to steady my resolve. The timing may be wrong but the decision is right. *It has to be.*

'I need to get out of this sun,' Hugh wheezes, looking unwell. 'Can we go back to the room?'

'Of course.' I bite my lip as I walk beside him, afraid of speaking and making things worse. I feel like I would do anything to take away his pain right now. Anything except return to a sham relationship.

Mercifully we bump into the concierge who has been making all Hugh's travel arrangements, and I get a moment or two's respite on the walkway. Hugh puts on a brave face while Laurent brings him up to speed on tomorrow's itinerary, and I wander on ahead trying to stay focused. I can't believe I'm actually doing this. I know there's a long way to go and many tears to be spilt, but part of me is almost excited – my new path awaits.

'Amber?'

That voice . . .

'Tezz!' I jump as I see him pacing towards the jetty, face devoid of its natural warmth. He looks like he means to speak to me, and in a fluster, not knowing whether to advance or run away, I lose my footing and keel back over the rope rail, plunging bum-first into the shallow waters below.

'Aaaghh!' My back grinds against the coral, water burbles over my face and for a second I can't remember how to get upright.

Next thing I know, three men are hauling me out of the water – concierge Laurent, mock-husband Hugh and ex-paramour Tezz.

'I'm fine! I'm fine!' I gasp for breath, realising I need to break up the party pronto.

'Are you sure?' Tezz may not be his usual pally self,

351

but there's enough concern in his voice to cause Hugh's face to darken. Oh no – he's looking for a valid reason why I would be ending the relationship and I can see him jumping to out-dated conclusions.

'Sorry! I'm such an idiot!' I scrabble away from six helping hands.

'Is there anything—?' Laurent begins as I race round to get back on the walkway.

'No, no,' Hugh answers for me. 'I'd better get her back to the room.'

And with that I'm bundled on my way. Mortified, absolutely mortified!

Back at the bungalow, Hugh closes the door and gravely states, 'I can't have you here like this.'

I look down at myself – by 'like this' does he mean all wet and squelchy and an embarrassment to mankind?

'I'll get a towel, tidy myself up . . .' I volunteer.

'I mean, we can't be under the same roof. Not when—'

I don't know whether he's stopping short of saying 'Not when you've just broken up with me', or 'Not when you're clearly carrying on with another man.'

Either way I simply gulp and say, 'I understand. I'll sort something out. Maybe Felicity could—'

'No,' he says, in an *Oh, no you don't* way. 'Allow me.' And with that he crosses the room, picks up the phone and says, 'Concierge please.' There is a short delay and then he says, 'Hi, Laurent, this is Hugh Garner. Yes, she's fine, but there is one thing you can do. Amber needs to fly back to the UK somewhat urgently . . .'

He's not! My heart starts to palpitate nervously as I sense the shift in power.

'Really, no damage done, it's another issue entirely. Could you possibly arrange the change in her ticket? For as soon as possible. Yes.' I endure a heart-hammering pause, and then he says, 'Tonight would be perfect.'

Tonight? I blanche at the prospect.

'Of course,' Hugh continues. 'I'll bring it over to you now.'

Oh my God – what have I done? I've been dealing exclusively with hypotheticals until now. I didn't imagine things would happen so fast. I didn't expect to see this new harsh side to Hugh. I feel caught out, like I'm being sent back prematurely. I don't know if I'm ready to face my life in Oxford yet and there's unfinished business with Felicity. How can I leave her with a big question-mark on her heart? The fact is, if Hugh changes the ticket I'll have no choice but to go. I certainly don't have the £1,000 plus it would cost to buy my own, and even if I did stay on, I doubt *Windstar* is given to accommodating stowaways.

'Hugh . . .' I begin as he sets down the phone.

'You should start packing your things,' he orders, robotically retrieving the paperwork from the drawer and moving towards the door.

'Um, wait!' I call him back. There is one small problem.

'Yes?' he stalls.

'I don't have a case. Remember it burst on the first day?'

He looks at me for a second as if I'm being deliberately obstructive, and then opens the wardrobe and pulls out his Louis Vuitton. 'Take mine.'

'Oh no, I'm sure they must have something in the shop I could use—'

'I'll get another one when I'm in Tahiti tomorrow,' he clips, lifting it on to the daybed and flicking the numbers round to release the lock. 'Just take it.'

I turn to thank him, but he's already gone.

Wow. With one short conversation I've managed to curdle the kind nature of my best friend. Sensing the beginning of a hyperventilation, I lurch out on to the balcony, desperately fighting the feeling that I am all alone in the world – just me and my great big mistake.

I can't bear to leave Hugh like this. Oh, please let the planes be full! I pant out my prayer. Let there be a non-exchangable, non-refundable policy on the ticket! Not that it would matter. Hugh would buy me a new one without blinking. He might even think I'll come to my senses when I get home. Maybe that's the plan – leave me to stew for a couple of days then offer to act like it never happened and everything will go back to how it was before. I gasp for air. *But I can't go back*. Not now.

For the second time today I find myself calling out 'Mum!', and my eyes fill with yearning to have her here to tell me that I'm doing the right thing – that the passion that has led me to this moment was real and worth it.

Without processing the thought I find myself tilting my head to avoid scraping it on the roof overhang and then lowering myself down into the blue. I'm already sopping. What can it hurt to get wet again?

I wade out until I'm neck-deep and then take a couple more paces, surprised to find that, even though I can no longer touch the bottom, I remain vertical and bobbing without so much as a swish of my arms. Wow. Who knew I could stand upright without so much as a rubber ring or armbands? I begin moving around with new-found grace and freedom, feeling as if I'm partaking in some kind of water deportment class. I even manage a small smile: seconds ago I felt hopeless and cut adrift and on the verge of hysteria; now I feel entirely supported. I relax a little more and let the water rock me gently, closing my eyes and imagining it's my mother rocking me in her arms.

'It's going to be all right, darling,' I hear her soothe, triggering the release of a flood of tears.

When you're in water it seems no big deal to cry. What's a little dribble from me compared with the vastness of the ocean?

As I release a flurry of old thoughts, I think back to when I was packing for this trip and how I hoped Felicity could magically bring back the bold person I used to be. Then along came Tezz, and the fantasy of being with him helped me dream up a new future for myself. Now, even if I have to move on without either of my muses, I'm glad for all the new feelings they've encouraged in me. I feel like they've given me an emotional map of how I want to feel – lighter and brighter and fully engaged in life. Not hiding from it, or hiding in someone else's life, like I have been with Hugh.

All those years I clung to him as if he was the last connection to my parents, but now it's just me and the water, and instead of feeling like I'm drowning, I feel buoyed up, like my soul is being refuelled. There's no need to grab on for dear life. I am magically supported in all that I do.

I sniff a final tear. If this is what has to happen next for me – the separation, the pain, the guilt, the introspection – then I will embrace it, because it is a life I have chosen for myself, not something bequeathed to me or something I have limpeted on to for the wrong reasons. I extend my arms, wiggle my toes and let the feeling of freedom filter into me.

And then I see Hugh stepping out on to the balcony and quickly pull myself down so the water rushes over my head, allowing my tears to merge with the lagoon water. Part of me would like to pull down deeper and feel my way along the bottom of the ocean until I can safely emerge on to a land where there is no one to hurt, but instead I come up for air and steadily swoosh back to the steps, hauling myself up to Hugh's eye level.

'There's a flight leaving tonight at 9 p.m.,' he tells

me. 'It's not direct, but it'll get you to Papeete in time for the 2 a.m. flight home.'

I can't believe he's done it. It's crushing to see him speaking to me like a stranger, shutting me out like this, but it's something I have to accept. This is the choice I've made, and I have to live with the consequences. Forcing myself to switch to survival autopilot, I step forward and say, 'I'm sorry.'

'Don't be sorry,' he clips. 'Just change your mind.'

I hold his gaze for a second, and then look down at the deck, grateful that all my inner organs are sitting quietly now, none of them making a fuss because they know how important it is for me to maintain my inner resolve. Seeing the pain in Hugh's face, it would be all too easy to say what he needs to hear – to reach out and tell him it's just the heat making me crazy and everything is going to be all right. But I know I mustn't because if I cave in now I'll only have to go through all this again a few months down the line. And the only thing worse than what I'm doing now would be to hurt him twice.

'Go home,' he instructs. 'Think about everything we have, everything we've been through together, and then change your mind,' he repeats.

I give a curt nod, acknowledging his request but making no promises.

'You won't have time to go over to *Windstar* now, but if you want to have dinner with Felicity in the room . . .' he tails off. 'Just leave the rest of the hotel to me.'

I sneak a peek at my watch, noting that we were due to rendezvous in less than an hour. 'You never even got to meet her,' I say, wistfully.

'I don't think tonight's the night, do you?'

I shake my head, feeling guilty that I have someone to comfort me when all he has is Sandrine, hardly the sympathetic type.

'I probably won't see you again before you leave, so . . .' He swallows hard in a bid to divert an impending wobble, ' . . . goodbye.'

Is this really it? Suddenly I feel like I may never see him again. I mean, of course when he comes back to Oxford there will be all kinds of things to sort out . . . but just in case, there are a few things I feel I should say.

'Hugh, I just want you to know that I never pictured my life without you in it. I'm sure we can get past this and—'

'Please, Amber. I can't—' He tenses, fingers raised to his forehead to push at the furrows. 'I can't listen to your voice saying these things to me.' He shakes his head. 'It hurts too much.'

I nod, pursing my lips. Best to say nothing, I tell myself.

He seems to struggle with himself for a second, and then he turns and leaves.

For ten minutes I sit on the floor, propped up against the door he has closed on me, stunned at what has just taken place. It's nigh on impossible to regain my former positivity with the image of Hugh's tortured face still so fresh in my mind so I try to recall my dad's advice about breaking situations down into manageable steps. (One – break the glass. Two – reach for the jewels. Three – scarper to the sound of alarm bells. I believe that was his mantra.)

So: One – change into dry clothes. Two – summon Felicity. Three – say '*nana*' to Tahiti.

Actually, I want to squeeze in a quick visit to Sandrine between actions two and three. There's something I want to ask her to do.

27

'*Cher*— Oh!' Sandrine greets me at her bungalow door. '*Non-non-non!* These red eyes are not a good look for you! What 'appen?' she asks, hustling me inside.

What to say? 'I . . .' I falter. 'I'm leaving early.' I decide to skip to the practicalities of the situation. 'Tonight, in fact.'

She looks aghast. Well, as aghast as her botoxed face will allow. 'Someone die? What is it?'

'Actually it's me and Hugh,' I say, taking a forlorn pew on the daybed. 'We've split up.'

I watch her face closely as she moves to join me. Definite underlying pleasure. And right now that's exactly what I want to see.

'But why?' she cries. 'Not because of his work? We have been so busy . . .' She gathers up the sprawl of papers beside me, as if to emphasise this point.

'No, of course not. I knew before I came that he

was going to be spending most of the time in meetings.'

If I'm honest with myself, that was a plus.

'Where is he now?' Sandrine asks, her vampy alter ego peeking through as she attempts to voice concern.

'Not sure, but not far,' I assure her, adding, 'I have the room for a few more hours and then I guess he'll be back there.'

I see a plan skitting across her eyes – something along the lines of a bottle of French champagne and a Dior camisole, no doubt.

'Is there anything I can do for you?' she asks, taking my hand, the picture of sincere sisterhood.

'As a matter of fact, there is . . .' I shuffle closer, each of us busily spinning our own webs.

'Tell me,' she implores.

'Well, I was hoping, if I leave you my number, that you might call me and give me an update. I just want to know that he's doing okay. Any time, it doesn't matter, just let me know.'

'Of course!' She accepts the request with Gallic ardour. 'I am happy to help.'

'And if you could shag him silly to take his mind off the fact that he's just been dumped, that would be marvellous.' This bit I just think to myself. She's already there mentally, after all.

There's a knock at the door.

'Ah, this is my evening cocktail – I like a martini while I dress for dinner, don't you?'

361

'Always,' I smile at her. She really is a different class of woman.

As she goes to the door and greets Mr Room Service, I remove the sheet of paper I inadvertently sat upon when I first arrived. Attempting to smooth out the creases of the fax, my eye is drawn to Hugh's name, triggering a flurry of latent suspicions. I quickly glance at the top of the page to see who she's addressing – some guy called Dirk at the American division of her Paris office – then flit across the lines, speed-reading a selection of increasingly alarming phrases: 'what a blessing he took Piers's place', 'candy from a baby' 'secured a number of private meetings in Manihi while he was distracted with his girlfriend'. In the background I hear the drink-bearer offering a little chit-chat about tonight's glorious sunset as he requests her signature on the bill.

'*Maururu!*' Thank yous exchanged, I'm forced to shove the fax back in amongst the paperwork, but not before I spot the ominous last line: '*the fool doesn't even know the Vahine Blue Pearl exists!*'

Shit! This is way beyond friendly rivalry. She is utterly intent on both screwing and humiliating Hugh with this deal. And to think I was hoping she could help ease the break-up pain with a little French kissing! If anything I have just exposed Hugh as being even more vulnerable than she may have hoped – not only is he seriously lacking in pearl knowledge (and what he thinks he knows is wrong, thanks to Sandrine), but he is now going to be emotionally

362

distracted by the departure of the woman he had hoped would become his Good Lady Wife. No wonder Sandrine was looking so gleefully predatory.

As she returns to the room and flutters around feigning grief at the demise of our relationship, it's all I can do to stop myself reaching out and plunging her face into her XXL martini and holding it there until she stops spluttering for good. But the only thing in my favour is that she doesn't know that I know what she's up to, so I have to resist. God! I can't believe she'd do this to Hugh, of all people. I was crazy to think she actually cared for him. But maybe that's it – maybe the fact that he turned her down is what's driving this revenge. No. That can't be right; it was years ago that she propositioned him, and as far as I know, there's been no intermediate contact. It is rather more likely, I decide, that she is simply a mercenary bitch.

'I must go and meet Felicity,' I say, getting up to excuse myself, and gritting my teeth as she pulls me into a '*Cherie*, I am sooooooo *desolé*!' hug.

'I promise I will take good care of him,' she insists as she guides me to the door.

Apparently that's French for 'kick him when he's down'.

'*Amber!*' Felicity is already at the jetty.

As I hurry towards her waving arms, I try to order my thoughts – so much to tell her in such a short time. Since we were last circling the island on a bus I've flown to Manihi, visited a pearl farm, played bride at a Tahitian wedding, learned to cook coconut-crusted sea bass, ended a four-year relationship and uncovered a scheme to screw Hugh. But not in the way I intended. The only thing I mentioned on the phone was that our dinner plans had been scuppered and she needed to get over here asap.

'I know it's only been two days, but it feels like I haven't seen you in an age!' she wails as we collide'n'squeeze. 'Bummer about dinner,' she continues, oblivious to my cried-out eyes in the darkness. 'Why the change of plan?'

Where to begin? I don't want to overwhelm her in the first thirty seconds, so I divert the attention back to her and ask for an update on Airport Guy.

'Oh God!' She rolls her eyes. 'Turns out Know-It-All Guy knew bugger all! It was all just a ploy to get in my knickers!'

'Did he?' I gasp.

'*Nooooo!*' she howls. 'He was seventy if he was a day!'

'Oh well, I suppose it's a compliment all the same.' I try to look on the bright side.

'Yeah, between him and Coco my ego's right back on track,' she grimaces. 'Anyway, I'm more interested in your love life at the moment – I can't believe I'm finally going to meet Hugh!'

'Ah . . .' I stall.

'What now? He's not working again, is he?'

'No.' I squirm, hoping this isn't going to ruin her sparky mood. 'We've split up.'

'*What?*' she squawks. 'When?'

'Not so long ago. In fact,' I take her hand, as if that will somehow soften the blow, 'I'm leaving in just under two hours.'

'Where are you going?' she splutters.

'Back to England.'

'*Nooo!*' she howls.

'It's Hugh's decision. Obviously I don't want to leave early and miss out on my time with you, but he has control of the tickets and—'

'Wait! Wait! This is too crazy!' she stomps in despair. 'Is this because of Tezz? Has something more happened there?'

'No, nothing,' I sigh. 'He's definitely got something going with Tiara.'

'You know that for sure now?'

'I saw them kissing with my own eyes.'

'Agony! Where?' Felicity gawps.

'On stage, in front of everyone.'

'Are you sure it wasn't part of the act?' she hesitates.

'Well, yes, it was, but it was more than that. You just don't kiss co-workers like that.'

'But they're performers. Different rules—'

'Trust me.'

Felicity looks increasingly despairing. 'This is all too awful!'

'It's okay,' I soothe.

'No it's not!' She stumbles to the edge of the jetty and moodily contemplates her reflection in the water. 'It's all my fault.'

'What do you mean?' I hoot. I just don't see the connection.

'Dragging you to The Paradise Room, egging you on about Tezz, making gibes at you about being "not discernibly unhappy",' she groans. 'I put the idea in your head that something wasn't right and I didn't even know what I was talking about! I was just jealous that you were sorted with a guy – a rich guy who proposes to you in paradise and wants to father your children.' She looks wretched. 'I know I've back-pedalled since but I sowed the seed. Now look what I've done!'

'Felicity, listen to me.' I turn her to face me, gripping her shoulders, feeling a little bit like I'm acting out a scene from a daytime soap. 'This isn't because of you, I promise.'

'Well then, how did it get to this?'

I guide Felicity over to the bench and sit her down. She obviously needs to hear a clear, logical explanation as to why a girl would cast aside a perfectly decent guy.

'I've known for a long time that something was wrong with the relationship, but I've always presumed it was me,' I begin. 'I knew it wasn't Hugh because people told me over and over again that he was perfect. And he really does have a million great qualities. But he's not perfect for me.' I take a breath. 'For so long I've bought into the propaganda of "Hang on to him – you've got a good one there!", but it didn't stop me feeling uneasy. Until now I couldn't put my finger on what the problem was. There are always just enough day-to-day niggles to distract you from the real issue, aren't there?'

Felicity shrugs, 'I guess,' but continues to look at sea.

'I thought it was just a phase – no one's happy all the time. And when unhappiness develops in such a gradual manner, you hardly notice the decline.'

'Until . . .' Felicity prompts me.

'Until one day you find yourself in the most romantic place on earth and you look at the man you're supposed to be in love with and you don't feel it. And this time there's no excuse – it's not because you had a bad day at work, or that you're tired or premenstrual, or you're missing your mum or you burnt the roux.'

'The what?'

'It's like a base for thickening sauces . . .'

'Oh.'

'It's that you don't love him. At least not how you're supposed to love someone.'

'And how's that?' She looks forlorn. 'How are you supposed to love someone?'

'With all your heart,' I say simply. 'You're supposed to love them because you can't help it. Because you wouldn't know how to not love them,' I sigh. 'Not because you *want* to. Not because it's a good idea or because you're going to try really, really hard until you do.'

Felicity nods in understanding and then raises her eyes to me. 'So I'm off the hook?'

'Absolutely,' I confirm.

'And Tezz? All that you felt for him . . .?'

'That certainly helped accelerate the process,' I admit. 'Or rather helped clarify things for me.'

'And you're sure that wasn't just lust?' Felicity tries to be tactful. 'I mean, other than the fantastic odds of having mind-blowing sex with him, what was it about him that you liked so much?'

I can't help but smile as I recall how I felt about him PMT (pre meeting Tiara).

'You really want to know?'

Felicity nods, intrigued.

'I liked that he makes everyone he's with feel special and noticed. I liked that his hugs are so intense it makes you wonder if he might secretly be an assassin assigned to squeeze people to death. I liked that he has more facial expressions than a cartoonist could draw and that he can do every line from *A Fish Called Wanda*. I liked that even when he's hamming it up he's still graceful. I liked that he laughs at his own jokes and that when he laughs he laughs *big*. I liked that he can wear a black angora Kangol hat in 100-degree heat. I liked that when he's performing he can identify the source of every whoop in the room and acknowledge that person without missing a beat or a lyric. I liked that he calls the old guy on keyboards "baby". I liked the fact that he managed to live in Vegas for ten years and still stay sweet. I liked that he didn't let his background or his upbringing define who he wanted to become. I liked that I can see the kid in him – like when he's tap-dancing he looks about seven and his tongue sticks out in concentration – and then at other times he's as calm and philosophical as Yoda. I liked that he's not afraid to show his vulnerable side and that that in turn makes him seem stronger. Most of all, I liked that when he looked at me I felt this bubbling electric joy like my heart was going to ignite and rocket into the sky.'

'Blimey!' Felicity reels, clearly having got more than she bargained for.

'Aside from all that . . .' I expel a long breath. 'There was just something about him that I felt belonged to me.'

'That's how I felt when I was looking at Airport Guy,' Felicity empathises, more than a little wistfully. 'I suppose it's possible that these guys are just steps or clues leading us towards true love?'

'Little signposts pointing us in the right direction towards the characteristics we really want in a man?'

'Exactly,' Felicity agrees. 'And you must have been on the right track with Tezz because your face lights up just talking about him . . .'

I can't deny that I feel something approaching inner radiance when I conjure up those early memories. But then I think of him kissing Tiara . . .

'Are you going to say goodbye to him?'

'I don't see any point . . .' I begin, and then stop for a moment to ponder this further. 'You know, now you mention it, I think I would like to. Even if it's just to say thank you. He doesn't realise it but meeting him has changed my life . . .'

'Well,' says Felicity purposefully, 'we're on the clock here, sister. We'd better get a move on.'

28

With all this heightened emotion I barely have enough puff to walk and talk as we march towards The Paradise Room, but somehow I manage to blab about Sandrine's evil pearl treachery, causing Felicity to become instantly incensed.

'Something must be done!' she bays into the night. 'That poor man!'

'I totally agree, but I can't think what,' I humph. 'The big deal takes place tomorrow and I feel like I should at least warn Hugh, but he can't even bear to be in the same room with me at the moment. Besides, I think it would just humiliate him further to hear this from me.'

'What if I tried to talk to him?'

'He doesn't know you from Adam. Or Eve.'

'Maybe that's in our favour.' Felicity develops a very particular glint in her eye. 'Maybe we could arrange it so that he feels he's the one who's unmasked the villain!'

'Blimey,' I marvel. 'I haven't seen that look since you got the netball team to go on strike!'

'I'm just thinking . . .'

'You so should have been a lawyer!' I smile. 'Or an activist. Or a super-hero. If you hadn't been so darn good at sports—'

'Yeah, and look where that got me,' Felicity snorts. 'Suburban tennis coach slash telemarketer! I bet if we looked up Miss Carla Dollop in the Headingtonian yearbook we'd find she's having the last laugh. She's probably head of some international corporation by now.'

'As a matter of fact, she's a fancy schmantzy casting director,' I reveal, still picturing her in sports kit the day of Sprintgate. 'Jackie Loh filled me in when I was looking for you. She's worked on a ton of big movies.'

'You're kidding!'

'Nope, and you know the real irony?'

'What?'

'She started as a runner.'

We chuckle and high-five. 'Go Carla!'

'Seriously, Amber,' Felicity says, getting back to the case in point. 'We can't let Hugh get screwed over like this, not after—'

'I so cruelly dumped him,' I finish.

'Not that I'm saying it was a mistake . . .' She holds up a finger.

'No.'

'But the man is seriously vulnerable. He won't be caring what pearls he buys. I know you said he was

372

your guardian angel, but right now he needs one of his own.'

I quickly check her back for wings. 'You?'

'Well, you won't be here. Who else?'

'Ladies!' We hear a familiar voice cry out and turn to find our favourite *rae-rae* ashimmer in a lurex mermaid ensemble having a sneaky ciggie out by the side entrance. 'I always like to dress nice for the seafood special!' she announces, posing coquettishly as we take in her fishtail skirt, shell bra and freshly-shaved chest.

'Fantasia, how much do you know about black pearls?' Felicity cuts to the chase.

'I'm Tahitian, darling.' She gives us a withering look. 'I know *everything*.'

'We need to talk,' Felicity insists.

Sensing intrigue, Fantasia eagerly accepts her request. 'Give me two minutes and I'll meet you in the bar.'

'Which leaves you free to say thank you and good-night to Tezz,' says Felicity as she bids me step inside ahead of her.

'You think I'm mad, don't you?' I say hesitantly.

'Oh, what do I know?' she shrugs. 'Your choices wouldn't be mine, but that's the beauty of all this, Amber – it's your life.'

Her words strike home. First there was life with mum and dad, then there was life with Hugh, but now, for the first time, it really does feel like My Life. And even though this next conversation has the potential to be hugely embarrassing, it's something I want to do. I feel like I've just invented a new policy on the spot – this new life of mine is going to be all about speaking up and seizing the day!

The restaurant is buzzing but backstage is deserted, so I head for the kitchen to see if Tony can point me in the right direction.

'Knock-knock!'

'Hey!' He looks up to greet me while his hands continue to move busily over a batch of coconut-milk sponges.

'Bad timing?'

'Only if you don't help me finish these hau pia cakes.'

'Tell me!' I say, speedily washing my hands in preparation.

'You can start by putting a couple of drops of strawberry essence in the whipped cream to turn it pink.'

I swiftly oblige – this will be my parting gift to the masterchef. As I whisk three bowls to an even finish, it dawns on me that I'm really going to miss Tony. He's such a fascinating person to be around. Even when he keeps you at arm's length, it's still intense. I look at him now, concentrating like crazy on coating each chilled desert plate with melba sauce, and imagine all the loving care he could bring to a relationship. It seems a terrible waste for him to hide himself away like he does. If I ever do come back here, I hope to find him using coconut milk for purposes other than cooking.

'I was hoping to have a quick word with Tezz,' I venture as I assist in the positioning of the lattice cookies.

'It's Wednesday,' Tony says as he adds a mint leaf to each dish. 'It's his night off. He's not here.'

My stomach plummets, but I determine not to give up that easily.

'Do you know where I might find him?'

'I can tell you exactly where he is, but you'd need a private plane to get there.'

'Another island?'

He nods. 'He's gone to collect Tiara's costumes. Won't be back until tomorrow.'

Again the carpet is pulled from under me.

'So Tiara's joining the show?' I try and hide my disappointment with small talk.

'Starts tomorrow. You know Malia got a record deal in Japan?'

I shake my head.

'You'll have to come and check out the new numbers.'

'Unfortunately it'll be in-flight movies for me. I'm going home.'

Tony stops what he's doing.

'I forgot to say – I had the conversation with Hugh. Basically he wants me gone. I leave tonight.'

If I didn't know better I'd actually think he looks disappointed.

'Well,' he says, recovering his composure. 'I, er, I hope everything works out for you.'

'Thanks.' I muster a concluding smile. 'And good luck with the restaurant – let me know if you fancy opening a sister branch in Oxford.'

'I will,' he nods.

'Okay.' I can't bring myself to say that wretched Goodbye word. It just doesn't seem enough.

'Did you have a message you wanted me to pass on to Tezz?' Tony asks, recalling my initial enquiry.

I think for a moment. 'No. I just . . . I just wanted to thank you guys for everything. It's been . . .' My eyes well up with emotion.

'Please don't cry on the cakes,' he cautions. 'If you're going to spill over, do it by the veggies. They could probably do with salting.'

I laugh, suddenly finding a list forming in my head of all the things I like about Tony. I may not have got the chance to tell Tezz how I felt, but it's not too late with Chef Perry.

'Do you want to hear what I like about you?' I say, sounding precisely five years old.

Tony raises his eyebrows in amusement, then demurs with a shy shrug. 'You know how I feel about compliments.'

'Oh, yes.' I turn to leave but then change my mind. 'Actually, I think I'm going to tell you anyway!' Once again bold in his presence, I step back to the preparation table and clear my throat. 'I like that you don't need to be liked. I like that you like the smell of Clorox floor bleach as much as freshly-baked bread. I like that you refuse to shag these women that offer themselves to you on a plate because it's not meaningful to you. I like that you can make a busy room still when you sing a ballad. I like your sensitivity and your dignity and your gravitas.'

'Wow.' Tony looks genuinely taken aback. 'You nearly had me putting the whipped cream on the lobster.'

'I've got more,' I tell him. 'I like the way you move through a crowded room like there's an invisible force field around you and that, despite having this ultra-sexual stage persona, when someone compliments you or makes a pass at you, you just smile serenely like you're the Pope!'

He cracks up.

'And most of all, I like it when you laugh,' I tell him softly.

He shakes his head and emits a low whistle. 'Well. You can sure dish it out!'

'Yes, I can!' I beam.

'But can you take it back?' He gives me a playful look.

It's been a hard day. I could certainly do with a boost before I face the long plane ride home. 'What could you possibly like about me?' I fish.

He strums his fingers on his chin for a second, and then smiles: 'I like the way you hum Aretha Franklin when you mash potato.'

I laugh. I'm so used to cooking by myself I didn't even know I did that.

'I like how enthralled you look when you're

studying a painting. I like that you speak your mind when you're speaking to me. I like that when you say you're going to do something, you do it.' He pauses to look me up and down. 'And I like that you've got the body of a supermodel and dress like you're sixty-two.'

'What?' I gasp.

'You know you do. I don't know why you do it, but I'm sure one day you'll get over it!' He chuckles for a minute, then looks serious. 'And I like that you've followed your heart, even though I know it wasn't the easiest route.'

'Do you mean that?'

He nods. 'I have to confess, I had you pegged as a heart-breaker. But now I understand you a bit better, I see how brave you've been. It almost makes me want to be brave too.'

'Really?' My heart dances triumphantly.

'Almost,' he says quietly.

I laugh and throw my arms around him in a farewell hug. 'That's nearly the best news I've heard all day.'

29

'We've got it!' Felicity pounces on me as soon as I emerge from the kitchen.

'Got what?' I'm still in a daze, so happy to have had the chance to say goodbye to Tony and yet so sorry that I won't be seeing Tezz again.

'A plan to save Hugh!' She looks delightfully mischievous. 'Fantasia called her pal at the Black Pearl Gem Company and she reckons we can infiltrate the deal tomorrow!'

'Infiltrate?' I hoot at her choice of word. 'Are you intending to disguise yourself as a pearl?'

Felicity tuts. 'As a matter of fact I shall be posing as a rival buyer!' she tells me, looking exceedingly pleased with herself.

'You? You don't know the first thing about pearls!'

'I only need to know about the high-end grade As they're dealing with. Besides, the main thing is to get the message across to Hugh that it's the blue pearls that are the most rare and coveted, not the peacocks that Sandrine has got him brainwashed over.'

I have to admit she's already sounding savvy, but I'm not overly convinced. 'How exactly are you going to muscle in on their negotiations? Surely that's private?'

'I don't need to be in the room with them. I just need the chance to exchange a few words with Hugh before he goes in.'

'But what if he asks you who you work for, or starts angling for some credentials?'

Felicity tuts as if I'm inventing problems for the sake of it. 'I'm not trying to sell him anything. He has no reason to mistrust me. Provided I look the part and I'm in the right place . . . Besides, I've got a Kiwi accent. I could make up any old name for a jeweller's and he wouldn't know any better. I mean, has Hugh had a lot of professional dealings with New Zealand?'

'None.'

'Well then.'

I take a moment to process the plan. It seems a bit flimsy, Felicity sidling up and casually tipping him the wink. I was expecting a flamboyant exposure of Sandrine's wicked ways, but I suppose the key thing is for Hugh to be enlightened.

'Well, what do you think?' Felicity looks expectantly at me.

With just minutes to go before I'm due to board the airport shuttle, I really don't have time to come up with an alternative.

'Do it!' I approve.

Felicity does a triumphant little dance and gives a thumbs-up sign to Fantasia, currently seating a party of four across the room.

'Oh, Amber, this is so cool!' Felicity cheers as we hustle back towards the hotel. 'Do you know what I've realised in the last half an hour?'

'What?' She really does look radiant – this must be good.

'I don't need a man, I need a *cause*!'

'A cause?'

'Something to believe in, something to fight for!' she enthuses. 'That's what's missing from my life. I'd forgotten how satisfying it is to rally for the underdog!'

'Do I sense an impending career change?' I query as we cut through the lobby to the walkway.

'Well, seeing as I don't have a job to go back to, it seems timely!' She laughs, then links her arm in mine. 'I couldn't have done any of this without you.' Her voice softens. 'Isn't it funny that we both came to Tahiti and got a whole new perspective – me on my calling, you on your relationship. Speaking of which, how'd it go with Tezz?'

Here I go again, threatening to rain on her parade. 'Um, unfortunately he's gone.'

'Gone?'

'It's fine,' I tell her, even though it's not. 'He's had to go to another island to collect some show costumes, so—'

'You're not going to be able to say goodbye?' She

looks stricken. 'Oh, Amber, that's such a shame!'

'I guess it really wasn't meant to be!'

'Oh, bollocks to that. There must be something we can do!' Her brain begins rattling frantically.

I reach out and smooth her brow. 'You're going to have to let this one go, Flossie. The shuttle is here.'

'Oh no!' she sobs, clinging to me.

I burrow my head in her shoulder and breathe in her hair. Having just found her again after an eighteen-year hiatus, it's too soon to part.

'*Mademoiselle Pepper, vous êtes prêt?*' The skipper approaches us, urging me to board.

It's probably just as well our farewell is so rushed – if I had the chance to linger longer I'd be tempted to bind myself to the walkway with the very rope I keeled over earlier today. As it is, as I take my last few steps I feel like I'm walking the gangplank.

As I turn back to give Felicity a final wave, I keep thinking there must be some mistake – that I'm going through the motions, playing along with this island eviction, but only because I'm secretly convinced some swashbuckler is about to swoop in, scoop me up and save the day! Instead my fate is sealed by the rev of the engine, which knocks me back into my seat and yanks me away from Felicity in a blurr and splutter of blue.

Gripping the edge of the boat, I hold her gaze until she merges with the island, now nothing more than a blur of green through my misty eyes.

30

At the airport everyone else seems to be rushing and faffing while I move in leaden slow motion. I smirk as the check-in staff inform me that I have to change planes in Manihi and can't help but wonder if Hugh requested that stop with the intention of pricking my conscience? How did I ever agree to be party to that wedding ceremony? I shake my head as I board, wondering if it's possible for the plane to lift off when it's carrying a passenger with such a heavy heart.

We power down the runway then tilt back and climb higher and higher and I watch the place that has given me a taste of real happiness shrink and disappear.

I close my eyes and play back all that has happened – my first view of Bora Bora from above, the flowers floating in the bath of the bungalow, afternoon tea with Felicity on *Windstar*, our tipsy dinner on the hotel terrace, Tony and Tezz prowling in their eye masks and feather headdresses, Fantasia presenting us with tiare buds, sinking down to the ocean floor to feed the fish, sunset aboard the catamaran, Marcel standing beside the painting of his grandmother, jet-skiing at full tilt, squeezing coconut milk down Tezz's torso, the kiss in the tree house, the frantic swish of grass skirts on Tahitian night at The Paradise Room, kitchen-time with Tony . . . I want to relive it all in real time to keep the memories fresh, but the images are coming in snatched flashes. I feel a chill. How soon before I feel like I'm watching someone else's home movie?

A lone tear weaves down my cheek. I feel so very sad.

As the flight attendant passes, I wipe the leakage away then move my fingers up into my hair, tracing my beloved beach bump and finding some solace in the fact that it's still sore. *Woah!* What was that? I look out the window and see that the plane is now shrouded in murky grey. As I search in vain for a clean patch of sky or sea, we start bumping and wavering. I instantly feel sick and force myself to inhale and exhale deeply. Then we make a sudden dip and there's a jolt that sends everyone's stomachs up to rap on the pilot's door then back with a smack. Nervous mutterings abound. I look at my watch. Eight more minutes until we're due to land. I can do that. When the clock ticks beyond the decreed time and we're still hovering twenty minutes later, my endurance skills are tested. Today is already in my Top Ten Worst Days of My Life, but I'm in no hurry to see it make the top spot.

Finally we bump-screech down. You've never seen a group of people deplane more efficiently. I stumble over to the all-too-familiar hut and dumbly follow everyone else's lead, claiming my suitcase ready for the next flight.

With the weather looking ever more threatening I decide to take out my sweatshirt. I kneel by the case, but then my hand stalls by the lock. Oh no. Oh no. Say it isn't . . . I tug at it. Locked! The numbers have swivelled round and I don't know the code. No doubt my dad could have jimmied this in a second, but sadly he didn't pass any of his practical skills on to me. Great. Still, seeing as all the bench space is now occupied, at least it's handy to sit on.

Just as I take a pew, there's a crackle and then a shock of lightning. I look over at a set of worried faces with walkie-talkies. This doesn't look good.

'I'll tell you right now, I'm not boarding that next plane in the eye of a storm,' an American woman tells her husband.

'Don't be silly, it'll be fine,' he says, trying to appease her with a pat on the knee.

'There must be another way back to Papeete. Can't we take a boat?'

'That would take you four days,' a local lady informs her.

'Sounds reasonable . . .' She looks imploringly at her husband.

He rolls his eyes. 'It'll be fine, Marsha.'

'Actually, it might not be,' the local interjects. 'If it

continues like this they may not be able to land in the first place.'

'You want to get a British pilot over here!' I chip in. 'They wouldn't have a job if they couldn't land in the rain.'

'It's the runway; it's not long enough,' the local explains. 'If there is rain, the plane cannot stop and—'

'Okay! Okay!' Marsha shrills, not wanting to add any more disaster news clips to her brain.

Right on cue it begins to rain. And then rains and rains and rains some more. The deluge almost makes me feel I'm right back in Oxford, but I no longer find any comfort in that sensation.

'Here it comes!' The local points to the sky.

I get to my feet and join the other passengers watching the small plane begin its descent, hover over the landing strip then bear up and fly on.

'Is that it?' It didn't look like they were even trying.

'I think they're going for another attempt,' the local decides.

We all inch forward, straining as far as we can without being saturated by the relentless rain. I notice there is now a fearsome wind gathering power, and before I can properly brace myself, it snatches my plane ticket right out of my hand!

'Oh no!' I cry as it does a tantalising midair pirouette before flick-flacking across the grassy bank which, I discover as I follow suit, has now turned to marshland. The muddy sludge spatters up my legs

386

and somehow hops into my mouth as I flounder forward trying not to skid into a horizontal dive.

'Stop! I need you!' I cry out, hoping the piece of paper will listen to reason. But it doesn't. It skitters ever onward until, apparently out of breath, it takes a breather, trembling against the spiky branches of a bush. Aha! I approach with caution as if afraid of startling it, but just as I make my lunge it whips out of reach, whisking upwards like a mortar board on graduation day. In response I make a jump my netball team would have been proud of and secure the blighter in my hand. I'm so triumphant I forget about landing securely and the ground skids from under me as I splat back to earth, my fall broken only by the squelch of mud.

'Perfect!' I sigh, staring up at the sky as the plane once again burrs by, this time making only a token gesture of descent. This flight is so not going to happen.

I blink away the rain falling into my eyes like drops of Optrex, then heave myself upright and give myself a quick once-over. I look like a Dead Sea spa treatment gone horribly wrong. Even if the plane did land they probably wouldn't let my Stig of the Dump self on board. And there's not a thing I can do about cleaning myself up – there's not even a toilet back at the hut. If only I was the kind of girl who carried a backpack of wetwipes wherever she went. Hold on. What's going on? I squint ahead of me. Everyone appears to be leaving – climbing into buses and golf carts and wobbling off on the handlebars of friends' bicycles. I break into a trot, trying to catch up with at least one person who can tell me what the new plan is, but by the time I'm back at base the place is deserted. I stand there utterly confounded. Now what? What exactly am I supposed to do? Is it customary to just cancel the flight and shrug your shoulders and go home? Will there be another one in an hour? If I was famous I might presume I was being Punk'd by Ashton Kutcher, but as I recall there was a distinct lack of art historian marks in his last series so I'm guessing that, yup, I'm alone and stranded and that's it.

The weird thing is, I don't seem to care. For a good thirty minutes I sit staring into space, just me and my suitcase and a plane ticket that looks like it's been finger-painted with chocolate mousse.

When I can finally get up the energy, I consider my options.

A) I wait here until the next flight, which frankly could be a week from now, I really wouldn't know.

B) I try to find my way to the Manihi Pearl Beach Resort where at least there would be a familiar concierge to consult.

C) Um . . .

Actually, I think that's pretty much it. I suppose I could try and walk into town, but I don't know the route and I seem to recall it was five miles and wasn't there some kind of ferry crossing you had to co-ordinate with? Maybe I'll wait here a bit longer, just in case everyone comes back.

A further thirty minutes down the line, the rain ceases abruptly as if Someone Up There just switched off a tap. I peer out from under my raffia shelter. The wind is now warm and I welcome the chance to get an al fresco all-over blow-dry, standing with my arms out and rotating for full effect. As I turn around I contemplate the runway. That could take rather longer to drain and dry off. And the low light is starting to get a little eerie. I really should try and find the hotel while there are still staff on duty. As far as I can remember there was just one track leading from the airport, and then it was a turning on the right. I don't know if it was the first or the third turning but I'm going to have to take my chances.

As I walk along, bumping the suitcase over rocks and twisting it down potholes, I almost want to laugh out loud. Ordinarily a situation like this would seem testing and tear-inducing but right now anything that prolongs my departure feels good to me. And look! Here's what's left of the *lei* I dropped two days ago – little more than a string of sodden pot-pourri, but at least I'm on the right track. In fact, this must be the turning here . . .

The suitcase drags a little more as I go down an even less groomed path, making quite an arrival fanfare as the now whittled, scraped and mud-clogged wheels resist every rotation.

'Urgh!' One final tug and I'm inside the door of reception. A millisecond later the heavens open again. This time the rain falls harder and faster and I'm convinced the already brimming swimming pool will overflow and race over my ankles any second.

'Madame Garner?' the receptionist starts, greeting me in possibly the least appropriate manner considering my current circumstances, but I smile regardless.

'You've got a good memory!' I beam back.

'How did you . . .?' He looks confused, checking his bookings to see how he could have missed me.

'I don't have a reservation,' I explain. 'I was on the flight to Papeete—'

'Ah yes, many of our guests were forced to return.'

'Any chance of another flight tonight?'

His eyes flick to the special effects rainstorm outside. 'I think not.'

'Okay.' I reach for my credit card. 'Then could I have a room for the night? It doesn't have to be over-water – anything will do. Just not *under*!' I jest.

'Oh, Madame, I am sorry but we are fully booked.'

My mouth falls open. 'You don't have anything?'

The receptionist looks wretched. 'Nothing.'

This really is not going at all to plan. I am wracking my brain for a solution when my peripheral vision senses a familiar form. Tall, slim, fluid . . . It can't be!

'Tezz?' I gawp, stumbling towards the bar, half suspecting he's some kind of wet-look mirage.

'Amber?' he says, amazed, further confounded by my rumpled, besmirched form. 'Damn, what happened to you?'

'Well, I entered this mud-wrestling contest and—'

'The mud won?'

390

'Exactly!' I laugh, and then my face freezes. As does his. We both know that our days of peppy banter are gone. In the awkward silence that follows, he might as well be saying, 'I can't believe you deceived me over Hugh!' and in return I'm frothing at the mouth over Tiara, still tormented by the image of their voracious kiss.

But instead of confronting him, I take the more English approach and opt for small talk. 'So did you get your costumes sorted?' I clip.

'How d'you know about that?'

'Tony told me.'

'And then you came—'

Oh God! He thinks I've stalked him here! 'No-no!' I assure him. 'I'm actually on my way home. I was supposed to change planes here but my flight got cancelled and there's not another one until tomorrow and—'

'Hold on, you're going back to Oxford?'

I nod.

'I thought you had another couple of days at least?'

'I did, but—'

'What happened?'

'Um . . .' I try to tread as carefully as I can. 'The guy I was with the other night . . .'

'Your husband,' he says coldly.

'Actually, he's not my husband. We did have a Tahitian ceremony while we were here, but nothing legal . . .' I stop myself from going on. I seem to be making things worse.

391

'Your boyfriend, then.' His face sours at my perceived pettiness.

'Actually, he's not that either. Not any more. That's kind of why I'm going . . .'

'You've split up?'

I nod.

'And now there's nothing else to keep you here?'

My heart tugs at the disappointment in his voice. 'As a matter of fact I would have loved to have stayed on,' I tell him. 'There's still so much I would have liked to do . . .' Now or never, Amber. 'In fact, I'm really glad I got to see you because I wanted to tell you how much meeting you has meant to me.'

He goes to speak but I hurry my next sentence out. 'Look, I know you're mad at me – justifiably – and that you're not free to reciprocate and that what happened in the tree house was a mistake—'

'A mistake?'

'Well, I'm sure Tiara would like to think it was,' I say pointedly. He's not the only one who's feeling deceived around here.

'I'm sure she would, but I don't think it was. At least I didn't . . .' He looks a little forlorn as he confesses, 'To be honest I rather hoped it was a beginning . . .'

'But . . . Tiara?' I can't believe he's being so flip about their relationship.

'Tiara is a beautiful girl, an outstanding performer and we're lucky to have her, but I have a strict no-dating policy with the women we work with. She was a little miffed about that at first, but she

392

understands that ultimately it's just asking for trouble.'

'So she wanted to, but you didn't?' I have to be clear on this point.

'And I should mention I wasn't her first choice!' He gives me a playful glint.

'Tony? She tried it on with Tony before you?' I hoot.

He grins back at me.

'Wow. Brave woman!' I coo.

Tezz laughs and shakes his head. 'You know, he's not so tough.'

'Actually, I do know that,' I smile, reflecting on our farewell hug. 'He's a great guy.'

Tezz takes a step closer. Suddenly he doesn't seem so remote. I'm ready to jump into his arms, but my head is still full of unresolved niggles regarding Tiara.

'So that kiss at the end of the Janet Jackson song?'

'Just part of the act. We've always done it that way. Well, perhaps not always with such vigour. She really went for it last night.' Tezz shudders slightly at the memory. 'We should probably think about dropping that end note.'

'I thought you were doing it to get back at me.'

'Yeah, well.' He gives a sheepish shrug. 'I don't suppose I resisted as much as I could have. It was just such a shock seeing you with this guy I didn't even know existed.'

'I'm so sorry about that,' I cringe, eyes downcast with remorse. 'I should have said something earlier.

I've been thinking about why I didn't and the best reason I can come up with is that I wanted us to have the chance to just be, no restrictions or complications . . .'

He nods compliance, but I feel I want to say more so that he really understands where I'm coming from.

'I've led a pretty quiet life up until now, Tezz. No grand passion. And I didn't mind, it seemed simpler that way, and it certainly never struck me that I was missing out. If anything I thought I was sparing myself untold angst . . .' I take a breath. 'Hugh came to me at a crucial time and he's been wonderful and supportive and a great human being, and everyone around me has always told me how lucky I am, how they wished they could have what I had. So I thought I must be lucky, but numb. I never felt any of it in my heart. And I put that down to my parents dying – that part of me shut down then. I didn't want to feel that kind of pain again – you know, love hurts . . .' I sigh. 'But then I met you.' I blink up at him. 'And there was this spark. And I felt this change in me, this new hope and a kind of *confidence* that things could be different. I started to think that maybe I could have the passion without the peril!' I laugh, suddenly self-conscious. 'I can give you a dozen fancy adjectives, but the bottom line is I like how I feel when I'm with you.'

'I like how I feel when I'm with you too,' he says, drawing me into one of his major-league hugs. Never was a chest and a pair of arms put to better use. If only all soul-bearing could be met with such a reward.

'Actually, I love it!' he sighs into my ear. 'Being with you makes me feel like I'm home, without any of the bad connotations that used to have!'

I beam back at him, knowing exactly what he means. Then we take a moment to seriously look at each other, excited by the potential for joy we seem to have tapped into.

'I think we should work on getting you to stay a little bit longer,' he decrees, gently wiping my mud-spattered face with the cuff of his sleeve.

His touch is so tender my heart shimmies at the prospect of a kiss but suddenly the bar is overrun with holidaymakers eager to rack up some sorrow-drowning aperitifs, and this time neither of us is willing to be the floor-show.

'Come on, let's go get you cleaned up!' He takes my hand and begins squeezing us through the crowd.

'Are you staying at the hotel?' I ask, hoping his room is nearby. It's still pelting down outside.

'Nope, I'm just here to meet Maeva, our costume-maker, for dinner. You have to join us!'

'Er, lovely, but where are we going to go to—' I hold out my crusty skirts at the door.

'Don't worry,' he says, tucking me into his armpit, 'I know where the maid keeps all the toiletries.'

'What exactly are you proposing?' I stall the dash.

'You'll see,' he says, propelling me on my way.

31

'Okay, put your hands out,' Tezz instructs.

We're rustling around in one of the huts set back in the jungle part of the hotel.

'Shampoo . . .' He squints in the darkness, holding the little plastic bottle up to the moonlight to check on the contents. 'Conditioner . . . Shower gel or soap?'

'Soap, please. I always feel that shower gel slips past the dirt even though it makes you smell nice.'

'Thanks for that.'

'No problem,' I titter as he checks for other goodies.

'Toilet cleaner we can do without . . .'

In the distance I hear some voices and give a furtive shiver. 'I feel like we're doing a job!' I whisper.

'Don't say that!' He switches around, suddenly serious.

'I didn't mean—'

'I would never take anything without the owner's

permission,' he insists. 'I'm cool with the staff here, and any time—'

'It's okay.' I rest my hand on his arm. 'I'm sorry I said that. I just meant it in a fun way.'

His face softens. 'I know.' He shakes his head. 'Sometimes I get kinda touchy about – well, you get it.'

'You know I do.'

He nods, smiling at our bond. 'I just never want to be that person. I don't even want to be around that kind of thing ever again.'

'You won't be,' I assure him. 'There's no need for you to be – you have your own life now. How about a towel?'

'Good thinking.' He grabs a pair and clicks the door back in place.

Together we weave further back through the staff huts and then off the paved path until we come upon a clearing which appears to be home to some kind of outside storage unit with stacks of crates and teams of plastic drums.

'You want to take a shower?' He steps out from under the shelter of the trees, flings his arms wide and turns his face to the sky. 'It doesn't get any better than this.'

'Are you serious?' I gasp.

'What,' he says, wiping his face, 'this isn't wet enough for you?'

'Well . . .' I can't deny the sky is still releasing torrents.

'Damn girl, you're awful picky! I thought you liked the rain?'

'I do, it's just that in this situation I'm normally wearing a raincoat.'

'You wear a raincoat in the shower?' He raises a teasing eyebrow at me.

I roll my eyes at him. 'Don't you?'

'Come on, Amber,' he entices, reaching his hands out to me. 'The water's lovely!'

I duck out of reach. 'But my clothes – I only just got dry!'

'Well you could always do this . . .' He pulls off his sopping T-shirt and flings it – splat! – into the sidelines. 'Better?'

Oh God, you have no idea, I sigh to myself, flashing back to when I first saw his wet torso on the beach. Then his skin was racing with lagoon water, now he's shiny and slick with rain. I can't decide which look I like better.

'Doo-de-doo-doo . . .' He hums the opening bars to 'Singin' In The Rain' as he begins capering like a half-naked Gene Kelly, jumping on the side wall and then clattering down the stepped crates, fuelled by that irresistible *joie de vivre* of his. I can't help but smile as I watch – he looks so happy, so free, as he tap-splashes around, doing turns and leaps and swinging around a palm tree in lieu of a lamppost. I wish I could do that!

'Okay, your turn.' He skids over to my side with a grin.

I shrink back, startled at his mind-reading. Me, dance with a dancer? 'I couldn't!' I bleat.

'Oh yes you could,' he says, taking my hands and spinning me out in a circle as the rain seeps into my clothes and splashes between my toes.

At first I feel tense and awkward, but soon I'm too dizzy to do anything but fall forward and relax into his arms, and before I know it my feet are clickety-clacking alongside his.

'Wait a second – you tap-dance?' He looks down at my feet as if he's addressing them personally.

'No. Well. I mean, years ago me and Felicity went to a couple of classes, but—'

'Oh my God!' he laughs. 'I thought I saw some form. Give me a double-time step!' He clicks his fingers.

'I'm wearing flip-flops!' I complain, suddenly self-conscious as my feet morph into a couple of sloppy beanbags.

'Uh-huh.' He nods in apparent sympathy before snarling, 'Nice try, but you're not off the hook yet – hand them over.'

'My shoes?'

'Your shoes.'

Before I can make any further enquiries he darts off with them, leaving me standing barefoot in the rain, pumicing my heels with the grit of the cement, trying to remember a single sodding step from my time at the Marsden Academy of Dance.

'Here!' He returns finally, handing me back my flip-flops, now with tough ridged shells taped to the heels and toes.

'Oh my God!' I laugh out loud at his ingenuity. I can't believe he did that!

'All the better to tap with!' he grins, helping me slide them on. 'Okay now – step-ball-change, step-ball-change . . .' he chants until I submit and start joining in.

'There you go!' he cheers. 'Now do this . . .' He rat-a-tats across the floor.

I follow his moves, gathering speed as my confidence grows. All that joy I've seen him convey on stage I'm now feeling too.

'Ha! You're great!' he cheers.

I swipe away his compliment. I can't hold a torch to him as he kicks out his legs in a move reminiscent of a Cossack dance.

'What about this?' He does the tilted-forward run with arms slashing at his side.

I try it. This is actually fun. My body doesn't normally get overly involved in my life – just gets me from A to B – but it's loving this chance to play. I'd forgotten how good it feels to dance around like a lunatic, not caring how silly you might look!

'Come here!' He swoops me into a galloping waltz, cavorting me around in grand sweeping turns. It feels so old-movie romantic it's all I can do not to fall into a swoon.

But then, out of nowhere, we hear the hard-core pumping bass of Fat Joe's 'Lean Back'.

'What?' I laugh. Who would be thumping out rap in the jungle?

'It's Kana, one of the staff,' Tezz explains, catching his breath. 'He can't get enough of the stuff.'

'Can you tap to this?' I challenge him.

Without a second's pause he's cracking the stone slabs with attitude, slapping his foot out and cranking a homeboy pose as he matches the beats with heel clicks.

I stand amazed. This is so much fun. I never want to stop dancing and I never want to be dry again.

'And for the finale . . .!' He gives me a Fred and Ginger dip, holds me there for a second, my back arched over his low arm, and then with amazing bicep control he ever so slowly eases me closer and closer to his mouth.

When we are just a breath apart I find my hand sliding up the back of his neck and allow myself to succumb to his pillowy lips.

This is even more beautiful than I remembered – it's as if we're creating our very own language, a new way to show how we really feel. This time I hold nothing back.

'You kiss so good,' he murmurs, pausing to gaze at me.

'You too,' I sigh back, my heart magnetised by his.

As his hands move into my hair, I notice a mischievous smile play on his face. 'Shampoo!' he announces suddenly, reaching behind me.

'Huh?' I'm still in a love-daze.

'Allow me,' he says, unscrewing the cap and splurging the iridescent liquid into his palm.

Lathering up, he smooths the foam evenly over my hair and then digs in, working it to maximum capacity until sudsy rivulets start to drip down my neck and on to my collarbone, slipping under my shirt. It's a bizarre sensation being soapy and wet, yet clothed. In a moment of daring I peel off my shirt and reveal my white cami-vest. Though the night is still warm, I shiver as his torso brushes past my now bare arm. He continues to move around me – I can feel his breastbone against my shoulder – as he pushes the white froth from my hair, encouraging the rain to swoosh it clean.

'Would madam like conditioner?' he asks, lowering his lips to the sensitive curve between my neck and shoulder.

'If sir would oblige,' I say, tremulously, leaning back into him as the right side of my body gets goosepimply with lust.

His fingers groove along my scalp, combing through the slippery liquid in firm, repetitive motions. Then he leads me to the shelter of the trees. The fall of the rain is broken by the canopy of leaves and I almost miss the water teaming over my body.

'What now?' I wonder out loud.

'Just letting it sit awhile,' he explains, smoothing my forehead. 'Isn't that what you people with hair do?'

I chuckle and reach up and let my hands caress his near-naked scalp, following imaginary patterns and ley lines.

'That feels so good,' he purrs, eyes flickering closed as he once again inclines his mouth to mine.

This kiss is even more rapturous and enveloping. Inside me a swirl of ribbons and streamers tickle every inner organ and then spiral heavenward. I feel like my heart will burst. I love him so much! Not love-love obviously – how could it be? I've only known him a matter of days! – but that version of love that zings from your heart and paints a permanent smile on your lips.

'What are you grinning at?' he asks as he leans back to study me.

'What do you think?' I reply.

He heaves a contented sigh. 'Okay, let's rinse.'

I move in utter submission to him, trusting that I'm in good hands. And such elegant hands. I can feel that thumb ring I admired early on brush against my temple as he massages my head and then eases my hair into a silken sheath down my back.

'Beautiful,' he admires, softly kissing my cheek before adding a seductive, 'Now, what do we have left to do . . .?'

'Soap!' I squeak, faint with loin-based yearning as my brain fast-forwards to the prospect of his hands over my fabric-free body.

'Uh-huh,' he growls.

Anything. I'd let him do anything with me.

'Tezz!'

What's that? I frown, distracted. Another voice speaking his name?

'Tezz – you out there?'

403

I can't tell if it's male or female, but either way they are persistent in their call.

'It's Maeva,' he sighs, the droop of his head letting me know that, for now at least, our al fresco amour is to be curtailed. 'I guess I lost track of time.'

I'm so thoroughly abandoned to arousal, it's a struggle to even consider simmering down sufficiently to sit at a dinner table and make civilised conversation. All I have to offer right now is a selection of appreciative moans. Not that I would have really got naked in a public place. *Would I?*

'I could see if she's got something you could borrow to wear?' he suggests.

I manage a nod.

While he's gone, I try and shake the desire from my body and then mentally run through their stage-wear – not a lot in the way of my usual bulky milkmaid outfits, so this is definitely going to be a departure.

He reappears. 'Here, try this.' He directs me to a battered old fence as if it's a boudoir screen.

I contemplate the scrap of black he's proffering.

'Please tell me these are just starter-knickers,' I protest as I try to differentiate between the waistband and leg holes.

'They're hot pants,' he tells me.

I don't believe this. 'Don't you have anything with more material?' I plead.

'Sorry, it's just the girls' stuff she's been working on.'

I look at my sodden skirt. I suppose I should be grateful that they don't perform in showgirl thongs. At least these are comfortably stretchy, if a little clingy. I ping them into place at the top of my thighs, thankful that Oxford is a city of cyclists.

'What about this top?' He swings a second item over to me.

I assess the swatch of purple satin and black fringing.

'It's not a top, it's a bra,' I complain.

'Don't be silly, it's got beading,' he scolds.

'Oh, well then,' I snort as I inspect the strands of jet which apparently drape over one's upper arm when worn.

'Just try it.'

Reluctantly I peel off my vest and then my own plain, wet, M&S bra and wriggle into the super-boosting bordello version. The good news is that it does fit. The bad news is that the balconette styling has given my boobs top-billing in a show of wanton sexuality. Short of using the tablecloth as a pashmina, I can't possibly sit down to dinner in this. People will start tucking dollar bills into the straps.

'Tezz, I'm really not sure . . .'

'Let's see.'

'No, it's too revealing.' I try to squish my boobs further into the cups but they defiantly spring back into place like a pair of feisty balloons. I'm on the verge of despair when Tony's reference to me having the body of a supermodel comes to mind. It seems hard to believe, but I guess he had no reason to lie. And now I come to think of it, Felicity said something similar the day I almost went swimming off the back of *Windstar* with her. Do I dare test Tezz's verdict?

'Okay, you can see, but only for a second,' I squeak. 'And just to show you why I can't go out in it.'

He steps around the corner and then instantly does a spin. 'Damn!' he hoots, scrunching up his eyes in disbelief and then grabbing my hands and holding them away from my body so I can't cover myself up.

'Woah!' he coos, nodding approval.

'See what I mean!' I squirm under his surveillance.

'I mean "woah" in a good way,' he insists, still agog.

I'm glad the lights are dim here. No one has ever seen me like this.

'I had no idea . . .' he breathes, then laughs at his own awe. 'So, what's Angelina Jolie gonna do now that you've stolen her body?'

'Don't be silly.' I bat away his compliment.

'I'm serious. I don't mean to stare, but . . .' Again he shakes his head, then smiles slyly. 'You don't know what you're doing to me.' He pulls me into an intense body-hug. 'I wish we could skip dinner.'

I can't believe I'm standing in front of the sexiest man I've ever met and yet I'm the one who's being admired.

'You know, you could have also worn this . . .' He reaches back round to his bag and pulls out a pair of long lycra trousers and a shimmery sheer top. 'But seeing as you look so hot in this . . .'

'What?!' I squeal. 'I can't believe you made me— *give me those!*'

'Just one more look!'

'Tezz!' I swat him.

'Okay, okay, but you're putting it back on later . . .'

I grab the clothes and hustle him back to the other side of the fence. Then I take a moment to look down at myself before I trade outfits. Can I really look as good as his reaction would suggest? I don't think I've ever wanted anyone to look at me in a directly sexual way until now. Suddenly I love the sensation. I've got body parts he wants to get to know better! I feel like I've got the best of both worlds – he liked me before he saw what was beneath the shapeless sundresses, and now he's utterly revved up. This is too exciting.

I quickly change, so much more at ease in full-length items, even if the trousers are Olympic-runner tight and the top does keep slipping off my shoulder.

'Ready?' he enquires, offering me his arm.

'Yup,' I smile.

I've never felt more ready or eager to step forward. Everything else can wait – the flight, returning home, the angst of the break-up. For now I'm going to immerse myself in this heady hedonism, and if this exquisite pleasure I feel from being with Tezz has to last me the rest of my life, so be it. It's already worth it.

32

Initially I'm a little thrown. We appear to be having dinner with the Tahitian equivalent of Eddie Izzard.

Maeva is a thick-necked, square-faced man wearing a conservative calf-length dress, purple button earrings and a matching necklace. Whereas Fantasia was flirty and coquettish – more of the John Leguizamo/ *To Wong Foo* persuasion – Maeva is solid and dignified and serious.

'Er . . .' I give Tezz a quizzical look as Maeva pauses to greet hotel manager Franck Vetier.

'I take it you haven't met a *mahu* yet?' Tezz looks amused.

'Just a *rae-rae*,' I shrug. 'Does that count?'

'Actually, there's quite a difference.' He ushers me out of earshot. 'Historically *mahus* were the chosen servants of royalty: they had real status and were renowned for their poise and discretion. Even today there's a great demand for them as staff – in the hotels or organising the island dance troupes – because they are so conscientious; real perfectionists, you know? You should see the work Maeva does on our costumes – the quality and the detailing is flawless.'

'That's so fascinating,' I coo under my breath as we take our seats.

There is definitely something about Maeva that commands respect. I try to dim the curiosity in my eyes so he doesn't feel overly scrutinised, and then the menu arrives and I am authentically distracted. 'Oooo, hot goat-cheese profiteroles with diced tomato sauce,' I salivate. 'Sweet potato soup with smoked fish . . .'

I remember nothing of the food I ate here two nights ago with Hugh and Sandrine, so this time I decide to lay off the vino so I can savour every bite. I don't want any of this memory to be blurry.

'Dariole de pomme golden à la crevette sauce pimentée,' Maeva makes his choice.

Tezz opts for the lagoon fish pâté. Me? Those profiteroles. And that's just the starters . . . For the main course we order grilled spiny lobster with parsley butter and Reisling wine sauce, marlin wrapped in banana leaf and seafood gratin, the prospect of which leaves me sitting erect and fidgety of toe in anticipation.

Things get better yet when Maeva informs me that because I have a business-class airline ticket I can, in fact, change my flight date as many times as I like – apparently it's one of the privileges you pay extra for.

'So I don't have to go back tomorrow?' I gasp, delighted at my reprieve.

'You don't even have to go back on Saturday. The choice is yours.'

I want to give every glass in the room a celebratory chink, but there is the small matter of accommodation.

'Tonight you will stay at my brother's house.' Maeva reads my mind. 'He is away in Rangiroa. It is all for you. And Tezz.'

'Really?' This is too wonderful.

'And tomorrow you will stay with me in Bora Bora,' Tezz chips in. 'And the next night. And the next . . . As long as you please.'

'Are you sure? I don't want to presume.' I'm suddenly shy. 'I mean, we hardly know each other.'

'All the more reason to spend as much time together as possible, wouldn't you say?' he shrugs, grinning happily.

'If you're sure . . .'

'In Tahiti we are very easy-going,' Maeva smiles knowingly. 'This is the Island of Love!'

'Well then, *thank you*.' I finally accept all invitations – along with the last of the breadfruit chips: perfect, firm, straight-sided chips that you can't tell apart from the real deal – and feel extremely blessed.

As we continue chatting I glean a little about Tahitians, including the fact that they are a very clean people who have several cold-water showers a day and use lime as a natural deodorant. It would also seem they have a mischievous sense of humour, especially when it comes to their governing country.

'God made France such a beautiful land and then,

so as not to make everyone else jealous, he made the French!' Maeva quips.

As I listen to him describing various aspects of Tahitian life, I ask myself if I could live here for real? I'd certainly miss all the creaking tomes and sniping wintry winds of home – no need for furry Yeti boots and pom-pom earmuffs here. I wonder, if I stayed would my clothing shrink to vest-tops and cut-off shorts? Would the Midas sun turn my pale skin gold? Would my hair be festooned daily with flowers?

As I ponder inwardly, I hear Tezz telling Maeva about my art historian background and then recount our recent meeting with Marcel.

'Perhaps you could help him with the exhibition?' Maeva suggests when Tezz is done praising the depth of my knowledge. 'Though art is in Marcel's blood, the business of a gallery is new to him.'

Perhaps I could.

'And if you want respite from Gauguin, if you want to be able to shake a hand with paint still fresh upon it, we have many wonderful local artists working here today . . . It would be my pleasure to introduce you to Maui Seaman. His paintings are so textured, vivid oranges and greens . . . And Linh Cao, her work is fun – young and decorative . . . And Jonathan Mencarelli, he specialises in sculpture in the round. You have to see his work *Rêve de Poissons* – this smooth, creamy maiden entwined with the ivory fish . . .'

Suddenly my mind is streaking ahead and I picture myself standing proudly outside a gallery of my own.

Perhaps luring customers with a few choice works on display at The Paradise Room and the promise of a state-of-the-art aircon unit . . . Tezz reaches across the table and squeezes my hand tight. The enthusiasm in his eyes reflects my own. Maybe my staying for an extended period isn't such a far-fetched idea after all.

'So many possibilities . . .' Maeva ponders the dessert menu. 'Personally, I recommend the soup and ravioli.'

I shoot Tezz a concerned look. Are we going to start the meal all over again?

Tezz chuckles at his friend's mischief. 'The soup is chilled watermelon with a strawberry liqueur,' he explains. 'And the ravioli is pineapple with a raspberry mousse.'

I swoon at the prospect of such inventive sweetness and sigh, 'I could get used to this!'

An hour later I'm standing behind Tezz as he unlocks the door to Maeva's brother's home. I feel a flicker of nervous excitement as we step inside, not quite knowing what will come next.

Without turning on the light he steps forward and enfolds me in the kind of everlasting hug that could keep me cruising on bliss for months – every muscle flex seems to infuse the embrace with more meaning. With just his arms and torso and breath he seems to be saying, *I'm so glad you're here. I want to slow down the world and linger in this moment with you. There may be things I can't say out loud but I want you to feel them . . .*

And I do. Just the nearness of our bodies feels so intimate and poignant. Perhaps it's premature to talk of love, but I really can sense our love blending – the double wonder of loving and being loved.

'Amber,' he husks my name as he leans down to kiss me.

As his lips meet mine I'm set adrift, moved by the intensity of both his ardour and his gentleness. To be simultaneously desired and cared for is a heady combination. One minute I'm in a rapturous swirl, the next we are oh-so-lightly breathing the same breath, teetering on the edge before we plunge deep, deep down.

I am so ready to surrender to him. He can have it all. This time I don't want to hold anything back.

'Wanna get horizontal?' he whispers playfully inviting me to join him on the futon.

It's a simple bed in a simple room, yet beyond sumptuous for me emotionally. I lower myself on to the soft cotton bedspread and smile as our bodies instinctively entwine and interlock. This feels so phenomenally good I can't imagine being apart from him ever again.

My heart is now pounding expectantly, and without thinking my hand slips up the back of his shirt, eager to be satisfied by the touch of his lustrous skin. He moans gently as I glide my hand up to his shoulder blade and drops his head to the side of my neck, nuzzling into me. I find myself emitting a groan of tingly delight and thrust myself closer to him.

'You feel so good,' he murmurs as he rolls above me so he can gaze down at me.

Wow! I can't believe his beautiful face is looking right at me! Those penetratingly dark eyes, that perfect pink mouth. I lift a finger to follow the precision V at the centre of his top lip, then slide it down to the matching plumpness of the lower. His mouth is just so beautiful, I have to kiss him again, and again and again.

As our hips press closer we slip our tops up and off, and as we come back together, the feeling is just so warm and silky and comforting I know there can be no better place on earth than right here, right now, and my face is overtaken by an outsize grin.

'What are you laughing at?' Tezz tilts his head, bemused.

'I'm not laughing,' I assure him. 'This is just a really big smile.'

'So you're happy?'

'You have no idea,' I beam.

And then his hips grind into me and I gasp at the electric sensations I'm experiencing. I never knew my heart and body could feel so open and engaged. The feeling builds with every kiss and movement. His hands in my hair, mine bumping over his ridged stomach, our remaining clothes cast to the floor, the twisting, the sighing, the urgency, the pleasure . . .

As we fall back on to the pillows, I'm atremble with awe at what has just taken place. I can't quite believe this is me, letting go like this. I feel relaxed yet elated – this is definitely the closest I've ever felt to another human being. I can't get enough of this eye-to-eye contact with Tezz.

'You're so beautiful,' he tells me, and for once I feel it. Right to my soul.

33

My toes slip into the luminous blue of the lagoon, so warm it barely registers as water. Even as I waft my feet back and forth I am more aware of silky sensuality than liquid. I squint open one eye to check that my legs really are immersed and discover I have been set in turquoise jelly from the knees down.

Shuffling forward on the decking, I extend my legs further, grazing my soles on the seabed, but it's only when I receive a wake-up pinch from the blanched coral that I truly recall where I am: paradise.

I know that for sure, not because of the limbo-ing palm trees, nor the musky-sweet scent of coconut oil perfuming the morning air, but because I have just been kissed in a way I have only ever dreamed about . . .

'Breakfast, my lady . . .' Tezz plants yet another winner on my lips as he sets down a small tray of pastries and papaya.

I never knew kissing had such range. The affection flows between us, and I feel my chest heave skyward.

'So, today, I was thinking . . .' he begins as he settles beside me.

'Yes?'

'Kana is taking a couple of hotel guests out to a private motu picnic – we could go along if you liked? Sneak off and find our own stretch of sand . . .' He kisses my neck. 'The plane to Bora Bora doesn't leave until 5 p.m., so we have plenty of time.' He works his way down.

'Mmmm,' I melt.

'Is that a yes?'

'It's always going to be a yes when you're doing that . . .' I sigh.

An hour later we meet two English girls and one Japanese, the best friend of Kana's Japanese wife, who is currently at home tending to their newborn babe.

Kana himself is a fine specimen of Tahitian manhood, with a Magnum moustache and curly chest hair creating a springy nest for his necklace of outsize sharks' teeth.

'Do you think those fangs are real?' one of the English girls quavers as she slides along the bench-style seating of his small canopied boat.

Her friend assesses Kana's tree-trunk chunky arms and heavily-inked skin and squeaks a yes.

Despite his alter ego as a kind of Crocodile Dundee of the Sea, he seems an amiable enough fellow and chats away to the Japanese girl in French as we pummel the waves, contending with the occasional heave up and thud down as the engine whines and whirrs us on our way.

All the while I lean happily into Tezz. It's amazing, the pleasure to be had from simply aligning yourself with another human being. When I used to rest on Hugh I would feel safe but almost instantly restless. With Tezz I feel like I've had every bone removed from my body and could lie here in a contented heap for the rest of the year. As I watch the English girl with her camcorder filming the rough island foliage rushing by to our left, I wish I had every moment I've spent with Tezz on tape so I could relive and relish each frame. Especially last night. I feel a stirring at the memory of those hours and hours of mutual adoration. It was like neither of us wanted to sleep because it would be like losing each other temporarily. Every time one of us shifted position, the other would snuggle closer and emit a sigh of contentment. And to think that by now I was due to be thousands of air miles away.

'Fish?' Kana grunts, bringing me back to the present moment by handing me a long piece of twine with a rock and piece of bait tied to the end.

I look at Tezz.

'Go on, try it,' he encourages me.

I look back at Kana. 'What do I have to do?'

He motions for me to lower the line into the water. I see now that he's stopped the boat in a patch of ultra-

418

blue, obviously a tried and tested fishing spot. Well, I guess I should at least give it a go.

Everyone watches as I feed the line deeper and deeper. Suddenly there's a tug and the twine indents my finger, leaving a sharp red line.

'I think it's caught on something.' I tug at it then immediately go to hand it back to Kana.

His English is minimal, so he mimes for me to start pulling up. I look around for help.

'You can do it!' Tezz cheers, a big grin on his face.

I pull and pull, ignoring the slicing pain of the twine, crossing hands with Kana as he assists me.

'Aaagghghhh!' I leap back screaming as an ugly yet strangely familiar fish comes flipping and struggling into view, its mouth gaping like a trapdoor so wide it could encompass my upper arm. 'Uuugghhhh!' I howl again as Kana swings it in my direction, sending me careening over to the other side of the boat into Tezz's arms.

'That's a beauty, look at it!' Tezz turns my head back.

'What is it?' I shudder, recognising the brown and white splotchy camouflage from the fish that had me darting out of the water the day of my wedding ceremony.

'Marbled rock cod,' Tezz informs me. 'One mother of a marbled rock cod.'

Cod? That doesn't sound nearly scary enough. Nevertheless I'd rather not share a boat with it.

'Are we going to throw it back now?' I ask innocently.

'Lunch,' Kana cheers, looking chuffed as he propels it into a polystyrene chest.

One by one every girl has a go, each screaming more than the last. Especially when one has quite a tussle on her hands and then pulls out nothing more than a fish head dripping fresh blood.

'Ewwwwwwweeeekk!' we all recoil.

'Shark,' says Kana.

We all blanche.

'What does he mean?' I grip Tezz.

'The shark saw the fish flipping in the water and went for it.'

'You're kidding?' I croak.

He leads me over to the edge of the boat, studies the water for a second and then says, 'There.'

A large light-grey form is making a rhythmic passage around the boat. This little boat that I really wish was *Windstar*-sized right now. I can't quite believe my eyes. 'That's really a shark?'

'Yes, ma'am.'

'Oh.' I try to sound as blasé as I can, but spoil it by letting slip an anxious, '*Oh my God!*'

When the other girls realise what's going on, they get in such a flailing twitter around the boat that we're soon in danger of capsizing. And all Kana can do is laugh – a big, Blackbeard, throaty gurgle.

'Can't we move on now?' one girl whimpers, looking pleadingly at him.

'One more,' Kana decides, launching a new line over the side.

We wait and wait, preparing for a Jaws-type eruption from the water, but instead he pulls up the prettiest flame-hued squirrelfish with a perfect crest of scarlet along its spine and scales of overlapping silver and crimson.

'Beauty and Beast,' I murmur to myself, casting a farewell glance back at the shark, relieved to be leaving it behind as we continue on to the island, only to be met by several of its smaller black-tip relatives waiting for us in the shallow waters where we moor.

Kana points out three within harpooning distance and then jumps into their private pool and wades ashore.

'Now what?' I gulp.

'We tread carefully,' Tezz advises.

'We're going to walk in the water where the sharks are swimming?' I can't believe my ears.

'It's the only way to get on shore,' Tezz explains. 'Honestly, it's fine. Look how casual Kana is.'

'Yes, but he's Tahitian. They're not going to bite one of their own,' I counter.

'You think you taste that good?' Tezz challenges, before biting down on my shoulder and adding: 'Actually, you do . . .'

The other guests are clinging to each other, looking equally timid.

'Come!' Kana beckons us over.

No one moves.

'I'll do it!' I am surprised to hear myself volunteer.

Everyone turns to watch as I lower myself rung by rung into the water. OhGodOhGodOhGod! I slosh through the water, afraid to even catch the shark's eye, just focusing on getting my feet up on to dry sand.

'Aaghh!' I do a little shudder-dance as I make it. 'Quick!' I beckon to the others.

Tezz sees everyone off the boat before lolloping through himself.

'You're so brave,' he says admiringly, bequeathing me a kiss when we are reunited.

'Never again!' I shudder.

'So you're not getting back on the boat?' he teases as he leads me to the shade of the raffia shelter.

I look around me: a deserted sandy isle sprigged with coconut palms and encircled by sheer turquoise waters. Despite my predilection for all things damp and grey, there are worse things I can think of than being marooned here with Tezz.

'Nope, I'm staying put,' I affirm.

While Kana sets up the barbecue and prods my cod and its pals with a stick, I find myself absorbed in the secret life of the sand. I am looking for a keepsake when I notice that every other shell is in motion. From the delicate little spirals as wee as a child's fingernails to the heavier, spikier cones, they all seem to be home to crabs of a corresponding size, scurrying around the beach like random backpackers. I crouch down and pick one up. Little legs flail for a moment then withdraw inside.

'You want to help me make the poisson cru?' Tezz calls over to me. 'Tony told me that you're quite the chef!'

'He did?' I puff proudly as I set the shell back down and follow him to the table.

'This is the one thing I know how to do because it doesn't require any actual cooking,' Tezz grins. 'So you take your cubes of raw tuna . . .' he tells me, releasing the Tupperware container and tipping the contents into a big wooden bowl. 'Add a cup of coconut milk.' He bids me do the pouring. 'Then the juice of a handful of limes. They actually just call them citrus here because sometimes they're yellow, sometimes green.'

'Uh-huh,' I nod, cutting the fruit and squeezing with all my might. 'So this is a bit like ceviche?'

'What?' Tezz blinks.

'It's a kind of Latin-American raw fish dish – the acid from the lime actually cooks it.'

'If you say so,' he shrugs jauntily.

I laugh along, for once feeling the expert.

'Then we add diced onions and tomatoes and cucumber and stir it all up.'

'Salt,' Kana reminds Tezz, coming over to check on proceedings.

I carefully jumble the contents till there's an even mix. Then Kana reaches in and takes a spoonful.

'Good.' He gives it his seal of approval.

'You eat it right away? No marinating time?' The outer layer of the tuna chunks may have gone opaque, but the inside is still raw pink.

423

'Taste,' he instructs me.

'I-I don't know. I don't really like sushi.'

Kana and his shark teeth won't take no for an answer. Tezz watches with amusement as I gingerly take a baby spoonful.

'Oh my God!' My taste buds zing with satisfaction. 'Oh wow – that's delicious! Totally melt-in-your-mouth.'

'Try these . . .' Kana removes some lids from previously prepared dishes – beetroot with sweetcorn, a leafy salad, a choppy potato dish . . . Then his pièce de résistance – a huge flagon of chilled blush wine.

Soon everyone is tucking in with gusto, having selected a cut of the fish they themselves caught.

'Well, I guess you were feeding the fish earlier today, now they are feeding you,' the one vegetarian in the group says nonchalantly.

'More bread?' Kana offers round the second baguette. '*Non?*'

Seeing that we're done, he walks to the water, baguette in one hand, cigarette in the other.

'What's he doing?' I frown as we follow him to the water's edge.

Holding the cigarette aloft, he places the bread in his mouth and ducks down till his chin is in the water.

'Is he crazy?' one English girl wails as a foot-long blue shark weaves up and takes a snag from the opposite end.

Within seconds there are five or six sharks all darting in to take a bite. Soon the baguette is nothing more than a piece of soggy mush dangling from his lips.

'This is better than Sea World!' whoops the girl with the camcorder.

'Do you think he takes the cigarette in there to burn them in case they get too close?' asks her friend.

Camcorder Girl rolls her eyes. 'Don't you think it would lose its burn once it's in the water?'

'Oh yes,' the first blushes.

We think the entertainment is done, but no sooner have we gone back for a top-up on the wine than Kana is at it again, this time flailing around with a heavy link-chain with a whole fish bound to the end.

'Here we go,' Tezz chuckles.

'What now?' I say fretfully as he begins to haul something heavy and reluctant up on to the beach.

It's a whole shark. A live, angry, wanting-to-get-back-in-the-water shark.

'Noooooooooooooo!'

Again Kana gets the girlie-screaming response that appears to motivate his behaviour as he holds it in place with a flip-flopped foot. He then grabs the writhing mass and indulges in a little playful midair wrestling, encouraging Camcorder Girl to step forward, eye blithely trained down the lens. Convinced she's about to star in her own snuff movie, I go to yank her back, but in the nick of time he returns the shark to the water with a dramatic splash. It scoots off at high speed, no doubt already plotting a return prank.

425

It's then that I decide there really is no way I'm wading back to that boat.

While the English girls sunbathe on the shoreline and Kana and his wife's pal flutter around the surface snorkelling, Tezz and I choose to languish in the shade of a sky-scraping palm.

As I settle on the sand I find myself instinctively adopting the knees-to-one-side pose of Gauguin's *Women of Tahiti on the Beach*. As I do, I realise how my many malign judgements about the artist have softened over the course of this trip. I knew that Gauguin had lived as a child in Peru (from the age of eighteen months until he was six), but I had never considered how that tropical idyll may have got under his skin until I felt the pleasure for myself. Now it seems only natural that he would crave a return to that brighter, more vivid lifestyle after one too many harsh grey French winters.

And there was I condemning him for abandoning his wife and children as if he had hopped on a flight on a Bounty ad whim, when in reality his painting had kept them apart for years as it was, and even when he did leave it took two months on a boat to get here. Besides, how many men leave their wives just to watch football on another woman's TV set? He left because he felt compelled to pursue his art, and he was hugely prolific during his time here, not lazing around getting a tan. What's more, Maeva put paid to any lingering doubts about him corrupting Tahitian women when she informed me that even today if a single white man visits the Marquesas Islands alone, he may find a native girl knocking on his door after dark, eager to create a light-skinned baby. Clearly different rules apply here.

I settle back into Tezz's shoulder. Even though I too am temporarily out of reach of all modern-day concerns, I can't seem to ignore the big countdown clock hanging over our heads. I could probably wangle an extra week off work if I explained my situation to Gilly, but what then? I want to let things between Tezz and me evolve at their own pace, but my head is demanding to know where this could possibly lead. Are any of the things we spoke of last night feasible? Could I really earn a living exhibiting local artists? I trace the source of my doubts to our impending return to Bora Bora. Knowing that Hugh is still there makes me feel extremely anxious, as if I'm in danger of this wonderful situation somehow reversing so that I wind up back with him, trapped again.

But no, I shake off my fear. That is not going to happen. I'm stronger now, more in control. Of myself at least. As for Tezz and the future, I just have to trust.

Two hours later I get a little boost of optimism to help me on my way.

Having sailed back to the hotel, bid a fond farewell to Maeva and shuttled back to the 'airport', we're now in line to board the plane. As Tezz and I clatter on to the tinny steps, we're each handed a traditional tiare flower by the attendant. Filing down the aisle, I remember Fantasia's explanation of the significance of where you place the bud and delay my selection by twirling the petals under my nose. As we take our seats I watch with delight as Tezz places his directly behind his left ear.

Taken.

'May I?' He now turns to me and repeats the gesture with extra finesse, leaning in to bestow the most heartfelt kiss upon my lips.

With sweaty tourists wrestling their hand luggage over our heads and kneeing us in the backs of our seats, this may be an unlikely setting for romance, but it actually feels more emotionally significant than when Hugh and I exchanged rings during our faux marriage. For this is a lovers' pledge. And for now that's all I need . . .

34

'Hey, isn't that your friend?'

Tezz directs my attention to the Bora Bora Lagoon Resort bar as we weave around the hotel en route to his pad. It is indeed Felicity. I wave my arms trying to get her attention, but she's deeply engrossed in conversation. With whom, I wonder? I know she's due for an early evening appointment with Fantasia – can they still be yappering?

'Why don't you go say hi,' Tezz suggests. 'I'll take your suitcase for you.'

'Are you sure?' I ask, delighted with the opportunity to tell her all my news.

'No problem. I've got to warm up and run through the set list with Tony. Take your time.' He blesses my lips with a kiss and then strides onward.

For a moment I watch him walking away and try not to dwell on the fact that it's actually Hugh's suitcase he's pulling along. Let's hope that the owner of those gold-embossed initials isn't propping up the spiral bar at The Paradise Room or there will be some nimble explaining to do.

I turn back to the hotel bar. I can't risk blatantly walking in, just in case Hugh or Sandrine are perched nearby. My best bet is to creep up to the window and call up to her.

When I get in position, having negotiated the waxy-leafed shrubbery, I find myself sinking a few inches into the soft earth and realise that the window is a good deal higher than I anticipated. I hear Felicity laugh, a tinkly, besotted gurgle and I know from that she's talking to a guy. I don't want to interrupt, but I have to let her know I'm back. I try jumping up to grab the ledge, but it's no use. I need a lift from below. Maybe if I wedged my foot against—

'Ms Pepper?'

Uh-oh.

I turn around and see – yes, of course it would be – Hiro. What must he make of me? First he finds me asleep in his towel stand, and now I'm trying to claw my way up the outside of a building.

'Do you need some help?' His tone suggests help of the psychiatric variety.

'No, no, I'm fine,' I breeze, bending down to inspect the markers on the plants as if I'm performing some kind of horticultural inspection. 'Just admiring your lovely *Freycinetia arborea*!'

'Indeed,' he muses, clearly unconvinced.

'Actually, I was trying to surprise a friend,' I confess,

430

pointing to the window above my head. I think it's important I reassure him that I'm doing something legit or he'll end up calling security and I can't have that. 'Unfortunately I'm not tall enough.'

'You want a boost?'

'What?'

'I could . . .' He offers his interlocked fingers as a stepping device.

'Oh no, no, really.'

'I don't mind.'

'Well . . .' Oh God, now what have I done? Still, it would be a help. 'Okay, if you're sure you don't mind. Here, let me take off my shoe.'

'Ready?' He bends his knees and braces his back.

'Ready,' I confirm.

Oop! He's really a lot stronger than he looks and I easily make it to head height with Felicity. Unfortunately her head is turned away. Fortunately so is that of her drinking companion. I say fortunately because it's a head I would recognise in a crowd of a thousand. It's Hugh's head.

'Down, down!' I bark, panicking and losing my footing. 'Aaagghh!' I fall back with a thud.

'What was that?' I hear Hugh's voice approaching the window.

Oh no! I yank Hiro on top of me to shield me from his eyes. Say he didn't see! Say he didn't see! I beg, cringing beneath Hiro's body weight.

'Ms Pepper?' Hiro sounds concerned. Make that afraid.

431

I peek out. No Hugh. Phew!

'I'm so sorry!' I scrabble out from under him, dusting off his uniform as we get back on to our feet.

'No need!' he says, quickly jumping back as my hand draws level with his waistband. 'I think I'd better be getting back to work.'

'Yes, yes, me too. Well, not work, obviously, but I'll be getting back to, um . . . whatever it is that I'm doing . . .'

'Goodnight!' he yelps, hurrying on his way, unable to withstand another nonsensical word from my mouth.

Well, I think he's learnt his lesson – next time he sees me behaving in a suspicious manner he'll just leave me to it.

I go to step out from the border, but immediately dart back and flatten myself against the wall. Hugh is leaving the bar, pausing to light a cigarette – that's bad news; he hasn't smoked since before he met me – and appears to be heading back to the bungalow.

'Felicity!' I hiss exaggeratedly once I'm sure he's gone.

'Hello?' I hear her confused voice.

'Look out the window!'

Her face juts over the sill. '*No way!* Amber!'

'Don't say my name!' I shush her.

'How did you— When? Why?' she flusters.

'Come down here so we can talk,' I hiss urgently, beckoning to her.

She looks furtively around her and then goes to climb out of the window.

'No!' I howl. 'Use the door, for heaven's sake.'

Apparently my absurd behaviour is catching.

As soon as she's within reach I drag her to a secluded dell of darkness beyond the pool.

'Firstly, in answer to your many questions, my flight got delayed in Manihi, I bumped into Tezz, we had a heart-to-heart and it turns out the hanky-panky we witnessed with Tiara was nothing more than a dance rehearsal, which left us free to . . .'

'Celebrate?' Felicity comes up with the perfect euphemism.

'Exactly!' I chirp, delighted. 'So now I'm back here for a couple more days at least.'

'That's fantastic news!'

'Yes, it is, but now to the more pertinent information.' I switch to a serious tone. 'That man you were talking to—'

'Did you see him? Isn't he yummy?' she beams.

'You know who he is?'

She nods her head vigorously, looking like she might explode from glee.

'Who?'

'Airport Guy!' she pips.

'*What*?' I gasp.

'I knew I'd find him eventually! I was having a drink at the bar with Fantasia, and he just walked in.' She clutches at my arm as if she can't believe her luck. 'All that chasing around after him, and he just waltzes right up to me!'

433

'Did he tell you his name?' Oh God, how am I going to break this to her?

She thinks for a minute. 'Do you know, we didn't even get into that! Don't you just love conversations when you skip all the formalities and the chit-chat and just get right down to it?'

'Right down to what?' I'm curious. 'What did you get down to?'

'All the good stuff – life, love, broken hearts.'

'Broken hearts?' Oh Lord, here we go!

'He's broken up with that woman I saw him with at the airport.' She gives me a 'see, told you they weren't a match' nod.

I pause to process this information and then realise that Felicity must have seen Hugh with Sandrine while I was in the loo, which would indeed explain the non-couple vibe.

'We talked about finding that special someone. He said he thought he had but now he was all confused. I said that would pass, but he said he couldn't imagine ever kissing another woman. So I moved a little closer and said, "Imagining will get you nowhere. You just have to do it."'

'*Felicity!*'

'Well, we're on holiday, aren't we?'

'What did he say?'

'He said he'd feel he was being unfaithful. Said he wasn't ready to let go. So I said, if he kissed me and felt nothing but guilt and discomfort, then he'd know it was too soon, but if he kissed me and had a positive response, then we could have some fun.'

'Gosh.' I blink at her forwardness. 'You're awfully persuasive, aren't you?'

'Years in sales, doll. I don't give up easily.'

'And then he kissed you?' I can't believe this!

'No, then he ordered us both a double shot of rum, necked his and asked for five minutes for it to kick in. So, to while away the time, I was telling him about how my mum would always have a swig of crème de menthe before a big court case on account of the double-kick of it steadying her nerves *and* giving her minty-fresh breath, and he leant over and kissed me!' She looks utterly star-struck at the memory.

'So it was a good kiss?' I venture.

'The best!' she trills, eyes aglow.

'And then?'

'And then he left.'

'Oh.'

'It's okay, he just had to have an early night. The good news is that we're meeting for drinks tomorrow night! He's got some gala dinner he can't get out of first, but afterwards . . .' She jiggles her eyebrows. 'Can you believe it?'

'Not really.' Truth be told, I'm stunned. It seems so out of character for Hugh to behave so rashly. But then again, he is thousands of miles from home with nothing to lose and a lot of pain to blot out. Besides, who am I to judge? Look at what I've been getting up to lately!

'I didn't let on that I'd seen him at the airport and

had spent most of my holiday trying to find him,' Felicity continues. 'Thought it might freak him out, and he did seem a bit delicate. Makes me want to mother him. And the rest!' she growls lasciviously.

This is too bizarre, listening to her letch after the man who made a ceremony out of his love for me the day before yesterday. There's no easy way to break it to her – I just have to say it.

Deep breath. 'Felicity, that man – he's Hugh!'

'You think?'

'What?'

'I mean he's definitely a little chunkier than Tony or Tezz, but—'

'Not *huge*!' I correct impatiently. 'Hugh! H-U-G-H!'

'Hugh.' She frowns, seemingly wondering why the name is ringing a bell. '*Hugh?*' she blurts suddenly as realisation smacks her between the eyes. '*Your* Hugh?'

'My *ex*-Hugh.'

'But that woman he was with—' she flounders.

'That was Sandrine.'

'Oh God. OH GOD!'

'It's all right.'

'No it's not,' she wails. '*Oh no, oh no, oh no!*'

'Well, it does mean that we're not going to be able to work the pearl scam we had planned, but other than that—'

'I can't believe I just kissed your boyfriend! I feel horrible.' She writhes in shame.

'*Ex*-boyfriend,' I remind her, trying to stop her pacing. 'And *he* was the one who kissed *you*.' I sound matter-of-fact, though inside I'm fighting some unsettling emotions.

'Do you hate me?'

'Of course not,' I insist. Not hate. I feel a little bit stung. A little too swiftly cast aside. There may even be a tinge of residual jealousy and nostalgia for all that is now past, but nothing that should hold her back. 'Let's sit for a minute,' I suggest, guiding her to the nearest bench.

'Oh, Amber, I can't believe it!' Felicity looks devastated as she kneads my hands in hers. 'I really thought we clicked . . . God!' She rails at the skies. 'Why can't I get a break? Why are you tormenting me like this?'

'Come on,' I urge, pulling her close. 'All is not lost. I know it might seem weird initially, but at least you know for sure he's single!'

She scowls at my feeble platitude.

'And he's definitely a good guy,' I carry on regardless. 'One in a million.'

'But there's no way he's going to fall in love with me when he's still in love with you,' she pouts. 'I mean, I envied what you had before I met him, and now—' She crumples into my chest.

I sigh and rub her back, wondering what I can say to make her feel better. All the time I envisaged palming Hugh off on Sandrine it didn't really faze me because I knew he'd turned her down once, and besides, she's hardly the girl-next-door he'd always dreamed of. But Felicity just could be . . .

'The truth is, it can't have been much fun for him being with me all those years getting so little love back,' I announce, feeling bad as I realise just how true this must be. 'This could be a revelation for him – the chance to get the love he deserves!'

'I'm so ready to love him!' Felicity smiles through her tears.

'I know you are,' I console her. And then a strange thought crosses my mind. 'What if I've been keeping him safe just for you?' I ask her.

Felicity looks confused.

'What if the reason I stayed with him so long was so that I could bring him to you – so you could both meet and fulfil your destiny together.'

'That's a bit far-fetched, isn't it?' Felicity laughs.

'I don't care,' I shrug. 'I think I might be on to something. What if this was all meant to be – you, Hugh, Tezz, me . . . We've all come to this place to make things right.'

Felicity ponders the thought for a moment, then concedes, 'I kind of like that idea . . .'

'So you'll give it a chance?'

'Okay,' she nods, a new determination coming into her eyes. 'But in the meantime, what are we going to do about those pearls? I'm even more invested now. We have to see that Hugh comes out on top. Hugh . . . Hugh Garner . . .' She drifts off, testing out his full name, unable to stop herself from taking the next step. 'Felicity Garner – hey, that sounds good!'

'Actually, it does!' I concur.

'So what do you reckon?' She hustles herself back on track. 'About the pearls?'

'Well, I think we're going to have to let the deal take place and then switch them.'

'When? How?' she splutters.

'Well, the ideal scenario would be at Los Angeles airport just before they board their respective flights – Sandrine to Paris, Hugh to London – but I don't think my presence would exactly go unnoticed at that juncture.'

'That's true,' Felicity sighs. 'Mind you, you'd make a good human diversion – Hugh would be totally thrown to see you. I know I was.'

'True, but it's really Sandrine we'd need to distract.'

'Didn't you say she's really into shoes?'

I'm lost in thought.

'Amber?'

'Come with me a second.' I take her arm and weave along the beach to where we can observe the over-water bungalows unnoticed. 'I think I've got an idea.' For five minutes I sit and study the bungalows, methodically thinking through every step I would have to make.

'Is this what they call casing the joint?' Felicity asks.

I nod and continue my silent process.

Felicity shuffles closer. 'Amber, do you promise you're all right about me going on a date with Hugh?' she asks in a small voice. 'I mean, I suppose that now you're with Tezz . . .'

'Even if I wasn't with Tezz it would be all right,' I

assure her. 'Any romance is well and truly over.'

'You're sure?'

I nod. 'I want you to go for it – you could be making two people I care about very happy.'

'I pray!'

'Okay, I think I've got it.' I clear my throat to announce the plan. 'Tomorrow night when Hugh and Sandrine leave for dinner, both sets of pearls will be locked in their respective safes. I already know the combination to Hugh's safe, and I'm fairly confident I could crack Sandrine's code.'

Felicity looks at me, intrigued.

'Family trick,' I shrug. There is one thing of use I remember my dad telling me.

'But how would you get into the rooms? Or did your dad leave you one of those spindly key-wizard things?'

'Actually, he always used one of my mother's hairpins.'

'Really?'

'No!' I scoff. 'Besides, I couldn't go in through the front door even if I had the key; someone might see me.'

'So how are you going to get in?'

'I'm going to swim up and enter through the coffee table.'

'What?' she hoots.

'You remember that glass cube with a sliding top?'

'The one we dropped bread down from? Oh wow, that's so James Bond!' she reels, getting it.

'I know!' I grin. 'All I'd need to do is find a way to

get a bit of height in the water, then I'd reach up, push open the glass, pull myself through and into the room . . .' The plan is coming together fast now. 'I'd get Hugh's pearls, then drop back down, swim across, get Sandrine's, swim back . . .'

'Wouldn't it be quicker if there was one person in each bungalow—'

'You're not doing this.' I stop her before she gets any ideas. 'It's too risky.'

'Don't be a spoilsport! Seriously, if I was in one bungalow and you—'

'No!'

'I want to do this,' she whines.

'I don't want you getting involved.'

'I'm already involved and I want to help. You know I can do it – I can swim better than you. I bet I can get myself up into the room quicker. You'll be lucky if you can even boost yourself high enough to reach the glass.'

'And remind me of your personal best for safe-cracking?' I taunt her.

'You've got Hugh's number – I'll do that one. If he walks in I just yell "*Surprise!*", tear off my clothes and throw myself on the bed!'

I can't help but laugh.

'Plus, once we're in, rather than swimming between the two we can just go out on to the balconies and throw the bags of pearls across to each other.'

'You want to throw a million dollars' worth of pearls across ten foot of water at night?'

'Come on, we were A-team netball – we can do this.'

'Does it bother you at all that this is illegal?' I ask her.

Felicity shrugs. 'What Sandrine has done is worse than illegal, it's *wrong*. We can make it right.'

I look at her resolute face.

'Come on, for old times' sake. For Headington School. Let's do it.'

I bite my lip and then succumb to an acquiescing hug.

'Oh wow, this is going to be so much fun!' she whoops, doing a little jig in the sand.

I hop along with her, trying to ignore the queasy sensation that has taken possession of my stomach. Some voice is nagging within, issuing a muffled warning, but the euphoria of being up to my old wrong-righting tricks with Felicity has me pogoing with such vigour I soon forget what that worry might be.

'Come on – let's go dancing!' she says, grabbing my hand and charging in the direction of The Paradise Room.

35

'Yow!' I raise my legs in the air and rotate my ankles. My feet are still throbbing from the dance-floor-pounding I gave them last night. The reinstatement of the Righteous Sisters put us in offensively high spirits, and we persuaded the majority of the cocktail-sippers to join us in bodily worship of the music of Soul Desire.

'I like that you girls are out there dancing with us,' Lexi told us on a break. 'Makes me feel like I'm not the only one working!'

Meanwhile Fantasia pretended to be in a huff on account of me 'crossing the line' with one of *her* boys, but then decided to forgive me, provided I shared some juicy details.

'Those swively hip movements Tezz does to "Hey Mister" . . . does he use them in his private life?' she was gagging to know.

I just gave her an enigmatic shrug. But the answer is yes. Oh yes.

The show itself was better than ever, with Tony giving the most eloquent rendition of Seal's 'Love's Divine' (and actually sounding like he meant it – hoorah!) and Tezz incorporating his Manihi 'Lean Back' tap moves, before changing mood to sing me a beautiful ballad whispering *Ua Here Vau la Oe* – I love you in Tahitian . . .

Later that night I had my most restful sleep of the trip, lying in Tezz's arms, soothed by the balmy breeze up in his tree house. So many times with Hugh I'd lie awake troubled by a vague feeling that I was letting him down. But last night I felt so relaxed, as if I'd finally found the place where it was enough just to be me.

The next day Tezz and Tony took Felicity and me parasailing off a friend's boat, which was – once I'd been assured there would be no surprise dunkings or ropes fraying to a tenuous thread – unexpectedly calming, a bit like having an out-of-body experience, floating high above everyone and everything. Not only did it give me a new perspective on the island, but it also prompted a new take on some of the things Tezz and I had discussed that night. He was talking about going back to Boston to visit his mum and sister, and how he wanted to make peace with his dad.

'There's been talk about us taking the show on the road, and though I always had this childhood ambition of performing at the Fleet Center, as an adult I've dreaded going back. It's almost as if I'm afraid of being tainted with all the bad stuff that used to go on there. But my dad is coming out of prison next month. He's talking about getting a fresh start, and I think it's time. And if you were there with me . . .'

With my new-found attitude it strikes me that for Tezz, moving forward means going home, and for me, it means leaving it. I wonder for a moment if Boston is where we might end up together. In many ways it would be perfect – he could dance for his hometown crew and I could work at one of the most prestigious art galleries in the country. And did I mention that their winters are absolutely foul? Relentless multi-directional rain and winds that could whip the very breath from you? Bliss!

So there I was, feeling contentedly optimistic, when the speedboat changed direction and sent me veering into the air space above the over-water bungalows of the Bora Bora Lagoon Resort. Suddenly my insides munched up as I imagined that later tonight I would be approaching these huts from quite a different angle.

'Please give me the nerve to pull this off!' I prayed as I was gently retracted on to the carpeted platform at the back of the boat, forcing myself to smile cheerily for Flossie's camera.

'You went so high!' she marvelled, helping me out of the harness, eager to take her turn. 'See if you can get one of me with *Windstar* in the background!'

I took her camera and snapped freely, posing between Tezz and Tony for one of those end-of-your-arm shots. Who'd have pictured this when I first saw them plumed and pumped-up on stage for the 'Freak Like Me' feather number? They seemed so aloof and unattainable then. Gorgeous but out of reach. Now here they were grinning either side of me, and I knew it was happening for real because Tony gave me a playful pinch, hoping I'd mess up my expression for the photo. But he could pinch all he liked – my smile wouldn't budge.

Come sunset Felicity and I excused ourselves, saying we needed some farewell time together before her date. If it went well with Hugh, we probably wouldn't be seeing each other again before her flight back to New Zealand the next morning.

'Don't be too late back – Tony's cooking saffron mussel soup!' Tezz winked.

'I won't!' I grinned, loving my new family set-up, cheerfully in denial of the string of illegal manoeuvres I was about to make.

'Stop twiddling your feet around and get those jelly shoes on,' barks Taskmaster Lacey. 'Hugh and Sandrine will already have left for dinner – we need to get a move on.'

I must confess, Felicity is proving a valuable asset to the mission. Earlier today she decided we couldn't risk being spotted as we slipped into the water from the hotel beach and suggested that instead we approach via the lagoon, which is why we are now sneaking a pair of kayaks off the back of the *Windstar*.

The plan is this: we'll paddle to a safe distance from the bungalows, slip into the water, stealth-swim the rest of the way, complete the pearl exchange, then return to the *Windstar* where we'll make a show of ourselves in the bar so everyone remembers seeing us on board, which means we couldn't possibly have been involved in any criminal activity at the Bora Bora Lagoon Resort, officer.

'I just hope the kayaks don't float off without us,' I fret as we make our first tentative strokes. 'It's not like they come with an anchor . . .'

'It's fine,' Felicity assures me. 'The water is barely moving, there's no current or tide here.' She holds her oar aloft. 'Ready?'

Together we increase our pace and move steadily forward in the black waters. Felicity definitely has the stronger stroke and pauses periodically to let me catch up. When she judges the distance from the bungalows to be sufficient, she signals across to me to stop, swings her legs into the water and sinks in up to her neck. I do the same. The water is still a pleasant temperature after a day simmering in the sun, yet I notice I'm shivering.

'You okay?' she whispers.

I nod back at her, unable to speak.

'See you on the balcony in five,' she instructs, breast-stroking onward.

I try to keep my movements smooth and even to create the least possible disturbance in the water, but my right foot inadvertently juts above the water as I attempt to surge forward and smacks down in a noisy splosh. Great way to freak myself out even more!, I tut, hoping my dad isn't looking down at me, disappointed at my lack of prowess as I approach the crime scene. There was he hoping to father his very own Artful Dodger, and instead he got an Art Historian.

My heart starts yammering as we draw level with our respective bungalows. Please let this pass without incident, I pray – no booby traps, no slip-ups, no arrests.

Suddenly I'm worrying about everything – cracking Sandrine's safe code, throwing the pearls across to one another, relocating the kayaks . . . But then I force myself to switch to professional calm. One thing at a time.

I position myself directly below the coffee table and then curse as I once again find myself a few inches shorter than required. Unable to reach the ledge as I'd planned, I'm forced to jump for it. Not easy on uneven coral. My first attempt fails, my second results in a splinter rammed into my middle finger.

'Yowww!' I grimace inwardly, swishing my hand in the water. No time to deal with that now. Just concentrate on getting up. I try to envision my feet being sprung with coils, and bend my knees ready to launch myself upward when suddenly I feel a pair of hands boost me.

'Got it!' I grab on, scrabbling my feet up to wedge myself in position.

'Told you I'd come in handy,' Felicity gloats before wading back over to her bungalow.

Now we're down to it, I realise I couldn't possibly be

doing any of this without her. Having an adept accomplice cuts the job time in half. Plus, knowing she's putting herself on the line motivates me to keep my side of the bargain. If it was just me, I think my nerves would have caused me to call the whole thing off by now.

But here I am, shifting position so I can manoeuvre the glass top, straining a couple of muscles as I do so. Apparently, carrying heavy art books and cycling between the library and the museum do not fully prepare a girl for the trials of cat burglary. Here we go . . . The glass gives way and I slide it across, making enough room to pull myself up on to the wooden frame. I reach around into my waterproof backpack and pull out a small towel – can't leave any drips that might betray my presence later. Once I'm sufficiently mopped, I drop the towel to the floor and shuffle over to the safe.

Right. Let's see if I can remember Sandrine's passport details correctly. I tap in a variation of six numbers. Third time lucky – her birthdate backwards. She really should know better. My dad always said that even the most savvy individuals go for the ease of using their birthdate as a code. I smile to myself, thinking that this at least would make him proud, then reach in and pull out the bag, taking care not to spill the cup of water beside it.

Again using the towel as a drip-catcher, I skid over to the balcony, slide open the door and step out into the night. For a second I remain still, pleading with my heart to resume a gentle patter and forgo the bongo-thump it's currently engaged in. When I'm sufficiently composed, I give a low whistle and Felicity comes into view.

'Got them!' she grins, white teeth dazzling. 'Ready?'

I still can't believe we're going to throw the bags of pearls, but dutifully set my quarry down and get my catching hands on.

'Go!' I hiss.

She throws them right into my body. I clasp them to me, puffing relief. One down, one to go.

My turn. Once again I'm gripped with nerves. I always was weaker at throwing long-distance – as goal shooter I only had to get it up and in the net. But that's all about precision. Felicity's reach is bigger than a hoop. I can do this.

'Now!' I call.

I'm about to release and project forward when *Windstar* blasts its horn and my hand jerks in response. Before I can even see where I've misthrown, I hear a splash.

Oh no! It's like the engagement ring box all over again – only this time there's real booty within.

I shoot a look of despair towards Felicity but find her gone. My eyes dart back at the water – the rings are too big for just the pearls, she must have gone in after them. I scrabble to the edge of the deck to peer down. Where is she? Oh God – if anything bad happens to her . . . Suddenly there's a rushing up from the water and she appears, breathless, holding the bag aloft!

I want to cheer but have to settle for a small arm-waving dance.

'I'm going back up through the coffee table,' she hisses at me.

'What?'

'I don't want to leave any suspicious puddles on the deck.'

'Oh, you're good!' I praise her.

I myself turn back inside, closing the patio door behind me. The pearls go back in the safe. I turn the lock, wipe away any fingerprints and go back down the shoot, entering the water with a little too much splash but hey, the job is done. Knowing that Felicity can pound water faster than me, I decide to get a head start getting back to the kayak. I'm making good progress, feet behaving this time, when I get a bad feeling and look back.

Oh no! My heart goes cold. The light is on in Hugh's room.

I flail around, not knowing what to do. Surely she wouldn't be crazy enough to flick the switch? Does this mean he's caught her? Or is she already away? I spin around in the water, trying to spot her. Again my heart starts to rat-a-tat-tat, faster even than Tezz's tap-dancing. Shit! Why did it have to be her? I swim a little closer, hoping for some clue as to what's going on. I can't hear any shouting. How would he react to finding her there? Has she had to resort to the throwing herself on the bed routine? Did he walk in to find her head in the coffee table like some kind of warped David Blaine trick? I swim closer still. Definite commotion. Please say she hasn't hit him over the head with a lamp!

Suddenly there's a posse of people running along the walkway towards Hugh's room – hotel people, security people. *Oh God!* There she is now, being marched outside.

'*Wait!*' I yell. 'I can explain!' I swallow a mouthful of lagoon as I attempt to swim and shout simultaneously. As I surge forward, a torch finds me in the dark and blinds me. I flounder on regardless, only to find myself being helped out of the water by two strong arms in uniform.

'*Amber?*' Hugh steps in front of me, beyond non-plussed. From the look on his face you'd think Neptune himself was taking his first steps on dry land. 'I d-don't understand . . . What the hell are you doing here?'

'It's not what it looks like! I can explain!' I blather, drowning in clichés. 'It was all my idea! I put her up to it!'

Hugh looks with increasing bewilderment at the pair of wet women stood before him. 'You two know each other?'

'Well,' I begin. 'I realise this may come as something of a shock, but this is my dear friend Felicity.'

He gawps at her, slack-jawed. 'You're Felicity?'

'Hi!' she smiles, giving him a cute little wave.

He reels back, incredulous. 'You're in this together? This whole thing—'

Uh-oh! I can see where his mind is going. 'No—' I hold up my hand, but it's swiftly placed behind my back.

'After all these years? Is this what you've been waiting for, to do a job on me?'

'Of course not!' Oh good grief! He's clearly been watching too many crime caper movies. I'm about to set him straight when the hotel manager François steps in. '*Excusez-moi*, Ms Pepper, do you or do you not have a valid reason why your friend here was caught with her hand in Mr Garner's safe.'

'I absolutely *do*!' I tell him earnestly. 'In fact, this can all be explained quite simply if you summon Madame Volereaux.'

'What's Sandrine got to do with this?' Hugh gruffs.

'You'll see,' I say, confident that I'm soon to be vindicated. I feel like I'm orchestrating some kind of Agatha Christie denouement, just waiting for a few missing players to take their positions. Mind you, we're not short on bodies – there's quite a crowd collecting now. Every face I've seen over the past week seems to be here.

'It wasn't really stealing,' I assure the assembled masses.

'Because . . .' a lone voice speaks out.

'Because,' I repeat, about to complete the sentence when I realise who said the B-word. It's Tezz.

I feel a chill as my eyes meet his. I can see exactly what he's thinking – to him I'm as in denial as his father.

'Honestly! It wasn't!' I protest, panicking, feeling him pulling back, withdrawing himself from my heart. *Noooo!*

'You know these women?' François turns to Tezz.

Tezz looks from me to Felicity and shakes his head sadly. 'Apparently not.' Then he turns on his heel and heads back in the direction of The Paradise Room.

'Wait!' I go to follow but find myself firmly restrained. 'Tezz!' I call after him, but he continues on his way.

My body slumps. What was I thinking? How did I not make the connection that this act, however altruistic, could be the ruin of our relationship? Of course I didn't plan on getting caught, but all the same . . . I whimper in despair and frustration. This is not going according to plan on any level. I shoot a look at Felicity. For some reason the gravity of the situation does not seem to have hit home with her – she still looks like she's having the time of her life. But then up sashays Sandrine.

'What is all this?' she frowns. 'Hugh, *cherie*, is everything all right?'

'I suggest you check your safe, Sandrine. This woman was just caught trying to steal my pearls.'

Sandrine's face spasms, contorting further when she sees me.

'Amber! *Qu'est-ce que tu—*'

Whatever she has to say, I don't want to hear it. In any language.

'Sandrine!' I cut in, smiling sweetly. 'Would you be

454

a love and go and get your pearls so I can explain to everyone what a deceptive, conniving bitch you are?'

As soon as my words are out I fear I may have played my hand a little too early. By the time she returns, she clearly has a strategy.

'I don't know what you're talking about,' she says as she approaches, going for maximum wide-eyed insouciance. 'My pearls are fine, everything is in order.'

'Are you denying that these are in fact your pearls?' I point to the 'evidence' pearls in Hugh's hands.

She takes them from him, borrows François's torch and shrugs, '*Mais oui*. These are Hugh's pearls for sure. I should know, I was with him when he bought them.' She turns back to François. 'I have twenty years' experience in the business. I don't make mistakes.'

Felicity and I exchange a look. Sandrine, to save face it seems, has claimed the pearls I swapped for her own. Now there is nothing to suggest that we weren't exclusively targeting Hugh. Damn. Now we're really in trouble.

36

In the short time I've been in the South Pacific I've experienced a variety of accommodations – the magical over-water bungalows of Bora Bora and Manihi, Maeva's brother's waterside haven, Tezz's cosy tree house and now a prison cell.

It's actually not that bad. There is no crime to speak of in Bora Bora, so there's little in the way of dank, rat-invested cellars with rusty old manacles hanging from the walls. The local police have managed to muster a room with some bars, though, so if you want to go for that classic pose of gripping them and trying to shove your face through, you can. The worst of it is that I can't see or speak to Felicity. I know she's made of sturdy stuff, but I feel horribly responsible for her plight and just pray there is some way I can get her off the hook.

'Mademoiselle Pepper?'

I eagerly acknowledge the guard on duty.

'You have a visitor.'

Oh, please let it be Tezz. I need a chance to explain. Same goes double for Hugh. If he could just learn *why* we were doing what we were doing, then I'm sure he'd drop the charges. I didn't get the chance to explain anything to him before we were removed and detained. (For some reason the hotel didn't want us discussing this matter within earshot of guests with safes brimming with valuables. Funny that.) I feel so bad when I think of him. First he comes away ill-prepared for a high-pressure business deal, then his girlfriend rejects his proposal and dumps him, then, as he sees it, the next woman who makes a move on him is only interested in his baubles.

'Sandrine!' I wasn't expecting her.

She pulls up a chair, crosses her legs and tucks them to one side like a Forties femme fatale. By rights she should be wearing a tilted chapeau, belted mac and stilettos.

'I think we can probably come to an understanding in this matter, don't you?' She speaks in a low, confidential tone.

I scowl back at her. She knows she's the one morally in the wrong, but I'm the one in the prison cell so I guess I'm going to have to hear her out.

'Go on,' I reluctantly encourage her.

She leans forward. 'Let us be direct: Hugh now has my pearls. I have his. It is not ideal, but rather than face the embarrassment of an investigation, I think it's best we leave things that way.'

This is not what I was expecting from her. I realise she's basically saving her own skin – she doesn't want anyone discovering her unethical activities – but at the same time, this does mean Hugh is going to come out on top with the better pearls.

'So what exactly are you saying?' I narrow my eyes. There has to be a catch.

'I'm saying that if you keep your mouth shut to both Hugh and the authorities, I will convince him to drop the charges.'

'Really?'

'*Vraiment*.'

Sounds good from a legal standpoint, but there's still a problem. 'How am I supposed to explain to Hugh what Felicity and I were up to?'

Sandrine rolls her eyes as if I'm being petty. 'Just say you needed one pearl from his collection to fund your stay here.'

'But that's stealing!' I want to hold out against that lie.

'And what you were doing was . . .?'

'I wasn't stealing, I was *swapping*,' I pout. 'I took nothing for myself.'

Sandrine tuts impatiently. 'Look, the main thing is to put this behind us. You want Hugh to go home with the highest-grade set of pearls, don't you?'

'Yes,' I sigh. 'That's all I was trying to do in the first place.'

'He doesn't understand what went on, but you know he doesn't really want to punish you. He's hurt, but he's not a hard man. I've told him already that there is no need to telephone his boss. For now, it remains between us.'

'How can I be sure you mean this?' I frown. 'I know you don't want a scandal, but I can't believe you'd give up your pearls this easily.'

Sandrine gives me a knowing look. 'You really want to know?'

I nod, finally realising that she's a few martinis gone.

She reaches into her pocket, pulls out a velvet pouch and unsheathes a gobstopper-size blue pearl. 'Because you didn't get this,' she smirks, gazing at its magical lustre. 'This alone is worth more than all the other pearls put together. I haven't let it out of my sight since I bought it. This, *cherie*, makes every other loss negligible.'

'I see.'

'So,' she lowers her voice. 'Do we have a deal?'

'I say nothing, and you get Hugh to drop the charges?'

'*Oui.*'

I can't see myself getting a better offer, so I say yes, it's a deal.

What an absolute mess. If I hadn't been so keen on playing the avenging angel, Hugh would probably have been satisfied with his pearls and maybe even had a dream date with Felicity and gone home with a little hope in his heart. As for me and Tezz . . . I can't even bear to think of the possibilities I have crippled there.

I make this bold step towards a new life, and, though as a criminal I may be classed as unarmed, I've somehow managed to shoot myself in the foot.

I watch with disdain as Sandrine gets to her feet. I want to blame everything on her, but really I've brought all this on myself.

'Just tell Hugh I'm sorry,' I call after her.

As she turns back to reply, she collides with a man entering the room. For a second they are a tangle of limbs and apologies in the shadows. Then I see that the man is Tezz, and Sandrine's hands are all over him.

'I didn't harm you, did I?' she simpers, fondling his biceps. 'Lucky you are so strong as to catch me!'

'Here, let me assist you.' He makes a big show of making sure she's securely upright, then offers his arm and escorts her out of the door.

What the hell is going on? Are they together? Why is he leaving with her?

Two minutes later he returns, alone, walks up as close to me as he can and says, 'So you weren't stealing, you were swapping?'

'She told you?' I gawp at him.

He shakes his head. 'I overheard. I was waiting my turn to come and see you and I heard the deal you struck.'

Deal? It makes me sound so guilty.

'I know I shouldn't have done it,' I groan. 'It's just that, at school, Felicity and I were all about righting wrongs, and we got carried away. I know there's no justification—'

'There never is.'

'Anyway, it was all a pointless exercise,' I slump. 'She had the Vahine Blue Pearl on her the whole time.'

'You mean this?' He rolls it towards me like a marble.

I stop it with my foot, then quickly lean down and hide it in my hand. 'You didn't!' I quickly replay their collision in the doorway. While her hands were all over him, his hands were apparently in her pockets.

'Oh my God! She's going to freak!' I squeal, rotating the heavy globe in my palm.

'Who's she going to run to?' he shrugs.

'The police?' I suggest.

He bids me roll it back to him. 'I'm going to take this to her now and see if she doesn't feel a little bit more like confessing to Hugh. She's going to have to come clean about the swap at the airport anyway – every pearl has a certificate, and they check them rigorously. I take it you didn't switch the paperwork too?'

I shake my head. I'd forgotten about that element. It would seem I really don't have the required savvy for this game.

'She can't take Hugh's pearls without the documents that go with them and vice versa. She probably knows that too. Yes, she'll end up with the Vahine, but at least this way Hugh and Felicity stand a chance of patching things up before he leaves.'

I'm stunned. 'I can't believe you'd do that. I mean, I'm thrilled, but I hate that you—'

'Stole for you?' he suggests.

'Really, you just borrowed it,' I quickly reason.

'No, I didn't, I stole. Because . . .' There's a long pause. 'Because of the way I feel about you.'

My heart flips, but then I watch his face crumple. 'I could really love you, Amber, but I can't risk this happening again. I've worked my whole life to get as far away from all that as I can.'

'*No!*' I cry, afraid of what's coming next. 'It won't happen again. It was a—'

'One-time thing?' He shakes his head. 'I've heard that too many times.' He leans a hand on the bar. 'Listen. I'll do this for you. I'll see you safely on a plane home, but that's it.'

My heart plummets and smashes on the rocks. 'That's it?'

'Your suitcase is with the prison guard. I've put a call in to the airline.'

'You're sending me home?' I feel sick.

'You understand why I have to do this.' He looks imploringly at me.

I want to dispute his choice but I can't. I think back to when he was a little boy, to the nights spent waiting for another knock on the door from the police, the empty justifications, *It's not stealing because* . . . If I was him I would have trouble trusting me too. I've done the one thing he has zero tolerance for. 'Yes, I understand,' I tell him, not wanting to do any more damage than I already have.

For a second he lets his head fall forward and rests it on the bars.

It takes every scrap of determination I have not to reach out and touch his Fuzzy-Felt scalp, to caress him back to me, to beg for one last kiss. But I know he could never feel good about us as a future concept now – he'd be forever questioning himself and me. I have to let him go.

He lifts up his head and stares deep into my eyes.

'It's okay,' I tell him, even though it's not.

He takes a deep breath, then steels himself. 'Goodbye, Amber.'

I open my mouth to speak, but there is no way I can tell this man goodbye. The best I can do is watch him shuffle towards the door, then close it tight behind him.

Now it's my turn to lean my head on the bars, exhausted from all the extreme emotions that have ravaged me in the last few hours. Since we got caught, I've been telling myself none of this is really happening, it's all a deranged dream. But that look of disappointment on Tezz's face is all too penetratingly real. As I replay our last exchange I feel a piercing sensation in my heart. It is devastating to me that I'm the cause of his pain. All I wanted from the first moment I saw him was to make him happy, to be the reason his big smile got even bigger. How could I have let this happen? How could I have been so careless with something so precious? Why couldn't I see how much I had to lose? I guess that trait runs in the family.

'Any advice?' I ask, looking heavenward. 'Or is it too late for that?'

No reply.

I fear it may be. Official charges aside, the worst possible sentence has already been passed. I now have to endure a life without Tezz.

37

'Wait, wait, wait!' Allegra holds up her hands, presiding over our library-corner gathering on my first day back at work. 'There's too much to take in, one thing at a time!'

'Go back to Gauguin's grandson,' Abigail pleads.

'You didn't seriously break-up with Hugh?' Gilly is still in shock.

'So technically Tezz is back on the market?' pipes a cheeky ear-wigger from the next aisle.

'Ladies, please! The last we heard Amber was in *prison*!' Allegra cries. 'I really think we should hear what happened next!'

'Well . . .' I take a deep breath and carefully explain that Sandrine did go to Hugh and set him straight, as Tezz intended. She copped to the fact that she had been deliberately misleading him for the duration of the trip and explained that Felicity and I were merely attempting to right that wrong by switching her pearl stash for his lesser booty. As far as I'm aware she didn't say sorry, or mention the Vahine Blue Pearl. In response, unable to face me, Hugh went directly to Felicity to verify the story. She told him everything, including the fact that she'd been pursuing him from the moment she first saw him at the airport.

'She didn't!' Gilly gasps.

'She did,' I confirm. 'She told him that she'd circled Bora Bora on a bus and surveyed the surrounding lagoon on a jet ski, checked every cabin on *Windstar* and ticked-off every hotel within a twenty-mile radius.'

'Wasn't he worried she was a stalker?' Abigail's nose shrivels up.

I shake my head. 'On the contrary he was flattered. For the first time in a long time he saw someone look at him with one hundred per cent devotion. Yes he was a little dumbfounded but his first words were, "You did all that for me?"'

'Awww,' Gilly and Abigail sigh, caught up in the romance of the scenario. 'And what did she say?'

'She said, "Yes. And when you kissed me in the hotel bar I knew it was all worthwhile."'

'Ohhhh!' The girls clasp each other's hands with misty satisfaction but Allegra looks disconcerted. 'You're being awfully blasé about your best friend making a move on your man.'

'He's not her man any more,' Abigail jumps in. 'Their relationship has clearly run its course.'

'What rot!' Allegra snorts. 'You don't give up a man like Hugh for a holiday romance!'

'Haven't you been listening to anything she's said?' Abigail gets defensive on my behalf.

'She's blown it with Tezz and now she's on the verge of losing her home, I don't see how you see this as a good thing.' Allegra turns to me. 'You said Hugh is buying out your side of the house, right?'

I nod. He proposed that on the plane, in between asking an awful lot of questions about Felicity.

'So here she is with no man, no place to live—'

'You can stay with me Amber,' Abigail interrupts Allegra's flow of negativity. 'My brother is away for a whole month so you can have his room and there's plenty of storage in the garage.'

'Thank you,' I smile at her, masking the chills I'm experiencing as it hits home that this is all happening for real. Until now it just seemed like a fanciful story to shock the girls but the fact is Hugh and I are done. I am alone. And up until a minute ago I was homeless.

'Just let me know when we can go to your house to get your things. I'm stronger than I look you know, I've lifted whole armchairs before now!' Abigail continues to offer her support, backed by Gilly.

'You can go this afternoon if you like, it might be easier while Hugh is at work . . .'

Oh gosh – this does seem awfully *soon*; I've only just got back!

'Probably a good idea to do it while he's out,' Allegra chips in. 'I suppose the tension between the two of you is murderous?'

I think for a minute. It's actually more sad than bad.

The hours and hours on the plane on the way home provided a kind of neutral air-space where we really got to talk things through and adjust to the idea of being apart while sat side by side, with no danger of anyone storming off mid-sentence. It was almost as if crossing through time zones at such an awkward time somehow bonded us. I don't think it hurt any that Hugh had a series of notes to read from Felicity (one for every two hours of the journey), her affection tempering my rejection. I guess that is the main difference between us currently – romantically he has new hope, for me it's nothing but regret over how things ended with Tezz. As much as I try to be philosophical about that I just can't seem to get past the feeling that I've blown the most wonderful opportunity of my life. It's not so much to do with having a man – I managed fine without prior to Hugh – but I really enjoyed myself so much more in his presence. Every time I think of him I have to turn away from the memory so I don't cry. I'll save my tears for when I'm alone tonight.

In the meantime, the questions keep coming from the girls: 'Are Hugh and Felicity going to meet again?' 'Is there really no hope with you and Tezz?' 'You'll still carry on working here, won't you?' 'If you're not going to eat your Rice Krispie Treat, can I have it?'

Together we sit and rummage through the debris of my situation, trying to find some guarantee that my life can be re-built and that everything will turn out for the best. I can see Allegra and Gilly struggling more than Abigail, who seems to understand that the relief of not having to live a lie with Hugh is way more than a consolation prize. I may not be doing a celebratory dance of freedom yet but there is definite comfort in knowing that I can make choices for the greater good of me!

'You know I was doing a little personal research on Frieda Kahlo while you were gone and I came across an interview with Selma Hayek,' Abigail muses as we head back to the Ashmolean. 'She said that adversity is the greatest gift in life. *But only if you embrace it.*'

I stop in the street, heart daring me to be brave. 'Okay,' I look Abigail in the eye. 'Let's go to the house now.'

Hugh hasn't put me under any urgent pressure to scoot but I don't want to live in limbo-land until I find a flat of my own. If I take this opportunity to move on physically, with any luck my emotions will soon follow.

'So that's the kitchen and bathroom and bedroom done. Nothing of yours in the lounge or the dining room,' Abigail busies. 'Anything stored in the loft?'

'No but there's actually a whole other room, just of mine,' I tell her, guiding her towards my den, fretting that this could be a bin bag too far. 'Are you sure it's all right for me to dump all this stuff on you?'

'It's fine, we've got plenty of storage space and even when my brother comes back you can stay on until you've got yourself sorted, it'll be fun to have you around!'

Fun may seem quite a stretch at the moment but I can see that I don't need to worry about being a burden to Abigail – it's as if all this time she has been waiting for permission from me to be a better friend to me. Look at her jumping at the chance to help me out here! I didn't see that coming so who knows what other good things might be on their way now I'm not so closed off. Speaking of which . . .

'Welcome to my hideaway,' I push open the door to my private quarters, letting someone other than Hugh venture in for the very first time.

'Oh wow! I wasn't expecting this!' Abigail laughs as she takes in the dark textured fittings. 'The rest of the house is so light and bare. This is like the inside of a jewellery box!'

Her comparison startles me.

'You know, one of those old caskets lined with red velvet . . .' she expands, running her hands over the seraphs and swirls of the wallpaper. 'It's so luxurious.'

'That paper is probably the most expensive thing I own,' I admit. 'And it's all got to come down.'

'We might be able to salvage it you know,' Abigail starts picking at a corner. 'If it's as heavy as it looks and you used lining paper . . .' She eases away the edging and then gets enough between her thumbs and fore-fingers to pull, stripping away an entire panel in one go. 'There! We can save it and use it on your new place.'

'Oh no!' I shudder. To me, this room now represents hiding and wallowing. 'Next time I'm going to do something different.'

'Blank canvas?' Abigail nods in collusion. 'Wonder what you'll go for?'

If I had to decorate this room right now, I know exactly what I'd do – I'd put a daydo rail a third of the way up to represent a coral reef and then paint sky blue above and turquoise lagoon below. And then pray for sunshine.

Abigail continues to peel away the layers. 'Could you grab me a couple of bin bags?'

'We just used the last one for my mum's throw. I'll have to nip to the shop. Which is actually more of a trek than a nip.'

'That's okay, take your time. And see if they've got a couple of boxes for your records while you're at it.'

I try to pace away my uneasiness but it's a battle against the wind just to get down the street. Ever since I've been back I've felt slightly at odds with the city. Half of me feels like I never went away, the other half has yet to return from Tahiti. Nothing looks quite the same any more. For one thing, it's strange to see so much paved ground when I've grown accustomed to sand and water. I'm just glad I've got my work. That always grounds me. And while I'm staying with Abigail I'll still have someone to cook for. Perhaps I'll grab a few bits now so tonight I can prepare a little treat to thank her for her moving skills? That nice Italian deli is just around the corner . . .

When I return the room is entirely white and Abigail is scrubbing away the traces of paste and lining paper.

For a moment I stand there bewildered, still dangling the shopping, feeling like I no longer have an anchor.

Abigail pauses, suds dripping down her arm and asks, 'How are you feeling?'

'A little bit exposed,' I concede with a gulp.

'End of an era, isn't it?' she acknowledges. 'Do you maybe feel a little bit hopeful, too?'

'A little bit . . .' I walk over to the window and begin to unhook the heavy velvet curtains, letting them crumple to the floor in a heap. (Rather like the voluminous dresses I decided to discard during the earlier wardrobe clear-out.) 'It's weird not knowing what's coming next but I'm looking forward to—' I falter, not really knowing how to complete the sentence. Obviously it'll be wonderful to have somewhere of my own where I'm free to express myself wherever I want, not just in a tucked-away nook, and it's going to be a huge relief to just be, as opposed to acting out a role I've been mis-cast for. But right now I'd settle for not worrying about Hugh and not missing Tezz with such an overwhelming intensity.

'It's okay, *really*,' Abigail senses my pain. 'Just the fact that you're looking forward is good enough for now.'

'Do you like beetroot?' I ask her.

She looks temporarily thrown then cheers, 'Love it!'

'Good, when we're done with all this I'm going to do some pink ravioli and a fennel and radicchio salad with rosemary foccacia . . .'

38

I look up at the calendar on the wall. I've been back in Oxford exactly six weeks, yet here I am, continuing to immerse myself in images of the islands. My excuse is that it's work.

Until we started researching our upcoming Matisse exhibit, I'd forgotten that the fluffy-bearded Frenchman had visited Tahiti in his sixties and that it was there he gained inspiration for his seminal gouache paper cut-outs – abstract interpretations of 'lagoon foliage' and frilly breadfruit leaves in royal blues and solid blacks and pillar-box reds in a style that revolutionised Modern Art. As well as summoning as many of those pieces as I can, I'm trying to put together a collection of his pen-and-ink sketches of native women and leaning palm landscapes. Gilly said she felt bad assigning me a daily reminder of 'Well, you know', but I told her I didn't mind – I'd be thinking about it every day anyway, wondering how different things might have been.

Things are certainly different for Felicity and Hugh. They're currently in Tokyo together – he had holiday to take, she had no job to go back to, and it was somewhere they'd both always dreamed of going. According to Felicity's recent phone call, they've spent nearly two weeks touring Japan, getting fonder of each other each day. Initially it was weird listening to her talk with such jovial familiarity about a man I once knew so well, but hearing about Hugh's inappropriate giggling fit in the Kenchoji Zen temple and the sake and champagne cocktail they created the first night they slept together (small shudder) at least helped ease the guilt I'd been sickened with. Hugh was obviously embracing a more equal relationship and had even forgone his five-star accoutrements when Felicity insisted it was her turn to pay for the hotel, ending up in one of those sterile dog-kennel cubicles the Japanese businessmen favour. Not that he slept a wink, so the two of them stayed up all night talking – something we never did – setting new standards of communication. I have to admit that sometimes it feels a bit weird if I think about them for too long, but two of the most significant people in my life are happy together, and that can only be a good thing.

As for me . . . I'm still at Abigail's, and rather enjoying the girlie company. Neither of us have had female flatmates before and I'm certainly finding the companionship a huge bonus. I have looked round a few properties with a view to buying, but I'm reluctant to put down roots when every day I'm still looking up flights to Tahiti, wondering if there is any point in me returning, wondering if I could try and convince Tezz that the episode with the pearls was a moment of madness, not me discovering my true calling. But it isn't just about me, it's about how I would make him feel – every time he looked at me he would see the girl who made him steal. He doesn't need reminding of that. I have to respect his decision, even if it leaves me crying myself to sleep every night listening to his voice on the CD.

So then last week I turned my attention to the Museum of Fine Art in Boston, checking to see if any jobs had come up there, thinking it would be the next best thing to be in the city where he grew up. Pitiful I know, but I just wanted to find a way to feel close to him again. I've also added Ticketmaster to my list of Internet favourites and check each morning to see if there's any sign of Soul Desire taking their show on the road. Nothing yet.

I have exchanged a couple of emails with Tony, but they're mostly recipe-related banter. Before I left Bora Bora he actually brought me a pre-cooked meal for the plane, with tin foil to peel back and everything. I had to write and thank him for that. He responded a few days later, brimming with excitement that his restaurant had been awarded three stars (top rating) in the new Frommer's South Pacific guide and business had never been better. I longed to ask after Tezz, but I didn't want him to feel compromised in any way so instead I focused on trying to convince him of the delicacy status of Toad in the Hole.

'Are you coming?' It's Abigail wanting to know if I'm ready to leave.

'In a while,' I tell her. 'I just want to see if I can track down some info on this silent movie Matisse got involved with. I was thinking maybe we could have it running on a screen in the room with his Tahitian works?'

'What movie's that?' Abigail's curiosity is piqued.

'*Taboo*. Have you heard of it? It's meant to be quite the masterpiece, same director as that Eskimo documentary *Nanook of the North*. The whole thing was filmed on Bora Bora.'

'Sounds cool. So you'll be a while?'

'Maybe.'

'Okay, well, see you at home.'

'Okay,' I smile back at her. She's really been great – always sensitive to when I need time to myself.

'It's just about healing now,' she told me on my second night. 'You're on a new path and everything will seem a bit strange at first, but you'll adjust and then you'll get stronger and then one day you'll be happy again, I promise.'

I very nearly believed her. Even though I still feel an agonising sense of loss whenever I think of Tezz, I'm grateful for all that he roused in me. It's almost as if he's given me this gift but I'm only halfway through reading the instruction manual, so I don't know how to fully use it yet. But when I do . . .

I sigh and swing round on my chair. I'm not in the mood for detective work after all. Neither am I ready to return to Abigail's yet. Perhaps I'll skip the bus and try pacing this restlessness from my body? I look out of the window. Still raining – perfect!

I shut down my computer, throw my paper coffee cup in the bin and strap my coat around me. As I pull my wool hat down to my eyebrows, I smile ruefully, remembering the bump on my head. I'm sorry to have lost this last connection with Tezz and quickly wind a coil of my hair under my nose and inhale. Coconut . . . I found a shampoo that reminded me of the one he lathered upon me in Manihi, and now I come to think of it, I used the last pearlescent blob this morning. I should pop into Superdrug and get some more. There – I have a purpose in life! I clatter down the steps from the office and stride towards the grand front entrance of the museum.

'Sorry, we're closed.' Stan is on door duty. He's a stubby, stubborn little man given to facial pucing at the slightest provocation. 'Bloody Americans,' he grizzles at me. 'They turn up here at 6 p.m. and wonder why the doors are locked.'

'Well the museums are open a lot later over there,' I tell him as I reach in my bag and prep my umbrella for the onslaught.

There's a rap on the glass pane of the door.

'I already told you – we're closed!' Stan snaps, but the rapping continues, gathering urgency.

Did someone just say my name? I look up. What?! *It*

can't be. I reel in disbelief. His peanut head may be shrouded in grey fleece, but it is, it's Tezz!

'Oh my God, open the door, open the door!' I urge Stan.

'He's not coming in!' he glowers. 'I don't care who he is.'

'You don't have to let him in – just let me out!' I bay, heart clamouring to get to him.

Stan rattles the lock open and I burst through the door like a racehorse leaving the starting gate at Aintree. 'What are you doing here?' I sputter as I propel myself into his arms.

'I was just in Boston,' he casually informs me as if it were the next village along. 'I went to see my dad—'

'You did it!' I gasp, jumping back. 'How'd it go? Was it weird seeing him after all this time? Did you get along?' I have so many questions. I know this must have been a really big deal for him.

'Actually, it was great,' he beams. 'We got along great.'

'Wow!' I breathe, trying to define the expression on his face. 'You look so . . . I don't know – relieved? Optimistic?'

'I definitely feel better for it,' he acknowledges, voice softening as he continues. 'It made me realise that if I could forgive him . . .'

I try not to get my hopes up, but seeing him in the flesh, it's too difficult not to.

'Then you could forgive me?' I gasp, full of hope.

'And myself,' he says gently.

My heart swells. This is too amazing! I don't know where to begin. I want to throw my arms around him and kiss him back to Tahiti, but I settle instead for tugging him under the eaves to shelter from a particularly robust tussle of wind, wishing Stan wasn't such a curmudgeon and would let us into the warm.

'Go on,' I shiver, not yet daring to believe the implications of him standing before me.

'Amber, what you did was insane. Way beyond foolish – the consequences could have been so dire . . .'

'I know.' I look deep into his eyes so that he knows I still have nightmares myself.

'I hated how willing I was to fall into the behaviour I worked so hard to get away from. It really made me question everything.'

My heart sinks. The forgiveness is clearly no fait accompli. 'Do you think you'll ever be able to think differently about it?'

'I already do,' he says simply.

'Really?'

'Before I left for Boston I had a conversation with Tony. We never get in each other's business, but he told me he was sick of seeing me moping around and that in his opinion what you did was ill-judged, but done with the best intentions. He said that I should forget the night of crime and find out how I feel about you without the palm trees and the sunsets and a bellyful of his fine cuisine.'

I laugh out loud. Tony Perry, you old romantic!

'He gave me your details.' He reaches into his

pocket and pulls out a damp scrap of paper, ink spidered from the rain. 'Your email, at least, and I remembered you saying you worked at the Ashmolean. It's such a weird name it kind of stuck with me!' He folds the paper back into his palm and moves closer. 'So here I am, and there are no palm trees, definitely no sun and for lunch I had a truly vile steak and kidney pie . . .'

'And?' I hold my breath, quaking with anticipation. 'How do you feel?'

He looks me directly in the eye and repeats my question. 'How do I feel?'

I nod, on tenterhooks.

'I feel like dancing!'

'What?'

'Yup, that's definitely it,' he grins as his feet start to splash-tap a beat on the stone steps. In one bold move he's out there, mingling with the million-strong parade of raindrops eager to match every click of his heel with a liquid pattering. Unfortunately his rain-dance is all too effective and the skies release a further barrage, pounding down so hard I can actually see individual drops of water rebounding from the ground like translucent jumping beans. Still he dances.

'Are you crazy?' I call out to him, delighted as he starts to spin on the spot, faster and faster.

'Crazy in love!' he hollers as his coat-tails flare out and his scarf whips around like a helicopter propeller.

Suddenly he stops. The rain is blurring his features

but I can see he's extending a hand toward me.

For a second I hesitate. I could let go in Tahiti, but I've had no call to since I've been back. Do I still have it in me? Before I can doubt myself further I take a stride forward and let Tezz gallivant me across the courtyard, currently resembling a large, square, flag-stone paddling pool. The faster he twirls me, the louder I whoop. I feel like a kid jumping double-footed into puddles. This is so liberating!

On the adjacent pavement people who were hell-bent on getting home before the rain seeps through to their underwear have ceased their head-down beetling to stop and stare, their own discomfort forgotten as they marvel at my deft-footed dance partner. I even catch Stan misting up the glass with his breath, scowly piglet eyes now wide with wonder. I know what he's thinking: 'I didn't think people did that kind of thing in real life!'

Neither did I! I chuckle to myself as we finally come to a halt and pant gleefully at each other. The moment has come. He lowers his face to mine and we meld into a kiss . . . It's nothing like the kisses in Tahiti – his nose is cold on my cheek and I can't feel his body through all the layers between us – but the warmth and sensuality of his lips conjures up mirages of moonlight and lullabies of lagoon waters sighing on the shore.

'Wet enough for you?' he smiles as he blots my rain-slicked face.

'Mmm-hmm,' I giggle, feeling like my future just stepped out of the shower, all refreshed and renewed.

He gives me one of his intense compressor hugs, and then, as he releases me, my eyes stray to the wrought-iron gate currently separating us from the rest of the world. I take a deep breath, step forward and raise the latch, setting the gate squeaking ajar. In turn Tezz offers me his crooked arm and enquires, 'Shall we?'

'We shall!' I zing, securing my arm in his.

I don't know where we're going. Bora Bora? Boston? Back to his hotel? All three in reverse? Wherever, whenever, I don't care.

All I know is that I'm going to be dancing all the way . . .

THE PARADISE ROOM WEBSITE

Visit <u>www.theparadiseroom.com</u> for exclusive photos, travel tips and behind-the-scenes scoops!

You can also email the author and link to a special Soul Desire musical treat.

This plane is leaving for paradise right now – click on it!

AVAILABLE IN ARROW BY BELINDA JONES

Divas Las Vegas

A tale of love, friendship and sequinned underpants

Jamie and Izzy, friends for ever, have a dream: a spangly double wedding in Las Vegas. And at twenty-seven, they decide they've had enough crap boyfriends and they're ready for crap husbands - all they have to do is find them. And where better than Las Vegas itself, where the air is 70% oxygen and 30% confetti?

But as they abandon their increasingly complicated lives in sleepy Devon for the eye-popping brilliance of Las Vegas, their groom-grabbing plan starts to look less than foolproof. And those niggling problems they thought they'd left behind - like Izzy's fiancé and the alarming reappearance of Jamie's first love - just won't go away...

I Love Capri

Sundrenched days, moonlit nights and Italian ice cream. What more could a girl wish for?

Kim Rees became a translator for the glamorous jet-set lifestyle. So, five years later, how come she's ended up in a basement flat in Cardiff translating German computer games in her dressing gown? Fortunately her mother has a plan to extract her from her marshmallowy rut: a trip to the magical island of Capri.

At first Kim refuses to wake up and smell the bougainvillea, but as she starts to succumb to the irresistible delights of cocktails on the terrace and millionaire suitors, she surprised to realise she's changing. And when she meets a man who's tiramisu personified, she finds herself falling in love. But how far will she go to win her Romeo?

arrow books

AVAILABLE IN ARROW BY BELINDA JONES

The California Club

What's your dream?

When Lara Richards jets off to glamorous California, the last thing she's expecting is to find her old friend Helen transformed from a clipboard-clasping frump into a shimmering surf goddess. The secret of her blissful new life? The mysterious California Club.

So the offer of guest membership - one wish guaranteed to come true by the end of their stay - is one Lara and her friends can't resist. Could this be Lara's chance to win her best friend Elliot's heart after ten years of longing? Or does the fact that he's travelling with his brand new fiancée mean that Lara will have to come up with a new dream?

On the Road to Mr Right

'If adventures do not befall a young lady in her own village, she must seek them abroad.' Jane Austen

Belinda loves America. Her best friend Emily loves men. So when they decide it's time to shake up their lives, they combine their two greatest passions in a fantastic road trip taking them from Eden to Valentine - via Climax - in pursuit of the American Dream Guy.

There's no shortage of men - a Casanova from Cazenovia, a male cheerleader from Darling and a tattooed trucker from Kissimmee. But is romance really the answer to their problems? And is two women in search of the perfect man such a great idea anyway?

Theirs is a journey of revelations and surprises, of cactus kisses and errant snowploughs, but above all it's a journey in search of love. And you think Thelma and Louise had an eventful trip...

arrow books

**Order further Belinda Jones titles
from your local bookshop, or have them delivered
direct to your door by Bookpost**

Divas Las Vegas Belinda Jones   0 09 941492 9   £5.99

☐ **I Love Capri** Belinda Jones   0 09 941493 7   £6.99

☐ **The California Club** Belinda Jones   0 09 944548 4   £5.99

☐ **On the Road to Mr Right**

Belinda Jones   0 09 944549 2   £6.99

Free post and packing

Overseas customers allow £2 per paperback

Phone: 01624 677237

Post: Random House Books
c/o Bookpost, PO Box 29, Douglas, Isle of Man IM99 1BQ

Fax: 01624 670923

email: bookshop@enterprise.net

Cheques (payable to Bookpost) and credit cards accepted

Prices and availability subject to change without notice.
Allow 28 days for delivery.
When placing your order, please state if you do not wish to receive any
additional information.

www.randomhouse.co.uk/arrowbooks

arrow books

WIN a fabulous Holiday to Tahiti and Her Islands with

Air New Zealand, Tahiti Tourisme and Turquoise Holidays are offering one lucky reader the chance to win a fantastic holiday to Tahiti and Her Islands. The prize includes two return tickets from London Heathrow to Tahiti (economy), 3 nights accommodation on Tahiti, staying at Radisson Plaza Resort Tahiti and 3 nights accommodation on Moorea, staying at Moorea Pearl Resort. The prize also includes return inter island flights, Tahiti – Moorea, with Air Moorea.

Your holiday should begin the moment you leave your home. With two new cabins – Business Premier and Pacific Premium, along with an updated Pacific Economy class, the latest on-demand in-flight entertainment system throughout, stylish new uniforms and a fresh taste to its unique New Zealand style meals and drinks service, the new look rolls out on selected long-haul flights during 2005.

The Radisson Plaza Resort Tahiti is perfectly placed on the North East Coast of Tahiti, just 7kms and 10 minutes from the hustle and bustle of the heart of the capital, Papeete. Revitalise and rejuvenate the mind body and soul in Tahiti's first Day Spa and Health Club where you can enjoy a range of pampering beauty and health treatments or a variety of fitness activities.

Air Moorea offers the best connection flights between Tahiti and Moorea with 40 flights a day. For more information on Tahiti and Her Islands, accommodation and air services visit www.tahititourisme.pf

Newly opened in June 2002, Moorea Pearl Resort is located on 21 acres of white sand beach on the island's magnificent north coast, just a 10 minute drive from the airport (15 minutes from the boat landing) and only two miles from Moorea's breathtaking Cook's Bay.

Turquoise is a specialist tour operator to Tahiti and Her Islands. For more information, visit www.turquoiseholidays.co.uk to request one of their award winning brochures.

To enter, answer the questions over the page, complete the tie-breaker in no more that 15 words. Complete the form and send it to The Paradise Room competition, Arrow Marketing Dept, 20 Vauxhall Bridge Road, London SW1V 2SA

Questions & Answers:

1. Who gives Amber a cooking lesson? ....

2. Which famous painter was nicknamed 'the Noble Savage'?

....

Tiebreaker: (complete in no more that 15 words)

'I want to go to paradise because ....

....

....,

Name: ....

Address: ....

....

Daytime contact number: ....

Email: ....

If you would like to receive more information about Random House books,
please tick this box ☐

If you would like to receive more information about Air New Zealand,
please tick this box ☐

If you tick this box, you give your consent for the Random House Group Ltd and Air New
Zealand to keep your details in a database for the purpose of sending you information
in the future about products or services offered by the Random House Group Ltd and Air
New Zealand. Your details will not be passed on to any third parties.